# ENES SMITH

# COLD RIVER RESURRECTION

## A NOVEL

# COLD RIVER RESURRECTION

Enes Smith 2009

This is a work of fiction. Names, characters, places, and incidents either are the product of the author's imagination or are used fictitiously. Any resemblance to actual persons, living or dead, events, or locales is entirely coincidental.

Cover design by Road's End Films
Cover text by Kent Wright

For additional copies, go to Amazon.com

ISBN: 145377713X
EAN 13: 9781453777138

Printed in the United States of America
Enes Smith Productions edition 2009

# AUTHOR'S NOTE

I am a Šiyápu, a white man, and as such, any mistakes I have made regarding Indian tribes, peoples, customs, and culture are mine alone. This is a work of fiction, from a Šiyápu looking in from the outside, and any relation to persons and events are from the author's imagination, and not related to real people or events.

The ideas that catch in a writer's mind are as eclectic as the writer's experience. I am a lifelong reader, bibliophile, cop, teacher, and writer.

Over the course of many months a series of unrelated newspaper articles lodged in this writer's brain: An article that chronicled the insertion of meth into the Wind River Indian Reservation in Wyoming by drug cartels; an article about a Bigfoot research expedition in Oregon; articles about mid-eastern terrorists attempting to set up a training camp in Oregon; and articles about terrorist organizations engaging in commerce with drug cartels.

While this is a work of fiction, the poison known as meth destroys far too many children in the United States, Mexico, and Indian Country.

## ACKNOWLEDGEMENTS

There have been many people who have contributed time and kind words, without whom Cold River Resurrection would have never happened:

Nancy Spreier, friend, consummate researcher, and constant believer, owed more than I can write; Annie Hausinger, for the journey of friendship and tireless copyediting; daughter Maddie Smith, beginning writer and one of my first readers; Tom Jones, fellow cop and most talented man I know; Michelle Jones, friend who cares enough to force me to write when I've lost the way; Trudy Held, webmaster and insightful reader; and my friend Lieutenant Avex "Stoney" Miller, Ret., of the Warm Springs Tribal Police Department, for his tracking expertise and stories about Indian Country.

For Tony, Melissa, Maddie, and Dani

and

Hunter, Halle, Samantha, and Justin


All my love

# Chapter 1

Cold River Indian Reservation, Oregon
Mt. Jefferson Wilderness Area
July 6


Jennifer Kruger had been lost for hours by the time she discovered the first body.

It was three o'clock in the afternoon, and she was on the eastern slope of Mt. Jefferson, trying to find a way out of the woods. Tall pine trees closed in on her, blocking the sun. She had been following a game trail, a small track that would disappear and then reappear every few feet. A low branch blocked her way like a crossing guard's arm. She shrugged out of her pack and crawled under the branch. Jennifer turned to face back down the tiny path. If she shifted and looked through the trees, she could see the bright flash of sun on Whitewater Glacier.

In front of her a rolling carpet of trees stretched down the slope as far as she could see. She hoped she could find a logging road, but it didn't look as if any trees had been cut this high up on the mountain. She knew she needed to keep going downhill.

The massive pine trees were so dense she had to constantly look back to the mountain to keep going east, or what she thought was east. It was such rugged country she didn't wonder why congress had given it to the Indians way back when. She tried to keep the word *lost* from taking over her thoughts. She shifted to a patch of sunlight and sat on the branch in the middle of the path.

*See, Jennifer, you can't be lost, the sun is shining.* She pulled a water bottle from her pack and scooted again so the sun hit her legs. The muted sounds of birds and distant running water gave her a sense of security she clung to, with a little nagging worry that she tried to push away.

*Gonna get dark soon, Jenny.*

She pulled a pair of jeans from her pack, raised up, and shrugged out of her hiking shorts. She shook her head at her legs, now a crosshatch of scratches. A bloody gash ran up the back of her right

7

calf; red bumps from mosquito bites covered her legs like angry measles.

Jennifer had shoulder length light brown hair tied in a ponytail. She was five foot four and athletic without working hard. She wore a blue long-sleeved shirt and carried a red backpack. She swung her pack onto her shoulders, adjusted the straps, and took a deep breath. Time to get going. She walked around towering old-growth trees, through bands of shadow and sunlight. She stopped. The trail angled uphill, to the north, away from the direction she thought she should go. She shrugged and started up the faint trail, and saw what looked like a break in the trees. A clearing. She picked up her pace and hopped over a branch. A clearing might mean logging, and no matter how long ago, there would be a road.

There was an opening, a football field away, through the trees.

Jennifer stepped off the animal trail and pushed through the brush. She came to a large rock and leaned back, looking at a patch of sky. The contrails of a jet thirty thousand feet above had a dreamy quality about it. She thought about what it would be like to be on that jet, going to Las Vegas, all the bright lights and people. She moved upright and pushed her way through the brush. Wilderness enveloped her. The last fifty feet to the clearing took her much longer than she had thought it would. It seemed almost full dark in the trees, but that couldn't be. She looked at her watch. It was just three thirty.

*Gets dark early in the mountains, don't you know, Jennifer.*

And suddenly she knew that she didn't want to spend the night in the woods alone, and what a fool she had been to leave their camp. She should have made Carl walk out with her, listened to the inevitable arguments, and put up with his company. Carl could be an insufferable prick, but she would gladly welcome the sight of him now.

She grunted, pushed through a Manzanita bush and lurched against a deadfall. She sat down hard, her breath coming fast, faster than it should. *Slow down, Jenny, slow down, don't panic.* She was sitting in a bush in the thick forest. There was no trail, not even an animal track.

*Okay, Jennifer, you little copy editor you, if you can spot a misplaced comma from across the room, how hard can it be to find a friggin trail?*

She slapped at a branch and then stood at the edge of the clearing. A rock slide long ago had cleared out an area the size of a supermarket parking lot. Small pine trees struggled to grow, some as high as three or four feet, growing around fallen trees and boulders. *Not exactly a pasture, but I'll take it.* She twisted out of her pack and dug inside for her lighter. With her lighter in hand, she set her pack down and looked around for some dry wood to burn. She realized now how quiet it was. The ubiquitous insect noise was gone. It was too quiet, and that unsettled her.

Birds chirping and twittering and the occasional rustle of small animals in the underbrush had accompanied her all day. She strained to hear.

Nothing.

It was as if she were in a sound booth, suddenly aware of her heart beat.

She pulled a dead branch out from under a log, and the odor hit her then, a heavy, stifling odor, something dead. The odor of something decaying.

She didn't want to look. Maybe it was a dead deer, but it was different somehow, coming now on a breeze fanning the clearing. Jennifer pulled the branch and started to turn. Her feet slipped out all at once and she fell to a sitting position, still holding onto the branch.

*Ohmigod, that's a shoe.*

She held onto the branch as the rotten meat odor blanketed her. She took shallow breaths through her mouth, holding onto the stupid branch. *Get up Jen, get moving.*

She had left their tent (and boyfriend Carl) at nine in the morning, determined to walk out of the wilderness, his life, and his crazy schemes, in that order. She had reminded him they weren't even supposed to *be* on the reservation. When she left camp, the July morning was warming up, and she had hummed to herself for the first hour. Then the trail had just quit and good old Carl had said there was only one trail in and out. After a while the trail just disappeared.

She had followed a twisting succession of game trails since then. Jennifer stopped humming at noon. By one o'clock, she was talking to herself. She thought of building a fire to attract someone, but she knew it wouldn't work in the dense woods. She thought more than once she would kill Carl for her cell phone.

Carl. What a loser. I deserve this, she thought. My life must be pathetic. I can't believe I let him talk me into going on another of his stupid expeditions. This time it was Bigfoot for chrisssakes. He had actually signed us up for a Bigfoot Expedition. Paid six hundred dollars apiece.

The idiot huckster Bigfoot leader told us we could be in the group that finally put the myth to rest, the group that found proof positive that Bigfoot, a large, hairy, bipedal ape existed in the forests of the Pacific Northwest. *Yeah, there was a hairy ape here in the Northwest. Until this morning, I used to date him.* I get back to Portland, I'm going to re-do Carl. He's an idiot.

*And you let them take your cell phone so it wouldn't scare Bigfoot!*

*You're an idiot, Jen, for going with him here.* Paying those scam artists all that money (teach us how to look for spoor, my ass) and letting them lead us to our overnight listening posts. The leader told us that Carl and I were most likely to see Sasquatch, since he was convinced the big hairy animal actually lived on the Cold River Indian Reservation. The Indians didn't talk about Bigfoot, he reasoned, 'cause they wanted to keep him secret.

*Well, no shit Jerry Garcia, the Indians didn't talk about Bigfoot because the hairy beast just doesn't exist.*

She let go of the branch, sat there and stared at the shoe. An ant, not just any ant, but a large black one, crawled out from under the suit pant leg, peered at Jennifer as if to say, "Come on down," and marched back under the cuff. Jennifer blinked. A man's dress shoe. *So this is what happens when you get lost, you die under a log.* Something was wrong here, very wrong. The shoe, a man's dress shoe, was attached to a leg covered with a suit pant. Grey with stripes. Above the suit pant (*don't look Jenny*) a white shirt with red and yellow stains completed the ensemble. Above that, nothing.

She finally got to her feet, her knees wobbling, and looked at the shoe. *A man's dress shoe.* She had the thought again, that something was wrong, aside from a body, the dress was wrong. A man wearing a suit, dress shoes, a white shirt.

*That's because he's not a hiker, Jennifer.*

How could that be? A man up here, dead, wearing dress shoes, and not just any dress shoes. That's a pair of Salvatore Ferragamo oxfords from Nordstrom, eight hundred a pair, no sir, no hiking boots here. But she couldn't see a pair, and she wasn't going to look any closer. She had seen only one shoe, and the head, well the head was missing. Must be under the log, you just can't see it.

But she knew that the head was missing, and it was just too much to deal with right now.

Jennifer backed up, her legs shaking. She placed her feet carefully, turned her head to look around, and walked back toward the trees. Ten feet, then twenty, the odor lessening somewhat, and she stopped and looked back at the shoe. She could make out the form of the body under the log, but she wasn't going any closer. She knew one thing though, Sasquatch, if he did exist, didn't hunt in downtown Portland. And this poor soul didn't walk up here in his Ferragamos.

This was no hiker. So, how did he get here? She looked out over the clearing. Rocks, scrub trees, crisscrossed by a few old-growth trees on the ground. Toward the middle, fifty feet away, she saw . . . something. Like a –

*Like a shoe, a shoe with a foot, Jenny. The missing Salvatore Ferragamo, brown lace-up oxford, ladies and gentlemen, don't Jenny, 'cause if you start . . .*

She bit her knuckle to hold back a laugh that once started, she knew would turn into a scream. She stood like that for the longest time, fear giving way to inertia. She knew at some level if she moved the fear would run until her heart burst, but her mind screamed

*Run, Jennifer, run as fast as far as you can, just run, Jen, runrunrunrunrun!*

The odor came over her again, a wave of decay, and she tasted death.

Breathe in, breathe out.

She had once edited a book for an NYPD detective, Jerry Biscoani, an energetic, likeable man who didn't have a nodding acquaintance with grammar or punctuation. His portrayal of crime scenes, however, was graphic and compelling, and the one thing she had never forgotten was his explanation of odor. "Odor is particulate," he had written.

*The sense of odor is triggered when particulates in the air hit receptors in the nasal passage and are interpreted in the brain. In other words, when you sense a certain odor, you are actually ingesting particulates (solid particles from the object you smell) that cling to the mucous membranes in the nose and give you that sense of odor. When you smell the decay of a dead body, you are actually ingesting particulates of dead flesh into your lungs. Dead flesh clinging to*

11

*alveoli, the clusters of air sacs in your lungs.*

Jennifer had been so grossed out by his description that she had called him up and asked specifically about particulates. "Well, Sis (Jerry had always called her 'Sis') it's like this. I don't ever make coffee in hotels where they keep the coffee pot in the bathroom, and I use airplanes sparingly." Gross.

Breathe in, Jenny, breathe out. She fell to her knees and leaned forward on her hands, her pack bunching up behind her neck as the acid came up fast in her throat and she vomited, hot, scalding. She vomited until nothing was left, gagged and spit, trying to get the taste out of her mouth, and then she gagged again, remembering Jerry's words. *Dead flesh clinging to alveoli.* Jennifer spit and moved her head to look at the shoe. She turned over and sat, then scooted away from her vomit. Her hands shook as she reached into her pack and removed her water bottle. She rinsed her mouth and spat, and felt a little better. She pushed herself up and stood, cold and shaking, even though the afternoon temperature was over eighty degrees. She felt weak, terrified, alone. She knew she needed a plan, needed to get some control. To get away from the death in the meadow.

"Build a fire, Jenny," she finally said, her voice sounding strange and far away. The sound of her voice scared her even more. She turned slowly, afraid of what she might see. *Or who might see me. Someone's watching me.*

And then she had a thought beyond all reason.

*Something is watching me.*

*Get some control, Jenny. Think!*

She took a step, and then another. She knew there must be some way to let people know where she was. A fire. Build a fire. Say it. Build a fire, make some smoke.

She whispered, "Build a fire."

But she wasn't going to spend the night anywhere close to that body, or any other body, no matter what. The dense forest was better. She walked away from the log, retracing her steps to the tree line. As she reached the trees, she bent over and began to pick up small pieces of wood, getting enough to start a fire.

*That's what I'll do, go back to the woods, put a tree to my back, start a fire, figure out what to do next.*

Jennifer bent over, reached for one last piece, and stared into the

12

vacant eye sockets of a human skull, inches away from her face, the skull seeming to mock her, the eye sockets cracked and broken.

She screamed, not a horror movie matinee squeal, but the scream of pure terror, its power and volume scaring her beyond all reason. She turned and ran, her pack bouncing on her back, brush punching her face and arms, and ran headlong into a tree, the bark smashing into her forehead, blood springing out, and she fell below the tree, alone and bleeding.

She lay like that as the sun slipped behind the mountain, the glacier glowing pink, and then red.

It was full dark when Jennifer opened her eyes. She had never confided in her closest friend the one thing she feared the most was to be alone in the woods in the dark with unknown wild animals. She told her doll, Nanna, that she would rather be stranded in Central Park at midnight. At least I could jog out of there, she told her doll.

She began shaking. *What am I going to do? I . . . can't think . . . I don't know, I'm afraid. Someone help me.*

Wild animals were here for sure, especially the ones chewing on Mr. Ferragamo Oxford back there. I'm alone and lost in the rugged wilderness with wild animals.

And dead things.

As Jennifer faded into unconsciousness, she knew not all the things to be afraid of at night in the wilderness were alive.

She soon learned that while animals could be territorial and make you part of their food chain, man was still the craziest, deadliest of all to inhabit the planet.

And walk the wilderness.

Her last thought was, *I want my Nanna.*

When Jennifer was two, her grandmother gave her a homemade doll, a canvas-covered human form without the eyes, nose, or mouth. The doll looked more like a dough figure, without much form, but Jenny loved it just the same. From her earliest memory, she was clutching the doll. She named it Nanna.

Nanna went with Jennifer to college (her friend Jill was the only adult person who knew this, and was sworn to secrecy.) Nanna had been re-covered more times than Jennifer could remember, but she was still Nanna. When Jennifer was troubled, she would find her Nanna and hold the old cloth doll, her comforter in a world not so nice. She would absently rub the cloth through her fingers like a tailor checking the fabric of a suit, or a latter-day Captain Queeg. When she caught herself rubbing her doll she would laugh, thinking that whether one used metal balls or cloth, is wasn't about the material.

She had left Nanna home for the trip to find Bigfoot. She didn't want to risk her doll in such a harsh environment.

Alone on the mountain, Jennifer moaned in her sleep and thrashed her legs. She turned over into a ball and twisted the tail of her shirt and pulled it up to her face. She opened her eyes to full dark. It was never completely dark in her apartment. Streetlights brightened the corners of her window in the middle of the night. She moved and pain lanced through her head, making her cry out. *Where am I?*

And then she remembered. The wilderness. And the dead things. She had never wanted to be in the city, any city so bad in her life. The places she had thought of as scary in New York City she would have willingly traded for the wilderness. She would gladly be in Central Park at midnight, to be able to jog a few blocks away from trouble and to civilization. The NYPD patrolled there, didn't they? Won't be any cops up here. She pushed up to sit. Her arms shook and the pain bounced in her head. As she sat up she saw that it was not completely dark. A half moon and starlight made the clearing behind her a place of shifting shadows.

*I want Nanna.*

The thought came to her without warning, that she really *did* want Nanna. Jennifer Kruger, a twenty-eight year old adventurer, sometime Deadhead who used to follow Jerry Garcia, owner of two cats, copy editor for a small romance novel publisher in Portland, and woman who sometimes thought she could handle just about anything - now just wanted her Nanna, her doll. She didn't want Carl, just Nanna. And she didn't care who knew. She would tell the world.

*If I live.*

For the first time, she began to have the notion that she would not make it out of the woods alive. You don't want to end up like Mr. Ferragamo Oxford back there, for things to snack on, do you? Something crashed far off, on the other side of the clearing, and she moaned.

*Gotta get out of here, gotta leave, gotta run.*

Pain flashed as she tried to stand, fighting panic. She whooped, fought for air, and got to her feet, trembling, her legs weak, her mind screaming for her to run.

If you panic now, Jen, she told herself, you are going to die here for sure. Make a fire, wait for morning, then make a huge fire, catch some attention. She shook, afraid of every shadow, every noise making her jump, and she slid down to her knees. She clasped her left hand over her right to stop the shake, then scraped up some twigs and fumbled in her pack for her lighter.

Jennifer woke in the night, the fire at her side a small mound of embers. She sat up slowly, her head a dull throb. She pulled her water bottle from her pack and took a long swallow, then another, and snapped the lid back on.

*If I make it through the night . . .*

A shadow moved in the clearing, dancing on the breeze. The shadow joined with others and then moved away, a solo disco of darkness and light. Jennifer didn't think she could possibly be more scared than she had been earlier, but she was wrong.

The shadow hopped on one leg, and where the head should have been, the moon peeked through. The lunar skull skipped on the shoulders of a one-legged man, a ghostly dance by Mr. Ferragamo Oxford.

Jennifer moaned and shrunk back against the tree, the bark lancing pain through her shirt.

*This is not happening, Jenny. This is a shadow.*

Instead of running, she was unable to move. Her mind screamed the insanity of what she was watching, her body a rigid knot as the shadows played in the dark. She clutched her pack to her face, and began to stroke the cloth as if Nanna were there.

In the early light of morning, the shadows were gone, and Jennifer knew what she would do. She wasn't going to take the time to build a fire. She stood and carefully checked her body, wiped her forehead, and ate an energy bar. She carefully took the items out of her pack: Two energy bars, a thirty-two ounce water bottle (minus a few swallows) a pocket knife, some rope, a lightweight sleeping bag, a piece of jerky, a star guide, a first aid kit, and a paperback by Michael Connelly, *The Brass Verdict*.

She stretched, ignored the pain, and walked to the edge of the clearing. She talked herself through the next part.

"Walk through the clearing, Jenny old girl, yep, just walk through it."

She started into the clearing, walking on a careful line to the remains of the man. He was in the same position as the day before. So he didn't dance after all. She stared at the remains. The ant (or its cousin) from the day before, scooted out along the leg, then hurried back out of sight. Well, more of your brothers will find Mr. Farragamo here when the day warms up. She looked around, thinking that whatever had been feasting on him might be back for another snack. She turned and walked toward the other shoe. She stared at the foot, and stepped back and took a deep breath. It was daylight, and she was going to get tough. Get out of here.

She began talking to herself again. "Walk through the clearing, Jenny. Walk to the nearest stream. Walk downhill to a logging road. Get the fuck out of here."

She had read somewhere that the Indians had logged the place to the point of unsustainable yield, whatever that meant, so there must be plenty of logging roads on the mountain. Find a logging road. Follow it down to a bigger road. Get saved.

A good plan.

By midmorning she was well beyond the clearing. The game trail she had been following ended at a sheer cliff of basalt rock, a hundred feet to the forest below. She worked her way around the cliff, sliding on her butt and grabbing branches to slow her journey. At the bottom, in the forest again, she drank deeply from her water bottle. She ate an energy bar and began walking toward what looked like another opening in the trees.

As she got closer, she could see the remnants of a large forest fire, some trees with upper limbs burned, and then she stood at the edge of a blackened, burned forest. Dark limbless trees pointed to the sky, like exclamation points (use sparingly, Detective Biscoani!). Across the scorched valley a rock wall stood watch over the desolation. As she made her way through the wasteland, it reminded Jennifer of pictures she had seen of Hiroshima after the atomic blast. At least she could see where she was going for the first time since she had entered the wilderness.

There! A car, a pickup truck in the burned out clearing. She began to run, a ragged scream coming out as a croak. As she got closer the pickup danced away, and she ran harder, dodging blackened trees. The truck changed into a tree and then a rock, and she sank down to her knees, too exhausted to cry. She sat like that until the sun was hot, and she rose up and started walking, the illusion of a truck already gone from her mind.

Jennifer walked aimlessly through the seared landscape. Tendrils of black dust rose up and swirled around her legs. A shadowy specter of ash floated behind her, marking her progress.

At the rock wall, she found another body. Her mouth was dry. Breathe in, breathe out.

Painted fingernails. Like her Nanna.

She took a souvenir.

No one's gonna mind.

Eventually she wandered away from the rock wall, back toward the forest. She sang to herself and fingered the fabric of her shirt, clutching the artifacts of her passing.

# Chapter 2

Cold River Indian Reservation
Sidwalter

"Daddy, I want to ask you something." Nine year old Laurel threw her bag on the floor of the Suburban and hopped into the passenger seat. She reached for her seatbelt and looked at her dad. It was an ongoing question, one that usually led to an argument.

"No. Not if it's about *Twati*."

"Daddy, why not?"

Smokey sighed. He grabbed the radio microphone from the console and announced that he was on his way to work. "Dispatch, be advised, I have my daughter with me."

"Copy, call Chief Andrews in his office."

"Three oh three, copy." Lieutenant Mark "Smokey" Kukup of the Cold River Tribal Police Department wore a gray and black uniform, kept his hair long, traditional, braided on each side. His face was Chinook, the high cheekbones and dark skin of the Columbia River Tribes. He looked at Laurel. Sometimes he thought she was a twenty-one year old in a nine year old body. He rarely said no. He had been in Afghanistan for three tours, much of Laurel's life, and it was hard for him to say no, but he was learning. He would hold firm on this request. She wanted to study with a *Twati*, an Indian doctor, a shaman. "Laurel, I don't want you to learn that type of stuff."

"*Ila* says I should. She says I have a gift."

"Your *Ila*, your grandmother, needs to speak to me about it first." He backed the SUV out from the log house he shared with his mother and daughter and pulled onto the drive. The house, barn, and outbuildings sat in a large grassy meadow. Behind the house the wooded slope ran for miles to the west toward Mt. Wilson. The driveway curled through the meadow, over a small hill for a half mile, and then ended on a wide gravel road that eventually led to State Highway Twenty-six, the Mount Hood Highway that ran through the reservation from Portland to Madras.

"Daddy."

Smokey turned to look at his daughter. She was so beautiful she

18

made his heart ache. She had her mother's face and shiny black hair down to her waist.

*Like her mother's face was once. Before Amelia started drinking again. Before the parties. Before meth, and her death when he was halfway around the world.*

"Daddy, couldn't I just learn a little bit?"

"Laurel, I will talk to *Ila* about this, just don't ask me. From what I hear, you already know too much *k'inut* (vision)."

"I won't ask until you talk to *Ila,* Dad, but *k'inut* is traditional, and you try to be a traditional Wasco, to live that way, right Daddy?"

Smokey nodded. Problem was, *Ila* had made all decisions for Laurel for the past several years, and in the eight months he had been home, it had been tough for all of them. And he knew Laurel was trying. His biggest fear was that he wouldn't be there for her.

They reached the highway and Smokey pulled out into the summer traffic. Eighteen wheelers interspersed with pickup campers, motor homes pulling boats.

"Daddy."

He smiled. Sometimes she reminds me of me.

"Daddy, do you *have* to go to work today? Let's go to Redmond, shop at Wal-Mart for stuff."

"I need to help with a narcotics search warrant. Stuff is what we don't need, Baby. But we'll go tomorrow and shop for *Ila.*"

"Daddy, weren't you supposed to call the chief?"

Smokey made the call, and when the chief came on the line, he listened.

"I'll be there in twenty minutes." Smokey flipped the phone closed. If they were activating the Tribal Search and Rescue team, they would have to put the narcotics search warrant on hold, depending on how quickly they found the lost person. Or the body. Sometimes these things ended in a rescue. More often than not, with the rivers and wild terrain they ended with a body recovery. Fifteen years ago three hikers had wandered into the wilderness area of the reservation and became lost on Whitewater Glacier. As far as he knew, they were still there.

"Uh, Laurel, we have a search and rescue activation. A woman is lost near Parker Creek."

"Do I know her? She a tribal member?"

"No."

"Indian?"

"No, *Šiyápu* (white) woman."

Laurel turned in her seat and cocked her leg up under her. "What's a *Šiyápu* woman doing up there on Mt. Jefferson?"

"Don't know, but she's been lost for over twenty-four hours."

"Can I go?"

"No."

"But Dad, you've been teaching me."

Smokey shook his head. No. He *had* been teaching her the traditional ways to track animals and humans. Laurel shook her head, side to side. She didn't give up easy.

"Laurel."

She hung her head down, then looked out at the crowded highway. "Anyways Dad, what's this *Šiyápu* woman doing up there in the wild?"

"It's 'anyway' not 'anyways' and I don't know, but I'm going to find out."

"Whatever," and then Laurel quickly added, "Daddy, I hope she's okay, this *Šiyápu* woman."

Smokey nodded. On these things he had his doubts. He had spent a lot of his life up on Mt. Jefferson, and even in summer a city person could last one night. Maybe. Two nights, remote possibility. Three nights, never.

"Is she pretty?"

"Laurel!" Smokey grinned, and then laughed. Since his return from Afghanistan the last time, Laurel had tried to play matchmaker. Smokey understood, but everything had its own time. Laurel was quiet as he drove into the Agency, the City of Cold River at the southern edge of the reservation. She started to say something as they drove down the hill, then closed her mouth and stared out the window.

She had been told she had a *gift*, that she could be a true seer, could make objects seem to be alive. A shaman. A witch was how he thought of it, but people with such gifts were often revered (or feared) within the tribe. Yes, he was traditional, but that didn't mean he wanted his daughter to take up such a consuming and possibly dangerous activity.

He pulled up at the community center where Laurel had activities planned for lunch. He leaned over the console and she threw her arms around him and kissed his cheek. He didn't think she could stay mad for long. He held her a moment longer than usual until she started to squirm, and he let her go.

"Call *Ila*, have her pick you up if I'm busy, or go to Aunt Nola's house. Okay?"

"Dad?"

"Uh –."

"Dad, if I can't study with *Twati*, can I have a 'MySpace?'"

Smokey just looked at his daughter. Laurel laughed, jumped out, and didn't look back as she walked into the center.

Cold River Tribal Police Lieutenant Mark "Smokey" Kukup watched for a moment after his daughter entered the doors to the gym, and slowly put the Suburban in gear. He thought later if he had known what waited for him up on the mountain, he would have run after his baby girl, taken her shopping at the Wal-Mart Supercenter down there in Redmond. Let someone else go up on the mountain. Or no one. Leave the dead their place.

*You've seen horror enough in four years in Afghanistan.*

But he hadn't seen this. And this new horror would involve everyone he loved.


Jennifer's eyes fluttered. She squinted against the sun, and closed her eyelids to feel the warmth. She was lying on a rock in the middle of an opening in the trees, the clearing from the night before a mile behind. The morning had been spent wandering, stumbling, falling, and finally she had crawled up on a rock in the sun, the mid-morning heat from the rock soothing, a stone womb to comfort her.

Nanna.

She clutched her Nanna, holding tight with her right hand, brushing the fingers of her left hand across Nanna's smooth surface. She held Nanna to her chest and fell asleep, dreaming of the doll she had left at home on her bed.

But Nanna was here now, keeping her safe.

21

# Chapter 3

Cold River Indian Reservation
Biddle Pass
Search and Rescue (SAR) Base Camp/Incident Command

"Call Portland Mountain Rescue, and call them now," Smokey yelled into his cell phone. "I want to tell them what we have, we may need them later, and bring that Bigfoot Expedition asshole to the trailer now. Drag him in here if you have to."

Fire and Rescue had set up the base camp on the flat area at Biddle Pass, an area flat and treeless enough to land helicopters. The logging road continued on toward the mountain for another three quarters of a mile before it turned south along Parker Creek. The white glaciers of Mt. Jefferson towered above the camp.

As SAR coordinator he knew that often the best place for a base camp was not the closest spot to the beginning of the search, but a place easily accessible for helicopters, multiple vehicles, trailers, with room to turn around. They could always set up a "spike" camp, a smaller satellite base camp closer to the search area.

He stood by the incident command trailer and looked around at the camp taking shape. What would appear to be chaos to the uninitiated - a jumble of SUV's, trailers, command vehicles, vans, horses, search dogs, and people, actually made sense to him.

Down the road on the other side of the large meadow, two SAR members were directing traffic for search teams. A search leader waved a clipboard. Team members signed in and then out again at the conclusion of the search, a tactic designed to not leave a search team member in the wilderness.

"Cheryl." Smokey called to a woman attaching maps to the wall of the incident command trailer. She stopped and looked at him.

"Call for a general meeting of all team leaders, four o'clock."

He turned and watched as an officer led a man into the command trailer. The man had long hair in a ponytail, wore surplus store woodland camo. Smokey closed the door.

"Sit." Smokey pointed to a bench on the wall.

"You want to violate the sovereignty of this nation, I should throw you in our tribal jail and see how you fare. What's your name?"

"Stan Perdue, but I didn't actually go on the reservation," he said. He folded his arms and leaned against the wall. Smokey stepped close to Perdue, and the man squirmed into the wall, turning his face away.

"You took money and put people on the rez, knowing that it was illegal, telling them that they would have a good chance of seeing Bigfoot here, didn't you?"

"Well, yes, but I  - ."

"Show us," Smokey said, pointing to a map. A detailed topographical map was on the table. Perdue walked over and put a finger on the map.

"Here. We walked the groups in on the Pacific Crest Trail from our base camp at Pamelia Creek. Then up to Hole-in-the-Wall Park, across Jefferson Creek, and up to the Parker Creek drainage." He tapped the map. "That's where Carl and Jennifer were camped, up there below the Whitewater Glacier.

"Where's Carl?"

"I saw him outside," Perdue said. "Look, I'm sorry, I –."

Smokey pointed to the tribal officer. "Get him out of here. Keep him in our custody until we figure out what he had to do with this woman's disappearance."

The missing girl's boyfriend entered and dropped on the bench without waiting for instructions. Smokey thought the slight man with constant frown lines on his forehead had the affect of a beaten dog. The boyfriend twisted his hands, looked up at Smokey, and then looked down at his lap.

"What's your name?"

"Carl Robbins."

"Well Carl, let's not waste time. Show us on the map where you last saw Jennifer."

Carl walked to the wall and stood in front of the map. "There." He pointed to a section of trail below Whitewater Glacier, the only trail on the map in that area, Smokey saw. A trail that eventually led to the base camp where they were now.

"What happened?"

"Well, yesterday morning we had a fight. Jennifer wanted to go, to get back to Portland, and I wanted to stay for another two days. She got mad, packed her pack, and left, going south on the trail, back the way we had come. After awhile, I got worried about her, and I packed up and walked back to the base camp off the reservation. I thought she would be there, ahead of me. When I got there, no one had seen her. She, uh, she must have taken a wrong turn."

Smokey leaned over. "Carl, look at me." Carl raised his eyes.

"Carl, did you kill your girlfriend?"

"What, no I –." Carl started up out of the chair. Smokey gently pushed him back down.

"Prove it."

"But she was *alive* when I left."

"You said you had a fight. Did you hit her?"

"No, I just talked, we –."

"How can you prove she was alive?"

"I don't know, I just don't know, except I would never hurt her."

"We need some information," Smokey said. He began asking questions as Sergeant Nathan Green took notes.

He learned that Jennifer had moved to Portland from New York two years ago, and was now working as a copy editor for a small publishing company, specializing in historical romances. She was five foot four, twenty-eight years old, and walked a lot for exercise. Mother in New Jersey. Carl said she had a sleeping bag, a bottle of water and energy bars.

"Carl, is she a quitter?"

"Uh, no, I don't think she is."

"She right or left-handed?"

Carl looked up, clearly surprised at the question. "Left." He held his left hand up. Smokey knew that in this case, the terrain would mostly direct her path, but it could be important. Lost people, especially when fatigued, had a longer stride on their dominant side. Without direction, a left-handed person would walk in a large circle to the right. He remembered a line from a comic: *Hire the left-handed, it's fun to watch them write.*

"Stay here, and don't touch anything." Smokey motioned for Nathan to join him outside. Around the trailer, the activity was more intense. Smokey walked to the side and spoke quietly.

"Have an officer take Carl to the department. Get the detectives to interview him as the suspect in the woman's disappearance, a possible homicide. If he killed her, we'll never find her unless he tells us where she is."

"I'll get them on it. F.B.I.?"

The F.B.I. had jurisdiction on Indian Reservations for the investigation of violent crime. Smokey sighed. He didn't want to, but they had to be told, and the case belonged to the Feebs if it turned out Jennifer was the victim of a homicide.

"Ask the chief to call the Bend office. Let's brief and show the teams where he said he last saw her. Some of them will want to go out tonight, set up portable radio repeaters. Computer map the area. Let's get started."

Jennifer's water bottle was long gone, lost in her wandering, stumbling journey. She worked her way down through thick brush; thirst pushed her toward the sound of water in a wooden, stiff-legged march. She stood at the edge of a fast-moving stream, holding her hand out on a large rock, and she settled down, then leaned forward to drink. She carefully placed Nanna beside her, and used both hands to scoop water from the stream. When she finished she picked up her doll and held Nanna close and rocked back and forth, thinking she should get up and clean her apartment.

*Maybe I'll wait here just a little while longer.*

The necessity and practical side of SAR operations was to find a lost person, and in some cases, to recover a body. The executive part of SAR, Smokey knew, was that one such operation could eat more of an annual budget than two or three homicide investigations. The logistics to provide food, equipment, overtime, fuel, and the sheer numbers of people needed was staggering. A homicide investigation could be scaled down. A search could be, but not before using thousands of hours of search time, sometimes tens of thousands of hours, and occasionally to no avail.

There was no way of knowing when a search might end. On the rez it ended with the location of the person or their remains.

There were fifty people at the briefing Smokey gave at the incident command trailer. If we go into tomorrow, he knew, there would easily be double the number of searchers.

"We'll have a helicopter up in an hour," Nathan said. Smokey heard the unmistakable rotor sounds coming from the north. He

25

stopped his presentation and watched as two small objects in the sky came toward them, became larger, and slowed as they reached the meadow. The Blackhawks overflew their location, and then came in from the west, flared, and landed across the road. When the rotors shut down and he could be heard again, Smokey said, "Two Blackhawks from the 939th Air Rescue out of the Oregon Air National Guard from Portland. They will stage here."

As they waited for the pilots and crew to join them, Smokey looked over the assembled group, noting teams from Wasco County SAR, Hood River Crag Rats Mountain Rescue Group, and a K-9 team from Tigard. If she wasn't found today, there would be more groups arriving tonight for a new and expanded search tomorrow morning.

Smokey finished with the assignments. The searchers left the meeting to assemble their teams. Some would drive back to Cold River, and then make the long drive to the other side of the Mt. Jefferson Wilderness area, to coordinate a search from the Bigfoot Expedition camp.

Hope we find her soon, he thought.

"Lieutenant."

Smokey turned and smiled at Sergeant Nathan Green. Green had been his mentor many years before, a man who was his uncle, his older brother, his best friend in one. Green was short and squat, a power lifter. A few criminals in federal prison had mistaken his short stature for weakness. If anything, Green's hair was longer than Smokey's. A long single ponytail was braided with leather.

"What's up, Big Brother, or as Laurel says, s'up?"

Green laughed. "Lieutenant, detectives want to know whether or not to stand down from the search warrant."

Smokey looked at his watch. Four-thirty. "No, let's help them with it. Get it over with. We may need them tomorrow if this goes badly." He followed Green to his car.

I sure hope we find you soon, Jennifer Kruger.

Smokey had been on a lot of successful searches over the years, but he had an uneasy feeling about this one, and he tried to shake it off as he drove back to the Agency. The last time he had had this bad of a feeling, he lost most of his platoon on a bare mountainside in Afghanistan. He had run out of *pishxu* (sage) on that mission. As part of his tradition, before touching a body, he would take a handful of *pishxu* and rub it in his hands, and then rub across his face, his chest, and up and down his arms. He had taken a bag of *pishxu* with him to Afghanistan. Before he left the country, he only had enough to rub between his thumb and forefinger.

They didn't find Jennifer soon.

When she was found, their world changed.

# Chapter 4

Whitewater River

At times during the day, Jennifer had moments of lucid thought. *Keep walking*, the voice said. *Just keep on walking.* The *stay put and build a fire* voice had long gone. Anyway, she was a long way from *stay put.* She had messed up that old wise advice a long time ago. She knew she was losing track of time and couldn't help it, anymore than she could help wanting to hold her doll. The fact that she really didn't have her doll, that she was cradling a replacement, was lost on her, even during those moments when she was sure she was awake.

Jennifer slipped into the comfort of illusion. Of hallucination.

Her thirst was overpowering, a constant companion during moments of clear thought and hallucination. She stood on the bank of a river, kneeled down, and began scooping water into her mouth. The water from snow melt churned past her. The river was too wild to cross. She turned and trudged uphill on a game trail, stepped around a boulder and entered the trees that seemed to reach the sky. A sky growing darker with each moment.

*Going to dark before long.*

She stepped slowly, the rumble of the rushing water fading with each step, the trees coming closer together. As she entered the forest, Jennifer stopped. Uncertain.

*You will die here.*

The thought jumped into her head before she could stop it. She had been having a good afternoon. A hike in the woods, some water to drink. She must have eaten something, but she couldn't remember. She didn't seem too hungry. Exhaustion and a large tree stopped her progress, and that was where she wanted to stay, even though it was not yet night. She curled tight, pulled her legs up and cradled her head with her arms, holding tight to her Nanna, an unconscious movement, her mind taking her away to the safest place she knew.

In her dream, she was sitting on her deck, holding Nanna, feeling the morning sun on her back, drinking a cup of black coffee and reading the Sunday Oregonian. Her safe place. The Willamette River gleamed below, and the comforting sounds of traffic drifted up to her.

Her fourth floor apartment was the perfect place.

Safe. Warm. No wild things. No dead things. No shadows. She dreamed of home.

She awoke in the wilderness, in the shadows with the dead things.

# Chapter 5

Cold River Indian Reservation
Tribal Police Department

Smokey walked to the front of the squad room and faced the assembled officers. The noise level dropped. Six uniformed officers and four detectives had been waiting to execute a tribal search warrant for possession and sales of meth. Some were on a scheduled day off and not too happy with him. Just part of my job, he thought, and waited for a few more seconds.

Officers Kincaid and Burwell were laughing about something and eating dinner from a large McDonald's bag. Across the table from them Officer Sarah Greywolf was putting on her duty belt, adjusting her gear. She looked up and glared at the two officers. Sgt. Lamebull was reading a Field and Stream magazine, his black hair rolling off the shoulder of his grey uniform shirt.

They aren't going to be happy when I tell them they might be joining the search team after the raid, Smokey thought. But now that they are here, they are as much conscripts as my great uncle when he was an Indian scout for General Crook in the Modoc Wars.

Kincaid slugged Burwell in the arm and laughed. Burwell pointed at the lieutenant.

"Way too much testosterone in here, Lieutenant," Sarah said.

"Looks like you got most of it, Officer Greywolf," Burwell said with a grin. Kincaid gave him a high five.

"I wasn't talking to you, Butthole, just about you," Sarah said, thrusting her face within inches of Burwell.

"Lieutenant Kukup, sir," Burwell said, "Officer Sarah is harassing me."

"Yeah, sex-shull-lee harassing both of us," Kincaid said.

"Knock it off," Smokey said. *Children.* I'm dealing with a bunch of kids. But he knew that they would perform with courage and professionalism when the time came.

"Okay, listen up." He turned to Officer Greywolf. "Sarah, chill!"

She stuck her tongue out at Kincaid and Burwell, sat down, looked at Smokey, and folded her arms. Kincaid blew her a kiss.

"Now!" Smokey said.

The room was silent. Smokey turned to Detective Williams.

"Lock the door please." What he was about to brief them on he didn't want to give to any person who wandered down the hallway.

"Detective Johns is handing out the tactical operations plan along with a map of the house, the area, photos of suspects, and our weapons and positions assignments. It's Detective Johns's plan and he will detail it later. Detective Williams has the informant and search warrant. He will go first."

Williams pointed to a picture taped to the briefing board. "This is Alberto Hermes. Some of you have met him before. Kincaid and Burwell chased him across the river into the State of Oregon a couple of months ago, took him to county, he bailed. He's wanted for numerous crimes, part of a bad group of illegals bringing meth from a superlab near Hermosillo in the State of Sonora, Mexico. He's wanted for multiple murders in Mexico. Just won't stay home."

Smokey knew that Williams had their attention now. Meth was king on the rez, not just here but in most of Indian Country around the United States. Most of it coming from superlabs in Mexico.

"As of one hour ago, Hermes was at the Littledeer residence up at Givens Heights."

"We have to deal with that little asshole again?" Sarah asked. "Last time we went up there with a search warrant, that little Eighteenth Street gangbanger shot at Frick and Frack here," she said, pointing at Kincaid and Burwell.

"Yeah, he's there, along with a half dozen of his slimy partners from the Eighteenth Streeters, plus whatever tweeker and open sore that might be hanging around." He showed pictures of a half dozen other gang members, all known to the officers from numerous arrests and street contacts.

"So you're saying, a normal dope search warrant," Sergeant Lamebull said, flipping the magazine on the table.

"Looks like all the food groups are represented all right," Sarah said. The officers in the room nodded and murmured their agreement.

"Okay, assignments, on the sheet." Lieutenant Kukup got their attention. "Burwell and Kincaid, AR-15's, perimeter east and west, lead car, get out fast. Rear is covered by two detective teams in place, one on the rocks above, a two-officer team in close. Okay, listen up."

The room was quiet now, officers studying their assignments, positions, faces of the gang bangers.

"Entry team, UMP submachine guns, Sergeant Lamebull first up, Sarah second . . ." Smokey continued with the assignments, looking over the officers in the room.

"I will bat cleanup, with the medic unit staged behind me. Listen up for Detective Williams. Vehicle assignments are on the tactical operations report. After Detective Williams is done, we meet at the cars in five minutes. We go in fast. As soon as we leave the parking lot here the entire rez will know we're going to raid something."

Sarah raised her hand. "Lieutenant, what about the search for the missing lady? Anything?"

"I was out there this afternoon. Woman's been missing for her second day. She had a bag, a little food. Just don't know. We'll use some of you in some capacity when this raid is over."

Burwell raised his hand.

"Yes." Smokey smiled. Burwell was young and energetic, had seen more violent activity in his first year on the reservation than most cops do in ten years, regardless of their department. He was cocky, and was getting the hang of it. He and Kincaid, the Blues Brothers.

"Sir, we heard the missing lady was camping on the rez, looking for Bigfoot."

"That's what we know so far."

"So Bigfoot exists on the rez then, far as you know?"

Smokey laughed. Time to stop this and get to work. "Only in your dreams, Officer Burwell." He looked at Detective Williams and motioned for him to continue.

Sarah held her thumb and forefinger up in front of Burwell, holding them about an inch apart.

"You heard the Lieutenant, Burwell, in your dreams."

It's gonna be a long afternoon, Smokey thought.

*It's gonna be a long afternoon.*

And then he had another thought. When he was a kid, camping up in the Mt. Jefferson wilderness with his uncle, he had heard things, seen things that he didn't talk about with anyone. Certainly not when he was in the white man's school up there in Madras.

*I hope this woman, whoever she is, doesn't hear and see any of the same things I saw. I had my uncle with me, and he told me to ignore*

32

*them, but my uncle was scared then, and he wouldn't let me talk about it. Not then, not ever. If she sees things and comes out of the mountains alive, she will not be the same.*

*I wasn't. I should talk to her. If she comes out.*

Smokey heard the detectives call the officers to their cars. He heard the voices far away, as if he were in another land.

*If she's still alive, this Jennifer Kruger, she certainly is in another land. A land closed for almost two hundred years, back in a time before computers, cars, airplanes, penicillin, a time of magic and superstition. A land closed before the conquest by the European invaders.*

*A time when beasts now forgotten roamed at will.*

*But we don't talk about them.*

# Chapter 6

Aboard 939th Air Rescue Squadron Blackhawk
Near Mt. Jefferson

While Smokey prepared the search warrant team, Sergeant Nathan Green was straining to see the countryside out of the side door of the Blackhawk. The nose of the helicopter tilted and they hovered a thousand feet above Jefferson Creek. Across the creek, off the reservation, the creek was the jumping-off spot for the Bigfoot Expedition members. Nathan leaned forward toward the pilot and observer. He pulled his microphone closer. "There, at nine o'clock, Hole-in the-Wall Park." He pointed.

"They would have crossed the creek there, and then on the trail to the northeast, under Waldo Glacier, to somewhere in the area of Parker Creek."

"Rugged country," the pilot said.

"It gets worse if she gets into the Whitewater Glacier drainage. Steep canyons, rock slides, dead trees crisscrossing every animal trail."

"Any trails at all in there?" the observer asked.

"Except for the Parker Creek Trail, the one that starts at the Hole-in-the-Wall Park, none."

"I have someone on the trail, looks like four people," the observer said. He pointed to the north.

"That's our group, tribal police officers, with the boyfriend. He supposedly is going to show us where their camp was."

"Why all the police?"

Nathan looked down at the hikers. "This boyfriend, Carl, he just might be lying. Their camping area, if there is one, may be a crime scene. We'll just have to see. Should know in a couple of hours."

They turned back toward the north, rising with the terrain to stay a thousand feet above ground level.

Rugged. It didn't get much worse than this, unless they continued on past Parker Creek.

"Search area?" the pilot asked, looking at a map on his knee.

"Let's stay within ten miles of where their camp should have been, at the head of Parker Creek. Even though she could be fifteen miles away now, hundreds of square miles."

"This won't be easy, with all the trees and slides," the pilot said.

"Never is," Nathan said, "never is."

"We might try the FLIR this evening, or at least in the early morning," the copilot said. FLIR, Nathan knew, was an acronym for Forward Looking Infrared Radar, a unit that tracked heat sources. Heat, as slight as body heat from one person (or deer, bear, or cougar) generated an outline of the mammal. It was also useful in finding campfires, or fires in general. Law enforcement had used the technology for years to locate marijuana growing operations. The military used it to find enemy campfires, engine heat, and soldiers.

The FLIR unit could, under optimum conditions, trace a person's movement through the landscape, with body heat lingering in the air. In some cases, you could see footprints that faded as the heat left them.

They flew him back to the base camp, and immediately took off to use the remaining daylight.

Whitewater River

Jennifer heard a noise and looked up. A buzzing noise. She just wanted to sleep. She clutched her Nanna and kissed the doll and closed her eyes. She had heard the noise before, but she couldn't remember where. The buzzing grew closer, then faded, and was gone altogether. Silence came back to her place.

*Helicopter. That's what it was. Helicopter. Sometimes they came up the Willamette River, through downtown Portland, not too far from my deck..*

*But they shouldn't be this close.*

*Good thing they went away. I need to sleep.*

# **C**hapter 7

Cold River Indian Reservation
Givens Heights Subdivision

Smokey looked over the line of vehicles ahead of him. They were two blocks from the target house when his cell phone rang. Surveillance team on the house.

"Smokey."

"Uh, bad guy number one is still here, we got at least seven Eighteenth Streeters in and around the house."

"We'll be turning on the street now."

"Right. See the first patrol car now, we have the rear and corners of the house covered."

"Copy."

The subdivision was spread out on a sagebrush hillside, each house on an acre lot, the target house at the end of the lane. The hillside rose up behind the house to a line of basalt rim rock, two hundred yards away. A detective was up there with a spotting scope.

The lead patrol car turned on the street, accelerated past a house toward the target house a hundred yards away, with four additional marked patrol cars, and four unmarked detective cars close behind, each car slamming around the corner. This run and shoot was the only way to do it in the daytime, and daytime raids were all they ever got.

*Go in fast, get the perimeter out and the entry team up. Hazardous, but the only way to do it.*

The house was a single story ranch-style house with nondescript grey siding. As Smokey rounded the corner with the ambulance trailing behind him, he could see eight or ten cars in the driveway and on the side of the house. Some had been permanent fixtures for years, left there for tenant after tenant to work around.

The lead patrol car slammed to a stop at the entrance to the driveway. The front doors flew open and Officers Kincaid and Burwell ran out, running fast to their assigned perimeter positions. Kincaid ran for a tree on the west side of the residence as Burwell ran for a vehicle on the east side, their submachine guns up and in firing position.

Smokey saw the rest of them come up fast, three patrol cars and a detective car, doors flying open and officers running for their assigned spots. Smokey stopped and watched as the entry team ran for a spot to the west of the front door. Sergeant Lamebull was followed closely by Officer Sarah Greywolf, her UMP machine gun at the ready.

*Bad guys have to know we are here by now. They get out and on the run, we're going to have trouble containing this.*

From where he was at the end of the line of cars Smokey could hear yelling from the house. The last member of the six-officer entry team got to the house, all of them low below the front window. Sgt. Lamebull held his hand up to wait, and the windows shook with a loud explosion from the rear of the house.

The plan was for the officers in the rear of the house to throw a stun grenade against the back wall, using the explosion as a diversion, and as a signal for the entry team to move.

Lamebull dropped his hand and an officer stepped forward with a steel ram, swung it back and rammed it forward into the lock. The door slammed open, the officer stepped back out of the way, and Sergeant Lamebull ran into the doorway and inside the house, followed closely by Sarah Greywolf and the rest of the team.

"Police with a search warrant! Get Down! Get Down! Police!"

Smokey heard the officers yelling from the open doorway. He walked forward along the line of patrol cars.

"Got some runners out the back." The detective on the radio sounded like he was running as well. And then, "Runner with a gun! In the back!"

Smokey was moving fast as he heard the last, running for the left side of the house, waving to Officer Kincaid, making sure Kincaid saw him before he ran around the corner.

Three shots in rapid succession from inside the house, a UMP submachine gun firing a three round burst. Shit!

They would have to take care of the situation in the house, and unless they call for more people in there, I'm staying on course at the rear, Smokey thought. He ran up to Kincaid.

*Good man, staying on position to cover his corner, even when things were going to hell.*

"Got at least three runners out the back, at least one with a gun, don't think we have any of them contained, Lieutenant." And then from Detective Williams at the rear of the house, "You guys see that first one, all the tattoos?"

"No, he's in the brush, somewhere south of us."

Yelling from the rear of the house.

"Two down in the back, one still on the loose. Spotters on the hill, can you see our third suspect?"

"Nope, still looking."

Smokey keyed his lapel microphone. "Freeze the action in the rear, keep who we have, we'll look for the runner later."

"We need help in the house!"

Smokey ran back around for the front door.

When Sarah ran into the house behind Sergeant Lamebull she began yelling, "Police with a search warrant, get down! Get down! Police with a search warrant!" Lamebull ran in straight ahead, Sarah hooked to the right, saw movement, two bodies on the floor, another running for the hallway, and two more standing in the living room, one with baggy pants, no shirt, jail tattoos on his arms, black bandanna on his head, holding a pistol in his right hand, backing away.

"Freeze! Drop the gun!"

Baggy pants raised his arm, and swung it around toward Sarah.

"Nooo, drop it!"

He continued the swing and the motion slowed for Sarah, and she yelled again, seeing movement from one of the tweekers on the floor, sensing an officer behind her, Lamebull yelling from the hallway, her UMP forty caliber machine gun lined up on the middle of baggy pants's chest, and he swung the gun around, throwing himself sideways as he brought it up, and Sarah fired fast, touched the trigger, a three round burst, the burst catching him center in the sternum, three rounds as one, almost the same entry hole, blood spraying out as he went down, his head snapping back as he fell.

"Get down, Asshole," she heard Sergeant Lamebull yell from her side at the other person standing in the room. The man dropped and she covered the remaining three with Lamebull, swinging her UMP on the bodies on the floor, looking at her sergeant.

She heard Sergeant Lamebull ask for more help in the house, and then ask for a medic unit immediately.

"Clear so far," Lamebull said as Smokey came in through the front door, followed by a medic team. "We still have to search the attic, the crawl space, and the runner outside."

Sarah lowered her machine gun as the three on the floor were handcuffed.

"You shot Jimmy, you bitch, you'll pay for – ."

Smokey moved forward, fast, jerked him to his feet, and pushed him to the door where Burwell waited.

"Get him in a car, now!"

Sarah watched as Martina, one of the medics, pulled her stethoscope away from the gunman's chest and looked up, shaking her head. Dead. She let herself be led outside by Smokey.

Kincaid came up and tapped her shoulder. Burwell put his arm around her and then followed Kincaid inside the house. She put her gun on safe and took the sling off her shoulder and handed the machine gun to Smokey.

"You alright?" he asked.

She looked up at him. "For now, Smokey. For now."

*So this was what it was like. Been shot at a lot of times, girl, but never shot someone. I should feel more, but I don't. I want my babies, they need me, need to get them out of the community center.*

"El Tee, can we get my kids from the center?" She was surprised at how calm she sounded.

"Soon," he said, sounding far away. They had too much going on. Drug raid gone bad. Woman lost, possibly dead. The smell of *pishxu*, sage, was strong. There would be more death.

Officer Sarah Greywolf motioned to the side of the building and Smokey followed her around the corner, away from the patrol cars, the drug suspects, the other officers. She turned her head to his shoulder, and the first tears came.


Near Hermosillo, Mexico


Enrico Alvarez stood alone on the platform and looked down on the workers below him. The large warehouse was brightly lit, even at midnight, the work continuing around the clock. From where he was the workers resembled white insects, their breathing apparatus looking like strange colorful antennae. He knew that he should wear a respirator like the workers, but he was only going to be in the weighing and packaging room for a minute longer.

The workers wore respirators so they wouldn't get addicted so quickly to the powder they were weighing. Once they got addicted, they made mistakes, and eventually would have to be killed or dumped in Mexico City with a habit.

Alvarez wore his usual grey suit and light blue shirt, with twin scars running down his cheeks, remnants of a childhood spent in the slums of Zihuatanejo, and later, Mexico City. He had shoulder length thick black hair that draped over the collar of his suit. He was short and fat, but no one had called him that for almost twenty years. A door opened behind Alvarez and a large man dressed in khakis stood behind him. His second in command, Roberto.

At a table below, a dozen workers meticulously weighed the powder and placed it in bags. The bags were then sealed in cans with various food labels for export to the United States. A woman suddenly became animated, waving her arms, urging the others around her to work faster, her long hair pulling out of a bun and falling on her shoulders.

Alvarez pointed. The man behind him spoke into a radio. Two men came in a side door below and grabbed her arms and pulled her from the room.

They turned walked outside and down a stairway. He waited for Roberto and they walked together to the adjacent building.

This one was not so brightly lit on the inside. Smaller, darker. Two men were bound and gagged, laying on the floor in the middle of the room, with a half-dozen guards standing over them. The bound men wore the uniforms of the local *policia*.

There are some good *policia*, and some bad ones, Alvarez thought. The bad ones, like these, thought they could arrest two of his employees. The good ones, they just leave me alone.

He walked up and held out his hand. Roberto placed a .45 caliber pistol in it, and Alvarez shot the first man in the head. The second one, maybe twenty-one years of age, Alvarez thought, began pleading.

"Por favor, Senor, I will do anything, just give me the chance, I will work for you do any . . ."

Alvarez shot him and calmly handed the gun to Roberto, walking to the door.

"Put them where we talked about," Alvarez said, "by morning."

Leticia Morales drove her aging Ford Taurus as fast as she dared, the *coche* shaking violently when she drove over 100 kilometers per hour. She was one of the few vehicles on the Blvd Luis Encinas Freeway as she sped through the dark morning toward the center of Hermosillo.

It was 5:15 in the morning and she was going to be late for a breakfast meeting at the hospital. She still had to drop her kids off at a friend's house on the way. Her four year old daughter was sleeping in the back seat, her five year old son munching *cereales* next to her in the front. The sun was coming up behind her as she flew past the Universidad de Sonora, took the off ramp and stopped for a traffic light in front of the museum, the formal columns guarding the massive front doors.

Something dripped on her windshield. Reddish black, thick, like softened ice cream. She reached for the wiper switch when another drop hit the window in the center, this time a splatter. *Aves?* Bird?

She tapped her foot and waited for a bus to cross. Her son leaned forward and craned his head to look up above the car, his right hand poised to reach for more cereal. He pointed.

"*Madre, La Mordida.*" He waved up at whatever it was above the car.

"*Madre, muy feo, rostro,*" he said, excited now, and Leticia thought he said, "Halloween."

She leaned forward and looked up as another large splatter of goo hit her windshield, and there was something up there, two something's hanging from the stop light.

*Cabeza?* A head. A *cabeza* with a *policia's* hat.

Cabezas, two of them, severed, blackened.

Two severed heads, swinging from the stop light, one with a hat, the other sporting a leering, lopsided grin, as if he knew some great and terrible secret, and Leticia began to scream.

Photos of the heads were on YouTube within the hour. By evening, as Alvarez was landing in Denver, there had been over a million hits worldwide.

41

# Chapter 8

Whitewater River

In the morning, Jennifer made her way back to the river and stood on the bank and gazed at the churning water. She carefully placed Nanna on a rock and scooped water up, spilling most of it, and drank that way until she was done. She pulled her doll up and struggled to her feet. *I think I'll go shopping today. Must be Sunday, I'm not at work. Maybe buy some clothes for Nanna. Give her a bath, she doesn't smell so good.*

SAR Base Camp
Biddle Pass

It had been a hectic night for Smokey and his officers. F.B.I. agents from Bend were investigating the narcotics raid shooting. He had found a couple of hours sleep, and now he could put this in a proper perspective – the lost Šiyápu woman Jennifer Kruger surely had a worse night.

Day three. She hadn't been seen for over forty-eight hours. If they didn't find her today, tonight would be her third night alone in the wilderness. He looked around the base camp. The assembled vehicles looked like a small city. Trailers, tents, helicopters, support vehicles.

He had enough searchers. Over a hundred people were involved now, and at this point, more would be hard to manage.

Smokey turned back to the command trailer and went inside for coffee. *The helicopter is our best hope now, and if she's dead, the infrared radar won't help. At least not for several more days.* He didn't want to think about it. Within two days, the search group would be down to a handful, with most searchers going back to their jobs, the thought being that the lost person didn't survive. Most search and rescue teams did not do body recovery, unless the victims were found early on in the search.

Smokey sipped his coffee and planned for the next phase. Something needed to happen. They needed to get lucky and spot her today. He watched as a Ford Explorer with the Cold River patrol vehicle markings drove up and parked by the trailer. Sergeant Nathan Green walked over.

"We get any more out of the boyfriend?"

"No, he might still be good for it, but we sweated him pretty good, setting up a polygraph for him today. She's probably lost, not a homicide."

"Either way, she's dead if we don't find her soon."

"You got that right," Nathan said. "You got that right, Boss."

Whitewater River

Jennifer spent the day sitting, but on occasion she would wander, mostly downhill, but often just take a few steps and then sit down again. She talked, mumbled, talked to Nanna, and wondered why she cried so much.

*I need to get Nanna some new clothes, and paint her nails again, the paint is fading. Maybe I will peel the fingernail paint off while we wait to shop. Give her a bath.*

Jennifer wandered down to the river to bathe Nanna. She really didn't smell so good.

That night, the animals came, following the ancient preferred tracking method, the smell of decay. Jennifer Kruger had a lucid thought, or as close as she got to clarity.

*Please someone, come soon.*

*You better come soon.*

# Chapter 9

Biddle Pass
SAR Base Camp

As Jennifer was praying for help, Smokey leaned against the side of the incident command trailer and watched the Blackhawks land in the meadow, the flashing red and green navigation lights reminding him of similar landings in a land across the world. The first one flared, followed by the second, the crews looking like aliens in their green helmets.

This would be their last general briefing. Many of the teams would be going to their respective homes tomorrow. A woman with the Portland Mountain Rescue Team limped up, stepping quickly on her right foot, her face streaked and twisted with pain.

The pilots and crew from the Blackhawks were walking across the road.

We must have over a hundred people here, Smokey thought. Three young members of the Cold River SAR carried a cooler into the lighted area in front of the trailer and were passing out water bottles and soda.

"We will hear from everyone, starting with the report from the officers who walked to the camp with Jennifer Kruger's boyfriend. Sergeant Nathan Green, you have the floor."

"We walked from the jumping-off place, at Hole-in-the-Wall Park, just off the rez, here." He pointed to the map on the wall of the trailer.

"We walked uphill to the Northwest, toward Whitewater Glacier, near Parker Creek. About three miles. Plenty of track on the trail of Mr. Robbins going in and out, track of Jennifer Kruger just going in. We went in about three miles and he showed us their camp."

"Do you think he killed her?" a member of the Blackhawk crew asked.

"I could be wrong," Green said, "but we spent a long day with Robbins, he didn't appear to be trying to hide anything, he talked about her in real time, not in past tense, showed us the camp."

Smokey knew what Green was talking about. Sergeant Green continued.

"Often when a suspect kills someone, they refer to them in past tense, because they know that they are already dead, they killed the victim. A slip that people often make. He didn't at any time today. Showed us the camp, said that he thought she was kidding, she had been saying for a day that she was tired of looking for Bigfoot, was leaving. Thought she would be back within a few minutes. When she didn't show up within two hours, he went looking for her on the back trail."

"You track her from the camp?"

"Back about a quarter mile, then she left the trail and crossed a large slide area. It will take some time to do some perimeter cutting around that large slide area. If she went across it."

"What do you think?" Smokey asked as he stepped forward. The searchers were quiet.

"I think, and I may be wrong, that she is lost, that the boyfriend didn't hurt her. Two reasons." Sergeant Green held up his hand.

"One, we tracked her out of the camp for a ways, and he didn't follow her. Secondly, he passed a polygraph this afternoon. He doesn't know where she is." He looked around.

"She's still out here, going into her third night."

Smokey caught Sergeant Green's eye as he left the front of the group and Green joined him. They walked around the end of the trailer. It was full dark now.

"Nathan," Smokey said softly.

"Kid," Sergeant Green said and smiled. He put his arm around Smokey. "How's my little brother I never had, my recruit from years ago, and now my boss?"

"What do you think?" Smokey asked.

"I think that she has had three days to walk on us, that even if she were dehydrated and delirious, she could get a hell of a long way, further than our current search parameters. That's what I think."

"Think she's alive?"

Green shook his head. "No way of knowing. People are pretty resilient. They also have a way of dying out here. And, I didn't say anything to the group, forgot about it actually. Saw a lot of animal sign out there, mostly bear, but a couple of cougar tracks. Mr. Bear not long out of hibernation, what with all the snow we have had. Who knows, maybe she can live another night with Mr. Hungry Bear. I know one other thing." Smokey looked at Green.

"We better find her tomorrow, or we ain't gonna."

They rejoined the group. Smokey listened as they heard from the other team leaders. Parker Creek drainage had been searched. Some of Whitewater River, but what a huge area. And she could be further along than that. Searches always started so hopeful. By this time, Smokey knew, people were starting to talk about 'body recovery,' and not 'rescue.'

Smokey listened to assignments. By tomorrow, they would lose most of their searchers. By the day after, they would be down to their own ten people. Then it would get hard.

*Where are you, Jennifer? Are you alive? Do something, let's find you tomorrow. Do something tonight.*

*Let's find you alive.*

# Chapter 10

Whitewater River

*I wonder where Carl went, he seems to be gone for a long time. Hey, Baby Girl, are you cold? My daddy used to call me 'Baby Girl,' so I call my doll Nanna 'Baby Girl' sometimes. Only sometimes. I need to wrap Nanna up.*

Jennifer looked around carefully as the sun went down. She sat, her feet splayed out in front of her, her breath coming shallow and fast. She had several moments of clarity today, unconnected moments, brief and fleeting, just moments when she knew where she was and at some point how grave her situation.

Grave. What a word. Grave. Well that's what all this beauty was. Nothing but a grave.

*I'm gonna die here. If not tonight, then tomorrow, can't go any further, just no more.*

I seem to have lost my pack and sleeping bag somewhere. Did I have it last night? She couldn't remember when she had last seen her pack and sleeping bag, or where. I must have had it last night. Must have, but I can't remember. Maybe Nanna knows, and she felt herself slipping into that comfortable mode, that place where Nanna wasn't something she found in the woods, a place where Nanna was a loving doll, a trusted life-long friend.

I don't want to look at what Nanna has become. I covered her with part of my shirt. What a nice moon, at least I can see. She looked out and down the canyon, where shadows moved in the light of the moon.

*That shadow down there, coming up from the creek, that shadow is moving, moving toward me and Nanna. I think there's another shadow behind it, moving. It's bright here with the moonlight, almost as bright as day, except for the darkness in the shadows. The shadows were not staying where they should.*

Jennifer heard a crash, somewhere downhill from her, not too far off.

*What was that?* And then she heard other sounds, grunting, snorting sounds. Coming closer. A shadow detached from the others, coming out of the trees down the hill from where she was, coming across a wide bare area, coming toward her. *Sasquatch!*

*Don't be silly. There is no such thing. Doesn't exist. That's not Sasquatch. That's a bear. A large, dark bear. And he's coming for my Nanna.*

Jennifer struggled to her feet, swaying, leaning against the trunk of the Ponderosa Pine she had been resting under, her heart pounding, and the shadow stopped.

"Go 'way." She yelled, then she yelled again, louder, and then she whispered, "Go 'way."

"Go away bear!"

The black bear stood up, sniffed, and looked up toward the tree where Jennifer was standing.

*He's looking at me!*

And she turned to run, her feet not working, pushing herself around the tree, as the bear dropped down on all fours and ran for the tree, a shuffling, quick run. Jennifer looked around the tree and screamed, ran a staggered imitation of a run, clutching Nanna, and she dropped just in time to avoid hitting a log, dove under the log, tight, pulling herself through a small opening, pushing herself backward with her feet, under a tight thatch of branches.

She screamed again as the bear hit the tree. In the dark Jennifer grabbed what she could, pushing rocks and dirt with her feet into the opening under the log.

The bear crawled over the log and pushed through the branches over Jennifer's head and she screamed, the horrible snout in the moonlight inches from her face, the warm breath making her gag with nothing in her stomach to come up.

"Noooooo."

The bear dropped back behind the log and pushed his snout into the opening where she had crawled, pushing his head under the log, and Jennifer pulled her feet back away from the small opening, the bear thrusting, pushing forward, touching her feet, and she screamed.

She pulled her feet back as far as she could, her back wedged tight against a rock, no place to go. The bear pulled his head out and snorted.

*He can't get me!*

*He can't have Nanna.*

Jennifer lay there, wedged under a log and broken branches, curled up tight against a rock at her back. The bear snorted, and she thought she could hear him move away.

*So tired. Go away bear.*

She dozed.

Once, during the night, she heard a crash, some snuffling, and she drifted off again, back at her apartment, the sun warm on her deck.

The bear shuffled off. He came back two more times during the night to check on his meal. On her last night, Jennifer dozed, mumbling, clutching her Nanna. She kicked her feet and dozed.

Her last night.

# Chapter 11

Aboard Blackhawk
Below Whitewater Glacier
0800 hours

The search resumed on the morning of Jennifer Kruger's fourth day alone. "We've got an hour of fuel left," Captain Roberts said. In the back, crew chief Scott Durning scanned the wooded canyon, looking for movement, for color. He hated to give up, knowing that once they left, the chances for finding her alive diminished.

He swept the terrain with his binoculars, following the river, the late runoff from the glacier making the river a white jumble of foaming water. He pulled the binoculars down and wiped his eyes, and as he did a flash of red caught the edge of the lens. There. He threw the binoculars back up. Where was it? He thumbed his microphone.

"Captain, hold."

The Blackhawk slowed, and then hovered.

"What you got, Scott?"

"Something, a few seconds ago. Thought I saw some color. Should be back behind us now, seven or eight o'clock."

"Want me to turn?"

Scott panned the area with the binoculars, back to the area he caught the flash. Couldn't be sure. The angle was wrong.

"Captain, one eighty, slowly, then back."

"Roger."

It took him ten minutes to find it. There. Almost directly below them, a hundred yards up from the water, in the trees.

"Stop. Below us and at nine o'clock, red patch, looks like a backpack."

"Got it."

"I got a sleeping bag, maybe a hundred feet away. Can you put us down?"

"Negative."

"Let me get my bag, drop me down."

The captain was on the radio as Scott gathered his pack that contained a complete medical kit and survival gear.

"Nearest ground unit's less than a mile away. They're humping it," Captain Roberts said. "They should be here before long. I can drop you to the east of the pack, that part with the trees down." Sgt. Coleman, the loader, helped Scott hook up, and then they dropped him into the wilderness.

On the ground, Scott waved them off, and the Blackhawk moved slowly away. He knew they would continue to search until low fuel forced them to return to base. He shouldered his pack and moved carefully over a large log. He yelled the lost girl's name, again and again as he walked. He reached the red backpack and picked it up. Lucky I saw it at all, he thought. This pack is worse for the wear, filthy, one strap ripped off, chewed. It's Jennifer's pack, same color, same brand.

Chewed?

He looked around and saw the bear sign, the tracks, the scat. He picked up the pack and called her name again, this time more aware of his surroundings. Although he was not generally worried about bear, it was a late spring, the snows just melting up this high, and they hadn't been long out of hibernation.

*They're still the biggest thing in the woods.*

The pack was light, can't be too much inside, Scott thought. He set it on the ground and opened the flap. *What the hell?*

Scott reached inside and pulled the contents out on the flap.

*Bones?*

Looks like animal bones in here. But they're not animal bones. He knew with a sudden, chilling certainty. These aren't animal bones. They're metacarpal bones. Human fingers, a wrist bone. A . . . dear God, part of a human jaw bone. What the hell's going on here?

Scott looked up and around, a complete circle from where he was kneeling. His body hair tightened up under his survival suit. He reached down and touched his Beretta 9mm in a shoulder holster under his arm.

"Blackhawk, this is Sgt. Durning."

"Go ahead Scott."

"Uh, I've got some weird shit going on down here."

"Say again, what?"

"Some weird shit, a pack with human bones in it."

"Human bones."

"Affirmative, human bones. It's her pack. Looks like her bag over there. And -."

"And," Scott continued, "a lot of bear sign here. Let me know if you see anything moving."

"Roger."

"Want us to let you know if we see Bigfoot?" Sergeant Coleman asked.

"Belay that," Captain Roberts said.

"Anything moving, you yell at me," Scott said.

Scott walked slowly as the helicopter moved away. He looked for sign, a footprint, anything that was made by Jennifer Kruger. He was joined by the Portland Mountain Rescue team twenty minutes later. They had a search dog with them. The Blackhawk left, Captain Roberts promising to return.

The dog found Jennifer ten minutes later.

When they carefully pulled her out from under the log, Scott thought she was dead. She looked horrible, cuts on her face, caked dirt, her hair twisted and matted, and the terrible smell of decay. She opened her eyes and mumbled. She clutched a bloody rag, holding it with both hands. She was alive.

Scott assisted with putting together a portable stretcher, and they worked quickly to start an IV. When they got the IV going, they carefully moved her out of her log fortress to a more level area. With the sun shining down on his back, not far from the bank of the Whitewater River, Scott Durning tried to remove the bloody rag (and whatever was in it) from Jennifer Kruger's hand. He hadn't told the rescue group about the contents of the pack. He had a bad feeling about this. He gently pulled on the rag. Jennifer clutched it tighter, her eyes wild, and he let go of it.

"You see the bear sign, the scratches on the log?" Harriet Jones, the team leader asked.

"Yeah," Scott said. "There was a lot of it around the pack."

"I can't imagine what she went through," Harriet said.

"Neither can I," Scott said, thinking of the contents of the pack. *Neither can I.*

In the end, they carefully moved her to the nearest logging road, taking turns with the stretcher and holding the IV. They met the ambulance an hour later.

# Chapter 12

Road 2168
Whitewater River Drainage
0945 hours

Smokey and Nathan arrived to see the rescue team come into sight a hundred yards down the hill from the old logging landing. They waited with the Cold River Fire and Safety ambulance crew at the end of the road. The team carrying Jennifer on a stretcher moved like a twisting, many-legged animal, chugging slowly up the hill. They picked their way around rocks and tree stumps. A man in a flight suit trailed the stretcher, holding an IV bag.

Smokey stood back as the medics transferred Jennifer onto a gurney, keeping the IV in place. Her face was swollen, blackened and streaked with blood, her right eye puffed out over her cheek. *She looks dead.* Her left eye blinked and moved from side to side, an unfocused nystagmus. *She doesn't know where she is.* The Cold River medics took over and moved the gurney into the ambulance. Smokey stepped back with Nathan and waited to hear something about her condition.

"No!" A croak from inside the ambulance. After a minute, Medic Carole Tewee came to the door.

"Lieutenant, can you come look at this?"

Smokey walked to the door, thinking that the woman may be aware of her surroundings. He looked in around Tewee.

"She's got a death grip on this bloody rag, and when we try to get it from her, she just grabs it tighter. It sounds like she thinks it's a doll, or something. I don't believe she is coherent, but we need to get an idea of what is going on with her."

"Can you sedate her?"

"Not too much, she's in bad shape, we'll be pulling out in a minute."

"Got it," a medic from inside said. And then, "Oh shit." He handed the bloody rag to Tewee. She unwrapped it. "Christ," she said, and twisted her face away. Smokey leaned forward.

*A hand. She's been holding a human hand. With painted fingernails.*

54

Tewee handed the rag with the hand to Smokey. He cradled it and looked closer, aware of the putrid odor, trying to look at it in a clinical fashion. The skin was starting to slough off, especially around the fingernails and at the fingertips; the hand had been severed at the wrist, not an animal separation, but it looked as if a sharp instrument had been used. *Surgical?*

What the hell happened to her? What did she find out there? *This changes things, won't be going home tonight.*

He found his voice.

"Sergeant Lamebull, take custody of this evidence." And then he added, "Paper sack, seal it for an autopsy later. In the fridge in the evidence room."

The people on the landing were quiet, the Portland Mountain Rescue team subdued, not as jubilant as they should have been, finding Jennifer alive. Sergeant Nathan Green directed them to a van.

"Lieutenant." The man in the flight suit came forward. He introduced himself. "Sergeant Scott Durning, 939th Air Rescue Group." He held up a red pack. "You need to see this, Lieutenant."

"What's in it, Scott?"

"Bones, Lieutenant. Human bones, I think."

*What the hell happened out there? What did this poor girl get into? And where?*

Smokey pulled the flap open and looked inside the pack. Like Sergeant Durning, he knew what the body parts were. Bones. Metacarpal bones, phalanges. They did indeed look human.

"You get GPS coordinates, where you found her?"

"Sure did," Durning said.

"We'll backtrack from there," Smokey said. Smokey looked up beyond the tree line to the snow-covered slopes of Mt. Jefferson, a mountain that had long-held secrets, even from the people who had always lived nearby. He knew he would be going up there within a few hours.

*What the hell did she find?*

*A human hand, a few days removed from its owner, a most certainly dead owner.*

*Human hand bones, the owner long since dead.*

*What the hell did she find?*

# Chapter 13

Mountain View Hospital
Madras, Oregon

"She's in pretty bad shape, not out of danger yet, but I think she'll pull through." Dr. Evans, the on duty ER doctor explained to Smokey.

"Is she talking?" Smokey asked, glancing through the curtain at Jennifer.

"Nothing that makes any sense. She cried out 'Nanna' or 'Manna' a couple of times, she flailed her arms around so we gave her a mild sedative. We can't give her too much, we're a little worried about her heart rhythms."

"What now?" Smokey asked.

"The main thing is to pump fluids into her, she's young, in good shape physically, keep her in bed until she's ready to get up. No broken bones that we can tell, a lot of contusions, bruises, we'll clean her up, that will help, and keep her here."

"Did she say anything about what she found?"

"No, but I heard that she may have found a body part or something." Dr. Evans said. He entered the curtained area by her bed and picked up her wrist, feeling for a pulse. A nurse was gently wiping her face. Even with the bruises and a deep scratch on her cheek, she looked a lot better than when he first saw her.

*She'll be pretty again.*

"How long you know me, Doc?" Smokey asked. They backed out of the enclosure.

"Since you were a snot-nosed kid." Evans grinned, put his arm around Smokey and said, "What do you need, Lieutenant?"

"Let your staff know that we will have someone with her twenty-four seven. Oh, and her room is not listed anywhere. We may want to move her each day."

"You mean have a guard on her?"

"Yes, at least until we know what is going on."

Evans held up a key ring and motioned for Smokey to follow. He walked to a door at the rear of the ER and motioned again for Smokey to follow. A gleaming white Mercedes sedan was parked just outside.

"You need one of these on the reservation, Smokey."

"Yeah, Doc, turn it into a rez ride, that's just what I need."

Evans laughed and they walked back inside.

Smokey stopped by the gift shop on his way out. Every hospital stay warranted flowers. He picked out a bouquet of wild flowers and saw a cloth doll with a bright summer dress, and took it to the counter with the flowers.

"You want to leave a message?"

"Uh, no. . .wait, I'd better."

*To Jennifer, We're glad you are safe. Your new Nanna. Lieutenant Smokey Kukup, Cold River Search and Rescue*

Smokey took the flowers and doll to the ER room as Officer Sarah Greywolf walked in. She looked at the flowers and raised her eyebrows but didn't say anything. Smokey gave her instructions, and knew that Jennifer would be safe. If anyone could get Jennifer to talk, he knew that Sarah would be the one to do it.

"Sarah, how are you?"

"Comes and goes, I'm okay. Never shot anyone before."

"You know, you need anything . . ."

She put her hand on his shoulder. "Yeah, now go." In any other department, Sarah would be on administrative leave for being involved in a shooting. On the rez, Smokey knew, you went back to work immediately, unless and until evidence unfavorable to the officer came out of the investigation.

He placed the doll in the crook of Jennifer's arm, touched her elbow and looked at Sarah. She shook her head and waved him away. Smokey left the ER and walked to his car, dialing Chief Andrews as he walked. It was time to go into the wilderness and find what the hell was out there. Then get back and talk to Jennifer. He drove out of Madras and north toward the rez. He told Chief Andrews of Jennifer's condition. He had a thought.

"Martin, does the F.B.I., the feebs, know about this yet?"

"I called the Supervisory Agent, Oakley, in Bend, and the Assistant U.S. Attorney in Portland."

*Shit.*

"Their reaction?"

"Not much yet, they're not too excited about the body parts. I believe the quote was, "You find a body, looks like they were killed on the rez, call us. Looks like they were dumped there, have fun."

"So their peckers aren't up yet," Smokey said.

Martin laughed.

"I find a body or two," Smokey said, "You can bet they'll be coming 'round, photo opportunity too much to pass up, they'll show up, tromp around in their Doc Martens, fuck up the crime scene, throw out some orders, and leave the work to us Indians."

"How do you really feel?" Martin asked, and laughed again.

"I need Sergeant Green to meet me, now, at the department, ready for two or three days in the woods. We're gonna backtrack, starting immediately. Find what's out there."

Smokey, a fifteen year veteran of the Cold River Police Department, Army Ranger, tribal member, and one of the best trackers in the country, wanted to find out what Jennifer saw. Find what was out there in the most rugged, isolated piece of wilderness in the country.

*Maybe I should let it remain a secret, the way the land had been forever.*

# Chapter 14

Whitewater River

When Smokey was five years old, his father would put him on a horse and have him follow tracks. He followed tracks of deer, elk, bear, cougar, and smaller animals like the *spilyay* (coyote), and weasels, raccoons, porcupine, and squirrels. Later on, he learned to track humans.

From the height of a horse he learned to find the trail of his quarry, and then track the mammal through different conditions. He learned shadow and the nuance of weather and time and how long different kinds of soil would hold a track.

The shadow on a track from a horse is different than the shadow he would see walking, or on his knees. He learned that shadow is best seen in the early morning, or late afternoon.

You could create shadow with a flashlight. That's what Smokey and Sergeant Nathan Green would be doing into the evening. Tracking with flashlights.

Smokey parked the Suburban on the logging landing where they had met the rescue crews with the ambulance to pick up Jennifer Kruger just hours before. He shut the engine off and looked over at Nathan Green. He wouldn't want it any other way – to be tracking, spending time in the woods, going into possible danger after the bad guy, than with Nathan.

Nathan Green, sixty-one years old, the uncle, the older brother I never had, Smokey thought. Expert tracker, taught me a lot of what I know about tracking, a lot of what I know about police work, too. He lets me play the uncle to his five kids. Nathan got out and stretched. Smokey watched this man, easy to laugh with, easy to like.

Smokey knew that Nathan would back him up in an instant with his life, if need be, and he had on several occasions.

I'm a lucky man, Smokey thought. To be here on this day, with Nathan.

"Hey, Nate, you ready?" Smokey got out and opened the back

doors of the Suburban.

"You worry about yourself, Lieutenant."

"Oh, I'm not worried. Just making sure that my elders are properly equipped."

Nathan snorted. "Elders my ass. I'll walk you into the ground, you'll be coming 'round crying, wanting me to ease up the pace, can't take it."

"So that's how it's gonna be, this trip." Smokey pulled his pack out and checked the straps. They were dressed in woodland camo Battle Dress Utilities with khaki-colored packs. They weren't trying to be found. If they needed stealth, they were ready. Smokey just didn't know what they would find.

*Or who.*

The pack was heavy when he shouldered it. He buckled the kidney belt, easing the weight on his shoulders. He and Nathan were self-sufficient should they become separated. They had sleeping bags, shelters, clothing, maps, compasses, hand-held GPS units, cell phones, radios, food, water, first aid, and a lot more. They each carried the department Glock forty caliber pistol.

Smokey opened a long gun case and removed the rifle. He handed it to Nathan, and pulled out another for himself.

"You expecting Mr. *Anahuy* (large bear)?" Nathan asked, as he took the rifle.

"Nope, but maybe his evil two-legged cousin."

"Bigfoot, then."

"The other cousin. Man. Much more dangerous of a critter than anything has ever come 'round walking in these woods."

"Amen, Little Brother. Amen." Nathan shouldered his rifle, a .308 caliber sniper rifle with scope, bipod and sling. Smokey did the same with his. They would be able to reach out and touch someone a long way off if need be, a half-mile or more. They both knew this was no longer a search and rescue mission. This was a hunt for bodies and the person or persons who put them there.

They picked up the trail of the rescuers and backtracked, easy to follow since there had been six of them carrying a litter and not trying to hide sign.

Smokey took one last look at the Suburban and they dropped off the landing into the forest. They walked out through a logged-over area with the new trees growing up about head high, and then into the forest, the white glaciers of Mt. Jefferson gleaming at them through the trees. The first mile was all uphill and he stopped in a small clearing, the waters of the Whitewater River down to his right. He looked over at Nathan as he came up.

"You got some sweat coming down there, Big Brother."

"Not as much as you, Little Brother. Maybe you need to go on a diet. Eat more roots and berries."

Smokey laughed and watched as Nathan looked at his GPS unit.

"Another ten yards, almost due west, where she was found." He put the GPS unit in a bag on his belt. "Beyond that, another couple of hundred yards to where the Air Rescue guy found her pack and sleeping bag."

Smokey leaned over the log and peered into Jennifer's hiding place. He reached down to his belt and removed his flashlight. The place in the rocks where she had wedged herself seemed incredibly small.

*What a warrior she is.*

He slid backwards off the log and looked at the scratches, the bark removed in some places, the scratches deep, wide apart.

"Mr. *Anahuy* was a big'n," Nathan said, bending down, looking at the tracks. "Looks like he was all of five hundred pounds, big for a black bear. This little woman, she's a fighter, most people would've given up."

"Yeah," Smokey said. He stood by the log. When Jennifer was here she had been on her last night, her last day, delirious, dehydrated, not sure where she was or even *if* she was. Her fight with the bear was instinctive, as old as man and woman, as old as mammals, fighting with instinct and adrenalin and fear and tooth and claw and muscle, no pain felt, to quit was to die. There was no calling 9-1-1 here, no yelling for help, no flagging down a cop, no locking the doors. This was down and dirty doing or dying.

*I admire you more, little girl, Jennifer. Wish I had known you. Get well.*

Smokey looked at Nathan and shrugged. "Let's go to where the pack was found."

Nathan led off, Smokey looking back at the crisscrossed logs where Jennifer fought with the bear and stayed her last night. He shook his head. Nathan was tracking uphill, through the trees, stepping around brush and over an occasional log, the Ponderosa Pine trees towering over them.

Nathan stopped in a clearing, brush and windblown trees giving an opening to the sky.

"Here. The Air Rescue Squadron guy found the pack here."

Smokey looked up at Mt. Jefferson. The sun was sinking over the top.

"Gonna be dark in less than an hour."

"I guess we move on, to the sleeping bag, check out the track in the dark. Might work better," Nathan said. They found the sleeping bag in ten minutes, using the GPS to guide them, finding a few tracks as they went.

At the sleeping bag, Nathan eased off his pack and dropped to his knees. He was looking for sign of Jennifer, so he could start tracking her. He looked around, slowly, out two to three feet, and turned in a circle to find her track.

"Fuck."

"What?"

"*Anahuy* brought her bag here, no sign of Jennifer. We have to go back to the place where she was found." Nathan picked up his pack and started back to the east, back toward the log hiding place where Jennifer fought the bear.

"Wait." Smokey held up his hand. "Here. A track, down toward the river." Nathan came over and looked.

"She had to have water," Smokey said. He watched as Nathan followed a track toward the water, abruptly turned and headed up the hill toward Mt. Jefferson, walking slowly, shining his flashlight down back and forth.

"You jump tracking, Big Brother?" Smokey asked.

"You know any other way to do this? We are in a hurry. We need to locate what she found. She had to go down to the river and then back up here again, and maybe back down for another two times. I'm going to find out where she went down to the river in the first place, and then backtrack from there."

Smokey watched in the dying light as Nathan found a track, then used his tracking stick to find another, and got up and walked down toward the river, then took an abrupt left and walked uphill.

"I'm marking this spot, going to find where she went to the river from here. She came up here. May work, may not."

"I'll get your pack."

Nathan walked uphill on a game track. Smokey carried the packs, watching from fifty feet back, providing cover for Nathan. As the sun went down behind Mt. Jefferson, Nathan used his flashlight, slowly, and then, "Got it. She went down here, came from upriver. We got it."

Smokey came up, his muscles straining with the two packs.

"What now, Big Brother?"

"We take a break, then track. Flashlights should work." Nathan straightened and looked at Smokey.

"Guess what, Little Brother?"

Smokey lifted his eyebrows.

"Mr. *Anahuy* had been following her, for some time."

"I thought as much. You're not the only one who can read sign."

They tracked for three hours, first to the north, the wrong way from where they thought she should be, and then followed the track back to the south, up higher toward the glacier, and then back into the trees.

They lost it on a slide area, rocks and dirt coming down through the trees.

"Let's stop here for the night," Nathan said, and then added, "if that's okay, Sir."

Smokey snorted. They ate dinner of sandwiches and jerky, and water. No fire. Smokey didn't know if anyone was out in the wilderness area or not, but they decided to take no chances. He rolled into his bag.

Smokey and Nathan lay in the dark at the edge of the clearing. Smokey had placed his sleeping bag with his feet facing the clearing so he could see the stars. Nathan was a murky shape a few feet away, using his pack for a pillow. It was an hour before moonrise. Smokey fingered his necklace, a leather cord with a small *spilyay* carved out of juniper wood. The coyote had been against his skin for a long time. Sweat and body oil had changed the light colored wood to black, as if a s*haman* had turned wood into obsidian.

He drifted, waiting for sleep. He thought his *uncle* must be sleeping, when the older man spoke.

"I see you still wear the *wahayakt*," Nathan said. He spoke in a murmur, almost a whisper.

"I thought you were sleeping," Smokey said. *How can that old man see what I'm doing?*

"No, just watching you, Little Brother."

"I've never taken it off since you gave it to me, Uncle. It served me well in Afghanistan. I was like two men. The Taliban said that I was an enemy who could be in two places at once. I fought, and you were by my side."

Nathan had given Smokey the necklace as Smokey was leaving for Afghanistan. It was a tradition, when a good friend was going on a hazardous journey, to give that friend something that had been used a lot, a *wahayak,* (necklace,) a pocket knife, something valuable to the giver. If the person with the object gets into trouble, they can take the object out and will have the strength of the giver, as well.

"Do you know the history of this *wahayakt,* Little Brother?"

"Just that it belonged to you, Uncle."

Nathan spoke again, this time a whisper. "It belonged to *my* uncle, my father's brother. He gave it to me before I left for the war of my generation. I wore it into Cambodia a year before Nixon announced we were going into that godforsaken jungle." Nathan chuckled, a low dry laugh, as if what he was remembering wasn't particularly funny, but there was no other way to think of it.

"My uncle fought beside me many a day," Nathan said. "I once carried two of my wounded buddies a lot of miles to a base camp, chased first by the Khmer Rouge and then VC. When I got there the commander was astonished that this little Indian could carry two heavy *Šiyápu.* I didn't tell him that my uncle was lifting also. He wouldn't have understood."

Smokey touched the necklace, thinking that he should have left it with Amelia, to help her with the alcohol, the drugs, the temptations of loneliness. He must have said her name aloud as Nathan interrupted his thoughts about his late wife.

"Maybe you should have Little Brother, given Amelia the *wahayakt,* but then you might not have made it back."

"Maybe not," Smokey agreed. *But then, she might have been able to use my strength to fight her devils.*

"Did I ever tell you about taking Amelia up here, Uncle?"

"No."

"When we first got married, she was nineteen, I was twenty-eight.

She had been going to college down there in Bend, at the community college, and when she got out for the summer, we used to hike up in this valley."

Nathan didn't speak. Smokey didn't expect him to, and thought about that summer. He smiled. After a time, he spoke again.

"We would pitch a small *ts'xwili,* and when it got dark we would build a fire and put a blanket out next to it. In the warm of the summer night we would lay together on the blanket and talk, look at the stars, and make love. Talk and make love and lay by the fire and hold each other until morning. On each trip, we would always pitch a tent, but I don't remember ever using it. We hiked in here several times that summer - Amelia would have our packs ready when I got home for the weekend. Later, when I left for war, we never talked about it, Amelia and me. We never talked about it when things got bad, but I know this was our best time. *Her* best time, and mine.

*Laurel was conceived up here, that summer. Ah, Amelia . . . we just never talked about it when things got bad for you.*

Smokey lay there for a long time, thinking of things past, of regrets, of things unsaid. His uncle snorted, then began to snore, a low rumble, and then he turned and quit. Smokey lay on his back and looked up at the stars, the dark sky giving way to moonrise, the starlight giving the forest a surreal quality, as if he were on the moon, or a moon of another planet. One of the moons of Jupiter. He drifted off to sleep. He dreamed of that first summer with Amelia here, with her by the fire. But his dreams turned to his night here with his uncle.

*Something moved in the tree line.*

*There in the forest.*

*In his dream, Smokey slowly reached over and touched his uncle. The snoring stopped.*

*Uncle, what's that in the woods, coming this way, something walkin?*

*Uncle, can you see?*

*Yes, Smokey, I can see things we were not meant to see.*

*A strange figure stood at the edge of the woods and looked at them, standing on two legs, covered with long hair, too tall for a bear, didn't walk like a bear.*

*I've seen Mr. Bear walk before, up on two legs. This shadow walks in a lurch, like the undead, like a shadow man on a stroll.*

*Uncle.*
*Can you see?*
*I can see.*
*Uncle, you have your eyes closed.*
*As you should, Smokey.*
*The hair figure looked straight at Smokey, raised his head and howled, a sound like Smokey had heard only once before, when he camped up here with his uncle many summers ago, a sound not unlike that of the wolf, only deeper, longer.*
*Uncle, my eyes are closed, what's that noise?*
*And what is that creature howling at us?*
*Smokey could see the muscles moving under the hair as the creature walked toward them. Smokey shivered, wanting to get up and run, to leave his uncle here, the sweat coming down his arms now.*
*The creature (Sasquatch?) What is this animal coming toward me? Must be a bear.*
*Uncle.*
*The creature is walking toward us, Uncle.*
*Get your gun, Uncle.*
*Won't do any good, Smokey.*
*The creature is walking toward us, now thirty feet away, I'm getting my gun. He's howling again.*
*Howoooooooooo!!*
*Close your eyes, Smokey.*
*Smokey closed his eyes, thinking that he should get Uncle's rifle.*

Smokey shifted in his sleeping bag and sat up, now wide awake, aching, the hair on his neck rigid, aching. He slowly reached for his rifle and felt Nathan move beside him.

"Did you hear that, Big Brother?"

Nathan grunted.

"What the hell was -?"

"Sounds in the forest, been here longer than we have, Little Brother."

Smokey looked into the darkness, listening, the forest quiet, not even small animals moving.

Quiet.

Then he heard it again, this time awake, the sound far off, a mile or more. He suddenly thought of Jennifer Kruger, alone in the woods all those nights, alone and dying, and he felt a kinship, a warm admiration that he hadn't felt in a long time. *How did she survive?*

"Go to sleep, Little Brother." Nathan turned over in his bag and was still.

Lieutenant Mark "Smokey" Kukup, thirty-eight years old, former staff sergeant in the U.S. Army, college graduate, a fifteen year member of the Cold River Tribal Police Department, and Cold River tribal member, lay in his sleeping bag in the woods below the Whitewater Glacier on Mt. Jefferson, wondering what the hell was going on. He wanted to go back to that time when he was here with Amelia, but the problems of today interfered.

A lost woman.

Body parts in the woods.

Something howling that you haven't heard before.

But then he knew.

*Yes, you have heard it before.*

*You and your uncle, Smokey.*

*Long ago.*


It was a long time before he slept, and when he did, he dreamed he was carrying Jennifer Kruger through the woods, running in the dark, stumbling, being chased by a large hairy creature. The creature went down on all fours and ran after them, and now it was up on two legs. Jennifer cried out and he ran again, running in the moonlight, not wanting to turn around and see what was chasing them, knowing that they had to get away.

Smokey slept, turning, sweating, running in the darkness.

# Chapter 15

Whitewater Glacier

Smokey opened his eyes to the incredible smell of coffee. It was early light, the sun not up yet to the downhill side, east of them. He looked over at Nathan and groaned. How does he do that so quietly?

"How'd you sleep?" Nathan was tending a coffee pot on a small backpacking stove. He handed Smokey a metal cup. Smokey sat up and reached for it and nodded.

"Uh, good, like a baby." They both knew it was a lie, but Smokey knew it was something they weren't going to talk about. Nathan had his sleeping bag rolled up and his pack ready to go, his rifle balanced on top of the pack. He handed Smokey a piece of jerky and walked to the place where he had marked Jennifer's track.

"I'll start here. Finish your coffee and breakfast." Nathan dropped down with his tracking stick and began measuring the stride, moving forward, slowly, down toward the river.

Smokey walked down to the place where he saw something in his dream, kneeled down, looking for sign, something to tell him whether or not he was crazy.

Nothing.

He looked up and caught Nathan looking, smiling, shaking his head. Smokey stood up, feeling foolish, and picked up their packs and followed Nathan, changing gears in his mind, forcing himself to think about the task at hand.

He wanted to cut her sign and jump ahead, do some jump tracking, try to figure out her path by reckoning and the lay of the land, go to where she must have passed. But he knew that would be an amateur thing to do. They needed to follow her tracks, no matter which direction, since they didn't know where she had found the body parts.

*And it could have been more than one place.*

Nathan tracked as the sun came up, first down to the riverbank, and then back up, Smokey following with the packs. When Nathan got ahead of him about fifty yards, Smokey would move the packs along behind him.

Smokey took over as lead tracker when they came back up from the river, the track now going south and a little west, up toward the glacier on Mt. Jefferson, following a game trail. Jennifer was wearing hiking boots, size six, Smokey thought, with good lug soles. Easy to follow on soft ground. He lost her track once on a rock shelf and after a few moments he walked across, getting on his knees on the other side and picked up the trail almost immediately. He knew they wouldn't always be so lucky.

He found a place where she had been running, the track harder to find, her stride longer and the foot strike not as distinct.

In the early afternoon they found her nest, the place where she had spent the night before her fight with the bear, her third night in the woods, Smokey thought. He found a wrapper and water bottle, photographed them, marked the coordinates with his GPS, and collected the evidence of her passing.

# Chapter 16

Mountain View Hospital
Madras

Jennifer raised up and looked around. Her head hurt so she lay back on the pillow and tried to swallow, her mouth dry from drugs. At some point during the night she knew she was in a hospital, that she was safe, but she wasn't sure what she was safe from.

I don't know how I got here, she thought. I must have been in an accident. I hurt. I just can't remember. She raised her right arm up. The IV tube followed her, the bandages on her hand hiding the needle. She lifted her left arm and saw bandages on her left hand as well.

*What happened to me?*

She dropped her hand and tried to sit up, and in the end, pushed the call button. A nurse arrived within a few seconds.

"Well, I see you decided to join us," the nurse said. She's young, about my age, Jennifer thought. She had the brisk efficiency that you want in a nurse. Maybe a little too cheerful considering that many people here don't actually go home. Home. Where is –? Portland, of course. My home. Seems so far away, so, so very different. It's as if I had been to a foreign land, traveled for a year or more, and can't remember where I went.

"My name is Mary," the cheerful nurse said, adjusting Jennifer's pillows.

"What happened to me?" Jennifer asked.

"I think I'll let the police tell you that."

"The police. Was I in an accident?"

"Well, sort of, but I can't say. Why don't you look at the flowers and I'll see if the police officer is still here."

*Flowers?*

The card was from a lieutenant, and said something about Nanna. Where was Nanna. She looked around and found the new doll under a fold of her blanket, different from Nanna, but a doll just the same. But how did this person know about Nanna?

Mary returned with a police officer in a grey and black uniform, a young woman with black shiny hair. Must be long when she lets it down, Jennifer thought. The woman held out her hand.

"Hi, I'm Officer Sarah Greywolf, Cold River Tribal Police." She reached over and patted Jennifer on the shoulder.

"Tribal Police, I don't understand, was I in an accident?"

Sarah pulled a chair over to the bed. "Kind of, you were camping and got lost, on the rez."

"The rez, I don't . . ."

"The Indian Reservation," Sarah said. "You were with a Bigfoot Expedition, and then camped on the rez, and apparently got lost."

*Ohmigod, Carl*

And then she remembered, a time that seemed like a year ago, driving from Portland to the Mt. Jefferson Wilderness area, camping with a bunch of fools like Carl, then camping on the reservation.

*I don't remember lost.*

*Yes you do.*

*I can't.*

"I remember walking, but not much else. I remember, I re- ." And then it came back to her, all at once, the finding of the body, spending the nights in the woods alone, the frightening sounds, the dead.

*The dead?*

*The dead man and the others.*

Jennifer shook, and pulled her blanket up around her with her gauze gloves. Sarah touched her shoulder.

"I need to talk with someone," Jennifer said. "I don't want to be alone," she added.

"I'll be here, or someone else, until the lieutenant gets back," Sarah said.

"Where is he?"

"Up on the mountain, looking for your trail."

"Oh. Okay, when he gets back then."

Jennifer lay back. So tired, I'm so tired.

She slept.


Parker Creek
1400 hours


Smokey enjoyed the day, as much as he could under the circumstances. They were in the tree line, just down from the snowfields, the forest thick with tall Ponderosa Pines, underbrush, and windblown trees crisscrossing the path. It was cool under the trees. Smokey and Nathan sat and ate a late afternoon snack.

"What you think, Big Brother?" Smokey asked. They hadn't talked much today, other than about the track, always the track, Nathan talking out loud, almost to himself, about the track they were following, how she was doing, whether or not she was running, wandering aimlessly, or resting.

They found a spot where she had apparently been sitting for several hours, a daytime sit, Nathan had said. It was too exposed for a nighttime bivouac. Within an hour Nathan stopped, pointing at a tree with brush around it. They stopped for a snack.

"I think that is where she spent the second night," Nathan said. "After that, who knows?" He shrugged.

"What do you think is out here?"

"A bunch of bodies, some new, some old." Nathan finished his snack, placed the baggie in his pack, and stood to resume the pace.

Maybe we'll find it today, Smokey thought.

*This place of death.*

Jennifer and Carl had been camping on Parker Creek. Smokey and Nathan had the coordinates in their GPS units. They were about a mile from the campsite. If there were bodies or body parts out here, they should find where Jennifer stumbled across them soon.

And they did. Smokey could smell death before they found any sign of remains.

Nathan stood upright and motioned for Smokey to join him. He held his hand out for his pack. Smokey handed the pack to Nathan, and then the rifle. They were in a level area, the trees thin here. A clearing with rock formations, downed trees, and smaller pine trees. Nathan had been following Jennifer's track on an animal trail, moving fast, the familiarity with her footprint an ingrained thing by now. Smokey looked up to the south, the direction of the camp, an area with thicker forest.

"Look," Nathan said, pointing at the trail. "She was running here, on her toes, see the stride, she was running full out, lucky to stay on the path."

Smokey leaned down and looked at the prints, the stride longer than he would have imagined for someone her size. The print was just the round part of the front of the shoe, a divot where she pushed off. He looked up the trail and tried to see her footprints without moving or walking on them. The odor came again, stronger this time.

"She's running from death," Smokey said, nodding down the trail.

"We may not find much, Little Brother," Nathan said.

"I've been watching Mr. Bear and Mr. Cougar tracks for most of the day. They might have been hungry as well." He carefully set his pack to the side of the trail, keeping his rifle in his hands. He pointed to the trail.

"Look carefully. If it's body parts we're after, some of them may be scattered by our animal friends, those not eaten may be scattered for hundreds of yards. Miles maybe."

Nathan removed his sketch book from his pack and quickly drew the trail, the location. He took a GPS reading and marked the trail with coordinates.

Smokey placed his pack beside the trail, opposite Nathan, and carefully looked around. He removed a pair of binoculars from his pack and scanned the clearing. There, at the other end. One hundred yards away.

Birds. Crows.

*A'a* on a log. Waiting for their turn to eat. The dead odor came and went on a slight breeze, but that was where he wanted to look first. He handed the binoculars to Nathan. They approached from different angles, keeping each other in sight, packs shouldered, rifles ready. Thirty feet away, Nathan held up his hand. He gestured to the ground in front of him with the barrel of his rifle.

"Bones. A femur and some others. Some flesh attached, not in very good shape."

Smokey watched as Nathan again removed his sketch book and handheld GPS unit, and wrote in the book. Smokey returned to his stalk of the log. The *a'a* flew off with a noisy protest, and then landed on another log, waiting for the intruders to leave them to their meal. He stepped forward, cautious, watching where he placed his feet, careful to not destroy evidence, footprints, anything that a person would leave in passing.

*That's a human skull, there in front of you.*

His scalp tingled, the skin on his head tightened, and he breathed slowly through his mouth. The skull was just there in front of him, lying next to a dead branch, an empty eye socket staring at him, accusing him for not being there sooner. A patch of hair, some scalp, but mostly cleaned, maybe by animals. He couldn't tell how long it had been there, with some flesh, a little decayed. If he hadn't been looking carefully, he would have missed it altogether.

"Skull here." Smokey pointed in front of him. Nathan looked up and over and nodded.

Smokey bent over the skull and looked closely. An adult skull, a little worse for wear, the lower jaw broken (chewed?) off, the upper teeth well formed, even, expensive, the lips gone (a delicacy) from carnivores and decay. Not a kid or someone from the rez. A hole in the right temple, bullet hole it looked like, entrance hole, the top of the skull missing. Well, this wasn't an accident, not with the body here. Enough for a dental comparison. He fumbled for his GPS unit and saved the spot. Nathan was walking slowly toward him. Smokey looked up and around. The mountain took on a sinister look, chilling in the afternoon heat, the July sun making the meadow hot. The crows were still making a racket on a log, watching the intruders stalk their meal.

"That's a head, not just a skull," Nathan said. He looked older just now, and Smokey saw what his friend would look like in twenty years. More wrinkled. More serious, the laughter gone.

"That's good, Big Brother. But I gave you a hint and you had a leg up on this one. Skull."

Nathan grinned. The grin faded and he went down on one knee to look closely at what was left of what had once been a human.

"That's not a contact gunshot," he said. Smokey knew what he meant but wanted to be sure.

"Why not?"

"With a contact gunshot to the skull, the pressure of the gasses would have caused greater damage to the skull than the bullet. The skull would have fractured, split in several fracture lines. So, not a contact wound. Probably not a suicide." He stood up and looked at Smokey.

"Let's see what the crows are so interested in. Then let's call this mess in."

Smokey came around the end of the log, the odor of rotten meat strong, his eyes watering, and saw a shoe, a dress shoe, and then a scrap of material, charcoal with gray stripes. A suit pant leg. Nathan pointed at the ground.

"Jennifer stood here. Her hiking boot print there, beside the shoe."

*So she had been here. This was the place. She spent the night less than a quarter mile from here. The horror she must have gone through.*

Nathan plugged in the coordinates and photographed the shoe and leg as it lay.

"Mr. *Anahuy*'s been here," Smokey said, looking at the bear paw prints beside and over Jennifer's hiking boot prints.

"Your call, Lieutenant. Do we move the remains to see what's left? Bear already moved it around."

"Grab on, Big Brother."

They pulled on rubber gloves and Smokey grabbed the shoe. As he pulled to remove the remains from under the branches, the leg and ankle started to separate. He reached down and grabbed the pant leg and pulled, moving the remains away from the log.

The leg was attached to a torso, bloody remains with the internal organs missing, one leg gone, one arm mostly gone. Remnants of what had once been a white shirt was wrapped around an arm. Incredibly there was a watch on a wrist and a gold ring on the left hand. Smokey pulled again, sliding the body another foot. *The head is missing, can't be the skull we saw, the skull has been here longer than this.* Smokey looked up at the sun to the west of Mt. Jefferson, thinking that it would be dark in a few hours, and the forest in the dark was a different place. *How did Jennifer survive this?*

Nathan sketched the remains, Jennifer's prints, Mr. Bear's prints, and photographed the area. Smokey opened his cell phone and saw that he had full signal strength. It always amazed him that he could be in the wilderness area and have a cell phone signal. They had a long way to go with their search, but he wanted to give their boss a heads-up on what they had found. He dialed Chief Martin Andrews. It was time to let their boss make some decisions.

*The dead man had a left hand.*

The hand that Jennifer carried was also a left hand. But not the same. And the hand Jennifer was clutching belonged to a woman, of that he was certain.

*Where's the woman? What the hell did you get into, Jennifer?*

# Chapter 17

Portland, Oregon
State of Oregon Medical Examiner's Office

"The hand is a young woman's hand, and she is, or most likely was, from twenty to thirty-five years old," Dr. Kathy Dornan said.

"How do you know that?" Chief Martin Andrews asked. He had known Dr. Dornan since she started as a pathologist with the medical examiner's office. Martin had been a Portland Police Bureau Homicide Detective, and Dr. Dornan had performed the autopsies on several of Martin's clients. She was now the medical examiner for the State of Oregon.

Dr. Dornan grinned. Martin knew she had to maintain a sense of humor or she wouldn't be able to do her job.

"Fingernail polish. Slight hand. And a color an older woman, like myself, wouldn't wear."

"Those reasons going to go in your report?" Martin asked.

"Sure, and some other, more technical stuff. But look at this," she said, turning the hand over in her gloved hand. "The hand was severed at the wrist joint, at the end of the radius and ulna. I say 'severed' because the instrument was as sharp as a scalpel. One of the fingers was chewed by an animal. The decay is consistent with a body being in the elements for about a week, so not too long before the girl found this. But I am guessing about the temperature during the day and night up there on the mountain. Cold at night in July, and warm during the day, right?" She looked at Martin.

"Yeah, thirty something at night," he said, looking closely at the hand. "Seventy-five or eighty during the day. If this was found in the trees, that would be about right. Up on one of the glaciers, then it could have been there a long time."

"And she carried this out?" Dr. Dornan said.

"She apparently thought this was a doll of her childhood," Martin said. "She was clutching it to her chest when she was found, didn't want to let it go."

"Poor thing." Dr. Dornan said.

"Which one?"

"Both of them," the doctor said. "I do want to see the body that this hand belongs to, if you ever find it."

"You sure there will be a body? Couldn't the person to whom the hand belongs be alive?"

"Oh sure, could be," Dr. Dornan said. "But in my experience, when you have a severed hand found by a lost hiker, and the hand was in a wilderness area, the body to which this hand was once attached, is deceased."

Martin nodded.

"And, by the way," Dr. Dornan continued, pulling off her gloves, "what's this about Sasquatch on the reservation?"

# Chapter 18

CNN News Affiliate
Portland, Oregon

Stan Perdue thought the CNN reporter, a thirty something woman with blond hair, was perfect. She would act skeptical, look tough, and was going to be astonished at what he was about to say. Bigfoot on the reservation. Body parts on the reservation, that was something else, and he wasn't going to talk about it. Territorial secrecy and sovereignty of the rez would work in his favor. He didn't want a flood of people traipsing around the area. At least, not until he was the one to find Bigfoot.

"This is Linda Chavez, CNN Northwest Reporter, and I'm here with Stan Perdue, leader of the Bigfoot Research Expedition. Stan led an expedition into the wilderness areas in Oregon this past week, most of it in the Mt. Jefferson Wilderness." She turned to her guest.

"Stan, of course you realize that many, if not most people, don't believe that Bigfoot exists." The CNN news reporter gave the serious news look to Stan. She would do well, he thought, and was perfect for what he wanted.

"Uh, well, you would have to explain that to the people who have actually seen the animal," Stan said. He was ready for this, and it happened at every news conference. When he was through with this one, he could charge more for the expeditions planned for next summer.

A lot more.

And it wasn't just about the money. It was about showing the world how something could exist and not be found.

"Didn't they just find a new species of shark last month off the Great Barrier Reef?" Stan asked, in his best evangelical voice. He was, in fact a proselyte for new converts, and he knew it. "And," he added in a softer voice, "wasn't a new species of leopard found in Africa just last week?" He smiled, and continued with a speech he had given a thousand times before.

"I'm sure that your facts about the location of the new species are correct," she said with a smile. "Why haven't we found a Bigfoot skeleton now, why not remains, or bagged a live one?"

"Linda, I don't live in an upscale tornado magnet doublewide. I have a PhD in anthropology. There are many species, and I might add, non-endangered species, that exist here in the Pacific Northwest and we rarely, if ever, see skeletal remains. Bear is one. I would like to hear from a hunter here in Oregon who has seen a bear skeleton." He sat back, waiting for a few seconds. When Linda Chavez didn't follow up, he began again.

"And what about cougar? There are reported to be three thousand to five thousand cougar in Oregon. Have you ever seen one? People do now, sometimes in town, like in Bend around Pilot Butte, but I've talked with hunters who have been in the field for fifty years, and have never seen a cougar. We get almost as many Bigfoot sightings as cougar sightings.

"I believe that Bigfoot is an ape, a descendent of the Miocene-period apes, and that we will one day find more evidence to support this. When we have populations of animals, namely the bobcat and gray fox that are almost never seen, it doesn't mean they don't exist. I doubt anyone has ever seen either in the woods, but we know they exist in Oregon, northern California, and other northwestern states." Stan stopped and waited for more questions.

"Now on a more somber note, Stan. What about Jennifer Kruger, the woman who was lost for several days. Was it worth it for your organization to have her go through this ordeal? Isn't she lucky to be alive?"

Now we're getting somewhere, Stan thought.

"I'm glad you asked that, Linda. Of course we are happy Jennifer was found, and that she is going to be alright. Whenever you go into a wilderness area, Linda, you accept that things could go wrong."

"It was reported that she was found on the Cold River Indian Reservation. Did you sanction a search for Bigfoot on the reservation without the permission of the Cold River tribal leaders, as told to us by the Tribal Council Chair, Bluefeathers?"

"We knew that Jennifer Kruger and her boyfriend, Carl, were going to camp on the reservation. We didn't think that it would be a bad thing, particularly if we found evidence of Bigfoot."

"So the end justifies the means?"

"No, not really, but there is a lot of information from certain individuals and families on the reservation of Sasquatch sightings over many decades, centuries, on the reservation. They don't really talk about it all that much, but almost every person I've talked with on the reservation believes with a certainty that Bigfoot exists there in the wild."

"So you purposely put people on the reservation, covertly?"

"They went in on their own accord. I didn't go onto the reservation, but I am planning to go back to that area tonight. Near the rez. See what I can see."

"Thanks, Stan. This is Linda Chavez, CNN News."

Yes, I'm going back to the area, Stan thought as he left the studio. Not just to the area, but back on the rez. To find Sasquatch. Only this time, I will be the one to find the biped. Become famous. Rich.

In the end, he saw too much.

# Chapter 19

Parker Creek

Smokey straightened up and watched Nathan roll the torso over. He didn't think the odor could get worse, that sickly, sweet smell of death, but it did.

*I'm gonna have to burn these clothes, go to the sweat lodge for a day. A warrior can't be this close to death and not be cleansed later. As soon as possible.*

Nathan tapped the back pocket area of the dress trousers and then reached down and unbuttoned the pants pocket on the left side. "I carry my wallet on the right side," he said, and he carefully reached in and removed the wallet.

"You don't carry a wallet," Smokey remarked.

"Well, if I did carry a wallet, it would be on the right side. Anyway, here it is." Nathan let the body roll back and stood with the wallet.

"Let's see who Mr. Dead Man really is," he said, and Smokey leaned over and looked. Nathan slowly opened the double fold wallet and a fat maggot rolled out and dropped on the ground by Smokey's feet. Smokey took a step back as Nathan removed an Oregon Driver's License. The photo showed a man with dark hair, thirty years old, with an address in West Portland. An Apartment. Said his name was Mohammad Kal-leed.

Nathan kept the license out and bagged the wallet in a plastic evidence bag. He bent down again and worked on the man's shoe, first untying it, and then carefully sliding it off the swollen, putrefied foot. Smokey put his arm around his nose and breathed through his mouth. The shoe was a brown oxford, a dress shoe.

"Let's see," Nathan said. "Mr. Kal-leed has expensive taste in shoes. This, and the other one that Mr. Bear has undoubtedly taken to try on somewhere, is a size ten. What you think, Little Bro, maybe five hundred at Macy's?"

Smokey pointed up.

"Okay, six hundred on sale."

"I think I should call the boss, let him know what we have found

81

so far." Smokey walked uphill from the dead man as Nathan bagged the shoe, and took more pictures of the remains and the evidence. He took his cell phone out and punched the speed dial for Chief Martin Andrews.

"Wait," Nathan said, holding his hand up. "Let's do a survey of the meadow, take thirty minutes in good light, and we'll have more information to give the chief. Maybe find the woman. Then call."

They started, and at the west end, near the tree line, found another shoe.

Nathan looked over at Smokey. "How the hell did he get here? See any tracks?"

Smokey had been wondering about that. How *did* the body get here? There were no roads, no mule or horse tracks, and no people tracks except for Jennifer's.

"Air drop?" Smokey asked.

"Yeah, I've thought of it. Air drop by a plane or helicopter. Don't see any other way."

"We're missing something," Smokey said. He thought again about Jennifer spending those nights up here.

"Nathan." Smokey stopped, looking at his friend. "We're still missing a body." He flipped his cell phone open and dialed. Chief Martin Andrews answered immediately. Smokey stood in the meadow and relayed what they had. *A fucking mess is what we have.*

"How long do you think the body has been up there?" Andrews asked.

"We figured some of the bones Jennifer found have been here over the winter, under the snow. The one body hasn't been here more than a couple of days. Hard to say, this is a big, rugged area, nobody comes up here." And then he had a thought, something that had been nagging at him for awhile. *The only people who know just how desolate this is, or who know how to get here, are most likely tribal members. An Indian told the bad guys where to dump bodies.*

"You find the person who lost a hand?" Chief Martin asked.

"Uh, no, we haven't found a woman."

"We'll have fingerprint identification sometime today, they tell me. Prints are pretty bad but they should be enough to get a name."

"We have a name on one of the bodies," Smokey told him. He gave it to the chief over the phone, name and date of birth.

"We'll send in a forensic team tomorrow. How long will it take you to hike out to your truck? I want to see both of you tonight."

Nathan held up his hand. Four fingers.

"Uh, Chief, the old man says we can make it to our truck in four hours. Was that four hours or days, Nathan?" Smokey laughed as Nathan held up one finger.

"See you tonight, Chief."

It took five hours of a punishing hump, too fast and hard to think. Smokey sweat through his shirt in the first hour, but he wasn't going to let the old man see how tired he was.

# Chapter 20

Cold River Tribal Police Department
2200 hours

Smokey stood in the shower and washed the sweat of the trail off of his skin. He tried to wash away the smell of death, but he knew that he would have to go to the sweat lodge and cleanse himself to get rid of the death he had touched and seen. He would put his BDU's in a plastic bag and seal it so he could burn them at a later time. Everything that touched death must be burned. He dried his hair and put on a clean uniform. For his meeting with the chief later he wanted to wear a uniform, no matter the time, since he didn't know what he would be doing after that.

He left the reservation, driving across the new bridge over the Deschutes River, the old one destroyed by a madman determined to protect the reservation and its peoples at all costs.

*Madman, hell, he was a courageous savior.*

Smokey made the fifteen minute drive into Madras thinking they needed answers, and fast. Who put the bodies there, and why? Bodies new and old - that didn't make sense. A conspiracy that they didn't need. People from off the reservation, of that he was sure. He had some thoughts about who might be in league with the killers. There are only a few people who knew their way around the remote areas below the glaciers. Jennifer was caught up in this, and he also had some idea about how the feebs would treat her. They would be sniffing around by tomorrow.

At the hospital, Smokey parked near the emergency room entrance, the only doors open at this time of day. There was a bright halo around the lights of the parking lot, a tired Honda Accord, the single car in the parking spaces making it seem even more deserted. The ER doc's Mercedes would be around the side, in an alcove, out of sight from mere mortals.

He sat in his car, dialed Chief Andrews on his cell phone and got his voice mail.

"Chief, this is Smokey, I'm at the hospital, will be back to meet you in about thirty minutes. Call me."

The ER doors slid open, whisper quiet, and he entered the hallway, the reception station ahead and on the right.

Smells like gunpowder in here, can't be, must be a transient memory. Something triggered by past visits to the ER. Both waiting rooms were empty.

He knew most of the receptionists. They were usually behind the glassed-in reception center, twenty-four seven, but this time, no one was there to greet him.

*Funny, and what's that smell?*

*And then he knew.*

*Blood.*

*Rich, coppery, the Godawful smell of blood and gunpowder.*

Smokey touched the Glock at his side and walked to the counter and leaned over. There was a pool of blood on the floor beneath the chair, a dark red corona circling the short blonde hair, the blue scrub suit turning green where the unexpected red touched it. Her body looked as if it had been thrown down, an afterthought, a discard. Her eyes were open, fixed. He tried to remember her name.

Delores.

Several things registered at once. Smokey pulled his gun and looked around. The hallway was empty.

*Gotta check her, can't go on without being sure.*

He looked through the waiting rooms, eyes going from left to right. Nobody here. He stepped around the side of the reception area to the door and entered, looked behind the desk and leaned over.

No pulse. Delores had no pulse and wouldn't be going home at the end of her shift. He straightened up and peered around the door, down the hallway to the opening to the ER examining rooms. The double doors were standing open, looking neglected, as if they were accusing him, mocking him.

*Why weren't you here when we needed you at the hospital?*

Smokey felt the hair stand up on his neck, his face tight.

*What the hell is happening here?*

And he knew with a certainty that this was about Jennifer, about the bodies up in the wilderness area.

*What could she possibly know?*

He stood in the doorway of the reception office and covered the hallway. He turned on his portable radio with his left hand and switched to the county frequency.

*I need my cell phone.*

He decided against putting out the call on the air, and reached over to the desk phone and dialed the county dispatch number.

"Dispatch."

"This is three oh three, Lieutenant Kukup, Warm Springs." He spoke softly, walked to the door and leaned out again, looking down the hallway, the phone cord trailing.

"Go ahead, sir."

"I'm at the hospital in Madras, the receptionist has been shot, the hospital is quiet, I'm going to check the hallways, need some help."

"Did you say *shot?*"

"Yes, shot, is deceased, I'm in uniform, gonna check further. I'll have my radio on, but very low."

"I'll call someone, people at home. All of my deputies and city officers are at a fatal accident, ten miles away. Get someone as soon as I can."

"Do that."

Smokey hung up, and had a wild thought.

*The Indians are here, where the hell are the fucking cowboys when you need them? Gotta do this yourself, Little Brother.*

He glanced out the door down toward the ER again and moved out, fast, toward the double doors. At the doors he paused, glanced inside, and then swung around the doorway and up against the wall inside. Doctor Evans lay sprawled on the floor on his side, his arms thrown over his head.

*Won't be needing that Mercedes anymore, Doc.*

A foot peeked out from under the center curtain of the examining area, a white shoe.

The nurse was crumpled on the floor in a pool of blood. *Looks as dead as the Doc.*

He cleared the room, walking quickly, moving from left to right, and walked quietly back through the examining room. As he approached the double doors, he heard a scream coming from somewhere in the hospital, and then a single gunshot.

*Jennifer!*

Smokey moved quickly then, down the hallway, his Glock up in front of him, leading the way.

He came to the end of the hallway, and looked around the corner to his right. The nurses station was empty. He looked past the station, walked to the next hallway, and looked left around the corner. The nurses station was empty because the nurse was in the hallway and looked as dead as the others. He thought for the second time

*What the hell did you get yourself into, Jennifer?*

Smokey walked past the nurse, realizing that he didn't know where Jennifer was, what room she was in. He slid into the nearest room and looked around.

Empty. He pulled his radio and turned the channel to Warm Springs Dispatch.

"Dispatch, three oh three."

"Dispatch."

"Who do we have at the hospital, guarding the SAR victim?"

"Officer Rhoan."

"Do you know the room number?"

"I believe it's one thirty-one."

"Contact three oh one, tell him that I need help like he did in the school. Ask him to stand by with as much help as he can call in. I'll explain in a little bit." Three oh one was the call sign for Chief Martin Andrews, and he would know what to do. There were thousands of people who listened to scanners and he didn't want this, whatever this was, to get out over the air just yet.

He was in one twenty-five. He went out and glided down to the door of one thirty-one and pushed it open. The bed was empty. Officer Tom Rhoan was sitting on the floor, under the window, his feet splayed out before him, his Glock in his right hand, down by his leg. His head was thrown back against the wall, his mouth open, a neat hole in his forehead, his eyes staring at the far wall as if he were examining a strange and wondrous sight. He wore his hair long, traditional, a braid down across his cheek.

*Aw, man. Tom.*

And then he had two thoughts at once.

*Now this is personal, very personal. And where the hell is Jennifer? She must be close.*

Smokey reached over and touched Tom's sleeve, and then went to the door. He went out of the room, fast and down the hallway toward the center of the hospital. He ran past patient rooms, most doors closed this time of night, some open. Images flashed to him as he ran past, an arm flung over a bed, an elderly woman with wisps of white hair sitting up in bed, croaking, "George, is that you?"

He came to a set of double doors and pushed through them without slowing, the doors slamming back as he hit them, and several things registered at once, his feet stopping almost before his brain told him what was in the hallway, twenty feet away.

Two men and a woman, the woman between them, wearing a hospital gown and trailing an IV line, the men dressed in dark clothes, wearing black baseball caps and ski masks, the kind you wear for extreme cold. The back of the hospital gown was open, the woman naked underneath, her body twisting with the struggle.

*Jennifer, they have Jennifer.*

And then he thought . . .

*nice ass.*

"Let me go!" She threw herself sideways against the man on her right, he stumbled into the wall as he was turning to look at Smokey, a pistol in his right hand. The man on her left was pulled off balance as well. He struck Jennifer with the back of his hand and she screamed, and the man then looked back at Smokey, and Smokey did the only thing he could do at that point.

He sprinted toward the men, yelling, "Get down on the floor, get down, get down!" And he pointed his Glock at the one on the right, the one on the left letting go of Jennifer and reaching for his gun, the one on the right swinging his gun around toward Smokey. Smokey shot him as he ran toward them, shooting three times, fast, hitting the man in the chest with all three and the man on the right went down, clawing at Jennifer as she stood there screaming. The man on the left pushed her away, bringing his pistol up and around, and Smokey shot him from five feet, the last shot hitting him in his left eye, his head exploding, the blood spraying the wall behind him.

The man's gun clattered away and he fell, dropped straight down as though his legs had been chopped off.

Jennifer put her hand up and swung at Smokey as he reached her side. He caught her hand, talking softly, holding his gun in his right hand. She looked at him, her eyes wide, wet with tears.

"Jennifer. Stop. I will help you." He put his right arm over her shoulder, feeling her shake. She tried to speak, the words not coming out.

"Jennifer, Lieutenant Kukup. I brought you the doll and flowers."

"You – ."

She slumped against him and then straightened. She looked down at the man who had struck her, stepped over and kicked him in the neck.

"That's for hitting me, you creep!"

A noise from down the hallway. People running. Maybe help was on the way, or hospital people. Smokey had shot seven or eight times, the noise should have attracted someone. He was aware that doors were opening, people standing in the doorways of their rooms, looking on, quiet.

A man burst around the corner, dressed like the other two gunmen, dark clothes, ski mask, carrying a short rifle, wearing a baseball cap, this one a Portland Trail Blazer's cap.

Unfortunate choice of caps, Smokey thought, and shot him.

Doors slammed, people ducking inside their rooms as two more men came around the corner. Smokey snapped off two shots, and the men disappeared.

"Come on!" He grabbed Jennifer and pulled her with him as he moved back toward the double doors, turning to shoot at the end of the hallway, wanting to keep the men back with suppression fire, and then they were through the doors, moving fast, Jennifer keeping up.

"Wait!" She slowed, pulling against Smokey.

"The room, I need to go back to the room." They stopped at room one thirty-one and pushed inside. Smokey closed the door. Jennifer walked to the bed and glanced back at Smokey, seemingly conscious for the first time of her open gown, trying to hold it together. She picked up the doll from the bed and held it, looking like a little girl.

Smokey walked to where Officer Tom Rhoan was against the wall and removed the officer's pistol from his hand and the extra magazines from his belt.

"I might need to borrow these, old friend," Smokey said, his voice husky, soft. He stood and saw that Jennifer was watching him, holding her doll.

"I'm sorry about your friend," she said.

"So am I," Smokey said. "So am I." He walked toward her and pulled the bedspread from the bed, handing it to her. "Wrap up, we gotta go. Now. I have a feeling those people aren't gonna quit just yet."

"But why - ."

"Don't know, but whatever you saw up there, they don't want you to recall. Let's go."

He opened the door slowly, Jennifer standing behind him, trying to look around his shoulder. The hallway was empty.

"Stay close," he said. With a look down toward the double doors, he entered the hallway and moved toward the ER, past the examining room with Doc Evans still on the floor, and out toward the front, his Suburban in sight through the glass doors.

As they got to the reception area he saw movement in the waiting room. A man walked unsteadily toward the counter, a man in his thirties, his face flushed with alcohol. He weaved and lurched to the counter. Smokey could smell the alcohol from where he stood.

"Hey, buddy," he slurred to Smokey. Smokey looked outside through the glass doors to his car. Two men, dressed in black, were standing outside, looking at the Suburban. Shit!

"Hey, buddy," the drunk said. "I can't seem to get any help here." He started banging the bell on the counter, pounding on it with his fleshy hand.

*Ding!Ding!Ding!Ding!*

Smokey held up his hand. "Hey, you don't want to be doing that."

Smokey stopped, Jennifer bumping into him.

"We gotta go back," he said.

"What, why?"

"People at my car. Let's back up, slowly. He watched as one of the men left the Suburban and walked to the entrance of the ER.

We're trapped!

The man continued to pound the bell as Smokey backed up toward the examining room with Jennifer at his side.

They backed inside the open double doors to the room. He could hear the drunk yelling.

"Hey, cop. I need some fucking help here!" It came out as *fushing* help, but Smokey got the idea. And then, "You Madras cops never help me, what a buncha assholes."

They reached the examining room and backed inside. The drunk continued to yell and pound.

*Ding!Ding!Ding!Ding!*

Maybe the saying was true, Smokey thought, that God helps drunks and little kids.

*Ding!Ding!*

A sudden burst of automatic weapons fire came from the front doors, and the bell clattered to the floor.

*Well, I guess not drunks in this case.*

*We need a car.*

# Chapter 21

Cold River Police Department
2330 hours

Chief Martin Andrews looked at the printout of Mohammed Kal-leed's driver's license. Guy has a heavy foot. Had. Several speeding tickets in the last year, all in the Portland area. A warning letter had been sent from the department of motor vehicles to his address in Lake Oswego. Expensive address. Mr. Kal-leed lived well.

The license plate on the vehicle came back to a Hummer.

Kal-leed had no identifiable criminal record. Martin was waiting for a call back from Detective Booker. Martin had called Booker at home and asked him to run Kal-leed through the federal computer system. Booker was retired F.B.I., now worked for the tribal police as a detective.

Martin looked up as a dispatcher stood in the doorway. He motioned for her to enter.

"Chief, Lieutenant Kukup is at the hospital in town. Says he needs for you to call in as many officers as you can find, says he has trouble like you in the school, says you would know what he meant."

*What the hell?*

A few years ago, at a school in Portland, Martin had been in a shooting. A very deadly one. What the hell did Kukup get into?

"The hospital, was he visiting the woman from the SAR? Jennifer something?"

"He called and asked for her room number, and then said to tell you to call people."

"Start calling, start with detectives, tell them it's mandatory, then call the sergeants, and maybe we will know more by the time they get here. Oh, let me know immediately if Kukup calls or contacts you."

She called back within a minute.

"Detective Booker on the phone for you." Martin put his phone on speaker.

"Chief, what the hell did we get into?"

"What do you mean?"

"This guy, Mohammed Kal-leed, he's on the federal terror watch list. Feds believe he is into laundering and finding money in the U.S. for terror projects here. Probably connected to meth as a fund raiser."

*Shit.*

"This computer hit is gonna raise some eyebrows. Expect to get a call. Someone is going to be calling the Portland Supervisory Agent soon, if they haven't already."

"So we can expect the rez to be crawling with feds with their peckers up."

"Yup, pretty much."

"I want you to come in, tonight."

"Uh, Chief, I have a date. A sleep-over date."

"Let her sleep, I still need you."

"Chief, do you know how many sleep-overs I get at my age?"

"No, and I don't want to. I still need you. Bye."

Martin broke the connection before Booker could whine again.

*What the hell is Lieutenant Kukup getting into? What did we get into?*

Before the night was over, Chief Martin Andrews, former Portland Police Bureau Homicide Detective, now a tribal chief of police for two years, had some answers.

*Smokey, where are you?*

# **C**hapter **22**

Mountain View Hospital

Smokey stepped around Doctor Evans. Without the blood he might have been sleeping. Won't be driving his big Mercedes around town too much after this night. He glanced back toward the open doors. Jennifer was right behind him, her eyes wide, clutching the bedspread around her with one hand, her doll in the other.

*Car, we need a car.*

*Mercedes.*

"Jennifer, go to the desk. Look for car keys, Mercedes keys." He pointed.

She hesitated, and then moved to the small office and held up a key ring, clutching her doll and bedspread in one hand. To Smokey, she looked like a little girl, eager to please her teacher. She held up a cell phone, and Smokey nodded. Good.

He walked to the open bay doors to the hallway, and risked a glance out. Two men, dressed in dark clothes like the others, were standing by the reception counter, both armed. They appeared to be arguing. One pointed down toward the ER examining room, and started down the hallway.

Smokey poked the barrel of his Glock around the corner and fired three times, fast, and ran back into the examining room.

Jennifer screamed.

"Jennifer, with me, now. We're going out the back."

He checked behind him, hoping the shots in the hallway would freeze the men in black for a few more seconds. He hit the bar on the door and ran for the Mercedes that was backed into the carport just in front of them. The lights on the Mercedes flashed. Jennifer ran for the passenger side, her blanket slipping, and Smokey ran for the driver's door. He grabbed the door handle and slid inside as Jennifer jumped into the passenger seat, her blanket now coming off, her gown up around her waist.

Smokey looked over at her. Jennifer held the keys up and glanced behind them.

"Keep your eyes to yourself, Mister," she said, and then added, "drive."

Smokey started the car, hit the gas and put it in gear all in one motion, the car lurching out of the carport, tires squealing. The right side mirror exploded as they turned into the parking lot.

Jennifer screamed, and then yelled, "Drive faster, you moron!"

They hit the street and the Mercedes bottomed out in a shower of sparks, and then they were flying down Tenth Street, Smokey keeping his foot on the floor as the T intersection at 'B' Street came flashing toward them.

*Moron?*

"They're coming after us!" Jennifer was turned in her seat, looking back. Smokey caught the headlights as a car slid out of the parking lot, two blocks behind. He slammed on the brakes, throwing Jennifer forward. They slid around the corner to the right, Jennifer sliding into him, and then they were around the corner and accelerating downhill, the big car going fast now, sixty, seventy, eighty, a red light on the highway three blocks down. Jennifer looked up, grabbed her seatbelt and pulled it around her.

"Gimme your seatbelt," she said, reaching over Smokey, and then, "corner!"

Smokey slammed on the brakes, thinking of how well the German engineers did their jobs as they slid through the corner, taking both lanes and the parking lane. Then they were rocketing up Highway 26, past Les Schwab Tires, Safeway a blur on the right, and up on the plains. The headlights behind them were dropping back, but stayed in his rearview mirror.

Jennifer arranged her blanket. She looked over at Smokey and gave him a little smile.

"I guess I should ask you, where are you taking me?"

"The rez." They were now in the country, the roadside a blur, passing the Oregon State University Agricultural Research Center, the speedometer passing one hundred forty.

"The rez?"

"Indian Reservation. Where you were hiking."

"I'd rather go someplace with electricity. Running water. Showers. No dead people. And no large hairy animals."

"Very funny. Whaddya mean, calling me a moron? This moron thinks he saved your life."

Jennifer didn't answer. She sat huddled in the seat, and finally asked, "Who are those men? What do they want with me?"

"I don't know," Smokey said, "but I would guess it has something to do with what you found up there on the mountain."

*But I'm gonna find out. This is my country. And someone killed my friend.*

Smokey slowed the big car as they approached the sweeping corner to the left, the road dropping down a long grade to the Deschutes River. Four miles, four sweeping corners, and then three miles along the river to the bridge and onto the reservation.

"Sit tight, they're gonna catch us here."

Jennifer held onto the shoulder harness with her right hand, Nanna in her left hand and swung her head around.

"They're right behind us!"

Smokey went into the corner at over a hundred miles an hour, the car wanting to leave the road, and then he accelerated downhill, flying toward the next corner.

*Sure hope nobody's coming.*

He used all of the road in the next corner, swinging wide into the oncoming lanes. There were no headlights coming at them, and as he reached the corner he jammed the accelerator to the floor. Jennifer screamed as the car drifted across the road and touched the guardrail with a spray of sparks. *Sorry about your car, Doc.*

"Jennifer, get the cell phone," Smokey said as they raced for the next corner, accelerating once again, downhill. Their pursuers swerved behind them.

Jennifer placed her doll in her lap and picked up the phone.

"Now what?"

"Dial 541-555-2396, talk to Chief Andrews."

"Indian chief?" She asked as she punched the numbers in. She looked impressed.

"No, police chief." Smokey wiped his hand on his leg, concentrating on the corner flying toward them, going downhill at over one forty.

*Ain't gonna make this one.*

"Tell the chief we're coming, and we've got company, same people who shot at us in the hospital. We need help at the border."

Jennifer relayed the information.

"Tell him we're three minutes out, or less, we're in a white Mercedes."

*Well, not so white now.*

Smokey touched the brakes, the car swerving to the left, saw the oncoming headlights as he came into the corner. Can't use all the road this time. A semi was coming up the hill in the far lane; the bad guys' car was right behind them.

They drifted into the oncoming lane, the headlights of the semi moving sideways, the big truck swerving to give them room, and then they were past. Smokey glanced to the side and then forward. He didn't have time to reflect on the fact that they missed the semi's wheels by inches at over a hundred miles an hour. They swept down through the last corner and flew along the Deschutes River, flat out now, the car up close behind them.

The rear window of the Mercedes exploded and Jennifer screamed. The glass sucked inward as the bullets struck the car.

"They're shooting at us!"

Jennifer screamed into the phone. Smokey swerved the big car and took up all three lanes. The dark waters of the Deschutes raced by on their left side as they reached the last corner before entering the reservation and safety. The last corner was a sharp left turn onto the Deschutes River Bridge.

*If I miss this one, we'll be in the swift water, and from that there's no return. Sure hope Martin has the officers get out of the way, we're coming through, should be able to see us now.*

Up ahead, across the bridge to the left, Smokey could see the flashing lights of Cold River Tribal Police cars. He was on the brakes, heavy, the pursuers' car coming up on his left as the Rainbow Market swept by on the right, the parking lot dark, deserted.

*Gotta get them on my right side or we're toast.*

If they're on the left, Smokey thought, we won't make it, they'll push us into the guardrail and over it and into the river, and we won't escape. Smokey hit the gas and jumped in front of the car as the bridge came up, the move saving their lives as the Mercedes was raked with automatic weapons fire, the bullets striking behind them, into the backseat area and trunk. The rear side windows exploded, and wind swirled into the car.

The other vehicle dropped back, just off their bumper. Smokey swerved to the left and tapped the brakes, forcing the pursuing vehicle up on their right, the bumper even with Jennifer's door. They swept onto the bridge, Jennifer screaming a constant shriek, her white face streaked with pain. Smokey swung his wheel to the right, smashed into the fender of the other car, the heavy Mercedes forcing the other car up onto the cement guardrail at the start of the bridge. The car flew up into the air and over the rail and hung there, suspended.

Smokey glanced at the driver, his face blackened, eyes wide, and then the nose of the car hit the water at ninety miles an hour, flipped over in a shower of spray, and sank.

Smokey stomped on the brakes as the Mercedes flashed over the bridge and past the patrol cars.

Chief Martin Andrews stood beside the road with his arms crossed, looking on as they flew by.

Smokey came to a stop in the parking lot of the Crossing Restaurant, and turned off the engine. The dashboard clock said they left the hospital in Madras seven minutes ago. He looked over at Jennifer.

"You okay?"

She smiled, a small uplifting of the corners of her mouth, but a smile just the same. She nodded her head. "Beats editing, most of the time," she said in a small voice, "but I'm okay, yeah." She looked at Smokey.

"You always treat people to this ride on the way to the reservation?"

"If I can." He put his hand on the top of hers, covering the bandage, bloody where the IV had ripped out. For what she had been through in the past few days, and then this deadly hospital stay, Jennifer needed a safe place to recuperate. To just be. He made a decision.

"Look, Jennifer, I'm going to take you to my mother's home, you'll be safe there, not many people know how to find it, and I promise you I will protect you. No matter what."

Jennifer looked at her hands, and pulled the blanket up. "I believe you will do that." She sat there for a few seconds, and then added, "I guess this means I can't go home just yet, doesn't it?"

"That's what it means, you can't go home." Smokey looked around at what was left of the car.

*Sorry about your car, Doc.*

He watched as Chief Martin Andrews and Sergeant Nathan Green walked toward the car.

*Now it's time for some answers.*
*Now it's time for us to go to war.*
*And I'm good at it.*

The smell of sage was so strong he almost wept.

# Chapter 23

Cold River Tribal Police Department
0200 hours

Smokey entered his office, left the lights off, and dropped in his chair. From where he sat he could look out his window at the Bureau of Indian Affairs Corrections Center, the perimeter lights making colorful halos above the razor wire fence. He rubbed his face, his hand coming away with the dried blood of his friend.

*I have to burn my uniform.*

He blew out his breath and considered what to do next. Whatever he decided, he would have to include his family in his planning. *Back to the old ways.* He was many things, as he knew most people were – father, former husband, tribal member, Indian, staff sergeant in the army, and police lieutenant. He had always known there was a hierarchy to his many roles. He understood the dichotomy of position. A poodle could be a ferocious carnivore when loose in the park after dark, but at home, that same poodle was a beloved pet and heeled to the master.

As a husband, Smokey believed that he was a failure. As a father he was trying, but he didn't think he was much good at fatherhood either. He knew the one thing that saved him was that Laurel adored and loved him unconditionally.

*I love her, too.*

He leaned back in his chair and rubbed his eyes. He pulled his hands away, mindful of the blood. Thoughts of the recent past were worse when he was tired. He couldn't see clearly into the future, especially when things seemed to be out of his control. Like now, with answers just out of reach.

Amelia had begged him to not go back into the Army after nine-eleven. She had begged him to find someone else to go in his place. Hadn't he done enough for his country? Smokey was determined to go and fight, and he thought that somehow her life would work out for her. He knew later that his urgency to get back to his unit in Afghanistan clouded his hopes for Amelia, that he held a benevolent wish that she would be okay. He knew at some level (pushed way back in his mind) that she might lose her struggle for life on her rez.

He turned and looked into the dark wall and thought about the past, looking with the benefit of years, and he was never kind to himself about what he had done. The arrogance of being right, of leaving his young wife and daughter to fend for themselves while he went to fight tugged at his soul.

He remembered the last time he saw Amelia, the day he left for his second tour.

He had carried Laurel on his shoulder and Amelia walked beside him into the meadow above his house. It was a cold morning in December, the sun bright in the sky. The frost on the grass glistened as it melted.

Smokey glanced over at Amelia. She walked with her head down, scuffing her boots. She was wearing jeans, a bright red and white ski jacket, her hair wound around her shoulder and down the front.

"*A'a.*" Laurel twisted in Smokey's arms and pointed. A large crow landed in a Juniper Tree in front of them.

"Mommy, look, *a'a.*"

Smokey watched with her as the crow looked at them. "She should concentrate on English," Amelia said. She kicked at a rock in the path. They stopped in the middle of the meadow and Smokey put Laurel down. She was three. She ran through the meadow and stopped, wind milling her arms.

Smokey knew that Amelia wasn't mad about Laurel speaking Sahaptin. Amelia had been distant, and hadn't spoken much since he told her he was going back to Afghanistan. She wouldn't meet his gaze. He looked at the mountains and snowy peaks ahead, the meadow etched in frost – and he wanted to remember this morning. It was as if he were looking in high definition, the mountain so clear and cold, and when he looked back at his house he could see the cloudy breath of the horses in his distant corral. Most of all, Smokey saw the slump of Amelia's shoulders.

"Smoke, I just . . . I don't know if I can do this, for a year or more, without you, I just think someone else can go over there to fight." She twisted around, away from him as Laurel ran up and pointed at the crow. Smokey glanced at his wife. At age twenty-five her face was puffy with alcohol.

"Maybe your partners can help you," he said, not able to keep the edge from his voice, and he was instantly sorry when he said it, but he knew it was out there now, and he could never take it back. Her partners. What she called her friends, her drinking buddies. He knew Amelia had been drinking her way through his last tour, leaving Laurel for longer and longer periods with his mother. She had slowed down for the months he was home, and when he received his new orders, she had started again, making little excuses to be gone, and in the last few days, she didn't even bother with an excuse.

The skin around her mouth drew tight, and when she glanced at him, he saw the pain in her eyes. Amelia mumbled something and he leaned in close.

"Amelia, what?"

When she spoke, the pain turned to anger, and she mumbled, louder.

"I said, fuck you, Smokey." A tear rolled down her cheek and Smokey reached for her and she put her face in his chest. She threw her arms around his waist and clung to him and sobbed. Laurel looked up at Smokey and then her mom. Smokey pulled Laurel into his leg and held both of them.

"Mommy crying." Smokey stroked her hair.

Amelia started talking without lifting her head.

"Smoke. I need you. I love you. I can't fight this without you . . . I can't fight this alone. And the loneliness. I . . . just . . . you . . . can't go."

He stood there and didn't know how to respond. He rubbed her back under her jacket. When Amelia finally lifted her head, the anger was back in her eyes.

Smokey left at noon. Amelia and Laurel and his mom stood in front of the log house. Laurel and his mom waved. Amelia stood there and stared as he drove through the meadow. He looked back one time. Amelia was already walking toward her car.

It was the last time he ever saw her.

She was dead in five months.

Smokey brought his head up and stared at the dark wall in his office.

*And you killed her, Smokey.*

After a few minutes, he stood and stretched. It was time to see the chief.

Smokey sat across from Chief Martin Andrews and closed his eyes. He opened them as Nathan entered and took a chair.

"Whoever these people are," Smokey said, "they have money, guns, and resources. They knew where Jennifer was, and they must believe she saw something up there and want to get it out of her. They killed everyone they came across in the hospital, just shot them and went on."

"What about Tom?" the Chief asked, his face grim.

"Doesn't look as if he had much warning. He was against the back wall of Jennifer's room, shot in the head, had his gun out." Smokey removed the pistol from his belt and gave it to Nathan.

"This is Tom's."

He drew his Glock and placed it on the Chief's desk. Chief Andrews looked at it.

"All hell is going to break loose here," the Chief said, "and soon. The Sheriff, Madras Police Department, the State Police, all are gonna want a piece of you for shooting up their jurisdictions. Not to mention that the rez is going to be swarming with F.B.I. Agents in about an hour."

"I'll get Smokey a replacement gun from the armory," Nathan said. The Chief nodded, and Nathan left the room.

"Officially, as of now, you are on administrative leave," Martin told Smokey. "Unofficially, I need your help with the Kruger woman, and I need your help with trying to figure out just what the hell happened here. A body dump, it looks like, with some people who have improved the human race by leaving it suddenly. But why here?"

"Well," Smokey said, "The Great White Father in Washington uses the Navajo for dumping nuclear waste. Why not dump bodies here?"

"You think the feds are responsible?"

"I wouldn't count them out, they have done worse things and pretended innocence," Smokey said.

"What are we going to do with Jennifer Kruger? Any ideas?"

"She went home with Sarah for a shower and to borrow some clothes," Smokey said. "They should be back soon, then I suggest we video an interview with her, should keep the local law enforcement and the F.B.I. off for a while, record a statement from me as well. Nothing will satisfy the feds until they can have one of their junior woodchucks interview her, antennae quivering and pencil poised, and all that. They are gonna want to wring her out."

"The F.B.I. will want to put her into protective custody," the Chief said.

"The feebs couldn't protect my virginity," Smokey said. "When she gets back, I will take her to mom's place. The junior woodchucks won't be able to find her there, off the paved roads, in the timber, and all that. Give us some time."

Martin nodded.

Nathan entered the office and handed a forty caliber Glock to Smokey, a box of ammunition, and two new magazines. He tapped Smokey's belt.

"Need your old magazines for evidence," he said.

Sarah leaned in the open doorway and knocked. Jennifer stood behind her. Sarah motioned Jennifer to a chair and introduced her to Chief Andrews.

"You look different, somehow," Smokey said. He grinned. Jennifer was wearing jeans, tennis shoes, and a gray sweater with a big green "O" on it.

Sarah snorted. "She was wearing a hospital gown when good ol' Smokey picked her up," she said. "A gown with no back in it."

Chief Andrews stood and approached Jennifer. "You feel up to talking about what happened, on camera?"

Jennifer said yes, and so it began, the interviews about what happened on the mountain, and then a separate interview about the events tonight. Jennifer was seated in an interview room with a small table and chairs, and Detective Johns asked her questions. Smokey watched from a television monitor in another room. Jennifer spoke in a low voice, slowly, and talked about finding the bodies, and then becoming thirsty and hungry, disoriented, and about being found. She didn't remember finding any other body or a "hand."

Smokey thought she was incredible; poised without being polished, giving matter-of-fact answers about the time she was lost. She concluded that after the first night, things began to get fuzzy, until she was completely disoriented.

"Tell me about tonight," Detective Johns asked, his voice encouraging, soothing.

Jennifer didn't answer right away, and to the uninitiated, she might have been stalling for time to collect her thoughts, to make up an answer. Smokey knew that she was trying to get it right, that she was taking her time before answering. And for all of her bravado during the flight to the rez, she looked scared. He knew from her file she was twenty-eight, but now with a leg crossed under her in the chair, the way she tucked her hair behind her ear and absently chewed her lip, she looked to be all of twelve.

"I was lying on my back in my bed watching television, a House rerun. The F.B.I. guy was in the hallway – he really didn't associate with us. Tom was in the chair, watching with me, and we would laugh together when something funny happened, or House did something totally outrageous. Did you know Tom liked that show?"

A lone tear rolled slowly down her cheek and she wiped it away with the heel of her hand. Smokey found his throat growing tight, and he felt a sudden kinship with Jennifer that surprised him.

*I will protect her with my life, for being a friend to my friend.*

"Then . . . there were a bunch of shots all together in the hallway, loud. I think that's where they shot the F.B.I. Agent. I jumped and spilled my juice, and looked over at Tom. House was yelling at a doctor on the tube, Tom's eyes were still on the television, getting big, and he struggled to get out of the chair, pulling his gun out as he stood up. And then . . . these men ran into the room and shot Tom as he was going to the hallway, trying to protect me."

She put her hands up and covered her face and spoke through her fingers. "They took me into the hallway and this wild man with braided hair and a uniform came and shot the bad men, and we raced for the reservation."

"Do you remember more?" Detective Johns asked.

Jennifer went over it again, started with the loud noises, and talked about what she remembered of the people, the sounds, the shooting. When she got to the part about arriving on the reservation, she sat back and closed her eyes.

"That's all I can remember for now."

Detective Johns looked up at the two-way mirror and stood up. He held up his hand.

"Jennifer, thank you for sharing this terrible time with me. If you think of something, please call me, no matter how late."

Sarah was there to take Jennifer out of the room. Smokey smiled at her as he entered.

He spent the next thirty minutes going through his arrival at the hospital and the aftermath, engaging the men taking Jennifer, the flight to the reservation.

"What do they want with the woman?" Johns asked.

"Whatever they want," Smokey said, "has to do with what she found, what she saw on the mountain." He stood up and nodded to Johns and walked out.

When he came out of the interview room, Nathan pulled him aside.

"I am going to personally go to stay with Tom's body, through the autopsy, and then bring him back for the dressing. Since this happened in town, they will insist on an autopsy, and when we get him back, I'll tell you about the plans for the dressing."

"Thanks. I wasn't thinking or I would have already sent someone."

"You've been busy," Nathan said. "Take care of her," he added, nodding at Jennifer.

"You can count on it, Big Brother. You can count on it."

Smokey walked outside, Jennifer trailing him, carrying a bag Sarah had put together for her. Smokey walked to a silver police patrol car and motioned for Jennifer to get in the front passenger side.

He drove out of the lot and down past the park. The red brick of the old Bureau of Indian Affairs buildings flashed by on their right, a daily reminder of the Great White Father's presence.

Jennifer pulled her borrowed jacket around her shoulders as they left the police department. She thought she would be fatigued, but she felt a strange exhilaration. She had recovered quickly from her ordeal in the wilderness. She was to have been released from the hospital later today, but the release came in a sudden way she certainly didn't expect. Her regimen of walking and jogging three times a week down by the Willamette River in Portland probably saved her.

The ordeal in the wilderness left her with an uneasy feeling, as if she had left something unfinished. She hadn't put that in place yet. She remembered seeing the dead body by the log. Sarah Greywolf told her in the hospital that she had been holding a human hand as if it were a doll, her Nanna, she was calling it. Little by little the days (and nights) in the woods were coming back to her, bits and pieces, but she was still missing chunks of time.

Smokey turned onto the highway, the opposite direction from the end of the chase at the bridge, Jennifer thought. The sun came up behind them as they drove up the hill and out of the town of Cold River, the sagebrush-covered hillsides still in shadow.

Jennifer had spent the last day in the hospital talking with Sarah. Jennifer had instantly liked Sarah. They were about the same age – but had such different backgrounds. Sarah was a single mother, Jennifer learned, and she had been a police officer for five years. Sarah was a Cold River tribal member. Jennifer thought that Sarah was pretty, with her long dark hair and dry sense of humor. Sarah made constant fun of Smokey, her first cousin.

Sarah had grown up on the reservation and gone to high school in Madras. She had lived on the rez all of her life, and knew *everyone*.

Jennifer was secretly glad that Sarah hadn't been in the hospital when the bad men (and that's how she was thinking of them, bad men) had arrived. She was sincerely sorry that the officer had been killed, but she also knew that she didn't cause his death.

Carl. What to do with Carl. The boyfriend. Ex-boyfriend, she corrected herself. He had been by the hospital once and stayed a few minutes. Nervous. Ill at ease. He clearly didn't want to be there, and apparently came out of a sense of duty or something. Carl needed to be back in his world, his realm of friends and co-workers in Portland, back at his insurance adjusting business where he could plan another of his conspiracy theories (they're hiding Bigfoot – whoever *they* are – on the reservation) and get rich quick schemes.

The problem with Carl was that he wasn't bad – he was just *there*. He was a nerd in some ways, and made his life okay by chasing conspiracy theories on his off time - aliens, Bigfoot, you name it.

But the problem is you, Jen, and you know it. You just *settled* for Carl. You had just *settled*. What your mom had done.

*Settled.*

Carl was never going to rock her world, or as her friend Allie used to say, Carl ain't gonna make you wet just thinking about him.

God, she had actually thought in the past year about marrying Carl – just to be done with it, and now the thought made her want to vomit.

Carl and I are so done, and we know it.

*Done.*

Jennifer had finally let him off the hook by telling him to go, that she would be alright, and she needed to sleep. The relief in his face was a little painful to her. Only a little.

At the top of the hill out of Cold River she looked over at Smokey, his features outlined in the instrument lights. Pretty good-looking man, even if he did have long hair. In braids. She idly wondered what his family looked like, his wife and child. Sarah had only said that he had a little girl.

"Well at least this trip, so far," he said as he guided the car through the corners, "is quieter than the last one."

"Thank God for that," Jennifer said. "I don't think I could stand too many more of those. Or survive them. And for you, your wife and family must be worried sick after they heard of what happened."

"I'm not married, and my family, they trust me to do the right thing," he said.

*He's not married.* Jennifer didn't know why that mattered, but it did.

Stop it, she told herself. And he is raising a little girl. Now she knew what Sarah meant that Smokey was raising his little girl. She had thought that it meant he was raising her with his wife.

*Jennifer, stop it right now. You've almost been killed, first in the wilderness, and then by a bunch of killers, and now you're thrilled because your rescuer is not married.*

But she was pleased. She smiled to herself. She looked at his hair, the long braids hanging down on his uniform shirt. Ohmigod. A man with braided hair. She thought of her younger years following Jerry Garcia around. There were men there with long hair. But they were not men.

This was a man.

"Smokey."

"Yeah?"

"Thank you for saving my life. After they killed all those people, I don't think they were going to let me go."

"Probably not."

"And who are those people? Are they from here? What did they want with me?"

Smokey turned left off the paved highway, driving through a wide meadow on a gravel road toward woods in the distance. He had told Jennifer that his mother lived in a traditional community on the reservation – up toward Mt. Jefferson, many miles north of where Jennifer was found. You had to be a guest to be there. Or a tribal member.

"We don't know yet. You must have seen something they're worried about. The bodies up there in the wilderness area."

"Maybe they think I did, but whatever they're worried about I didn't find after all. A body or two, some have been there a long time, according to Sarah."

"Sarah talks too much," Smokey said.

"Don't you be picking on my Sarah," Jennifer said.

"Your Sarah," Smokey said, smiling.

"Yeah, and those people, they can just leave me . . . leave all of us alone."

"It's too late for that," Smokey said. "They brought death to a friend of mine, and brought death to the reservation, to a sacred place. They will have to pay."

Jennifer suddenly knew that he meant what he said, that the bad men (whoever they were) who had killed his friend and those people at the hospital, were in trouble. She had seen him in action, and he didn't need a committee to decide what needed to be done.

*My life has been on hold until this point.*

I've been marking time, she thought. I've lived more (and feared more) in the last week than in my entire life. I know that life can't be all adrenalin, but it's like I've been waiting for something all my life – something to happen.

*Maybe this is it.*

Other than spending time down in Eugene at the University of Oregon (everything in the state was *down* when you lived in Portland) she had lived in the city of Portland all of her life.

Something was happening. I don't want people to kill me, and I didn't plan this, but I can't get out of here. Not yet. I know that.

And you're not as afraid as you should be, Jennifer, old kid.

*I can't just go back to Portland and pick up my old life again. Not with those men out there, and Smokey seems to understand it. I don't want to, and I'm not sure I can. I miss my apartment on the river, but I can edit books from any location.*

I'm gonna do this. I'm gonna stay alive and help Smokey and the others find these people. I'm gonna remember what I saw up there.

Jennifer Kruger, search and rescue victim, kidnapping victim, victim of some very bad men, wished later that she had just gone home and found a new apartment. Worked it out on her own.

She had found death on the mountain, and it still followed her these days.

And visited those around her. Her new-found friends.

Sarah.

Smokey.

The people they loved.

# Chapter 24

Cold River Indian Reservation
Sidwalter

Jennifer looked out at the woods. The trees didn't seem so threatening now when she was in a car with Smokey. The sun drifted up through the trees behind them as they drove slowly through a large meadow. Wildflowers littered the grass like bright red and yellow discarded confetti. A herd of horses stood off to the left, ears up and watching the car, waiting for a sign to run.

"Those your horses?" Jennifer pointed.

"One or two of mine might be mixed in there. Most are wild mustangs; we have a lot of them on the reservation."

I really am in the wild west, Jennifer thought. She looked up ahead and saw the house, a long low structure with log siding. A covered porch with a railing ran full length across the front. A lazy trail of white smoke rose out of the chimney.

This isn't a teepee. It looks like Bonanza. She half expected Pa, Hoss, Little Joe, and Hop Sing to come out on the porch. If that happens, I'll know that I really died and am forced to live in a surreal world, where Indians have running water, cars, electricity, resorts and casinos.

A three-car garage was off to the side, and then what looked like a shop and barn in the back. Corrals. A haystack. One of the biggest stacks of wood she had ever seen. As they parked behind a Suburban, she nodded at the wood.

"Get cold here?"

"In the winter, very cold. But on most mornings, winter and summer, my mother uses wood to cook breakfast."

Smokey opened the door of the car and started go get out. Jennifer picked up her pack and stepped out as the front door of the house burst open and a blur of movement shot toward them. A girl, about eight years old Jennifer thought, ran toward the car, her black ponytail bobbing, her white tennis shoes flashing. She wore jeans and a red hooded sweatshirt.

"Daddy!" The girl threw herself at Smokey and jumped. Jennifer thought he would have fallen had he not braced himself for the certain onslaught. The girl wrapped her arms around him and kissed his cheek.

"Hey, little girl, ease up," he said, laughing, "and speaking of up, why are you awake so early?" He kissed her on the forehead.

"I asked Grandma to wake me up when you were on your way home. She said you called."

Jennifer stood at the front of the car and waited. Smokey made the introductions.

"Jennifer, I'd like you to meet Laurel, my daughter. Honey, this is Jennifer, the woman I told you about."

Laurel lifted her head up from Smokey's shoulder.

"You the lady who was lost?"

"That was me," Jennifer said. *Woman he told her about? What else did he tell her about me?*

Jennifer held out her hand.

"I'm very pleased to meet you," she said. Laurel waved.

"Well, let's go in and meet my mother," Smokey said. Jennifer hung back as they started to move toward the front porch area. Smokey whispered something to Laurel, and the girl jumped down from his arms and held a hand up to Jennifer.

"Come on, take my hand," she said. Jennifer reached out with her bandaged left hand. Laurel grabbed her hand lightly, smiled up at her, and pulled.

"Come on, Jennifer. Aunt Sarah told me all about you. I'm going to introduce you to Grandma. The others are still sleeping, but when you meet them, they won't bite."

Jennifer had a sudden fear, afraid that these people, Smokey's family, wouldn't like her, would think of her as an intruder, and she just wanted to be away.

*But you don't have any other place to go, Jen.*

Jennifer looked to Smokey for help. He shook his head, smiling. She let herself be pulled inside. A large living room looked out over a deck in the back, with floor to ceiling windows. A big screen television stood in the corner, a news channel on, the sound down low. Jennifer had several impressions at once. Leather couches and chairs, bead work, baskets and animals on the walls. Pictures of family.

Smells of coffee. Breakfast.

A short round woman with long gray hair stood at a wood stove in the far corner, stirring a pot. She looked up and smiled. Jennifer let herself be pulled that way, thinking that the woman had beautiful eyes.

"Grandma," Laurel said, still pulling, "this is Jennifer, the lost lady that Daddy found."

"I'm very happy to meet you," Jennifer said, holding out her right hand.

"I'm Catherine," she said, "but everyone calls me 'Cat.'" She moved Jennifer's outstretched hand and gave her a hug.

"Welcome to our home."

Jennifer tried to move back to make the hug a quick, superficial thing, but Cat moved closer and gathered Jennifer in her arms. Jennifer stiffened, and then stopped struggling when Cat looked into her eyes from inches away.

"Welcome to my home, child. Sarah said that you had been through a lot, that you were special, that you needed us. You will heal here and find peace." And with that, the woman let go, and Jennifer stood there, not knowing what to say.

"Thank you for everything," she finally said, and then she looked around.

"Where's Smokey?"

"Oh, he's getting his clothes ready to burn," Cat said.

*Burn?*

"The clothes he wore when they found the bodies, the uniform he wore last night during the killing. Death clothes. He has to burn them, never to wear them again. And then he has to go to the sweat lodge and purify himself from death."

A man who could drive a Mercedes like Jeff Gordon, a man who was a police supervisor, a father, was a man who embraced a tradition and religion that she couldn't comprehend.

Cat held up a cup of coffee and Jennifer took it, the aroma of the coffee and breakfast melting her remaining resistance.

*A home. That's what this is.*

*A home.*

*And that's what you have been missing, Jen.*

She had a thought and tried to push it away, but it remained.

*Death follows you, Jen.*

*Followed you to the hospital.*

113

*To the reservation.*
*To this family.*
*This family that I have been missing all my life.*
But death did follow her. And had she known then what form it would take, she would have borrowed one of the cars out front, driven to Portland, and taken her chances at her apartment.
*Please, God, don't let death follow me here.*

# Chapter 25

Near Hermosillo
State of Sonora, Mexico

Enrico Alvarez walked through the long metal building, a business owner looking at the pride of his labor. Years before *anfetamina cristalizada* was produced in Mexico, the buildings had been constructed as chicken barns.

The drying shed had rows of tables with long thin metal pans holding the finished product, crystal methamphetamine. Once known as a poor man's cocaine, a niche drug produced by West Coast biker gangs, most of the methamphetamine used in the United States came from labs like the one he owned, Enrico knew. And it was a good business, with many of his countrymen becoming addicted as well.

Enrico had started his tour at his chemical plant, where pre-cursor chemicals were measured and mixed. The methamphetamine chemical plant resembled a modern chemical lab, where the workers wore white coats. Thanks to me, Enrico thought, even Mexico's El Presidente won't mess with us.

When they were getting established, they had come to the attention of the federales. Enrico had taken two police officers hostage, filmed their last moments, and in a sudden vision of clarity, he had placed their heads on metal poles and put them in the town square. A lighted sign on the poles demanded respect. Then in a moment of genius he had posted the video on YouTube for the world to see. For the police to see. For the El Presidente.

For the other cartels to see. It wasn't anything new – the Islamo Fascists had been doing it on television for a long time, but it was new to the drug cartels.

He knew what he was called, what was whispered so quietly as to not be a name at all, *el morbosa*. The ghoul. He had been placed in charge of establishing lucrative meth routes, worth billions of dollars, into Norte America, and to take care of the competition. The competition was fierce, and deadly.

With the drug cartels in Sinaloa and the Gulf going at each other, Enrico and his backers had stepped into the void. And had done so relatively unnoticed until the past year. When they got big.

Thank you United States of America for shutting down the local meth manufacturers in the U.S. Thank you amigos. We now have a market beyond our wildest dreams.

Thanks again, amigos.

Enrico got to the end of the drying shed and stepped into the sunlight. He put on a pair of dark sunglasses, waited for his entourage of guards and bankers, and walked the fifty feet to the next shed. It was identical to the others, at least from the outside. With his sunglasses on, he might have been mistaken for Manuel Noriega, the Panamanian strong man. Enrico's dark and menacing good looks were not diminished by childhood chicken pox and a knife scar running down his left cheek from his eye to his chin. At five foot seven, he was shorter then Noriega, but had more powerful shoulders and arms.

He dressed as always, blue dress shirt, khaki slacks, black sport coat. He carried an FN-7 in a shoulder holster, the weapon of choice with the American Secret Service. If it was good enough to protect the president of the United States, it was good enough for him.

Two guards ran in front of Enrico, their assault rifles at the ready, and opened the door to the next building. Enrico walked through the door and took off his sunglasses. The nervous gaggle of bankers came in behind him. They had been flown here in a private jet, and would be taken back before the end of the business day. It had been Enrico's idea to bring the bankers here. They didn't know exactly where they were, and by bringing them here, it would ensure their cooperation and silence forever.

This was the packaging room. Methamphetamine was meticulously weighed on scales and packaged for transportation to the United States. At the far end of the building, the packages were vacu-sealed in large plastic containers, and then carefully washed and wiped down.

The washing might be unnecessary, since they put so much meth in the United States that their losses to the cops there were not only acceptable, but expected and needed, so the cops there were looked upon as doing something. The percentage of losses to seizures were far less than a grocery man's produce losses.

Acceptable spoilage.

Enrico Alvarez liked these tours. The bankers were impressed and subdued. As they exited the packaging building, they walked to another, newer building, not one of the chicken sheds, but one constructed specifically for the new drug business. The building had its own guards, surveillance system, and electronic alarms. It was for counting, sorting, and packaging money, and he reserved it for the end of the tour. Even the ones from the wealthiest banks would raise their eyes at the sight of so much money. There were hundreds of millions of U.S. dollars in one room. His counting machines, surveillance cameras and surveillance command and control centers were as good as any casino in the world. Enrico had, in fact, attended the G3 World Gaming Trade Conference in Las Vegas this past October, to keep up on the latest in surveillance equipment.

A man wearing a beige linen suit entered behind them and quickly caught up with the group. Enrico turned as he heard his name. Roberto, his second in command, called to him.

"Ola, Enrico. You're wanted in the main house. I'll take over for you here."

Enrico raised his eyebrows.

"He say why?"

"It's about the business in the United States, the situation with the bodies on the reservation."

Enrico nodded.

"All in a day's work, amigo. A lesson."

He walked out into the sunlight, thinking that to do something right, he would have to do it himself. Did these people he hired to clean up in Oregon not think that he would notice their failure to bring him the woman from the hospital?

How hard could it be?

He would have to do it himself.

He would go back to this reservation, a critical link in the distribution system. The idea of using places in the United States where local law enforcement can't go was pure gold. The Indian reservation system with sovereign borders in Norte America was perfect for dealing drugs with just the tribal police to deal with.

He would get this woman, this Jennifer Kruger, bring her back to Mexico. Enrico was a firm believer in showing the troops how to do something.

117

Bring this woman back to Mexico, here to the factory at Hermosillo.

Maybe put her head on YouTube.

# Chapter 26

Cold River Indian Reservation

The heat came off the rocks and penetrated Smokey's skin, working its way into his bones. He didn't have time for a cleansing sweat, so this would have to do for now. He closed his eyes and thought about the events of the past few days.

He had been thinking about the bodies in the wilderness area, particularly the man, Kal-leed. To have an Islamic fascist here on the reservation was not impossible. The upper end of the reservation was only seventy miles from Portland. In the war on terror, Portland played a part. After September eleventh, seven Portland area people conspired to travel to Afghanistan to wage war on the United States. One was killed in Afghanistan and the remaining six eventually pled guilty to a bunch of charges and were sent to prison.

But why dump a body here? Smokey lay back, feeling the heat from the stones.

And then there was the secret al Qaeda training camp that an Islamic entrepreneur tried to set up in Bly, Oregon. That was a joke, but it was attempted. The joke was on them. Smokey had been to Bly. The good ol' boys in Southern Oregon made the cast of Deliverance look downright normal. The first time someone was seen wearing a kaffiyeh around Bly, they just wouldn't have been heard from again.

"Squeal like a pig" would have taken on a whole new meaning.

If Kal-leed was on the terror watch list, who killed him? Was someone going to start a war and use the rez for a dumping ground? It didn't make sense, unless Kal-leed had pissed off some of his comrades. They might decide to use the rez as a place to put bodies. But that didn't explain the older bones. And what about the hand that Jennifer found? Where did that come from, and who did the hand belong to?

A better question, he knew, was where is the body now? He hadn't talked with Jennifer about it, but he wanted to interview her and see if she could reach back in her memory and discover more about the woman's hand. Where did she find it? Did she see a woman's body? Did she see other bodies?

The feds had a role here, but he didn't know what. From experience he knew that asking them for a straight answer was futile.

They were protected by explaining that he either didn't have a need to know or have the right to know.

Smokey stood up and opened the flap. He stepped out into the bright day. The mid-morning sun filtered through the forest in white streaks, the tall Ponderosa Pines looking like shiny giants. The cool air on his skin felt good in contrast to the heat of the sweat lodge.

He started on the path through the woods that led to his mother's house. He stopped on the trail and looked through the trees back toward the sweat lodge. He could see the white presence of Mt. Jefferson towering through the trees. The snow on Whitewater Glacier sparkled in the sun.

A wild area.

A sacred area.

Someone had defiled it.

He turned and started back to the house.

What would have happened if Jennifer hadn't found the bodies, hadn't found the hand? More killings gone unreported? More bodies on the rez?

He needed to talk with Jennifer.

It was time to get some answers.

It was time for her to lead him to the body.

# Chapter 27

Mt. Jefferson Wilderness Area
Hole in the Wall Park, 1100 hours

Stan Perdue folded the map and looked across Jefferson Creek to the reservation lands. He had decided that he wasn't going to leave until he had proof positive that Bigfoot lived on the reservation. He felt certain that the sanctuary of the tribal lands had afforded the large biped a place to thrive. Hell, the Indians had plenty of legends that spoke of Sasquatch. Stan had food and supplies in his pack, and he and his girlfriend, Amy, each had a camera.

Even though he ran the Bigfoot Expeditions, Inc., across the country, this little trip wasn't part of that organization. BFE was for tourists, for those adventuresome souls who could shell out a thousand dollars each for some quality time in the woods to look for something that they believed existed.

Or wanted to believe.

"You sure we should go over there?" Amy asked. "What about the sign that said, 'No Trespassing?'"

"That's just to scare people away. Besides, what are the Indians gonna do, shoot us?"

Stan could see that Amy wasn't so sure that they wouldn't. She nibbled at her lower lip, and put one foot forward, tentative, as if Stan would change his mind.

"It will be okay," Stan said. He sighed. He needed for Amy to go with him, he needed the extra hand with the gear. Otherwise, he would have gone alone. With her along, he would have to mention her in any journals, articles, and publicity this generated. And he would have to mention her in the best selling book he was sure to write.

He was going to have an encounter with Bigfoot, of that he was certain. He had dropped a good portion of his summer's profits from the Bigfoot Expeditions for the camera, a camera fitted with the latest night vision device he could buy. He had night vision goggles for both himself and Amy. Since Bigfoot was nocturnal, they would be able to hunt for the animal at night.

Finally, there would be a film to go along with the 1967 Patterson film. Only this would have the latest technology, a digital movie that could be copyrighted and sold. Every time the film he was about to take of Bigfoot was played, be it on the internet or television, his name would be connected with it.

In October, 1967, a man named Roger Patterson filmed an encounter with a seven feet tall upright biped giant in Bluff Creek Valley in northern California. This huge ape-looking creature was walking at a diagonal toward Patterson, and changed forever the way people thought about Bigfoot.

It was the only film available for over forty years.

Stan Perdue had grown up watching the Patterson film, the several minutes of sixteen millimeter film of poor quality.

The Perdue film, as this was going to be known, would be more famous. It would be of good quality, and if they had some luck at all, they would be able to track Sasquatch for a long time, maybe even off the reservation. He didn't have a gun for protection. He had a gun used by field biologists that would insert a pellet into an animal, and allow tracking with a laptop computer with a satellite link. .

He could track the animal from his farmhouse a thousand miles away, and use the tracking to write a series of books on Sasquatch.

*I'll be more famous than Jane Goodall.*

*As famous as Jacques Cousteau.*

*As rich as I want.*

"Okay, Amy, ready to get your feet wet?"

Stan looked across Jefferson Creek, picked out his path along the creek bed, and stepped in the icy water.

They made good time early on, the hike easy around the base of Goat Peak. After an hour, Stan held up his hand and stopped. Sweat ran down his back between his shoulder blades. He leaned forward and loosened the straps to his pack. Amy came up behind him, smiling.

She loved the trail and the wilderness areas, and she loved to hike. Stan knew that she would ease up once they started the hike, even if they were on the reservation. He helped her with her pack. They were overloaded, and he knew it, but it couldn't be helped. His pack was sixty-five pounds. Amy's was fifty, at least ten more than she should have had. But she had a good amount of their food, so her pack would be getting lighter.

"Okay, let's take a break here," he said. He spread out the map on a rock. Carl, Jennifer Kruger's boyfriend, had marked his trail. They were going into the Parker Creek area to the camp where Carl and Jennifer had spent a couple of days. From there he would try to find out where Jennifer had been. She had seen something, and Stan was willing to bet that she had had an encounter with Bigfoot. She either couldn't tell, or the Indians had convinced her to not tell. Either way, he wasn't going to let them officially make the discovery. He was the one who had spent most of his adult life chasing the elusive giant. He looked out over the forest spread below them. This was perfect Sasquatch country. The animal could have survived here for thousands of years, with only an occasional encounter with man.

The hike in from the Cabot Lake trailhead had taken them all of yesterday afternoon and evening. They had been on the trail for three hours this morning. Thirteen miles of trail with heavy packs. Amy leaned over his shoulder and looked at the map.

"How much further?" she asked.

"Only about three miles. Another hour, hour and a half. Then we'll set up camp and rest. Look for Jennifer's trail."

"Deal," Amy said. Stan folded the map and put it in the pocket in his hiking shorts. He picked up Amy's pack and held it for her. She looked so cute in her shorts and blue hiking shirt, her blonde ponytail and her muscular legs. Stan even liked her tattoos. Maybe she would take on a more important part in his book. He could afford it. She was a great companion.

They started off on the trail and the woods closed in around them. The heat and brightness of the July sun filtered through the trees. Stan had a sudden flash of fear, something he rarely felt in the woods.

*What if we don't make if out of here?*

He turned and looked at Amy. She smiled at him and blew him a kiss.

"Move on, buddy," she said. "I don't have all day, we have a Sasquatch to find."

Stan laughed and shook his head. He faced forward and started off, thinking that he was a lucky man. He had a great hiking companion and they were in the wilderness on a wonderful summer day.

He had the thought again.

*What if we don't make it out of here?"*

123

They didn't.

# Chapter 28

Near Hermosillo
Sonora, Mexico

Enrico Alvarez drove his Hummer on the paved driveway past an army of groundskeepers, the main house coming in and out of view on the hill above. He waved at the  guards at the gate and continued on. He would have one more set of guards to go through, but it was more or less automatic, since he had picked the guards himself.

The Boss, the Patron. Even the people in the city who didn't directly work for the Boss, called him that. Out of *respecto*. Out of *temer*. The Boss once told him that people would either respect him or fear him, and he didn't care which.

"If I can't get people to respect me," the Boss said, "then I know I can get them to fear me, and fear is more reliable. I think I would rather they fear me."

Enrico had taken the words to heart. He didn't even bother with respect. He drove up to the main house, a long, beige three story structure, with a red tile roof and an inner courtyard that held two swimming pools, a tennis court, and a bowling alley. The Boss loved to bowl. Enrico parked at the gate to the courtyard, and walked past the guards as they came to attention.

The Boss was sitting at a table under a palm tree, watching across the grass at some children bowling at an outdoor lane. Having the childhood of privilege we never had, Enrico thought. The Boss waved him to sit, and raised his hand slightly for a waiter. Two waiters were standing at attention behind the palm, like pets waiting to be praised.

"Coffee," Enrico said, settling into his chair.

"I don't see how you can drink that stuff in the afternoon, in the heat," El Patron said. The Boss was getting old, or older, in his eighties, and had been at this game a long time. He had started with *marihuana*, and had been a coke dealer, and now major meth manufacturer. He knew all about treachery and what money could do for and against you. He wore what he always did, a navy blue suit, with a white shirt and no tie. He reminded Enrico of the old movie Mexican moguls, the land barons of old Mexico, the Boss having grown up

125

watching those old movies. A full head of white hair, large white goatee.

"I want you to send someone back to the United States, see to the problems the Jihadists have created in their rush to get some of our money."

Enrico nodded. It was not time for him to speak yet.

"In many ways they are like children, having little patience, wanting one thing and seeing one way to get it.

"Deadly children," he added, "but children just the same." He sat back.

"I've been thinking about this," Enrico said, and took a sip of his coffee.

"The middle eastern people we have been dealing with have no method of learning of our operation. They can take off a dealer or two if they find out who they are, but we don't publish our troop movements like the United States government and media do. We don't advertise our every move. They don't know us.

"We can move at will in the U.S. because we have fifty million people there who look like us, came from Mexico, speak the language, and work there. We are a part of the economy now."

"We are already at war with the Gulf Cartel and the Sinaloa Cartel. We don't need another one."

"We are at war with everyone who isn't at this table," Enrico said softly.

The Boss smiled, and nodded his head. "You learn well."

"You taught me, Patron. But we are at war with the government of the United States, and that will cost us over time. We can use them, with their new-found fear of the Islamic fascists, and we can be a useful ally to them. Look at how well the heroin dealers in Afghanistan have done. The DEA, the U.S. troops, they leave them alone. All to fight the fascists.

"We will help them find the Jihadists, a few at a time. If a few Indians on reservations up there get in the way, so what? We'll treat them like we treat the peasants here.

"So you see, Patron, I can't send anyone to the United States. This is something I have to do myself. I will leak information to the F.B.I. and the D.E.A. and get them to lay off of our major routes for a while, and also give them the information I have about how the fascists are getting into the U.S.

"I will even give them a shipment or two, just to keep our people on their toes." Enrico laughed.

"First, clean up the mess in the woods up there, get the woman," Patron said, serious now. "I don't want the other cartels to use this information against us, to hurt us, and it could." He waved his arms at his immense house, toward the guards in the front.

"Take what and who you need, Enrico. Just get it done."

Enrico nodded, got up and embraced the Patron, and walked to his Hummer. He dialed a number on his cell phone, and said, "Get the plane ready. One hour."

*Now I go to the United States on a business trip. To take care of some business that should have already been taken care of.*

*The woman.*

*Jennifer Kruger.*

*And whoever was with her.*

# Chapter 29

Cold River Indian Reservation
Sidwalter

Jennifer stretched and slowly opened her eyes. Laurel sat on the floor beside the couch. The girl's eyes were closed, her head on Jennifer's blanket.

"She didn't want to miss you when you woke up," Smokey said, bending down and touching Laurel's hair.

Jennifer sat up, leaving Laurel on the blanket. After Smokey had gone to "sweat," whatever that was, his mother Cat had given her a blanket and pointed to the couch. "I'll get a bedroom ready for you today," she had said, "but for now, I hope the couch is okay."

Jennifer had not realized how tired she was. Now that the adrenalin was wearing off, she had been ready to sleep. She had fallen asleep as soon as she pulled the blanket up. She thought she must have been asleep several hours.

"What time is it?" she asked.

"Almost noon," Smokey said. "How about some lunch and then we will talk, you and I, and try to figure out why these people want to kill you. After that, I will meet with the F.B.I. and my chief."

The way he said 'F.B.I.' made Jennifer think that he didn't want to do it, but that it was a necessity.

"I don't know what we'll find out that I haven't already told you," Jennifer said, "but I'll do whatever you want."

*What I want is a shower.*

"Can I take a shower first?"

"Of course."

Laurel sat up and rubbed her eyes. She looked up at her dad and grinned.

"Wow, Dad, you sure got some of those dudes who jacked Jennifer."

Jennifer looked on as Smokey stared at his daughter.

"Laurel, how'd you . . ." he asked.

Laurel held up a pink cell phone. "It's all over the rez, Dad, and Daddy, do you think they will come after Jennifer again?"

"No!"

As Jennifer listened to father and daughter, she didn't think that Smokey said 'no' with much conviction. Then she had a thought that would become reality in a short time.

*They're coming after me again.*

*Here.*


Jennifer let hot water run over her back. The heat felt so good that she didn't want to stop. She worried that she might be using too much, since there had been several children watching television when she left the living room. Okay, time to get out. She turned the faucet off and stood in the steam. She opened the shower door and felt for a towel.

Laurel held a towel up in the doorway.

"Thanks." Jennifer wrapped herself in the towel and stepped out. Laurel stepped back and stood there, looking up at Jennifer.

"You're welcome," she said.

Jennifer thought it strange she didn't feel self-conscious around this kid, this stranger, and shrugged at her comfort. She usually didn't like to share her bathroom with anyone.

"My daddy said you are one tough girl," Laurel said.

"He did, did he?" Jennifer laughed.

"Yep. Know what else?"

"What?"

"I think he likes you, my dad, I mean."

Jennifer felt herself blushing. She wrapped the towel tighter. Laurel snatched another towel from the rack and held it out. "For your hair."

As Jennifer wrapped her hair, she thought about what Laurel just said.

*It shouldn't matter, Jen. You just met these people.*

And then she had another thought.

*But you know you feel good, and welcome here.*

She smiled and walked into the adjoining bedroom where she had her clothes laid out. Someone had placed socks and panties on the bed next to her borrowed jeans. Laurel trailed her out of the bathroom and stood as Jennifer toweled herself dry. She looked at Smokey's daughter and could see the dad there. And the dad's attitude. Laurel didn't appear to be afraid of anything.

Jennifer sat on a bench and patted the space beside her. Laurel plopped down.

"You're very pretty," Laurel said, a smug look curling her mouth.

"Thanks, you're very pretty yourself." She stood and pulled the jeans up. "Tell me, Laurel, tell me something about your daddy."

"Do you like him back?"

"How could I not? He saved my life, didn't he?"

They both laughed, and to Jen, it was the best feeling she had had in a long time.

They were still laughing ten minutes later when then entered the living room, Jennifer with her arm resting easily on Laurel's shoulder. Smokey gave her a look of surprise, and Jennifer grinned at him.


After a lunch of soup and bread, Jennifer followed Smokey out the back door and onto the deck. The view was tremendous – a mountain meadow with a barn and corrals to her left, and at the end, a forest of Ponderosa Pine trees, and above the forest off to the left, the white glacier-covered slopes of Mt. Jefferson. Mt. Wilson, a smaller mountain was off to the right.

"I don't think I could ever get tired of this," she said.

"I never have." Smokey stood beside her. "What was that all about, you and Laurel, laughing?"

"Girl stuff," Jennifer said, and then added, "she's a great kid."

"Yeah, I know," Smokey said, turning toward her, "but with Laurel, she hasn't warmed up to a new person since . . . well, for a long time." He shook his head.

"How many *new* friends do you bring around her?"

"None! I mean,-."

"I would never have believed you could be at a loss for words," Jennifer said.

"Not usually." He pointed to a table on the deck. "Let's go take a look at a map. I'm going to ask you to remember what happened to you, what you saw, and try to put it in perspective on a map." He moved to the table. "It may not be easy," he added.

Jennifer pulled a chair over next to Smokey. A map of the reservation, with adjoining Mt. Jefferson Wilderness area, was spread out on the table.

"Did you and Carl have maps of the area?" Smokey asked.

"Yeah, we did, and I looked at them occasionally so I was pretty familiar with where we were, what the maps looked like."

"From talking with Carl, you entered the rez here, at the 'Hole-in-the-Wall Park.'"

"Yeah, and it sure looks different on the map than on foot. See here," Jennifer said, pointing, "that switchback trail, dropping into the canyon of Jefferson Creek, is a steep one. Then we had to climb out the other side on the reservation. In the trees mostly, at the base of Mt. Jefferson. Carl, you know Carl?"

Smokey nodded. "We had him at the Search and Rescue base camp."

"Just so you know, Carl is an idiot. We are done as a couple. I can't believe that I settled for that guy." She looked closer at the map.

*You're saying too much Jennifer.*

"Okay, here," she pointed, "after we left Jefferson Creek, I don't know exactly where we camped, but it took us a half day or so to hike in. Had to be quiet, which is not how I like to hike, I like to sing, talk with my companions, remark on the rocks, trees, flora and fauna, and all that. Carl, that jerk, said we had to be quiet, so we could sneak up on Bigfoot, freaking Sasquatch."

Jennifer looked up as Laurel sat in a chair next to her.

"Laurel." Smokey jerked his head in the direction of the house, his braids flying.

"Daddy, can't I stay? Pleeeze?" She scooted her chair closer to Jennifer. "I want to hear what Jen has to say as much as you do."

Jennifer turned to Smokey. "It's okay with me."

Jennifer smiled at Laurel, who immediately grinned back. Jennifer saw Smokey looking first at his daughter, then at her. He shook his head, slowly, defeated.

"Okay, I can't win with both of you. And since when did Jennifer change to Jen?"

"It's what I like to be called," Jennifer said. She pointed at the map. "You know how to read a map, Laurel?"

"Of course. Daddy taught me a long time ago."

"I'll get some coffee," Smokey said. Jennifer watched as he walked inside, shaking his head.

Laurel laughed.

I could get to like this kid, Jennifer thought. She walked to the edge of the deck and looked out over the tree-lined slope. Laurel stood behind her. The back yard area was not lawn, as she would have expected, but the undergrowth of a forest, with juniper trees and a large Ponderosa Pine just off the deck. The ground was covered with pine cones and dead branches.

Her attention was drawn to one of the sticks on the ground.

*It moved!*

Jennifer looked closer, knowing that she had imagined it. There. Again.

*The stick moved again, an undulating motion. A snake!*

"Laurel, did you see that?" Jennifer pointed to the stick and turned to look back at Laurel. The little girl was at her side, staring out at the branches on the ground.

"Yeah, the stick moved."

"But how?"

"I did it, but don't tell, Daddy doesn't like for me . . ."

"Laurel!"

Smokey stood behind them. He held a tray with coffee and cocoa.

"Laurel, I told you, no *Twati!*" He set the tray on the table and glared at his daughter. Laurel shrugged. "Sorry, Dad," she said, but Jennifer didn't think she sounded too sorry.

Jennifer turned to Smokey, and decided to remain quiet.

*What did I just see? Whatever it was, Smokey is pissed at his daughter.*

Jennifer looked at the sticks again as Smokey waved her over. She didn't think that this was the time to ask about that illusion she saw, but if she continued to hang with the Indians, she was going to find out. She would make a point of it. She joined Smokey at the table and looked at the map.

"When we got out of the Jefferson Creek canyon, I don't really know how far we went to the camp," Jennifer said.

"Here, this is where you camped with Carl," Smokey said, making a circle with a green marker. "Here, on Parker Creek." He traced their trail from where they entered the reservation to their camp. Jennifer and Laurel leaned over the map. Jennifer thought of the first night and day at the camp.

*I was so bored. Carl fiddling with his gadgets, the camera, the listening devices he was sure would work. I had packed some of the stuff in for him. Good thing I brought a paperback. By day two at the camp, sitting around waiting for night so Carl could look around for Sasquatch, I was ready to go. But no, he had to stay. Our argument did get a little out of hand, me calling him a little jerk off, loading up my pack with just my stuff and stomping off in a huff.*

*Not very smart, Jen. Look what happened then.*

"I was bored," Jennifer said, and shrugged. "I couldn't take another day of not talking, just sitting around waiting for dark. So I left."

She looked at the map.

"I'm not sure where I went from there, but I thought I was backtracking. I thought I had a pretty good handle on what our trails looked like. But I don't know where I took a wrong turn."

"We found the bodies here, by trailing you," Smokey said.

"But that's way over on Parker Creek. I don't think I walked that far the first day. I left camp after breakfast, say eight o'clock, and I think it was about three or four in the afternoon when I found the bodies. So I could have walked, how far?"

"You went four to five miles, as the crow flies, but hiking on animal trails and tracks, you walked at least ten miles. That's the best Nathan and I can come up with.

"Take your time," Smokey continued. "Think about that first day, maybe you will remember where you went, what you saw. You and I both know that it's important to somebody. Important enough to kill a lot of people."

Jennifer traced the map with her fingers. Laurel grabbed her left hand and squeezed. Jen smiled, lost in the thought of that day she left Carl at the camp.

*I had a good day, that first day after leaving, I was good in the woods alone. I was pretty content, thinking that I could get most of the way back to the Bigfoot Expedition base camp, then read and talk and wait for Carl to come out.*

*But I didn't count on finding a body, some body parts, did I? Thought I was pretty tough, going it alone out there. The trail petered out, and then I just walked on animal trails. I knew I was lost. Lost my little ass in the woods, took a wrong turn, went the wrong way, trying to prove something to Carl. And when I knew I was lost, I saw an opening in the trees, and*

"I found a clearing, thought I would make a fire." Jen blurted the words, excited now, remembering how and why she came to the place where she found the body of the man.

*The body. The man, what did Smokey say his name was? Kal-leed something. A narco-terrorist, Smokey called him. Someone trying to kill us with drug money. Glad he's dead.*

*I remember looking at the leg of the man, of the shoe, a hiker, no, not a hiker, dress shoes, slacks, missing parts, ah God, he's missing parts. And the skull. I remember the skull, and then it was night.*

"I sure didn't want to spend the first night alone, after finding the dead man," Jennifer said, quiet now.

"That was the beginning of some very bad nights, I can't remember the next one, but I'll try. Let me think."

Smokey smiled, reassuring.

Laurel squeezed her hand, smiled a knowing little girl's smile.

*She's a beautiful girl, and will be a stunningly gorgeous woman. I wonder if she knows that.*

*Cold. Stiff. I got up from the first night alone, scared, hungry, eating a bar from my pack. Nanna, I want my Nanna more than anything in the world. I found . . . I saw something.*

*Think, Jen.*

*I saw*

*And then I found Nanna.*

*And I ran.*

"I remember what I found, I found my doll, Nanna" Jennifer said. She spoke slowly, measured, in a monotone, as if in a trance, her mind on the mountain, her eyes taking in a horrific scene. "But how did I get the hand?"

Smokey opened a folder and removed three pictures. Jennifer watched as he placed them face down on the table.

"Laurel, this is where you leave us," Smokey said.

"But Dad, why can't I . . ."

Smokey looked at his daughter. Laurel got up, gave Jennifer a hug, kissed Smokey, and walked inside the house.

Smokey waited until she was gone. "Do you remember where you found your doll?" he asked.

Jennifer didn't move, made no effort to look at the pictures.

*No. I don't remember. It was on the ground, I was running. I was running from the bodies in the meadow, and then during the day*

"It was daytime," Jennifer said, "and I had been running."

*I was running and then I tripped and fell down and saw my Nanna. I grabbed her and looked around at the trees, the sky, no one here, but what was my Nanna doing here? I picked her up and then I ran. I looked back and saw the trees, the big rock wall where Nanna was. There was a sheer rock wall, going up fifty feet or more, a tree on top of the cliff with a branch out sideways, like a stick person holding his arm out over Nanna.*

"I know where I found her," Jennifer said. She spoke quickly, excited now, still seeing the rocks and the tree.

"There was a tree, a distinct tree, with a branch sticking out like an arm, a pine tree I think, and I picked up Nanna, the hand, under the tree at the base of a sheer rock wall. Maybe a fifty foot high rock wall."

"We should be able to find that," Smokey said, "although Nathan and I didn't see a rock wall in our travels there." He looked at the map and drew a line showing their trail. He consulted a notebook, and then put an x in the Whitewater River area where Jennifer was found.

"Can we fly over it?" Jennifer asked. "Maybe find it from the air. It can't be too far from Kal-leed's body. I found Nanna the day after I found the bodies."

"We can fly it, but flying it means taking the feds with us," Smokey said, "and that carries with it another set of problems."

Jennifer reached for the pictures and picked them up. She turned the first one over and placed it on the map in front of her.

*A hand. A small hand, severed at the wrist. Red fingernail polish, with some kind of pattern in gold. Trailer camp nails, we used to call them. A hand photographed on a blue background. No blood. Looks like it has been under water, wrinkled. Turn over another picture Jennifer.*

She turned over the second picture.

A piece of cloth, a dirty piece of cloth.

"Is this -?"

"We think that cloth is from your shirt, the cloth you had Nanna, the hand, wrapped in when we found you," Smokey said.

Jennifer shook her head.

*I just don't remember.*

She turned the third picture over. A woman, a young woman, in an obvious jail photo, her unsmiling face staring at the camera.

"Is this –"

"This is the woman . . . was the woman whose hand you found," Smokey said. He looked at his notebook.

Jennifer stared at the picture.

*I've never seen her. I don't think I saw her on the mountain. I can't remember what I saw by the cliff. I don't think that I saw her. What was there?*

She shook her head. "I don't know her." She put the picture down on the map.

"Her name is Georgia Sherell. She worked the street in Portland."

"And she was with Kal-leed," Jennifer said, "she was with him when he died."

"Probably so," Smokey said.

Then let's go find her, Jennifer thought. And let's go find the cliff. Find out what I saw.

*I need to know.*

*How bad could it be.*

*Bad.*

# Chapter 30

Cold River Indian Reservation
Parker Creek

"How much further?" Amy asked.

Stan took his pack off and sat down beside it. He pulled the map from his pocket.

"Two, three miles, toward Whitewater Creek Glacier," he said. "Where Jennifer Kruger walked, from Parker Creek to Whitewater Glacier. That's where we will find Bigfoot, tag him, or her (this got a smile from Amy), take pictures, then get out of here."

"Be famous," Amy said.

"Be rich and famous," Stan said. He pulled his tracking rifle from his pack. "We shoot Bigfoot with this, we can track him during the next year, wherever Bigfoot might travel."

Amy nodded. She had heard this before. She watched as Stan removed a small case from his pack.

"With my mini-laptop, we can track Bigfoot from anywhere in the world."

We might need to, Amy thought.

*We might need to be anyplace but here.*

# Chapter 31

Cold River Tribal Police Department

Smokey parked and saw a virtual caravan of Suburban SUV's and unmarked Ford Crown Vic sedans.

*Feds are here.*

Nathan met him at the back door and grabbed him in a bear hug. "Glad you made it, Little Brother."

"Me too."

"Come with me." Nathan motioned Smokey toward the hallway. They walked past the records officer and Smokey put his finger to his lips, hoping she got the idea that they didn't want anyone to know he was there. She put her arms around him.

"I'm not here," Smokey said.

"Didn't see you," she said, and walked back to her desk.

Smokey dropped to a chair as Nathan closed the door. He was tired to his core, could go to sleep here right now.

"I just need a few minutes sleep," he said, and yawned.

"Feebs are raising hell in there with the chief," Nathan said, "and the chief wants you in there. Told me to find you quick."

"You found me," Smokey said, his eyes closed. He started talking, told Nathan about the morning with Jennifer and her description of the rock wall.

"U.S. Attorney is mad as hell, was yelling around about you, maybe the chief, hiding her witness," Nathan said.

"Her witness? Jennifer?"

"Yup."

"Fuck her."

"Yup." They both laughed.

"Between you and me," Smokey said, "can you find out where that rock wall is, talk to some of the elders?" Nathan nodded.

The door opened and Chief Martin Andrews entered. He closed the door and sat at a desk, looking at Smokey, then Nathan.

"Feebs are pretty upset. The U.S. Attorney is upset. They want Jennifer Kruger, and the coordinates to the location of the man in the meadow."

"We gonna give it to them?"

"We have to," Martin said. "They will get it one way or another."

"What about Jennifer?"

"She's their witness. They want to put her in a protection program for the time being."

"She have a choice in this?" Smokey asked, his face getting red, his fatigue making thought difficult. He wanted to sleep. He got up, glanced at Nathan. "Let me know, Big Brother," he said.

Nathan nodded.

Smokey walked out with the chief.


The conference room was filled with suits. Most Smokey knew from working on other cases in the past. James Russell, Supervisory Special Agent for Oregon, F.B.I., and oh my, Julie Sturgis, *the* U.S. Attorney for the State of Oregon, a presidential appointee who had survived the purges in D.C. Smokey thought she looked a little uptight as he entered the room. Pissed was more like it. But she was tough, and he liked that in her.

She had two of her Assistant U.S. Attorneys with her. One of them, Kelly Devans, a fifty year old prosecutor, was assigned to Indian Country prosecution in Oregon, and was the person who prosecuted most Indians in U.S. District Court. He was a pretty good guy, hard worker, and didn't blow too much smoke.

More F.B.I. suits, six more in all. Two of the young agents Smokey had worked with before, and they had to be watched. Olson, his blond hair said surfer dude, Rafael, dark hair, serious. Full of themselves. Rafael a loose cannon, would use Indian Country to get where he wanted to go. Thought of everyone outside of Washington, D.C. a "local," with Indians below that designation.

The other four were a mixture of people waiting to find a station they liked well enough to retire: A middle-aged woman from Sioux Falls; a gray-haired man with a paunch, an old Russian specialist until the Ruski's no longer mattered; a CPA from San Francisco who looked very uncomfortable, as if the Indians might start scalping at any minute; and the supervisor from Bend, Oakley, a good cop who had gone as far as he could with the F.B.I. without completely compromising his integrity.

Oakley wasn't going to be able to stop what was going to come next, Smokey thought.

Martin made introductions. Smokey knew that this isn't going to be an event where we all shake hands. He nodded as each person was introduced in turn. He had met all of them except the new Assistant U.S. Attorney, Theresa Barrett.

Julie Sturgis led, as was expected. She stood up, moved her gray suit coat back with a hand and placed it on her hip, as if she were in court addressing a jury. No nonsense. She looked at a police report, probably my report, Smokey thought, and then addressed the room.

"Well, Lieutenant Kukup, sounds as if you have been busy." She looked at Chief Martin Andrews, and then finally at Smokey.

He didn't answer, and knew he wasn't expected to.

"The hospital is one issue we'll get to in a few minutes. I want to hear about the bodies in the woods." She looked at Smokey. In fact, they were all looking.

"As you know from my report, Sgt. Nathan Green and I were at the landing when Jennifer Kruger was brought in from the woods by the mountain rescue group. She had a hand with her, probably a female hand, looked as if it had been severed."

He told them about the backtracking, the days and nights spent in the woods. He got up and walked to a map of the reservation on the wall.

"We started here, near the Whitewater River, and the track took us more or less south toward Parker Creek." He looked at the F.B.I. supervisor from Bend, Oakley. "We have GPS waypoints all along our trail," Smokey said, and smiled.

"We don't use smoke signals too much any more."

That got a smile from Sturgis, and then she was serious again.

"On the morning of day three, we found the bodies." Smokey described the body of Mohammed Kal-leed as they found it. The billfold. The missing head.

Russell held up his index finger.

"And you didn't find a female body?"

Smokey shook his head. No.

"How do you think the bodies got there?" Oakley asked.

Smokey looked around the room. "Nathan Green is as good a tracker as you will find. I'm pretty good myself. Mr. Kal-leed didn't walk in. It would help if I knew when he was last seen intact. In Portland, or wherever."

Russell looked at Sturgis, and she shook her head. No.

Smokey was tired. Too tired. He felt the anger coming up, and found he didn't care if he controlled it.

*Business as usual with the feds.*

Smokey removed a notebook from his pocket. He handed it to Martin.

"Chief, my notes for our backtracking, with GPS notations along the way, with Mr. Kal-leed's location. I can copy them for you."

Martin nodded. He called his secretary and Smokey handed her the notebook, explained the pages to be copied when she came in. The room was quiet until she returned, handing the notebook and copies to Chief Martin Andrews.

"I have a question of you all," Smokey said. He looked at Sturgis, the power in the room. She nodded.

*Permission to speak in my own land. Control, Smokey old kid, control yourself. If you go off, you will lose credibility. Try.*

"The hospital. Who were they, and why did they want to kill Jennifer Kruger?"

Sturgis sat, looked at her notepad, and then up at Smokey.

"Well, at some point we can get to that. What we need to do is to get Ms. Kruger, talk with her, and keep her in a safe place."

"With all respect, U.S. Attorney Sturgis, you all had her once, and weren't able to keep her safe. I see that this is business as usual with the feds. We're not only the 'locals,' we're just a bunch of po' Indins."

"Lt. Kukup," Chief Martin Andrews said quietly.

"I had a friend killed," Smokey continued, the anger rising, "and the same people tried to kill me, and I want to know!"

"Well I had a friend killed, too," Agent Rafael said, yelling at the end, coming up out of his chair.

Oakley pointed at Rafael, told him to sit down. Rafael glared at Smokey, and then slowly sat back down. Smokey glared back.

They were all looking at him now, Sturgis not flustered, just looking.

"As far as you feds protecting Kruger, give me a break. You guys won't be able to find her, let alone protect her. Good job in the hospital." He looked at Oakley, and then at Sturgis. Smokey watched as Oakley raised his hand. He directed his remarks to Sturgis.

"Permission to say something," he said.

She nodded. "Of course, we are all here to get to the bottom of this, to find the people responsible."

I don't believe that for a minute, Smokey thought. They are all here to protect whatever they think they need to protect.

"I've known Lt. Kukup for quite some time, we have a good relationship," Oakley said, "and, it's my understanding that he has a secret security clearance with the department of defense, a former Ranger in Afghanistan and Iraq, assigned as active reserve, isn't that right, Lieutenant?"

Smokey nodded.

Sturgis looked up at Smokey, a curious interest on her face.

"How about I fill him in, with Chief Andrews, and then go talk with Ms Jennifer Kruger? We'll all get what we want."

Smokey stood. He looked at Oakley, then at the U.S. Attorney, and left the Chief's office.

*Well, I could have handled that better. I need some sleep.*

# Chapter 32

Cold River Police Department

Smokey slumped in the chair in Nathan's office and closed his eyes. Nathan was looking intently at his computer screen.

"Tough duty in there, huh?" he said.

"Yep." Smokey closed his eyes.

He knew that Martin would be looking for him in seconds. He had needed to make a point, and now he needed to calm down. In the end, the feds wouldn't care if he lost a friend, if he was tired, but they would care if he didn't give them Jennifer Kruger.

But he wasn't going to do that. They would lose her. He would take Oakley to her, and then keep her safe himself.

*She's the key to what was going to happen next.*

There was a knock on the door and Chief Martin Andrews entered, followed by Oakley. Oakley walked over and shook hands with Nathan.

"Good to see you, Sergeant Green."

Nathan stood and shook hands, and then walked to the door.

"You can stay, Sergeant," Oakley said.

"Not on your life," Nathan said. "I know when I don't want to know." He chuckled and walked out, closing the door behind him.

Oakley took Nathan's chair.

"Kal-leed was, is, a Muslim, part of a group of terrorists who are operating in and out of the United States, planning to destroy lives and property. He was raising money for the terrorist operations by dealing with Mexican drug cartels."

"Meth cartels," Smokey said, keeping his eyes closed.

"Yes, meth cartels, and in particular, a new and violent one.

"Kal-leed lived a pretty good lifestyle in Portland," Oakley continued, "and his lifestyle was part of his cover. He had many sides . . . a terrorist, a druggie, and . . ." Oakley paused and looked at Martin, then Smokey.

"And he was one of ours."

Smokey opened his eyes. "He was talking to the feds?"

"That's right," Oakley said. "He was talking to us, and we were paying him. Giving us information on the druggies, and we were working on getting information about the terrorist's plans."

"And he was killed," Smokey said. "But you don't know who did it, the druggies or the terrorists, right?"

"Pretty much right," Oakley said, "but it was probably the druggies. He was living a fast lifestyle in Portland, starting to come to the attention of his fellow terrorists who were cramped up in an apartment. Kal-leed had a Mercedes, and a lot of women. He wasn't so sure that he was going to meet the seventy-two virgins when he died, so he was doing his best to find them in Portland in this life."

Smokey snorted. "Seventy-two virgins? In Portland? So you're saying he was a pedophile?"

Oakley laughed.

"We just hadn't maneuvered him into the situation where he was comfortable telling us about the terrorist activity, but we were getting close. He wanted out. Someone got to him first."

"What about the girl's hand?" Martin asked.

"We think his latest 'virgin,'" Oakley said, "was Sherell, a hooker. We don't know why she was killed, or where the body is, but we do think she was murdered."

"They want Jennifer because of the hand," Smokey said. "Somehow the woman, the ex-girlfriend of Kal-leed, had something they want. There is something on the body, something they have to retrieve. The hand is the key."

Oakley made arrangements to meet Jennifer at Smokey's house in the morning and left to join the rest of his group.

Smokey opened his eyes and looked at Chief Martin Andrews. "So, Chief, what do you think he left out?"

Chief Martin Andrews laughed. "Almost everything, Lieutenant. We know we can count on the feebs to leave out just about everything, and pretend that we think they are keeping us in the loop. Things just don't change."

If I weren't so tired, Smokey thought, *I would laugh.*

By the time he saw Oakley in the morning, a lot more people were dead.

# Chapter 33

Sidwalter

Laurel moved quietly around her room as Jennifer napped. She wanted to reach over and touch Jennifer, but decided instead to sit at her desk and watch Jennifer sleep.

*I really like Jennifer, hope Dad does too, but he sometimes is too quiet for his own good. Oh, I know that she's a Šiyápu, but that doesn't matter, there are some pretty good ones. She is so funny. She and I talk like my girlfriends, like my partners, and I like that. She seems to know what I think and like and we sometimes laugh the same, and the same time and at the same things. I showed her my plans for my very own "MySpace" and I think she thought I was way too young. Oh well. I told her my dad wouldn't let anything happen to me, that if someone tried to hurt me, that person would be in a lot of trouble. She looked at me like she knew that and she said she trusted my dad to take care of anyone around him.*

*Then she said the funniest thing. She said she thought that people must feel better around my dad, that she felt safe when she was with them.*

*I told her that I had always felt safe, except for the time when my friend Owen at school dared me to climb the elm tree in the school yard and couldn't get down. I told Jennifer that I liked her and she hugged me. She smells good. I told her that I seen my dad looking at her, looking at her when she walked away, and she laughed and said that she had already caught him doing that. I like her laugh.*

*I have decided that I wasn't going to let them go off without me, that if Dad and her go somewheres I am going with them, even if I have to sneak along. My dad won't stay mad at me for long.*

*He never does.*

# Chapter 34

Southern Oregon
Aboard Lear N783PA

"Bring him with you," Enrico Alvarez said. He spoke softly into his cell phone. The Lear slowed down as it lost altitude over Crater Lake. They were heading due north for a straight-in approach at The Sunriver Resort Airport. He listened, smiled, and snapped the phone closed.

He had leased a private lodge out of Sunriver, a resort community south of Bend, Oregon. He would be far enough away from what was to happen, yet close enough to be on the Indian Reservation in an hour. He could even have the Lear brought up to the airport in Madras.

Enrico looked out over the green carpet of forest as they made their approach. He liked it here in the United States, but only for a little while. It was fun to go, but he didn't exactly trust the people he had paid to keep his identity from being known. He traveled as Fernando Rodriguez, a businessman from Mexico City. In fact, the plane was registered to a legitimate business in Mexico, and he had a very clean passport in the name of Rodriguez. But still, the *federales* in the U.S. might get a wild hair and find out who he really was. They wouldn't be able to resist arresting me, he thought, even after all I have done for them. He looked around the plane.

Roberto sat in the rear seat. He was as ugly as sin, Enrico thought, with scars on his face and small dark eyes. Enrico smiled. Roberto was the one who carried out the  beheadings, and he seemed to have a taste for it.. He trusted Roberto as much as he trusted anyone. Roberto liked to hurt people.

In front of Roberto were the Curillo brothers. Justine was not particularly bright, but loyal and ruthless. Jason, the younger brother, could fly anything. Helicopters, this plane, anything. He had been an officer in the Mexican airforce, until he was jailed for flying powder on the side. Enrico got him out and made him more wealthy than he could imagine.

After landing, they will take a limo to the lodge. Then he would have the gang leader brought up from the reservation, a deadly little Native Gang meth dealer.

Not as deadly as me.

Not by half.

The gang leader was a useful *gusano*, a worm. A *gusano* who was expendable. Once I get the information I need, Enrico thought, the worm was dead, and another young gang banger would immediately take his place. One who worked for Enrico.

*Find the puta who discovered Kal-leed's body, and the hand of the whore. She doesn't know what she has seen, but she might put it together. Kill the Indian who interfered with his men. Kill his family so the Indians will know to stay on the reservation, to never deal with us again. Take the woman, this Jennifer, back to Mexico with us. I just have to make sure it's done right. That's why I'm here.*

*Too much at stake.*

*Do it right.*

*Make them fear. Keep the feds close. Keep them needing me to route out the terrorists.*

*Make billions.*

# Chapter 35

Kah-Nee-Ta Resort and Casino
Cold River Indian Reservation

Supervisory Special Agent Dennis Oakley sat in the Chinook dining room of the resort. Below the deck, the golf course wound along the river; the sagebrush hills glowed orange in the dying sun. He thought of the action about to take place. He would be lucky to have any credibility left with the tribal police if the U.S. Attorney had her way. They were all seated at a long table with Julie Sturgis holding forth. Oakley's boss, James Russell, sat to his right. The rest of the table was laden with U.S. Attorneys and lesser F.B.I. agents.

"We need to get this woman, what's her name?"

"Jennifer Kruger," Oakley said. He just wanted out of the room, away from this political confab. This was not going to end well.

"Right. We need to get this woman into our custody and quiz her again. She knows something, more than she remembered to tell the tribal detectives. Someone wants her bad." She said 'tribal' with her mouth turned down, as if she had bitten into something sour. "Where is she now?"

"Lieutenant Kukup's house, or somewhere with him." Safer than we could keep her, Oakley thought. He decided to say what he thought.

"We could interview her again, leave her in the protection of the tribal police. That's where she says she wants to stay," Oakley said.

Sturgis frowned at that, her brows arching in a pose he had seen before in court. A junior attorney down at the end of the table laughed. Oakley suddenly hated his job, the stupidity and arrogance of many of his co-workers, of federal attorneys in general.

Oakley looked up at Sturgis and spoke, his voice raising to carry the table. Russell stiffened beside him, a salad fork stopping halfway up from the plate.

"Lieutenant Kukup, 'Smokey,' is no beginner. I know of his service. He still belongs to an Army reserve outfit, was a ranger with three tours in Afghanistan, took part in some of the early fierce fighting in the hunt for Osama bin Laden. He's as good as you get, and his service to this country is part of the best. Let me tell you about Lt. Kukup: Staff Sergeant Kukup was awarded a Bronze Star in the fighting around Kandahar. His unit commander thought he should have been awarded the Medal of Honor." Oakley looked at them and went on, telling of Smokey's fighting ability, his loyalty. A story he realized was futile with this group, but nonetheless, needed to be told.

"Jennifer Kruger will be safe with Lieutenant Kukup." He finished, and waited for the inevitable response.

Sturgis didn't buy it. And Russell, his boss, wouldn't intervene. Russell didn't get to be the F.B.I. agent in charge of Oregon without a keen sense of politics. His job was like most of the hierarchy of the federal government. And Julie Sturgis was a political appointee who was subject to being replaced at any time by the Attorney General.

He let a breath out slowly. There were some good people at the table. Some talented people, most from middle class, average homes. But something happened to many, if not most of them when they became a fed. Washington, D.C., and those who climbed up the corporate federal ladder to get there (usually over several bodies of their co-workers) became more important than the people in the communities around the country.

It occurred to Oakley that he couldn't win this, and that in his failure to convince them to keep the Kruger woman on the reservation, that she would lose as well. Maybe lose her life. He had no illusions about the feds ability to protect her. They could protect her, until they lost interest or Sturgis got what she wanted and then Jennifer Kruger would be tossed out of the federal loop, out on her own, without a thought from his boss and the U.S. Attorney. He knew it wasn't personal with them. It was the way they operated. And people like Jennifer Kruger were the losers.

We lose, too, Oakley thought. People just don't want to work with us, don't trust us. We treat them like shit, and they resent the hell out of us. And I don't blame them.

Sturgis stood up. All of the minions at the table looked at her.

Oakley looked at the fading sunlight and waited for her verdict.

"Okay, I'm sure that Lt. Kukup has some skills courtesy of the army, but what we need is access to this woman, and to do that, I want her in Portland."

Oakley turned to look at her. He smiled, more to himself than to her, but she took it as approval.

"Glad you feel the same way, Agent Oakley. Pick her up at first light. Use our helicopter and take her to Portland."

Oakley stood up, not looking at the others. *People are gonna die over this decision.*

*He just didn't know how many.*

*Or how soon.*

# Chapter 36

Sidwalter

"What's that, on the wall above the television?" Jennifer sat on the couch with Laurel and pointed.

"It's a *waxwintash*, silly. Everyone knows that," Laurel said, laughing. "It's a basket worn around the waist for carrying berries."

Jennifer laughed with her and pointed at a drum in the corner. "Okay, smarty, what is the drum called?"

"*Kiwkiwlaas*," Laurel said, "and . . .'

"Yes I know, *everyone* knows that." As Jennifer hugged Laurel she looked out at the deck. Smokey was sitting at the table, alone with a cup of coffee. She nudged Laurel.

"Hey, kiddo, I'm going to talk with your dad for a minute. 'Kay?"

Laurel jumped up and pulled on Jennifer's hands. "Great idea Jennifer, let's go."

"Just me this time, you come out later."

Laurel nodded, all knowing, and ran to play with her cousins. Jennifer stood in front of the sliding door to the deck and watched Smokey, thinking about the life he and his daughter had here. A family, and she was envious for the first time in her life. She thought she had a family with her cat and her friends in Portland, but this was so much more. She slid the door open and walked out on the deck. Smokey patted the bench beside him without turning around.

"How'd you know it was me?" Jennifer asked as she sat down.

Smokey smiled and sipped his coffee, looking out at the forest. "I've lived here for a few years, and do you think Laurel would be this quiet?"

"No, I guess not." Jennifer was quiet while Smokey drank his coffee. When he started talking, she knew better than to say anything. She wasn't always a good listener, but now she had to be or he might not talk about himself again. He stared at the trees and at first he talked so softly she had to strain to hear. She came to realize that he was talking as much for his benefit as for hers, maybe mostly for his benefit.

"Ten years ago I was a guest lecturer in a college class, a career day, down in Bend at the community college. I wore my Ranger uniform, and in fact, I had just graduated from Ranger school at Fort Benning, Georgia. Amelia was in the class, and of course I knew her from the rez. I knew her family, her parents. The last time I remember seeing her she was in middle school, a gangly kid. Now here was this young woman, and for the first time I really saw her as a woman." He smiled and glanced at Jennifer. She nodded, thinking, *keep going, keep going.*

"Now she was sitting in the front row, and I thought *wow*, and I mean *Wow*. She was so damned beautiful, I couldn't take my eyes off her. She asked intelligent questions, was beautiful, did I tell you she was beautiful? And was completely different from my perception of her on the reservation. I had heard that she was a party girl in high school, but I had still thought of her as a kid.

"I was twenty-eight, Amelia was eighteen. After the lecture she asked if she could buy a soldier lunch. We went to the cafeteria – I couldn't take my eyes off of her – the way she moved, the animated way she talked. We went to a movie that night, left after thirty minutes and just drove the sixty miles back to the reservation and talked. We talked most of the night.

"Something happened to both of us that night, and we became inseparable. When I wasn't working and she wasn't in school, we were together. We got married three months later. Laurel was born the next year."

Jennifer watched, not wanting to move as Smokey sat holding his cup, smiling at his coffee. *He's thinking of the good times. As it should be, Jen.*

"I think she did okay for awhile during my first stint in Afghanistan. When I went back for the second tour, she really lost it. I had heard that she was partying with her partners, drinking heavily and getting into meth, leaving Laurel with my mother for days at a time, and then . . ." He put his hand over his eyes and lowered his head. Jennifer didn't know what to say, and thought she should touch him.

*Don't do anything, Jen.*

Smokey leaned on his hands and shook his head. "I don't know . . . I don't know why I'm telling you this, I just-." His voice was husky, soft.

"Shhhh, it's okay," Jennifer whispered. She wanted to touch him but didn't know if she should. "It's okay – I want to hear you, after all, you saved my life."

Smokey sat there for several minutes, and Jennifer thought she had said too much, and then he started to speak again, this time stronger, different.

"By my third tour, she was already dead. I deserted them, both of them, thought it was for a noble cause, but I deserted them just the same." Smokey looked up and turned to Jennifer. "I want you to know this because I see the way Laurel looks at you, the longing in her face for everything to be okay."

"I don't know what to say Smokey, but she's a great kid, and you haven't deserted her. You see the longing in her eyes when she looks at me, I see her when she looks at you. She worships you, and from what I've seen, you're worth it."

"I just don't want to desert her again," he said.

"You won't, Smokey."

When Jennifer thought about it later, she wondered why she had said such a thing. He deserted them both, in a way she couldn't foresee.

*And it just wasn't fair.*

# Chapter 37

Sunriver Resort

"I want the woman alive, and the head of the Indian lieutenant," Enrico Alvarez told the assembled men. He turned toward Roberto. "Do we know where this *casa* is?"

Roberto nodded and pointed at a large man with a shaved head, and prison tattoos on his arms and neck. "This is Armando, from the reservation. He knows the house. His men have been watching it. The woman and Indian lieutenant are there. We will take them in the night."

"*Por favor, Patron.* What do we do with the others, the old woman and children?"

"*Todos ellos asesinato* (kill them all)."

Enrico Alvarez looked over the dozen men, the assembled weapons, and nodded.

*The woman and the head of the Indian. He would have the Indian's head on YouTube by morning.*

# Chapter 38

Parker Creek

The late afternoon sun gave Mt. Jefferson a shining that Amy thought magical; the glaciers on the mountain glowed orange and red. The colors changed and flowed on the ice. The glaciers appeared to move as if they were living, breathing beings. She sat on a log, waiting as Stan fussed with his equipment. The waters of Parker Creek rushed by far below, twinkling through the trees.

"Amy, look at this." Stan rose from his packs. He held a small object in his hand.

He loves his gadgets, Amy thought, and she suddenly forgave him for dragging her way the hell up here, away from the comforts of her place in Albany. She looked again at Mt. Jefferson and thought the view might be worth the price of hiking without a shower. Stan was, like most men she had encountered, a large boy, adventuresome, excitable, and at times, helpless. She should be happy with that. His obsession with Bigfoot was the one thing that she would change if she could. She turned back to examine the piece of equipment he held in his hand. It was about the size of a small flashlight, a black plastic tube.

Amy turned it over in her hand and examined the object. She knew that Stan wanted her to guess what it was. There was a dark lens on one end, so it wasn't a flashlight, she reasoned.

"A laser pointer?" she said, wanting to get started with the guessing game. She didn't think that was what she was holding, but it could be close.

"Pretty good guess," Stan said. He smirked.

"A laser pointer flashlight?" Amy said. She handed it back to him. She stood up and stretched. She wanted to camp for the night. Enough of this game.

"It's used for tracking," Stan said.

"Tracking what?" Amy asked, losing interest.

"Blood." Stan handed it back to her. Amy held it, shook it, looked at the object again.

"Whose blood?"

"Any blood," Stan said. "It's an infrared blood tracker. When you shine this on blood at night, it glows green. You can track a wounded animal this way, lead you right to them. It's a Carnivore TRAX Blood Tracking Light. I can mount this on a helmet for hands-free use." "Great," Amy said. "I'm glad we have it." She tried to sound sincere, so Stan wouldn't get his feelings hurt and then she would have to deal with *that*. She was tired. And hungry again. She looked around. She could camp anywhere.

"Stan."

"Huh?" He picked up his gear.

"Can we camp now? I'm tired."

"How about an hour," he said. Amy thought he sounded a little put off, but, hey, he was the one who wanted her to go on this rodeo.

"One hour."

"Yep. One hour." He pointed to the north, to an area below White-water Glacier. "See that area there, that knoll? One hour. That's where we should camp tonight."

"It's a deal," Amy said, and started off, thinking that it would take them more than an hour to get there. She heard the helicopter before he did.

Amy walked on the animal trail behind Stan. When they had started off, she could see the knoll where he said they would be spending the night, but now it was lost in the trees. They were winding their way around a side hill, using animal trails and avoiding downed trees as much as they could. Amy looked up and didn't think that they were any closer to their destination. She looked around Stan. There was a clearing ahead, a break in the trees.

The sound came to her and she knew at once what it was. She had lived near Good Samaritan Hospital in Portland for a time, and heard Air Life flights day and night, until they became a part of the background noise. But she always was conscious at some level of the life flights. The flutter of the rotors. She stopped.

"Stan." He kept walking, a soldier in their army of two. One foot in front of the other.

"Stan." Amy called louder. She pointed up.

"Helicopter."

Stan looked up and pointed. Down to his right. The sound was getting closer. She saw the helicopter then, flying up the mountain, on a course that would take it directly over them.

"Here!" Stan yelled, jumping forward toward a large Ponderosa Pine tree. He bent down under the branches and motioned for Amy.

Amy trudged over and crouched beside Stan under the branches of the tree.

"They won't see us here," Stan said.

Amy wondered just how smart they were for trespassing on the reservation, looking for a creature that most people didn't believe existed. She suddenly wanted to be home, out of the wilderness and back on her block with her friends, her car, her job. She dropped her pack and watched as the helicopter came toward them.

The craft was green, a military Blackhawk. That much she knew from watching the movie Blackhawk Down, and from watching all of the news footage from Iraq and Afghanistan. But what if they landed and did happen to see them? She didn't want to know what would happen then.

"Stan."

"What?" He didn't look at her, but she could see his eyes were bright. He was excited, and that was when she started to get mad.

"Stan," she yelled, fear rising with her anger. "Stan, this is bullshit, we're gonna get in so much trouble. Let's go back when they leave." But she knew he wouldn't, and she would stay with him, like the script of a grade C horror movie, she was going to stay with him to the scary end. She wasn't going to get lost like that other woman.

The flutter of the rotors grew louder, the turbine whine adding to the noise.

It's coming right for us, Amy thought. *How do they know where we are?*

She knew the thought was irrational, but she had it just the same. They *were* here illegally, and she didn't know what the Indians would do if they were caught, but it wouldn't be pleasant.

*It's slowing down.*

"Stan!" Amy yelled and tugged at his sleeve. "Stan, it's slowing down."

He pulled his arm away and stared.

The Blackhawk slowed and crawled slowly over the trees. The big machine settled into a hover just off the ground. Amy could see the helmeted pilots, their green helmets and dark visors giving them an unearthly look.

The helicopter dropped out of sight behind a line of trees, and Amy could tell that it had landed when the turbine shut down. She had a sudden and crazy thought to walk up to the crew, say she was lost, and get a ride home. But that wouldn't be fair to Stan, and she didn't feel that they were in any great danger, *except for getting thrown into an Indian jail for trespassing.* Stan pulled items from his pack and came up with a pair of binoculars. He walked slowly toward the helicopter.

"Are you crazy?" Amy grabbed his arm, her whisper fierce and harsh, louder than she wanted. *Why am I whispering?*

"We need to see what they are doing," Stan said mildly. "Let's leave the packs here, take a look, and then come back here for a snack."

It made sense, but she didn't want to go. Like a horse afraid of losing the herd, Amy followed, more afraid of being alone and lost than following Stan in another one of his adventures.

They crawled the last twenty feet, settling at the base of a large tree. Stan peeked around and brought the binoculars up and looked for what seemed to Amy to be a long time. She realized as they got closer that the engine had not shut down completely, but was running at an idle. She listened to the subdued whine of the turbine, the whisper of the rotors.

*What the hell are we doing here?*

Stan handed Amy the binoculars. She slid under the branches and brought the binoculars up. The image of the helicopter and men came into view. Her first thought was that they were too close. There were two men in suits outside the helicopter. She hadn't seen them in the fly over, but they were in charge, directing the crew members with them on the ground.

*Ohmigod. It looks like they are loading a body.*
*A body?*

She ran her tongue over her lips, her mouth suddenly dry, and she watched as two crew members in their olive drab one-piece flight suits and matching helmets clumsily carried a body. One of the crew held the body at the knees, the lower legs bouncing as he walked.

She hit the zoom on the binoculars and looked on as they placed it on top of a body bag.

*The body has dress shoes? That doesn't make sense.*

*Where's the rest . . . fuck me. Oh, fuck me. The head is gone. Missing. Maybe . . .*

Her hands started shaking and she lost the image, her fingers locked and bloodless.

*Gotta go. Gotta get out of here. Now.*

Amy tried to steady her hands and watched in horror as the crew loaded the body bag. She put her head down on her arm. The turbine went from a whine to a scream, the rotors thrumming, and the helicopter lifted off. Amy felt this, heard this, but didn't see it. She didn't need to. She just wanted out of here. She crawled back to Stan.

*I want to go home.*

Amy sat on her pack under the branches of a tree and watched as Stan walked to the helicopter landing. He walked cautiously, bent over as an old man might walk, and looked at the ground. She waited to run in a split second if another body with no head should suddenly appear.

Stan stopped, and Amy shook her head. Might as well join him. I've already decided I'm not going to be like that other girl, get lost alone. As she walked she hoped that there wasn't anything gross to see. The sun was getting lower, crouching above the cleft between Mt. Jefferson and Mt. Washington.

*Be dark before we know it.*

And Amy had another thought. *I don't want to be here.* She got to the spot where the helicopter had landed. Stan walked around the area where the body had been found. He turned and smiled to her and gave her a thumbs up. Jesus. He was enjoying himself, in his element, excited.

"Nothing here," he called, and waved.

Bullshit, Amy thought. I'm not going over there. This is close enough. She folded her arms across her chest, and waited. Eventually he would come over.

"Stan."

He looked up and moved slowly toward her, as if he were in trouble.

"Stan, can we go now?"

159

"Sure, nothing here, just wanted to be sure." He looked around and down the slope, and pointed. "We'll move off a ways, and set up camp." He walked down the slope, and Amy followed.

"Yeah," Amy said. "A long ways." She knew that they couldn't get off the reservation tonight, but it wouldn't hurt her feelings if they left for good tomorrow.

"Stan." He stopped and turned around.

"Stan, what *was* that, what did we just see?"

"A body, looked like, someone died here, got dumped here, not our concern."

"I *know* it was a body, but what was *that*, what did we get into?" When he didn't answer Amy stood with her hands on her hips and glared at him. "I'll tell what we didn't see, Stan!" she yelled. "What we didn't see were any Indians, you know, Native Americans. Those people were federal government people. And they knew there was a body here."

"Well, -." Stan said.

"Well what?" Amy yelled.

"Well, let's hike for a bit, get away from this place."

"Fine!"

He turned and started down the slope. Amy followed him in the dying light for the next thirty minutes, heading deeper into the wilderness of the reservation. A continuous thread ran through Amy's head: *Why am I here?* And *I'm gonna kill him.*

When they finally set up camp, it wasn't far enough from where they saw the body to suit Amy, but it was getting dark, and it would just have to do.

In their small tent, Stan busied himself with his gadgets, happily back on the trail of Bigfoot. He assembled a small air rifle and placed a dart in the chamber.

"If I can get this dart in one, it plants a small transmitter under the skin, a little bigger than a grain of rice."

He opened up his mini laptop and turned it on. A map of the area appeared. "See this dot, here?" He pointed to the screen. "That's where we are, the software will track the dart for years, much like satellite GPS, only in the reverse. We can track Bigfoot no matter what, map out its route for a year, write a book about it, become famous.

"And rich."

If the creature existed, Amy thought, it might just work.

Amy awoke in the tent to full dark, before moonrise. She lay in her sleeping bag and listened. A noise. Something crashed far off, and then it was quiet. She was almost asleep when she heard something . . .

*Walking?*

Outside the tent.

She reached over and felt Stan next to her.

She thought she would never be so scared ever again in her life.

*She was wrong.*

# **Chapter 39**

Sidwalter

Smokey walked into the living room and handed Jennifer a cup of coffee. She sat on the couch with Laurel. The TV was on. The other kids and his mother were arranged around it like an attentive and colorful school of fish. Jennifer, across the room and behind the others, sat with her legs under her. With bandages and bruises, Smokey thought she looked beautiful.

Better be careful here, he thought. He knew how adrenalin, fear, and escape from near death brought people closer together. Maybe this isn't real.

"How far are we from where I was found?" Jennifer asked.

"Maybe thirty miles in a straight line. Our house is on the edge of the same wilderness, just further north and a little east."

She motioned for him to sit.

He shook his head.

"Can't. Got work to do. And," he nodded toward his mother and the others, "they're leaving." A loud noise from the TV made him turn to look. They were watching a rerun of the series "24" and Jack Bauer was yelling "Everybody Down!!"

"What do you mean, work to do?" Jennifer asked.

*They are coming for us!*

Smokey didn't reply. He looked at Laurel and Jennifer, and knew what he had to do. He smiled. He went over to his mother, waited for a commercial break, and then bent down.

*"Kala."*

She waited for him to speak.

*"Kala*, when the show is over, you take the kids to Sarah's house, stay there."

She patted his hand, nodding. He walked back to the couch.

"You, too, Laurel. Get something packed."

"Dad. I'm staying here. With you and Jennifer."

He was torn, putting her out of harm's way would also mean that he couldn't protect her, couldn't know how she was doing.

162

"What am I missing here?" Jennifer asked. She looked first at Smokey, then at Laurel.

"*Kala* and the kids are going to Sarah's house in town. Laurel wants to stay here with me."

"And her," Laurel said, snuggling against Jennifer.

"What you're missing," Smokey said, his voice quiet, "what you're missing is that someone will be coming for you. I want both of you to put a small pack together. Something for a couple of days in the country."

Smokey entered his bedroom. When he came out a few minutes later, he looked like the warrior he once was. He wore battle dress utility black pants, a black camouflage shirt, and a black vest. The vest held ammunition for his pistol, rifle, and shotgun – a radio with an earpiece, and other equipment of a modern warrior. He tied his hair back with a leather thong.

He had a short-barreled shotgun slung across his back, and held UMP submachine in his right hand.

He nodded at Jennifer and Laurel, said something to his mother as she assembled the kids, and quietly slipped out the back door.

Jennifer shivered as Smokey disappeared.

*What have I brought on these people?*

Smokey wouldn't let me leave now if I wanted to. But it wasn't fair that my lark in the woods should bring this on them. I'm scared, afraid of what is coming, scared for this little one with her head on my shoulder.

*Admit it Jennifer, you feel protected at the same time.*

*Yeah, I do. What a family.*

She reached down and stroked Laurel's hair.

Smokey stood on the deck and waited for his eyes to adjust to the dark. He walked off the deck, a silent shadow to join another shadow.

Nathan was similarly dressed. His face was blackened with camouflage paint; his eyes glistened in the darkness. He handed Smokey a night vision headset.

"Good to see you, Big Brother," Smokey said. "Up kinda late for you, aren't we?"

Nathan stared at him. "Figured you needed someone to do the heavy lifting for you, Little Brother. The team is in place." Smokey didn't need to talk with them. He knew they would do what was needed when it was time. Two officers walked by, carrying long rifles with night vision scopes, shooting pads and painted faces. They disappeared up the hill into the dark. Smokey knew that they could cover the entire house except for immediately in front. There were two more at the beginning of the driveway, two in the woods by the meadow Smokey knew, and two with assault weapons by the haystack.

Should be enough.

*Unless the maggots know we're ready for them.*

A car door shut in the front of the house.

"*Kala* and kids leaving," Smokey said.

"I'll watch them to the highway," Nathan said. He spoke quietly into a small microphone.

Smokey watched him melt away. One second Nathan was there, and then he was gone.

Big Brother was good.

*Gonna need him before the night is over. Of that, I'm sure.*

"You can use this one," Laurel said. She handed a green backpack to Jennifer. Jennifer put the backpack on the bed and put her meager possessions inside. She hadn't thought of her place in Portland for days, really thought about it, and now she wasn't so sure that what she had there was important at all.

*This is what I have, some borrowed clothes in a borrowed backpack.*

Laurel handed her an old army coat, and Jennifer tried it on. She held the sleeves up, her hands buried inside. Laurel looked at her and giggled. Jennifer turned and looked at her image in the mirror, and started laughing.

She looked like a street urchin, lost in a big coat. Laurel looked in the mirror and shrieked. Jennifer threw her arms around Laurel and they collapsed on the bed, laughing. Jennifer tickled Laurel and she shrieked again. Jennifer laughed until tears ran down her cheeks, and she realized she hadn't felt so good in a long time. Laurel stopped laughing and went to the closet.

"Hey Jen, hold on." Laurel stood on her tiptoes and tried to reach the top shelf. She jumped and still couldn't reach.

"Want some help?" Jennifer grabbed Laurel and lifted her up to the shelf. Laurel grabbed something and Jennifer set her down.

"Thanks." Laurel turned and was holding a small revolver.

"Laurel, is that thing real?"

*This kid has a gun.*

Laurel nodded. "Of course it's real. My dad taught me how to shoot when I was little."

"Do you really think you will need that?"

Laurel shrugged. She checked the cylinder and put the gun in her pack. She looked at Jennifer and then jumped at her, tickling her in the ribs, and Jennifer fell on the bed again and grabbed Laurel, pulling her on top.

Jennifer laughed, and then had the thought again.

*This kid has a gun.*


Smokey found them that way.

*God, they're beautiful.*

Laurel saw him first, and quit laughing. Jennifer looked up at the fierce, dark figure.

Smokey smiled, bent down and kissed first Laurel, and then Jennifer. He spent a second longer on the kiss with Jennifer, smelling her hair. He straightened up and watched Jennifer's face. She smiled, and then grinned.

"More, please, kind sir," she said. Smokey just stood there, not knowing what to do. He knew what he wanted to do, and he tried to push those thoughts out of his mind.

"Yes, please, more sir," Laurel said, and fell into Jennifer's arms, laughing so hard Jennifer thought the kid wouldn't be able to stop.

In the end, Smokey joined in and tickled first Laurel, and then Jennifer. He laughed until Jennifer brought his face down and kissed him back.

"Gross," Laurel said, but she was smiling as she said it.

Smokey sat up, afraid to look at them for fear of another new round of laughter. When it was time, he told them what they had to do.

The assault came just before dawn.

# Chapter 40

"Smokey, this is Nathan." Smokey leaned back, invisible in the dark. He pressed his earpiece. Nathan spoke quickly, his voice urgent.

"Smokey."

"Uh, we have two dark SUV's coming down the highway fast. Just crossed the Northern border onto the rez. These guys are cooking, close to a hundred. Be at the Sidwalter turn in a few minutes, way they're going."

"Are they feds?"

"Don't think so," Nathan said.

"Leave them be," Smokey murmured.

*So it starts. Hope we planned this right. Maybe we should have more people here. But I can't leave the rest of the rez unprotected.*

*I should have taken Laurel and Jennifer out, but I can personally watch over them here.*

Smokey walked to the corner of the house. The barnyard, corrals, and haystack were on his right. The front porch of the house was dark. The only lights on were in the house, a subdued lamp light coming out of the front windows. His Suburban and a Honda were parked in front.

*Should look like we're home.*

"Vehicles turning off the highway," Nathan said. "They just turned their lights out. They're going fast down the gravel."

"Copy," Smokey said. *They must have night vision.*

"Smokey to all units. They'll have night vision." Microphone clicks told Smokey that the officers heard. There was no need to call each one.

*What am I forgetting?*

"They're five minutes out," Nathan said.

Smokey stood in the dark beside the back corner of the house. He looked down the driveway toward the meadow. A horse snorted, then squealed, hoof beats a nervous rattle as they moved around. The horses had been nervous all night, people moving around, and now fast-approaching cars.

He looked behind the house, and walked quickly to the back door. He was beginning to get a very bad feeling about the entire operation. Two Suburbans, carrying killers like the ones in the hospital, could have six or seven people each, a dozen or more. Weaponry, maybe more than assault rifles. But, this is our ground. He looked at the back door.

*I should have evacuated Laurel and Jennifer. Should have taken them out of the fight. What was I thinking?*

Smokey tapped on the back door. Jennifer answered immediately. Laurel peeked around Jennifer, her face under Jennifer's arm. A soft light from the kitchen highlighted them.. They were both wearing their packs.

Cute.

I must look like an alien to them with my face painted, night vision goggles on my forehead, guns strapped on. Jennifer's eyes were large and white. Laurel had seen this look before.

"When the shooting starts, lay on the kitchen floor," Smokey said.

"Are they coming, Dad, the bad people?" Laurel asked. Jennifer just looked.

"Less than five minutes. Lock the door. Nathan and I have keys." Smokey pulled Laurel closer, and kissed her on the cheek. "Take care of Jen."

"I will Dad, and Dad, you come back and get us."

He nodded, and closed the door.

"They're one mile from the driveway," Nathan said on the radio, louder now. Smokey moved to the corner of the house, thinking of the layout and where he positioned the officers. He looked over to his right at the darkened barn. Sarah would be there. He pulled his night vision headset down and the image of the barn, corrals, and haystack jumped into view. Nathan would follow them in.

*We're as ready as we can be.*

*Or so I think.*

"The lead van's slowing for the driveway," Nathan said. Smokey had the radio turned down to its lowest setting, his earpiece loud, causing his head to jerk up. He strained to see down the driveway from the rear of the house. They would come through the trees in the meadow, then around a small knoll. When they passed the corral and haystack, they would be in front of the house.

He heard the tires crunching on the gravel. Smokey caught a glint of starlight on metal, and then he saw the first vehicle as it passed the pasture. The second was close behind, a deadly, malignant train. He pulled his night vision down.

*Something sticking out the window of the Suburban.*

*Shit.*

*Looks like . . .*

Smokey keyed his microphone as he watched in horror as the first van skidded to a stop fifty feet in front of the house. The doors flew open in the blue light of the night vision and the men on the right side of the SUV pulled up a long tube. The second vehicle van slowed and stopped.

*An RPG!*

*Rocket propelled grenades. Why didn't I think?*

"RPG! Fire on them!" Smokey screamed into his microphone and ran for the front of the house. He pulled his automatic rifle up and fired as he ran, sprinting hard toward the men getting out of the lead Suburban. He had a sense of firing coming from the barn and haystack, officers firing and yelling.

The driver got out and Smokey fired a burst into the chest of the dark clad figure. The man dropped and Smokey slowed to take aim at the figure with the RPG lining up on the front door, and Smokey fired another full burst. The bullets hit the assailant in a sudden spray. The RPG fired as the man went down, the sudden flare of the rocket blinding Smokey with the night vision. Smokey jerked the night vision up and watched as the rocket flared up and over the roof of the house and exploded on the side of the haystack.

He felt bullets slam into the house inches from his head, and he dropped down and back around the corner. He grabbed a new magazine and slammed it into his rifle as he came back around.

Nathan came from around the haystack, looking like a figure from hell in the light of the growing fire. His night vision hung on his neck as he ran toward the Suburban, yelling an ancient war cry.

Figures from the SUV's were on their knees, firing at Nathan. Smokey jumped up and fired, hitting two in a single burst, and ran to the third and shot him in the face. Blood sprayed black in the dark. At least two of the assailants made it to the corner of the house and disappeared. He felt a tug on his sleeve as a bullet hit his arm. He looked up the driveway.

The black clad men in the second Suburban were out and firing, running toward the house, two with RPG's, and one went down with a burst from officers in the trees.

A rocket slammed into the front door. The explosion blew Smokey back on his knees, and two figures ran for the open door. The door frame burst into flames.

"Nathan, get the back!" Smokey yelled. Time slowed for Smokey as the figures moved in slow motion. The second Suburban moved up and Smokey emptied a long burst into the windshield on the driver's side. The driver's body jerked in a spray of blood. The engine screamed and the wheels sprayed gravel as the large SUV swerved to the left around the first vehicle, across the barnyard and slammed into the burning haystack. Burning bales fell on top of the vehicle.

Bullets buzzed by Smokey as he threw himself on the ground. He fired short bursts at the men running for the house. A fusillade of shots came from the officers on the hill and the man with the RPG went down. The rocket touched off and screamed down the driveway.

*One RPG to go.*

Smokey reloaded on his knees, yelling, screaming at the men who would try to kill him and his family. The dark man with the RPG stopped and aimed the rocket at the front window of the house from a distance of thirty feet. Killing distance for those inside. The other man was standing, firing at Smokey. Smokey felt a sharp sting on his arm, and then a slap on his neck.

*How fucking dare they.*

And suddenly he was filled with a rage that he hadn't felt in a long time, a familiar and frightening feeling, like a terrible and painful hand had gripped him, a hot flash of light jumping through his body.

The RPG slammed into the window and the explosion blew into the living room, the flash a brilliant light of destruction.

The figure who had been firing at Smokey ran for the front door, obscured by smoke as Smokey fired, then stopped.

*Laurel's inside.*

The man with the RPG was trying to get rid of the tube and bring his rifle up when Smokey ran up to him and shot him in the face from a distance of five feet, blood and brain matter spraying out in clumps, and the man dropped, a leg bent under him, as if the string on a puppet had been cut. Smokey turned and ran for the house, screaming Laurel's name.

When Smokey had left them by the back door, Jennifer looked at Laurel in the dim light, and pulled the girl into her arms.

"You scared?" she whispered.

"Yeah, a little. But Dad usually takes care of things."

"What do you think we should do?" Jennifer asked, giving Laurel another hug. This child I could care for, she thought. And then she had another thought, this one deeper, more to the core of who she was, thoughts that she hadn't had for a long time, if ever. Thoughts that she knew most people put off and never looked inside to answer.

*Why am I here?*

The answer came quickly.

*You're supposed to be. This is meant for you.*

She was in a strange house, a house she didn't know existed until a day ago, with people she just met, and people she didn't know were outside trying to kill her, for reasons that she couldn't fathom.

*But you know you're supposed to be here.*

If anyone asked, she knew that she could not tell why she felt that way, but in a crazy way, she knew she was right. Laurel tugged on her arm.

"Jennifer." Laurel tugged.

"Jen, come with me. I think we should stay here, in the pantry, on the floor." Jennifer let herself be led into the pantry, a large walk-in closet, and they sat on the floor, the single light on the kitchen counter their only reference. The pantry was dark.

"Dad says that when shooting ever starts, you should lay on the floor in most instances, and get out of the way of the bullets."

Jennifer put her arms around Laurel. *How does she know all this?*

"Can we turn a light on in here?" Jennifer asked. Laurel pulled a flashlight from her pack and switched it on. She jumped up and closed the door and then sat back down next to Jennifer. Laurel put the flashlight under her chin and shined it upward, making her face look ghoulish. She laughed.

"Stop that," Jennifer said, and laughed with her. They both jumped when the first shot exploded outside.

The explosions and screams from the front of the house made Jennifer want to put her hands over her ears and shut out the noise of men dying.

*What if something happens to Smokey?*

She started to get up, and Laurel held on fast.

"We can't leave," Laurel whispered, her voice fierce, her hold on Jennifer as strong as an adult's.

"But what if-."

An explosion thumped into the house. Cans fell from the shelves above them and thudded to the floor.

"Ow!" Laurel cried out as a can fell on her head. Jennifer leaned over Laurel and tried to protect her from more falling food. The floor was a jumble of cans and packages of food.

The gunfire was almost non-stop outside.

"What do we do if the bad people (she had thought of the people after her as the 'bad people' since the hospital) come in here first?" She didn't expect an answer from Laurel, but the girl pulled her head from under Jennifer's arm and reached in her pack. Jennifer picked up the flashlight from the floor and set it on a shelf.

Laurel pulled the silver revolver from her pack and pointed it at the door.

"We'll shoot them," Laurel said, matter-of-factly.

Jennifer looked at the small revolver. In the city, no way. Here in this land, it just made sense.

"I have to ask," she said, looking closely at Laurel, "do you know how to use it?"

Laurel gave her a look as if she were a pure fool. "Of course, Dad has been teaching me to shoot since I was five or six."

*Of course, what an idiot you are, Jennifer.*

"I'm not supposed to have it unless he says," Laurel added, "but I think this might be a time when he would say."

"Is it loaded?" Jennifer wanted to take this back as soon as she said it, but it was out. The look she got she thought she might deserve, a look reserved for complete and utter fools. Village idiots.

"Well, let's hope we don't have to use it."

But somehow, she knew in her heart, the way the week had been going, the way people were relentlessly trying to kill her, that Laurel would have to use the gun, and judging from the sounds outside, the explosions, the shots and screams, they would have to use it soon.

She huddled with the precious child of a most unusual man, thinking that the kid was the one in charge, the protector here.

As it turned out, Smokey wasn't the first one to arrive at the pantry door.

He had his own problems with survival.

# Chapter 41

Smokey ran through the front door. A lamp on the end table in the corner shimmered through the smoke. Shreds of a blanket draped around the shade like a street person's clothing. One end of the couch was missing, the remainder blown into pieces. Batting hung on the walls. The HDTV television *Kala* had been so proud of was a smoking ruin. Small fires burned around the room, one going fairly well in the corner where the television had been.

*The house is going to go.*

Smokey looked toward the kitchen and the back of the house. Smoke hung in the air, getting thick now, swirling up the walls and on the ceiling.

*The lamp is on. Amazing. The bulb didn't break and the room is destroyed.*

He was dimly aware of shouts and gunfire outside, and somewhere out front another blast shook the house. He started to move toward the kitchen so he could walk around the corner to the back door and get into the pantry off the laundry room.

*Those men who came in will kill you and Jennifer and Laurel if you don't get moving and stay frosty. You've done this before.*

The sight of his mother's house in flames, familiar belongings and surroundings slowed him down. The war in Afghanistan was horrible, but at least it wasn't his own turf, his own house.

He brought his UMP .40 caliber assault rifle up and took a step toward the back. His radio snapped with his name.

"Smokey!" Nathan's voice, a scream.

"Smokey, behind you, front door!"

Smokey threw himself down in mid-step, twisting as he fell, and a burst of automatic gunfire slammed over his head, inches away from killing him, the shock wave of the bullets buzzing over his right ear, and he flipped over in mid-air before he hit the floor and brought his gun up close, holding it against his chest, pushing the barrel around so he could shoot. He hit the floor and fired a long burst at the dark figures coming through the front door, a dozen feet away.

Shots and screams came from the back of the kitchen.

*The pantry.*

Five shots, a thirty-eight.

*Laurel's gun.*

Smokey's burst caught the closest one up high in the chest and neck, and he dropped. The second dark figure threw himself down and out of the doorway, firing as he went down, a fusillade of bullets stitching the floor beside Smokey.

*Shit!*

The gunman was outside the doorway, the barrel of the gun now rounding the corner, lining up on Smokey.

Jennifer stretched her left leg out. The cans and boxes that had fallen from the shelves surrounded her as if she had jumped into a dumpster to hide. She held Laurel close and tried to give a hug, but Laurel shrugged her off, pointing toward the door, a foot in front of her leg.

"They'll come through there," Laurel whispered. She pointed to the door with the short barrel of the pistol. Another blast shook the house and Jennifer flinched. She held the flashlight up toward the door, her hand shaking, making the glow dance on the door. She tried to steady the light, and Laurel chuckled.

"Hey, keep the light still, will yah?" she said, and grinned up at Jennifer.

A burst of gunfire came from somewhere in the house, from the living room, Jennifer thought. Laurel reached over and touched Jennifer's hand.

"Keep it on the door," she whispered.

Jennifer was scared, and it would have been worse if she had been alone. She knew she must look strong for Laurel, but she was thinking that the nine year old was the strong one here.

*Smoke. I smell smoke.*

She was suddenly aware of smoke in the pantry, first the smell, and then a swirl of it around the light on the door.

"Laurel," Jennifer whispered. Urgent.

"Yeah, I see it. The house is on fire," Laurel said matter-of-factly. "Jen, we are going to have to move soon." Jennifer tried to stand, tried to be quiet as the cans slid off her legs.

More gunfire came from somewhere in the house. Jennifer stood and reached down for Laurel. She caught the girl's arm and pulled her up until she was standing next to her, slightly in front. Jennifer moved the flashlight toward the door again and Laurel brought the gun up as the door was thrown open.

Jennifer screamed. Her flashlight caught a hooded figure with a short, wicked-looking rifle. The hooded apparition backed up and brought the barrel of his rifle up to Jennifer's face. She saw another figure behind him. Laurel fired, screaming, the flash from the barrel of the little gun brighter than the flashlight.

Jennifer dropped the flashlight and held Laurel as the girl fired, firing all five rounds in succession, as fast as anyone could, one blast hitting the hooded figure in the face, blood and brain matter and bone spraying back on the second man. The hooded apparition dropped out of sight. A bullet struck the second figure and he spun around and went out the back door so quickly that Jennifer thought she might have only imagined him there.

"Shit," Laurel cried, "Shitshitshit." She was shaking and crying, and Jennifer held onto the shaking girl. She hugged her and held her. More shots and shouts from the living room, and the smoke grew heavier.

*We have to get out of here soon, Jennifer thought. This girl, this wonderful girl saved our lives.*

"I forgot," Laurel sobbed, and held up the gun with shaking hands, "I forgot where the bullets are," she cried, "and I only got one of them, and now Daddy needs our help, and he's going to be mad at me for cussing, and . . ."

Laurel turned her head into Jennifer's waist and sobbed.

"Here." Jennifer took the box of shells from her jacket pocket. "I took them, remember?"

Jennifer crouched in the doorway and put her right arm around Laurel, trying not to look at the dead man on the floor, inches from them.

"Laurel, hand me the gun."

Jennifer took the gun and looked at it. So small for so much damage.

"Now show me how to load it."

175

Jennifer's hand shook once, and then steadied. A week ago she would have refused to even look at a gun. To hold one. Now it seemed . . . it seemed so right.

Necessary.

Survival. No justification. No platitudes. No second amendment speeches for or against.

Survival.

Laurel helped her swing the cylinder open.

Jennifer began shoving shells into the cylinder, one by one. The smoke was making it hard to breathe.

Survival.

# Chapter 42

Smokey pushed himself backwards from the open doorway where one man lay dead in a dark shadow. He was vaguely aware of a fire somewhere outside that was growing in intensity, the shadows from the flames flickering inside the open front door. A sudden burst of gunfire from outside by the Suburban was followed by an enormous explosion from the side of the house in the direction of the barn.

Smokey covered the front door with his rifle and tried to push himself back into the kitchen to get some distance from the door, to get around the corner and get to the pantry. To stand up here was suicide, he knew, so he kept the door covered. The smoke was getting thicker, giving him some cover and at the same time, making it harder to breathe.

Smokey tried to remember how many rounds he had fired, most of a magazine, and as he watched the door, he pulled the magazine out from the rifle and slammed in a fresh one. A gun barrel slid around into the doorway on the right side and Smokey fired into the doorjamb. He jumped to a crouch, continued to fire, ripping bullets into the wall where the gunman must be, firing the full magazine, yelling, until the man fell into the doorway and crumpled.

*No time to waste.*

*Laurel.*

*Jennifer.*

Smokey reloaded as he crouched and ran to the kitchen. The corner of the living room was now engulfed and he quickly peeked around the corner through the smoke to the pantry door. He shook his head. Blood from a wound above his eye seeped into his eyelid. He wiped a sleeve across his face, smearing blood. A dark figure lay on the floor in the doorway of the pantry, the back door open, smoke rolling out from living room fire.

Smokey covered the door with his assault rifle.

"Laurel!"

"Dad?" Her voice quavered. Then she yelled, "Daddy?"

Smokey stepped into the doorway and there they were, Jennifer holding the gun, looking up, and Laurel jumped into his arms.

"Daddy, I shot the gun, shot the bad men, and I –." and then she sobbed, clutching Smokey like a baby monkey holding onto her mother. Smokey looked at Jennifer.

"The second one ran out the door," Jennifer said, and held the gun up for him to see. "You look terrible," Jennifer said. She held her sleeve over her mouth.

"Been busy," Smokey said, and let Laurel down to her feet. He looked back toward the living room. "We need to get out of here, now." He reached out and grabbed Jennifer's hand. He moved toward the back door, holding onto Jennifer with Laurel between them.

Nathan was just outside the door, his face covered with soot and blood. He motioned them to the deck. Smokey leaned against the tree and took a deep breath. Jennifer collapsed into a chair, the deck a surreal light show with flames from the front yard flashing over the roof. Light from the burning barn illuminated the trees.

"We get them all?" Smokey asked.

"Mostly," Nathan said, looking up toward the hill behind the house.

"Got the ones in front and at the barn, two in the front door, one at the pantry, and one a runner up the hill, from the back door."

"I winged him," Laurel said from under Jennifer's arm.

"Yeah, I know, precious child," Nathan said.

"He was behind the other one, I think I hit him in the shoulder," Laurel said, sitting up, her arms around Jennifer.

A muffled *whump* from the living room caused them all to jump. Smokey looked to Nathan.

"The runner?"

"Got three after him. Good blood trail. They're maybe a minute behind."

Smokey lowered his voice, looking at his daughter and Jennifer. He moved to the end of the deck. Nathan moved with him.

"Their orders."

"Find the runner, quiz him."

"How?" Smokey knew it wouldn't be pretty. He would let his people protect him. Someone had declared war on us, and now they were going to find out what war was like here. We fight as a family.

*Nathan, the older brother I never had, a man I love as much as I love my life, a man who stood between death and my family was*

178

*waiting for me to answer. I couldn't tell them to be easy. And they weren't about to hear that from me now.*

"Boss," Nathan said. "Smokey, Little Brother."

Smokey waited.

"Boss, we ain't gonna water board him. Besides, that's illegal now." He gave a short laugh. "We do not plan to invite the fucking congress to the interview. These pieces of shit came here to kill us all, and they found out that it just wasn't quite as easy as they thought. We killed them all, except for the runner." Nathan turned and spit on the ground. Smokey waited for him to continue.

"He will tell us all he knows, up there on the mountain when we catch up with him, any minute now. Then we're gonna let him join the others in the front yard."

Nathan drew his finger across his neck. "Dead."

Smokey nodded.

"Meet me here, five minutes," Smokey said, and the older man moved to the corner of the house and disappeared around the side.

"Jennifer." Smokey looked over at the two of them in the chair. They looked up.

"I'm going back inside, and . . ."

"No, Dad, you can't do it, it's burning down." Laurel looked wildly around at the house, flames visible now through the kitchen window.

"I'll be one minute, less," Smokey said. "You two wait by the tree." He helped Jennifer to her feet and kissed her on the lips. Her eyebrows went up as he held the kiss.

"Thanks for being with my daughter," he said as he pulled away. He reached behind her and pulled Laurel up and kissed her on the head. Smokey led them to the tree off the porch.

He ran into the house, lurched for the bedroom, grabbed their packs and ran back for the door as the kitchen burst into flames.

He stumbled onto the back deck and coughed up black gunk, gasping and coughing as Laurel and Jennifer came to him.

"Get ready to move," Smokey gasped. "We're gonna find the woman on the mountain."

*When they found her, Smokey wished he had gone alone.*

*Or not at all.*

# **C**hapter **43**

Smokey led Jennifer and Laurel around the house away from the kitchen, and stopped when he heard Laurel cry out.

"Dad!"

She pointed to the barn. It was fully engulfed in flames, and Smokey dimly remembered an RPG hitting the siding, one burying itself on a wild shot in the haystack. The hay was burning on the end, and it would be a total loss.

"Dad, the horses, I'm going." She started to run around Smokey, and he caught her, grabbed her arms.

"Laurel, they're out, Nathan let them out, ouch, stop, stop!"

She turned her head and looked up at him, her face covered with soot. A single tear rolled down, and she shuddered.

"Can't let go now, *Miyanash,* we have a long way to go." She nodded, and reached out for Jennifer's hand.

*God, what she's been through. What have I done to my Miyanash, my child?*

And then he had another thought. *I didn't do this to her, and the people who did are gonna pay.*

When they got to the front of the house in the drive, Smokey knew that he couldn't make it any better for Jennifer and Laurel. The front drive and yard area was littered with the casualties of war – bodies lay crumpled where they died, a body next to a dark Suburban was on fire. Both vehicles that brought the assault were on blazing, the house burning with two bodies in the doorway, the hair of one burning, the smell something that Smokey had smelled many times before.

The amazing thing was that Smokey's Suburban was intact.

"Go," he said, pointing to the Suburban.

He helped Jennifer into the passenger seat, and she pulled Laurel in on top of her. The girl curled into Jennifer's lap and put her arms around her neck.

"Go do what you have to, and come back to us," Jennifer said, and Smokey touched her hair and shut the door. The SUV was facing the house, off to the side of the burning assault vehicles, and it looked to Smokey that Jennifer would have a ringside seat, like an old outdoor theatre.

Jennifer and Laurel watched as the roof fell in. A shower of sparks shot up into the dark sky. It reminded Jennifer of a video of an active volcano, except this wasn't a volcano, this was a home for people she was coming to care about.

"Jennifer?" Laurel pressed against Jennifer's chest, her voice muffled."

"What, Honey?"

"Sorry about Nanna."

"What . . . oh, my doll, Nanna, oh Honey, wait, she's in my pack." Jennifer twisted and reached around, pulling Nanna from her pack in the back seat.

*She's thinking of me when her house just burned down.*

"Now she'll be our doll," Jennifer said, and handed Nanna to Laurel. "We'll share her. After all, your daddy bought her."

Laurel nodded, and clutched Nanna much the same way Jennifer had, and closed her eyes.

Smokey jogged to the back of the house, the flames bright and hot on his skin.

Nathan waited in the trees behind the house. He looked at Smokey, then peered closer.

"What?" Smokey said.

"You looked in the mirror lately, Little Brother?"

"Nope. You?"

"Well," Nathan said, looking within inches of Smokey's face, "you got a lotta blood on your face, looks like a couple of bullet zips in your right arm, other stuff. You might want to wash up so you won't scare the ladies."

Smokey snorted.

"Scare you, you mean."

"Little Brother," Nathan said, quiet now. "I will protect the little one, my daughter as well as yours. You know she shot those two?"

*Fight as a family. We fight as a family. Used to, anyway.*

*Now we do again.*

Smokey nodded, not allowing himself the time to think about putting his daughter into a situation where she had to kill or be killed. He pointed to the trees.

181

"Let's get it done."

They walked to the men crouched in the trees, fifty yards up from the house. It was hot even this far from the flames.

The overall effect of the flames from the barn and the house made the men look like demented demons. Camouflage paint and blood from wounds made them look like they had just journeyed from hell.

Smokey stood close to his team. They were all dirty, some with blood on their battle dress utilities, their own or the enemies', he had no way of knowing. Most he had known for years. Nathan, his friend and older brother and uncle; Lamebull, long braided hair, quiet, grim face. He nodded, ever polite.

"Lieutenant."

"Sergeant," Smokey said softly.

He looked over the group in the dark, and felt a love for them he couldn't describe, and he knew that those who had been in combat would know how he felt. But these people were more than that to him, they were his own, they were family fighting for his family. The Šiyápu here, officers Kincaid and Burwell, they were his brothers. They had been before today, Smokey knew, brothers in arms in uniform, but today, they became his brothers for life, fighting for his family, putting their lives in harm's way for his home.

"El Tee." Sarah leaned forward and spoke. If Smokey hadn't known her from when she was a toddler, he wouldn't have recognized what he saw. Her face was painted black and green with camo paint, then covered with soot, dirt and blood. A cut below her right eye was oozing blood down her cheek. She took a swipe at it with her left hand (the right one held a UMP in a sling) and he noticed a deep cut on the back of her hand. The swipe made her face look more fierce and terrible, frightening, except that her Kevlar helmet had slipped down over her forehead, looking too big, her face small and fragile. And dirty. He had never seen her look more lovely.

He looked around. All of them. Lovely.

"Sorry about your house, El Tee," Sarah said.

Smokey nodded, not trusting himself to speak. He cleared his throat, and spoke to Sarah.

"Officer Greywolf, give me your report." He raised his voice a little and addressed all of them.

"I'll take verbal after-action reports here, now, and then you will write about what happened. All reports go to Sgt. Green, period. Go ahead, Sarah."

"Well, me and Plug here," Sarah said, "we surprised them, that's for sure. We were at the side of the haystack." Plug, Officer Danny Smith, stood behind Sarah, his face a mirror image of hers. Danny was short and squat, hence the nickname "Plug." He held a UMP submachine gun, wore a Kevlar helmet, had long braided black hair down his back, over his pack.

"Me and Plug, we pretty much covered the driver's side of the cars, and when they came out shooting, we opened up, mostly on the second Suburban, got two coming out, and then one in the lead car. But those rockets, Jesus."

"Plug, you talking?" Smokey asked.

Plug shook his head. Sarah smiled, and continued.

"One of the ones in the front car, back seat, came around and ran toward the haystack. He made it about halfway, and we got him. He never saw us, you think, Plug? But you told us to hold, and we knew you were fighting on the other side, and in the house, but we held there. Okay?"

Smokey nodded.

"Oh, and Smokey, sir?" Sarah looked at Smokey and he nodded.

"Did Laurel really shoot the guy inside the back door?"

"Yeah," Smokey said, looking down.

*What the hell have I done to my baby girl?*

"And she shot the runner," Nathan said.

"Smokey, El Tee," Sarah said, touching his arm, "she'll be okay, this family will take care of you all."

Smokey didn't trust himself to speak. He pointed at Detective Johns, who was in assault gear like the others.

"Uh, Kincaid and Burwell and I were on the north side, in the trees, the passenger side of the vehicles, not nearly as close as the haystack. We put some fire into the second Suburban, but the first ones were out and engaged before we could be effective. I think Kincaid came up and got one of the rocket shooters."

Smokey looked around.

"Okay, Sergeant Lamebull."

183

Sergeant George Lamebull, at sixty-three, the oldest in the group, had always deferred to Smokey, even though he had twenty years more police experience. And for that, Smokey was grateful.

"Lieutenant," Lamebull said, his voice deep and soft, "Lieutenant, we have Cubby, Two-shoes, and Stoneface up the hill, after the one your *miyanash* shot. Stoneface is out front, tracking. We get what we need, we put him where, in the yard with the others?"

Smokey shook his head. "No. We take his gear, leave him on the hill."

*Jesus, what did I just say, what did I just do? Give an order to kill a man when they catch him? As a cop, you can't do that, buddy. War. We're in a war, and we didn't start it, and this intruder was going to kill my miyanash, my Laurel. Fuck him.*

Smokey looked back at the house. The heat was reaching out to them, even at this distance. If he thought now what he and his mom had lost . . . he shook his head.

"Sergeant Lamebull."

"Sir."

"You take care of the hill. Get verbal reports only, replace all gear of the officers involved, get their weapons."

"Uh, they won't use guns, sir."

"Replace their gear, then."

Lamebull reached over and touched Smokey's arm, and walked up the hill and disappeared in the darkness. Smokey watched him until he couldn't see the figure, and turned back to the others.

"Sergeant Green."

"Boss."

"Check all gear, replace ammo, get after-action reports in writing, to you only, go to the Simnasho fire-hall and get some sleep. Get ready to go again. This ain't over. But first, wait for Chief Andrews, bring your cars up and wait at the edge of the trees by my driveway. Oh, and have the medics check all injuries. Sarah might want to get a date again."

Sergeant Nathan Green laughed, as did the others. Sarah stuck her tongue out at him.

They started to file past Smokey, and Sarah stopped.

"El Tee," she said.

*Soft, with care, concern. Love.*

Smokey gave her a smile, wanting to encourage her, so she could finish. He knew her.

"El Tee, the others want me to tell you something. This is from all of us, me, Plug, Kincaid, Burwell, Johns, all of us." The others nodded, murmured.

"This was for the hospital." Her voice grew husky, cracking at the end. She waved her hand. "Let me finish. We love you, all of us, even Burwell," she laughed and blew her nose on her sleeve.

"We love you, your *miyanash*, your baby girl, and we will always protect you, but this was for Tom. They executed him at the hospital, and he was one of ours."

Sarah grabbed Smokey and hugged him, and walked past. Each in turn, Burwell, Kincaid, Plug, and the rest, gave him a hug, and left him alone with Nathan.

*What have we done?*
*What are we about to do?*

When he thought about it later, he would have stopped it here.

# Chapter 44

Kah-Nee-Ta High Desert Resort and Casino

F.B.I. Supervisory Special Agent Dennis Oakley followed a line of people toward the two Blackhawk helicopters that were warming up in the parking lot of the casino. It had been roped off to accommodate the crews and machines. It was just after first light, and the boss wanted to get the woman and be back in Portland before the workday started. For some of these people, this would be their first time in a helicopter.

The drab military machines were, he knew, a show of force for the Indians, and anyone else who might be watching or interested in what the feds were doing on the good ol' rez. They were there courtesy of the power of the U.S. Attorney Julie Sturgis, who had good traction inside the Beltway. It had been rumored that she was on a short list to replace the current Attorney General, a man embattled since the day he took office last year.

Sturgis was in the lead. Her dark hair bounced down the back of a flight jacket that she was making look fashionable. She wore tan slacks and carried a black briefcase. Always in charge. Behind her and trying to keep up was the new Assistant U.S. Attorney, Teresa Barrett. Barrett struggled with two briefcases and a bag. Someone didn't tell Barrett that they were going for a helicopter ride, as she was wearing a dark pin-striped suit with a knee-length skirt. Barrett, short and blonde, must have been good in law school and have some skills, or she wouldn't be here, but her newness to the job made her appear vulnerable, scared.

I sure wouldn't want to be second to Sturgis, especially as a woman, Oakley thought. Behind Teresa Barrett was the other AUSA, Kelly Devans, the Indian specialist. He was a pretty good guy, but was supporting his boss by dutifully lining up behind them.

A helmeted crew member tried to help Sturgis into the lead helicopter. She waved him off and climbed in unassisted. Teresa Barrett needed the hand, and Oakley stopped and admired the view as she handed the briefcases up and then took a hand and was lifted aboard.

Stop it Oakley. Pay attention to what's going to happen. Sturgis had wanted him in the lead helicopter, since he was the one designated to take Jennifer Kruger to Portland and interview her again. His boss, James Russell readily agreed. Oakley was the only one who had had a prior relationship with Lt. "Smokey" Kukup.

Oakley followed Russell to the lead machine and looked over as the rest of their crew walked to the other helicopter.

Oakley took a seat inside, sitting on a jump seat next to Teresa Barrett. He smiled at her and gave her a thumbs up. She gave him a grateful smile back, and looked a little sick.

He leaned over and cupped his hands to her ear. "Been in a helicopter before?"

"No." She shook her head.

"It'll be fine," he said.

The helicopter lifted off and headed west, moving slowly, coming up over the light standards in the parking lot. Teresa Barrett did indeed look as if she were going to lose her breakfast.

Oakley looked out at the sun as it peeked up over the Mutton Mountains to the east. The resort was in a valley, surrounded by beautiful hills of grass, sagebrush, and lava rock formations on the mountain tops. As they gained height, Mt. Hood towered to the north, to their right, and ahead and slightly to their left, glacier-covered Mt. Jefferson. They were heading west, to the edge of the forest past the traditional community of Sidwalter, to the Kukup ranch. To get Jennifer Kruger.

Gonna piss off the Indians.

Won't be the first time.

The flight wouldn't be long, probably ten minutes in all, since they could have driven there in forty minutes from the resort. Oakley was thinking of how he would try to make this right with Smokey and Martin Andrews.

The pilot first told them of trouble, five minutes into the flight.

"Uh, folks, we may have a problem." Oakley looked up ahead as the pilot pointed out the windscreen. "Smoke, a lot of smoke, coming from the coordinates, or close to, where we are supposed to take you."

"Slow us down a little, and let's take a look," Russell said.

Oakley glanced over at Teresa Barrett, and now she looked both pale and green at the same time.

Oakley leaned forward and watched as they flew to the tree line, then came up slowly on the smoke.

"Jesus Christ," the pilot muttered. He spoke urgently into his headset. Oakley heard him tell the pilot of the second Blackhawk to take a holding position up at five hundred meters above ground level, to stand off a kilometer. Oakley strained to look out at the fires below. What had once been a house was almost completely burned out, the wall on one end still standing; a haystack was burning, and what had once been a barn was completely destroyed. In the yard a tree was on fire, with no apparent attempt to put it out.

A large SUV was in the front yard, and looked as if it had been bombed. Oakley could see a number of bodies on the ground, one smoldering.

*Fuck me. What the hell happened here? This looks like a war zone.*

Oakley unhooked his seat belt and moved between the seats, leaning between the pilot and co-pilot for a better look. He pointed.

"Is this mess where we were supposed to land?"

The pilot turned slightly.

"Yes sir," he shouted. "These are the GPS coordinates that were given to us for the landing.

Oakley looked back at Russell, and glanced over at Sturgis. She didn't look any too good either. Back to Russell, who pointed down to the floor with his index finger.

Oakley held his hand up, and turned to the pilot.

"See any sign of life?"

The pilot pointed. "There. An SUV with two people standing beside it." Oakley looked and saw the green Trailblazer. Looked like Police Chief Martin Andrews, and Smokey. Oakley looked at the tree line and pointed. Two additional SUV's, people wearing battle gear around the vehicles. He turned back toward Russell.

"Sir. The chief of police and his lieutenant are on the ground, look okay." Russell motioned down again.

"Let us off," Oakley said to the pilot.

He put the Blackhawk down a hundred feet behind the police car, two hundred yards from the house. When the crewman opened the door, the smell of burning bodies came to them. As Oakley and Russell jumped down, Oakley looked back in the cabin of the aircraft and watched as Teresa Barrett vomited on her boss's briefcase.

He thought then that this would not end well, that this entry into Indian country where things were going to shit in a global way, was going to make all of them vomit, if they were lucky, before it was over.

Oakley watched as Sturgis climbed out and jumped to the ground, and turned and yelled something to those inside the helicopter. She was bending down under the rotors and stopped That was about where the smell of the bodies would hit her. Okay, *fine*, Oakley thought.

*Welcome to war on the rez. And that's what this was.*

*War.*

*Hope the U.S. Attorney for Oregon is having a good time. Maybe the rest of the feds will get their shoes dirty before this is over.*

*But they all would.*

*He knew it.*

*Because he knew stuff he didn't tell the Indians. Couldn't tell them. And that was a damned shame.*

# Chapter 45

Smokey heard the choppers before the rest of them did, a product of his recent tour in Afghanistan. The team had pulled their vehicles up to the tree line behind Chief Andrews. He waited with Nathan. The officers were shedding gear and cleaning wounds. The choppers came in from the east and slowed.

*Here to pick up Jennifer. How thoughtful of the feds to let us know.*

Smokey watched Nathan cup a hand over his ear piece, and then motion to talk.

"They have the runner," Nathan said.

"Make sure they know there are choppers in the air," Smokey said.

"They know, they won't be seen."

"Anything yet?" He knew it would be fast.

"They'll call me. I'll be on your hip, Boss. Oh, and Boss," Nathan said, waiting.

"Yeah?"

"The troops, all of us, we need to *laatlat*, in *xwayatsh*. We have touched the dead."

Smokey felt it too, a growing dread of having touched the dead. They all needed to sweat in a traditional sweathouse.

Before the helicopters arrived, the team moved through the killing ground, gathering intelligence on the invaders before all of the evidence disappeared into the federal system, never to be seen or talked about again, at least not to them. It required the touching of the dead.

Smokey moved to the SUV with Sarah at the back tailgate. She was looking at the approaching choppers; Plug was trying to wipe the wound on her hand.

"Hold still," he said, looked up at Smokey and grinned with a missing tooth.

"It talks," Sarah said.

Smokey thought that they were the first words he had heard Plug say in months.

"El Tee," Sarah said, wincing as Plug applied an antiseptic. "El Tee, did Laurel really shoot that guy at the back door?"

"Yeah, and the runner."

Sarah touched his arm. "She'll be okay."

*Yeah. One way or the other. But what have I done to my daughter?*

# Chapter 46

Oakley stepped off the Blackhawk into a war zone. The barn and house were blazing ruins. Black smoke poured from what was left of a haystack, and bodies were scattered on the ground as if they had been thrown there by a careless war god. There was a body halfway in the doorway of what had once been a farmhouse. The upper part of the body was on fire, the legs sticking out as if the person were taking a nap.

The smell of the burning bodies was stronger here, away from the Blackhawk. Russell walked toward Chief Andrews, holding his hand out. Oakley looked back at the scene. An SUV on fire in the haystack and another in front of the house; an assault team of a dozen men.

*Oh, Christ. One of the bodies on the lawn has an RPG launcher. What the hell? This was an all-out assault by a well-trained and equipped team. Who are these people? Some of Kal-leed's or from the cartel?*

*Oh shit. Maybe both.*

*Fuck me, this is a mess.*

Oakley turned to walk toward Chief Andrews, when several things happened at once:

Julie Sturgis was moving away from the Blackhawk, walking purposefully toward him; Teresa stumbled out of the helicopter, moved a few feet away, and sank to her knees and put her head down; the gas tank of the front SUV blew up with a sudden whoosh, and some ammunition cooked off with a barrraaack and Oakley ran for Sturgis, pulling her the rest of the way to the Chief's car. He looked over at Teresa Barrett. She didn't even look up from getting sick all over again beside the Blackhawk.

Lieutenant Kukup ran from the trees to help Teresa.

Oakley stayed with the car, watching as Smokey scooped Teresa up and jogged with her to their car. The Blackhawk's rotors picked up speed and the big chopper lifted off, leaving them on the ground.

With the Indians.

Oakley met Smokey and took Teresa from him, sitting her in the front seat of Chief Andrews's car. He put his left hand on the back of her neck and eased her down. An explosion from the remains of the house sent debris down over the front yard. Teresa gripped his arm hard, her eyes wild, not seeing, a string of saliva dripping from her mouth.

"Teresa! Look at me." Oakley bent his head down in front of her, inches from her eyes. "Look at me," he said, softer.

*This kid needs medical help. She's in shock, lost a lot of fluid, and at this rate is gonna need an IV soon.*

Smokey leaned in and looked at Teresa, his long braids hanging down in front of his uniform shirt. He stood up behind Oakley.

"We have an ambulance on the B-100 road. I'll get them to look at her." Oakley nodded.

"Smokey, what about your team?"

"Got some scratches, but okay."

Holy shit, Oakley thought. They did all this? Against a trained, equipped battle team? Oakley shook his head. He continued to hold Teresa's hand and waited, looking around at the absolute fucking mess. Well, he had heard of Chief Martin Andrews and company in Peru, they all had, and they were capable, he would give them that. But, look at this.

*Welcome to the rez, Teresa.*


Smokey stood to the side and waited for his cue to talk. Chief Andrews started. He addressed Russell and Sturgis.

"So, to what do we owe this unannounced visit by the two most powerful feds in this sovereign nation?"

"Uh, Chief," Russell started. Chief Martin Andrews held his hand up.

"Let me guess. You were going to pick up Jennifer Kruger, without so much as a kiss my ass to Lieutenant Kukup?" The chief looked at Russell and Sturgis. Smokey thought they were looking as green as the woman in the car seat. He waited for his turn.

Chief Andrews swept his hand around (a gesture he must have picked up from watching the tribal council members, Smokey thought) and had them all look at the carnage.

"This is Lieutenant Kukup's family home, their tribal land, and it has been invaded by what looks like a well-equipped team, a well-financed team of killers. They tried to kill Smokey, his daughter, Jennifer Kruger, and members of his team."

"Doesn't look like they succeeded," Oakley said.

Smokey looked at the chief. Andrews nodded.

"My turn," Smokey said.

*Keep it cool, keep the anger down, won't help with the feds. Besides, Oakley is a good one.*

"Someone," Smokey said, raising his voice, "someone owes my mother a new *nishaykt*. Owes me a new barn and some hay for the winter." He looked over at the assembled group, aware that the ambulance had arrived and two crew members were leading Teresa to the back doors. He had the attention of the feds. He was dimly aware that an SUV had pulled up alongside the ambulance, driven by Sarah.

"You have a hell of a crime scene here, Madam U.S. Attorney." He pointed around his property, with his finger stopping at Sturgis.

"You feds need to tell us who these people are, the ones who came unannounced much like you did today. Oh, you come here with your Blackhawks and your shiny clothes from town, and whether or not you will admit it, you look down on us poor Indians, you don't think we know that?"

He had their attention. Chief Andrews told him to go ahead with this, to put the feds on the defensive so they could get the people out of here while the feds were somewhat in disarray.

"You," Smokey said, pointing at Sturgis and Russell, "you have a crime scene here. My *nishaykt*, my mother's *nishaykt*, my daughter's house. My mother had a life's worth of valuable items inside, valuable to real people, not store bought stuff made in China like you Šiyápu fill your houses with. It doesn't matter that much to me, but I had a few ribbons and medals in there, given to me by the Šiyápu army for fighting in Afghanistan and elsewhere. But here on the reservation, where I have to fight for my family myself, you come with your helicopters to take a woman with you, a woman who doesn't want to go with you." He looked around.

"Where the hell were you all earlier this morning, with your helicopters and your shiny pants from town?"

Smokey could see Jennifer and Laurel listening, watching from his SUV.

"Oh, and you should know, there's a few more dead around here, two at the haystack, one inside what used to be my back door."

Smokey looked at Sturgis as he said this, and then walked to the driver's side of the SUV.

"Uh, Lieutenant Kukup, where are you going?" Sturgis found her voice. "We need to talk to you and Jennifer Kruger."

She walked over to the car as Smokey got in behind the wheel. "We really do need to talk. Leave Jennifer Kruger here, talk with us. Where do you think you can go?"

"Somewhere to keep her alive," Smokey said, starting the car, "and somewhere to find out what just happened here."

Jennifer leaned over Smokey, looked at Sturgis.

"Look, I don't know who you are nor do I care. I'm going with them." Laurel struggled over Jennifer's lap and moved her head next to her father.

"You, lady, we fight as a family. That's what we're gonna do. My dad will protect us. Jennifer and I will protect him."

She leaned over and put her arms around Jennifer as Smokey rolled the window up. He didn't trust himself to speak. He put the Suburban in gear and turned around, looking at his place for one last time. As he turned for the driveway to go out to the Sidwalter road, his team stood up and saluted, Sarah's salute the sharpest, Plug's a little sloppy, but Smokey was never more proud, more caring for them, wouldn't trade them for any military unit he had ever served with.

*What the hell just happened here? Three tours in Afghanistan and I lost Amelia to loneliness and drugs. And Laurel is getting so attached to Jennifer, a young woman I don't know much about.*

*Maybe you should get attached too, buddy.*

*But she's a Šiyápu.*

*So what, as Laurel had said. Tutu likes her, Daddy, and so should you.*

Chief Martin Andrews walked toward U.S. Attorney Julie Sturgis. She was in a huddle with Russell, the F.B.I. Special Agent in Charge of Oregon. The feebs, they do like their titles, he thought. He waited until they looked up.

"Well, folks. Let me show you around your crime scene."

# Chapter 47

Parker Creek

Amy took the steaming cup of coffee Stan handed her and gratefully took a sip. Stan had them up before dawn, the events of the evening a distant, bad dream, or so Amy hoped. He told her (and she believed it) that they may have been the first people to camp in the area for years, maybe decades. The Parker Creek drainage on the eastern slopes of Mt. Jefferson was a sacred area to the Indians, and in any event, the Indians didn't camp here.

It was still quite dark. The lamp in the tent made their movements exaggerated shadow people on the walls. Stan had a plan, a plan in motion to see if their visitor in the night was really Bigfoot. He believed, and it actually made sense to Amy, that the giant biped was nocturnal, and had a place to bed down not far from here. He was explaining it to her on the map and she tried to listen, but really, all she was going to do was follow Stan. Unlike that woman who got lost, Jennifer, Amy had a cell phone and an extra battery. She was damned well going to use it if she got separated or lost. She had full power, full bars here, must be hitting a cell site on one of the mountains.

*If Bigfoot really does exist, he (or she) won't have trouble finding us now. And what was that last night? Was it Bigfoot or was it a bear or just what the hell was that? I really want to go home. This is getting to be scary bullshit.*

She came out of the tent and stood looking to the east, straight down the slope of the mountain, wishing the sun would come up. The moon was down, but with the starlight, she could see fairly well. Stan consulted a GPS unit, and pointed.

"This way." He started off, and turned to look back.

"Stay close, Amy."

When she caught up with him, he started off again, walking carefully, trying to be quiet.

Amy wanted to laugh, but she knew if she started giggling, it would be hard to stop, and would earn the wrath of Stan. She kicked over a rock in the dark and it made a clacking sound as it dropped down the hill.

Stan turned and she could feel his glare in the dark.

"Sorry," she whispered.

They walked for an hour, Stan stopping every few minutes to consult his GPS unit. During the night, he had programmed a route he thought would lead to the animal's home.

Amy thought she could see a lightening of the sky to the east, on the top of the Mutton Mountains, but that might have been wishful thinking. Daybreak was an hour away or more, but that didn't mean she didn't want to see where the hell they were going.

The smell came to her all at once, a physical thing, an overpowering smell, a putrid smell of something long dead. She gagged as Stan held up his hand for her to stop.

Stan turned around and leaned back to whisper.

"Bigfoot may be close, be as quiet as you can."

"Stan," Amy whispered, louder than she wanted, "Stan, that's just some dead thing. Let's go around, get away from it. Besides," she said, looking closely at him, "bad smells are dead smells, decaying meat. Fuck!"

"Okay, we'll wait for first light, but be quiet."

Amy sat on her pack and folded her arms around her chest. Whatever smelled bad was close. There was no breeze on the mountain this early in the day. It could be within feet.

Amy pulled her t-shirt over her nose.

"Stan."

"Huh?"

"Stan, this smell is really awful. Let's move back some, then you can come up and look when it's daylight."

"Okay."

It must be getting to him too, Amy thought. She picked up her pack and turned to go, trying to breath shallow breaths through her mouth. She stepped on something soft, her foot sliding, and she fought for balance, and stepped forward to firm ground.

*Oooooh nooooo*

*The smell is so bad, and what did I just step in?*

Stan stopped behind Amy, and then he broke his earlier rule about no flashlights. He shined his light on the area around Amy's feet. A human ribcage, a piece of clothing, a scattering of cheap jewelry, thedeath grin of a jaw, some teeth missing, the jaw partially covered with decayed flesh, some bare parts.

*A dead person.*

Something, some scavenger (Bigfoot?) had pulled the body from its grave, the lower part still buried, the other arm missing a hand.

An aluminum container poked out of the ground like a forgotten thermos.

*Stan we gotta get outta here.*

Movement to her right, toward the glacier.

Something big.

Something upright.

Amy screamed before she could stop herself. Stan fumbled with his pack and brought out the stupid tracking gun. He brought the gun up and fired a dart at the shape, dropped the gun and jerked up his pack. Amy had never wanted a real gun so bad before in her life and she started to run.

She knew the other girl had done this, the one who had gotten lost, the girl must have panicked and run, but I'm gonna get the hell out of here, Amy thought, with what was left of her sanity.

*Gonna run until I drop.*

Amy ran with the pent-up energy of the scared, an adrenalin jolt a thousand times more powerful than an energy drink. She ran with the same chemical jolt that had saved countless historic men and women from death at the hands of predators. She ran with the scant knowledge that Stan was running behind her, her fear infectious, and warranted.

They stopped at their tent, out of breath.

They had found the prize.

A large hairy biped.

A much sought after dead woman with secrets.

Worth killing for.

Over and over again.

# Chapter 48

Laurel fell asleep before they made it to the highway. She snuggled against Jennifer in the front seat, clutching Nanna, the shared doll. She needs Nanna a lot more than I do, Jennifer thought. Laurel snored softly, sleeping away the horrific events of the early morning. Jennifer stared out at the sun rising on the trees, trying to think of what she should do next, but her brain wasn't functioning. Smokey slowed on the gravel road as they approached State Hwy 26. He stopped over a hundred yards from the pavement. He reached over and touched his daughter.

At six a.m. summer traffic was already in full swing. Pickups with campers pulling boats; motor homes; swarming clouds of motorcycles with baby boomers on shiny new bikes; moving south through the Central Oregon Cascade Mountains, headed to one of the many high lakes south of Bend. Hwy 26 was the main east-west highway running from the Portland area to Madras; then Hwy 97 through central and southern Oregon, connecting with Interstate 5 in northern California.

Jennifer knew that Hwy 26 was the main highway going through the reservation. Few people strayed off the highway, unless they were on one of the BIA roads going to the resort at Kah-Nee-Ta. Smokey had told her that to be any other place on the reservation, unless you were Indian, meant that you were trespassing. He told her that she had been trespassing when she and her boyfriend had gone onto the reservation wilderness area.

Jennifer put her hand on Smokey's right arm and let it rest there until he relaxed. His arm was streaked with soot and blood, veins showing on the muscle. She kept her hand there as he brushed Laurel's hair.

When he spoke, Jennifer could heard the emotion, the worry, in his voice.

"I don't ever want to put her in that kind of danger again." "You didn't," Jennifer said. She gripped his arm harder. "They did, and she wouldn't want to be any other place. I know how much you love her, but for Laurel, you are her world."

"And as her father, I want her to have a life, a future, whether I am around or not. I already lost her mother, I can't lose her."

He shook his head and put his hand over his eyes.

"I can't," he whispered.

"You won't," Jennifer said.

*And I will do whatever I can to make sure you don't lose Laurel.*

Jennifer shifted toward Smokey and slid Laurel down in the seat. The child was getting heavy. Laurel snorted, mumbled something, and nestled her head against Jennifer's shoulder. Jennifer kissed Laurel's head and saw Smokey looking at them. He leaned toward her. His face, like his arm, was smeared with soot and blood.

*He's beautiful, with all the blood and soot and face paint, he's beautiful, and you can't be thinking this.*

*Jen. You can't be thinking this.*

*Why not?*

*He's the most beautiful man I've ever seen.*

*And he's gonna kiss you.*

Jennifer leaned on the center console, holding Laurel with her right arm, and smiled up at Smokey.

He leaned down and brushed his lips on Jennifer's. She opened her lips slightly, and kissed him then, pressing her lips into his, and she felt something drop away, and felt so, just so right. Smokey pulled back slightly, and then began kissing her lips gently, and she didn't want to know what it would be like to not be around him. Her breathing stopped, and then she gasped, and he leaned back away from her, smiling.

*OhGod OhGod OhGod Jennifer what just happened to you, Oh God Jen, Oh I want to kiss him again, he's so beautiful.*

"Smokey?"

"What?" He mouthed the words.

"Kiss me again." She was surprised that she could speak at all.

He nodded. As he leaned toward her, still smiling, she whispered. "And again."

Near Sunriver

"Puta!" Alvarez threw the phone across the room. He'd been trying to raise the team for the past hour. The phone call from the meth house on the reservation gave him the answer. The team should have reported to him by now, should have killed the cop who took out his men at the hospital, and have the woman with them. His vehicles were on fire, his men dead. Federal helicopters there. Shit, shit, shit.

He yelled at Roberto. "Get me some people! Get the helicopter ready! I will do this myself! Today! Get ready! Arriba!"

*How can I put this woman on YouTube unless I have her?*

Highway 26 near Sidwalter

Smokey leaned his head against Jennifer. She didn't trust herself to speak. Laurel snuggled on Jennifer's right shoulder. Smokey had his cheek on her other shoulder, and Jennifer felt as if she couldn't be more content.

*Yeah, right Jen. Here you are on an Indian reservation, been shot at how many times? And the people who are trying to kill you aren't going to give up any time soon. And how long have you known Smokey? And Laurel? And aren't you a Šiyápu, as they call it?*

*Stupid, is what you are.*

*But she knew that in her life she had never felt so alive, so wanted, so needed.*

*So family.*

*Okay, it's settled.*

*You're staying with them.*

"Jennifer."

Smokey was looking out at the highway. He pointed to his left, north.

"We go that way, I can take you to your apartment in Portland. I can probably find the woman on the mountain with my team. That way we let the feds and Portland Police Bureau take care of you."

Jennifer shook her head.

No.

He swung his arm across to the right. South, toward Cold River, the agency. "We go that way, we'll go to the agency, get some things . . . some weapons, gear, camping supplies, and head for the mountain. Find the woman with the missing hand. It won't be pretty, or easy."

Jennifer smiled. "Ain't been easy since I stumbled upon the bodies. I thought we were going to fight together as a family."

*Gotcha there, buddy.*

"We already did that," Smokey said. But he was smiling.

*I go to Portland, a piece of me that I've been looking for will be lost. I'm not gonna go that easy. I know he likes me. And he needs me on this. Time to let him know how I feel.*

"Besides, Lieutenant Mark Kukup, 'Smokey,' what will you do with Laurel?"

"Mom is going to take her and the other kids shopping at the Wal-Mart superstore down there in Redmond later today. Get them some of the clothes they lost."

*Let him know, Jen.*

"Smokey?" She grinned.

"Huh?"

"You see my ass there in the hospital?"

"Yeah," he said, his voice suddenly husky.

"Don't you, sometime when the time is right, want to see the rest?"

# Chapter 49

Madras
Cross Keys Station Inn

Smokey entered the lobby carrying two large duffle bags. The clerk, a girl barely out of her teens, looked up and he could see her sudden fright. Her hand hovered over the phone, as if she thought about calling the Madras Police.

"I have a pre-paid reservation," Smokey said, and that seemed to calm the clerk somewhat. He had cleaned up a little at the Cold River Police Department, but too damned little for civilization. He got some of the camo paint and blood and soot off, but not all.

"Been in a fire," Smokey said lamely, and it didn't look as if that helped the clerk at all. He pushed his credit card across the counter. The clerk picked it up as if it was radioactive and swiped it through the machine. She pushed it back with a fingernail.

Smokey had decided that they would get a room for a few hours, to get away from the reservation and get some sleep before they started for the mountain. Jennifer followed, holding Laurel's hand. Laurel was asleep on her feet, clutching Nanna.

Smokey held the elevator door open and Jennifer shuffled in with Laurel. Laurel put her arms around Jennifer's legs. The door closed and they were in their own capsule, riding up to their third floor room. Jennifer leaned against Smokey, and he put his arm around her and pulled her close.

"We need to get some sleep," Smokey said. He yawned. He had been this tired before, but worrying about Laurel and Jennifer didn't help. He hadn't slept well since he was on the mountain the last time, a couple of days ago, with Nathan.

*Had it only been two days ago?*

In the suite, Laurel lay on one of the beds and curled up. "Let's get her clothes off and under the covers," Smokey said. Jennifer helped, and they pulled her dirty jeans and sweatshirt off, leaving her in her t-shirt and panties, little girl panties with red hearts. Jennifer pulled the covers back and they rolled Laurel in, the girl already snoring, clutching Nanna. Smokey kissed her and pulled the blanket up. Jennifer sat on the bed and smelled her clothes.

"I really smell bad," she said, and pulled her sweatshirt off.

"You, lady, first in the shower." Smokey handed her pack over, and Jennifer trudged into the bathroom. At the door, she turned and looked at him.

"Thanks." She went in and closed the door. He heard the water start, and Jennifer singing something. He sat heavily in the chair.

*This better work out. Don't know what else to do. We need to get to the woman's remains on the mountain, get there first, can't trust the feds to keep us in the loop.*

*We need to end this. Make whatever it is they want public, take the secret away. Get Jennifer's life back.*

Smokey pulled a large garbage bag from one of his duffle bags. He placed it on the floor and removed his boots, carefully placing them inside the bag. He then eased out of his torn, stained t-shirt, BDU pants, shredded and bloody, and socks. With a glance at the bathroom door, he stripped naked and put on a pair of old jeans. These too would find their way into the bag when he had showered.

He placed a rag on the table and pulled guns from his duffle. He disassembled two Glock pistols, a UMP submachine gun, and the five-shot Smith & Wesson .38 that Laurel had used. He was cleaning the weapons when the shower stopped. Jennifer came out in a cloud of steam, wearing a white robe, a towel around her head. She stood by the door and watched as Smokey assembled a Glock, loaded it, and stuck it in his waistband.

She walked over and sat in a chair opposite Smokey, toweling her hair. Jennifer nodded at the bag with his clothes and boots.

"For the cleaners?"

"To burn. They touched the dead."

Jennifer started to say something, and stopped. Smokey waited, and when she didn't speak, he told her. After all, she was a Šiyápu, and as such, didn't know what was required of a warrior when he touched the dead. She was worth it, and he was, he knew, caring more and more for her, she was just so . . . worth it.

"I was wearing these clothes when I touched the dead. As such, they are unclean, can never be cleansed or worn again. They must be burned. I will do that soon. And I have to sweat, but a long hot shower will have to do until I can properly sweat."

"Okay." Jennifer gave him a slight smile.

"What, Jen?"

"Well, if you keep this up, you will need a lot more clothes."

"No kidding." Smokey stood up and leaned over and kissed her. He straightened and removed clean BDU's and underclothes from his pack, placed a pair of boots by the chair. He turned for the shower.

"Good idea," Jennifer said. "You don't smell so good either."

Smokey stood under the hot water and thought about his sweathouse. This would have to do. He washed the blood, soot, and pieces of his enemies from his skin. When he walked into the room fifteen minutes later, Jennifer was under the covers with Laurel, both of them sleeping.

He finished cleaning the guns, reloaded them, wrapped them in cloth and placed them in the duffle bag. He placed one of the Glocks on the nightstand. It just wouldn't do to go into the world (or the motel room) unarmed. A gun zipped away in a duffle was akin to being unarmed.

Smokey checked his equipment. Lightweight sleeping bags, jackets, ammunition, freeze-dried food, water bottles. He assembled packs, called for a wake up call at noon, and lay down on the bed.

Smokey was asleep in seconds. He began dreaming almost as quickly.

*In his dream Smokey walked on a dark trail, alone, the dark so complete he couldn't see his feet. The mountain was above him, he knew, even though he couldn't see it. He walked in the burn area from the Lightening Complex fire of the summer of '07. Trees with branches burned off, black spires, some rising up a hundred feet, spires like dead sentinels to guard the mountain. Black clouds of ash puffed up around his feet and lower legs.*

*He thought he was alone but he wasn't - there was movement in front of him. Something large, something that had lived on the mountain as long as the people had lived here, for thousands of years. Something that owned the mountain. He felt his body tighten. His hair rose in an age-old challenge to danger. He turned to run and jerked his upper body around, but his legs remained on the path, his feet pointing toward the large shape on the path.*

*The shape stood on two legs, tall, about eight feet, Smokey saw, but he couldn't make out what it was.*

*Legend.*

*That's what it was.*

*The shape moved, slowly, away from Smokey, down the trail, and then stopped, and the upper body turned back, as if the shape/thing was watching. Wanting him to follow.*

*He took a step, then another, then followed at a good pace, not winded, just following the large shape/thing through the burn area. It was lighter now. Starlight made it easier for him to see.*

*A black landscape with black sticks reaching up to the stars.*

*Black ash rose up around the shape, now fifty feet in front of Smokey. They continued on, toward a rock ledge.*

*I know where this is, Smokey said.*

*The ledge where Jennifer found the hand.*

*This is the place.*

*The shape/thing sat on the rock ledge, a ledge high above the trail, and Smokey walked up and stopped, looking up at it.*

*Legend.*

*The thing in the legend.*

*His hair rubbed on his clothes, sweat trickled down his back.*

*What do you want, shape/thing?*

*To show you what you must do.*

*It didn't seem strange that he was talking without opening his mouth, that he was having a conversation with something that didn't exist, that he was standing there doing that, that he could understand the thing. The shape/thing didn't exist, and this was a dream, had to be.*

*But it isn't a dream, Smokey, you just want it to be.*

*The shape/thing pointed, raising a long hairy arm, pointed down the trail.*

*Walk there.*

*Look there.*

*Don't want to, Smokey said. He knew he sounded petulant, as a child, and hoped the shape/thing would understand. Something was bad, there were shapes in the trail.*

*I can't go there, Smokey said, been too long since I have been to the sweat lodge, have to burn all those clothes now, can't wait, don't want the dead to touch me again.*

*Walk there.*

*Smokey looked down the trail and walked slowly to the first thing.*

*Big Brother. Nathan.*

*Nathan, the man who was his mentor, his big brother, lay on the trail, his hand missing, his eyes open in death.*

*Nooooooo!*

*Not Nathan, what will I do without him to guide me through life?*

*Smokey looked back toward the rock shelf, toward the shape/thing.*

*Gone.*

*He turned to leave, to wake up, but this wasn't a dream. This was real.*

*Keep walking.*

*The shape/thing's voice. Keep walking.*

*A lump in the trail. A smaller shape. The one I wanted and needed after Amelia died, the one Laurel and the mountain has picked for me, one my mother likes, the Šiyápu woman who as much as told me she is mine. She and I have something, you know?*

*Jennifer lay on the trail, both feet missing, dressed in the white robe of the motel, her eyes open, a doll in her hands.*

*Not a doll. The painted fingernails of the woman. The woman at the ledge. The woman with the answers.*

*Keep walking.*

*But I want to touch her.*

*Can't, she's dead. Not properly buried.*

*Keep walking.*

*Another lump in the trail, a smaller lump.*

*Of course it's familiar. Any dad would know what his kids look like when they are sleeping.*

*Laurel?*

*Nooooooo can't be my baby.*

*I can't look. It's light enough to see. Can't look.*

*Won't look.*

*Laurel lay in the trail, her t-shirt with Bart Simpson staring up at him, her legs bare, with little girl panties, white with hearts, clutching*

*Nanna in one hand, a nickel-plated .38 Smith & Wesson revolver in the other.*

*Smokey dropped to his knees, screaming, crying, tears running down his cheeks, and pulled her up, cradled her, holding her close to protect her from harm.*

*She's just sleeping, Smokey. Just a little girl, sleeping.*

*She's so cold.*

*He turned to run. He screamed her name.*

*Laurel! Baby girl!*

*He cradled her, and fell to the trail, curling up around her.*

"Smokey!"

He curled up tighter.

"Smokey, it's Jennifer. Smokey!"

Smokey opened his eyes. The black trail was gone.

"Laurel?" He croaked, and thrashed around.

"Smokey, it's Jennifer, Smokey you're dreaming. Smokey!"

He opened his eyes and sat up. The room was dim with the curtains closed.

*Jennifer?*

"Jennifer?"

She sat on the bed and put her head on his forehead. "Smokey, you had a bad dream, you were screaming."

He looked over at the other bed. Laurel was sitting up, watching.

"Sorry," he whispered.

Jennifer gave him a hug, and he gave Laurel a little wave. She swung her legs out of bed and jumped into his bed and threw her arms around him.

*Both still alive. God it seemed so real.*

He grabbed Jennifer and pulled her on the bed, put his left arm around Laurel held them close.

*Jesus, I had lost them.*

"Dad," Laurel said. "I think you were dreaming."

Smokey nodded. Yes.

"Daddy. I'm hungry. And," she said, jumping up, "I have to pee." She sniffed her arm, "And shower. I stink." She ran into the bathroom and closed the door.

Smokey looked at Jennifer, her face inches away.

"In my dream you were dead, you and Laurel."

Jennifer pulled back. Only then did he notice that she was wearing a green bra and panties. The robe was gone.

*Green?*

"We're okay, as you can see, and sometime, if you . . ."

"Yeah I know," Smokey said, "If I play my cards right."

"You can find out that I'm not dead."

"I like green," Smokey said, sitting up in the bed and watching as Jennifer put her jeans on. She pulled a t-shirt on over her head as Laurel came out swaddled in a large towel.

"Okay you two," she said, ran to Jennifer and gave her a hug. "No time for that."

Smokey smiled at Jennifer over the top of Laurel's head. She grinned.

"Besides," Laurel said. "I'm starved." She ran to the bed and pulled clothes from her pack.

"Take me to the Black Bear Restaurant, Daddy. Take me and Jennifer now or lose us forever."


On the way to the restaurant, Smokey wondered how he could be so lucky. He shivered.

The dream seemed so real. He knew luck was not real, it was made. And it could be taken away.

On the mountain.

And that's where they were going.


*In the end, he wished he could have taken it back.*
*Never gone back to the mountain.*
*Never with the people he loved.*

# Chapter 50

Cold River Indian Reservation
Bald Peter Mountain, Forest Road 6574

Smokey shut off the engine and looked out over the valley below them. Jennifer leaned against the passenger door with her arm around Laurel. They both had their eyes closed, the events of the night and lack of sleep catching up with them. In the end, Smokey had decided to keep Laurel with them. She had grown up in the mountains, he could keep an eye on her, and he gave in when Jennifer and his daughter told him that they didn't want to be separated.

"Besides, Dad," Laurel had reasoned, "I protected Jen once, and I can do it again."

Smokey wasn't so sure that he bought her line of reasoning, but he didn't tell her otherwise.

At just after noon, it was hot. He had left the air conditioner in the Suburban off, not wanting to start their hike in a blast of heat. He got out and walked to the front of the car and leaned against the hood. They were parked on an old logging landing at the top of Bald Peter Mountain, the closest road to the area where Jennifer had found the hand.

Down the slope the tree line was at mid-mountain. To his right the burn area of 2007 was a black slash in the forest. Mount Jefferson rose up in front of him, dominating the landscape. The mountain had always been a part of his life. His family home in Sidwalter was on the northeastern slope of the mountain, twenty-five miles from here. What they were about to do should be a walk in the woods, and even though it was rugged territory, it wasn't that far as the crow flies.

*We need to find the woman and the reason for her being here. And if the reason isn't apparent, we'll leave and deal with the rest of it later. Maybe I should take the fight to the bad people. Go on the offensive with some warriors. Leave Jennifer and Laurel home.*

They were laughing about something when he walked to the back of the SUV.

"What?" He smiled as he got to the back. They were getting too chummy.

"Daddy, we were thinking, Jennifer and I, that you really know how to show two girls a good time." She had her arm around Jennifer's waist.

"Stick with me," Smokey said. "You haven't seen anything yet." He opened the back door and removed a pack. He wore camouflage pants and a sleeveless camo shirt and "boonie" hat. He had a pistol belt with pouches for ammunition and other gear. In the back of the SUV he laid out a small submachine gun, an H & K UMP, and a short-barreled .308 caliber sniper rifle. Both had slings. He handed packs to Jennifer and Laurel; a small one for his daughter, a medium sized pack for Jennifer. When they put on their packs, he handed the machine gun to Jennifer.

"Let me know if this gets too much for you," he said.

She put the sling over her head and adjusted the rifle.

"It's fine. Just show me how it works sometime."

"Daddy," Laurel said.

"What?" he said, not looking back. He started down the trail. They had to go down into the Parker Creek area, Laurel knew, before starting toward the mountain.

"Daddy, you think I can stay with Jennifer until our house is built again?"

Smokey didn't answer. He motioned for Laurel to join him. She ran up to him and he dropped on one knee, and untied the leather thong that held the carved figure of the *spilyay*, the coyote. As Jennifer looked on, he explained the significance of the necklace.

"This is a *wahayakt*."

"I've heard of it before, Dad, but I thought it was a necklace of a *spilyay*."

"It is, but it is much more than that. If you are about to go on a hazardous journey, if a friend gives you something that is special to that friend, well then, if you get into trouble, you can call upon the *wahayakt* and you will have the strength of the friend as well."

"I will be as strong as you?"

"Stronger than me," Smokey said with a grin. He kissed Laurel on her cheek and stood up. Jennifer met his eyes and nodded her approval, then shook her head slightly side to side and smiled.

"Laurel, I carried this in Afghanistan, Uncle Nathan carried it in Viet Nam. It has a lot of strength with it."

Laurel held up the necklace to show Jennifer, and Smokey walked down the steep trail toward the trees. The July sun was right above him, and it was getting hot.

Laurel and Jennifer had a plan. When things returned to normal (and even at nine, Laurel didn't think things were ever going to be quite "normal" again) she was going to go to Portland and spend a month with Jennifer. They would get up late, play video games, play with dolls, then go down to a little restaurant by the Willamette River and have lunch.

And then shop.

Unless, of course, her dad wanted to spend the month with them.

That would be cool. Get him off the rez. They didn't have a house anyways.

It felt good with her dad, to be out with him, and she knew she was lucky. A lot of her school friends didn't have dads or even moms to take care of them and were being raised by *tutu* or aunts. She didn't think of her mom much, but it was hard for her when her dad was gone to that place, Afghanistan. She had looked it up on a map and that didn't mean much, just a place on the map that was a different color from the other places on the map. A kid at school, Dean Whinishut, said that her dad was killing Al Qaeda, over there, that some rag heads had bombed the World Trade Center. That had scared her, since she was in pre-school when her dad first went there, and she had cried. She cried a lot the first time her dad went there, and cried when he left for the second time, but he wasn't gone long then, he got hurt, and he came home.

She told him that he couldn't go back after that.

That Šiyápu chief of police, Chief Martin Andrews (Dad liked him) had hired her dad back.

And now this stuff. But her daddy would always protect her, and would protect Jennifer, she knew that. He always would, no matter what happened.

He will always take care of me. And I will take care of him.

*My daddy. And now there's Jennifer. If I have to drag him to her place in Portland, I will, but I won't have to drag him, you know?*

Jennifer lagged behind, slowly walking downhill behind Laurel, listening as Smokey and his daughter bantered back and forth. The day was beautiful. The sun was warm, and as they entered the tree line, the shadows created by the Ponderosa Pines were welcome and comforting. The mountain view was blocked by the trees now, but she caught occasional glimpses of the snow fields thousands of feet above them. The mountain had been so much a part of her landscape the past few days, she was used to it.

*Smokey. Ah, God, what do I do?*

Jennifer knew that it would be all too easy to forget her life (such as it was) in Portland and come here. She knew that she could be a mother to Laurel, and she and Laurel both knew it. Laurel was so sweet, had such a need for a mom that it was almost painful to watch.

*And maybe you have a need, too, Jen. You have been so careful, so aloof, so just alone, that maybe it's time. After all, Jen, you will be thirty this year. Admit it, you're good with her, and you like her. Could come to love her. And you can edit books from here.*

Smokey. Maybe it's just a foxhole kind of attraction. People attracted to each other because they have been thrown together in stressful situations. But that was just her way of protecting herself, because she knew at every level that the attraction she had for him was real, and was returned. She thought that they both knew it, and they were feeling their way through the newness.

*God, I wish I weren't so awkward in these things. But I am, and maybe that's good. Don't want to be a slut. Or, maybe I do, but don't want to appear to be. And it's good that he is awkward, too. It's cute.*

She had asked Laurel about Smokey, and Laurel told her that he hadn't dated, hadn't seen anyone since he had been in Afghanistan, since her mother had died a few years ago.

"He's been waiting for you," Laurel had said, grinning, and Jennifer blushed. This kid really wanted them to get together, and Jennifer worried about that, too. What if it didn't work?

Her sweatshirt was wet between the straps of her pack, and she stopped to pull it off. She looked up the trail and saw that Laurel and Smokey had stopped, fifty feet ahead. Smokey bent down and said something to his daughter, and they both laughed.

Jennifer smiled. Their laugh about her made her feel good. Part of them. She stuffed her sweatshirt in her pack and walked toward them, wearing a sleeveless top, jeans and tennis shoes. A beautiful day in the mountains, with two people she was falling helplessly in love with.

She pushed away thoughts of why they were here . . . looking for a body with answers.

She walked up in the shadow of a large pine tree and threw her arms around both of them.

"Hi, guys. Want to kiss me?" She laughed as they both kissed her, Laurel tickling her in the side. As she danced away from the tickle, Jennifer saw Smokey looking at her, serious, questioning.

"What?" she said, dancing away from Laurel.

"Well," he said, "we decided that we both like you. That, well, that . . ."

"That we want to keep you," Laurel yelled. She threw her arms around Jennifer, and they hugged. Jennifer looked over Laurel's hair, smiled at Smokey and nodded.

"I want to keep you two, also."

"For sure?" Laurel said.

"For sure."

Ohmigod, she thought. Here I am, wearing borrowed jeans, borrowed tank top, borrowed tennis shoes (and they all fit pretty good, thanks to Sarah Greywolf) with people I just met, and I feel like I belong here. I could use a few less bad guys shooting at me, but I would never have met Laurel and Smokey. And, Jennifer girl, they did put their lives up for you. Don't forget that.

I haven't even missed my cat. What's up with that. And now I know that people who don't have a life, have a cat.

Plant people.

Chia pet people.

Goldfish people.

Might as well have a gerbil.

A gecko.

Mom had been telling me that I needed to get out more, to have someone else take care of my cat. She never liked Carl. She didn't think he could produce anything resembling a grandchild worth spoiling, and the little bit I told her in the past few days had mom salivating. She was a realist. She didn't worry too much, thought that if I survived, I would go on an ovulating quest.

.

Well, Mom, I certainly have tried to speed things up in the past few days. And if I'm not ovulating, I must be close. I feel like I'm in heat when I get around Smokey.

Laurel had asked a lot of questions, like, "Have you ever been married?" And "Do you like kids?"

Oh, and the great question, "Will you and Daddy give me a baby to take care of?"

Jennifer had blushed again at that one, but she thought about what her answer should have been.

"Yes! Yes! Yes!"

But that had been a day ago, a day before the house burned down, before the shooting, a long time ago. Now she would have said a lot of things. Things she would answer tomorrow. When they got back.

After all, what could happen here in the mountains?

Just a hike, let Smokey take care of the yucky stuff.

After all, we are alone.

Aren't we?

# **Chapter 51**

Near Sunriver Resort

"We know where they are? Right?" Enrico Alvarez glared at the gang banger, his voice flat and hard. His killing voice, his soldiers whispered. He was sitting by the pool with a towel around his middle. A waiter appeared with lunch and he waved him away.

"We have them in sight," Roberto said.

"And where are they?" Alvarez asked.

"They just left their car, up on a logging road. They are walking toward the mountain."

"The woman's there, right? And the *policia* we're going to kill?"

"Yeah, and you're gonna love this. The cop's little girl is with them. Makes it easy to see them, she's wearing a red shirt." He grinned.

"Show me," Alvarez said. "I want to see where our men are."

Justine put a map of the reservation on the table. "Here is where we think the hooker's body is. We have been able to hike in there since they stopped flying the search and rescue helicopters. They will see the cop and the woman coming."

Alvarez leaned over the map.

"We have another group following them from the landing where they parked. From long distance, using spotting scopes and GPS systems, we know about where they are going, so our people shouldn't be seen."

Alvarez grunted. He had seen it all, and knew that his men could still fuck it up. "How far is this, from the Madras Airport to the spot on the mountain, by helicopter?"

"Uh, maybe fifteen minutes, if we know right where to go. They flew fire suppressant helicopters out of the airport for the 2007 Lightening Complex fire in the same area on the reservation. Ten to fifteen minutes. The airport is only two miles from the reservation if you fly straight to the river."

"Get the chopper there, standing by at the airport. We'll bring the Lear up from Sunriver. This better work or Kal-leed and that Indian cop won't be the only ones rotting up there on the mountain."

Alvarez waved lunch over.

"Kill the cop," he said. "Don't hurt the woman or the *nina* if you can help it, especially the woman. If the *nina* gets killed, so be it. If the woman and kid are alive, they'll be going back with us."

"We'll show them a good time before they die."

# Chapter 52

Cold River Indian Reservation
Biddle Pass

Smokey leaned down and studied the trail. They were walking toward Milk Creek through stands of trees. The burn area from the Lightening Complex Fire of 2007 was just ahead. A single burned tree stood up like a black pencil marking the edge of the burn. The tracks on the trail had been bothering him for an hour, and now he studied them.

They were too new.

"Hey, Dad," Laurel said, walking up behind him, "Jennifer wants to . . ."

He held his hand up for her to stop. "Wait here, I want to see the trail."

"Okay, me and Jennifer are going to take our packs off and have some water."

He waved at her to go ahead and looked at the impressions in the trail. The sun highlighted the ridges in the tracks. Smokey followed them with his eyes to a shady patch, then out in the sun again. This wasn't right. He had known it for the past hour, but since he knew pretty much where they were going, he didn't need the trail for that. He had a GPS position for the ledge where he thought they would find the woman's remains.

He thought the footprints might turn in a different direction, and had been made by day hikers, some tribal members up here for a picnic. But they had gone on too far.

There should be tracks on the trail through Biddle Pass. Tracks from the searchers. The search ended four days ago.

*But these tracks are less than four hours old. These tracks were from someone ahead of us, and the tracks were going in, none coming out.*

Three people, three men, three different boot sizes and prints.

*Do I tell the other?. Yeah. Tell them. They need to know.*

"Jennifer, Laurel." He called quietly, aware now for sure that they were not alone.

"We're taking a break, Dad," Laurel said. They laughed. "Yeah, Dad," Jennifer said, and giggled.

He didn't want to ruin their mood, but there was nothing else to be done.

"Hey, guys, I want to show you this." He waited, looking for some sign that he might be wrong. Laurel came up and leaned on his shoulder.

"What's up, Daddy? Or as my friend Tim says, 'sup?"

"I'm looking at tracks here, three men, carrying packs. Maybe four hours ago, six at the most."

"How do you know they are men?" Jennifer asked, leaning in over his left shoulder.

"Length of stride, shoe size, weight, although the weight is not always a determinant. And I've tracked enough people to know. These prints are men's boots, and they are all carrying fairly heavy packs. They walk differently with a pack on, not used to the weight, don't pick their feet up the same way as a normal walk, the heels dig in more. With the packs, they are all well over two hundred pounds."

"You sure?" Jennifer asked.

"Yeah, he's sure," Laurel said.

"Here, I'll show you," Smokey said, "but first, you have to let me up." He walked back up the trail, above where they had stopped.

"Look, this is Jennifer's print. See the shoe size, the length of stride." He pointed to the trail. "And look at Laurel's. Smaller, length of stride. Those prints up there are men."

"What's it mean?" Jennifer asked. She had a worried look on her face. Smokey was instantly sorry for spoiling their day.

"It means three people went up this trail this morning. Maybe hikers. Just stay alert, okay?"

"Okay Dad." Laurel walked down and picked up her pack, looked at Jennifer, and shrugged.

"You sure know how to ruin a hike, Daddy, you sure do."

"Wait a minute," Jennifer said, looking down at the trail. "How do you know that these aren't some of the searchers, the ones looking for me. I mean, there must have been a lot of people on this trail when I was lost. Maybe it's just their tracks."

Smokey took a knee and motioned Jennifer closer. Laurel bent down on the other side.

"We're in a volcanic region, and what looks like dirt on the trail is pumice, very light, porous, and crumbly. Tracks form easily in pumice, but they also lose their shape quickly. Look at this one here." He pointed at the side of the trail.

"This is a track, an old one, now just a large, unformed, rounded impression. The wind for the past week has almost obliterated it." Smokey shifted to the middle of the trail.

"This track, one of the three new ones, is just starting to crumble on the outside, with a line of dirt filling the inside, where the vibram tread is. The more dirt on the inside, the older the track is. Four hours."

*I should turn around now, take them both back. Come back with Nathan, war paint on, full tactical gear. Be ready to take out people if necessary.*

*Ready to kill them.*

Smokey did the next best thing. He pulled the sling of the sniper rifle from his shoulder and carried it at port arms. He started down the trail, following the unknown tracks. But he knew in his gut that the tracks represented a lot of trouble for someone.

A lot of trouble for us.

He looked down the trail. He stopped, removed binoculars from his pack and scanned the countryside. He knew one thing in all of his years up here. The mountain didn't care about mere humans, tribal or not. He put the binoculars away and looked at the two women he loved.

In a few minutes they would enter the burned area, an area where they were exposed, with little or no cover if trouble started.

The area of his dream.

# Chapter 53

Below Biddle Pass

"I don't care if we haven't taken a movie of Bigfoot yet, I want out of here," Amy said. Stan was such a fool sometimes. He was determined to wait one more night, even after finding the remains (and there really wasn't much remaining) of the woman. She had gone along with all of his shit to this point, even helping him move the tent closer to where the woman was, thinking for some reason that Bigfoot was close by. That just didn't make any sense.

"Stan, are you listening to me?" He was in front of the tent, fooling with his dart rifle.

"Stan!"

He looked up. Amy couldn't see any interest or concern in his look, and that made it worse.

"Stan, just wondering, do you have a real gun in that bag of crap you carry with you?"

"You know I don't like guns, Amy. They just cause problems." He went back to wiping a cloth on his dart gun.

"Well, someone has been killing people here on the reservation, maybe putting dead people here, might be a good time to rethink the whole gun thing. I'm pretty sure Bigfoot is going to be none too happy about you shooting it, him, her, whatever, with the dart gun. I don't know or care, all I know is I want to go back to Albany. That town never looked so good. It might even smell better, certainly better than us by now. Stan are you *listening* to me?"

"Yes, Amy," Stan said, sounding to her like he was bored, trying to humor her. Keep her quiet.

"In fact, Bigfoot is probably heading for the next county with all your chatter." He lowered his voice. "See that rock face over there? I'm gonna be there this afternoon, hiding with the dart gun. May stay there all night. Then, no matter what happens, if I see Bigfoot or not, we'll hike out in the morning. Satisfied? Only, it would help if you could be a little quieter."

She looked at the rock face across the canyon, near where they had found the woman.

*This is way too close for me. I'm not going with Stan tonight, I'm gonna stay in camp and then get the hell out of here in the morning.*

Amy had to admit, Stan's idea of being set for life appealed to the part of her that wanted to set up a preserve for the animal, a large tract of land, maybe in Montana, or on the upper peninsula rain forest in Washington State. So she would go with Stan after all this afternoon. She had come this far.

"When we gonna get the hell out of here?" the Eighteenth Street gang member whined. Roberto glanced at the tweeker. He wanted this to be over as well, to quit fucking around in the United States. He also wanted to be rid of the little asshole they were saddled with on this particular hike. He wondered if the boss would let Justine kill the gang banger before they left. Leave him on the mountain. But they had needed him to get them on the trail.

They had hiked in during the morning. Everything had changed with the disastrous assault on the cop's house. Well, this was the cop's last day on earth.

They set up in a large group of trees, on the hillside near a shear rock outcropping, close to where they thought the hooker was. This should have been over days ago, Roberto thought, except for the lost woman.

"Roberto." Justine was laying over a log, looking through a spotting scope. A sniper rifle was propped on the log next to him. Roberto kneeled down.

"Roberto, I see them, on the trail, there." Justine pointed up toward the round mountain, back the way they had come. "About to enter the burn area."

"How far?" Roberto asked. Things were going to happen quickly now.

"Maybe a mile. If they go to the cliff, they will pass within two hundred yards of us. The little girl is wearing a red shirt. Spot them pretty easy from now on.

"We need to take them close if we can, but the cop is good, don't want to give him a chance. We'll take him first, then capture the woman. I don't want to get into a foot chase. Take them close."

"How about I take the *nina* first?" Justine asked, picking up the rifle and looking through the scope.

"Take the cop first, no mistakes."

Justine grinned, still looking through the rifle scope.

Roberto kneeled and looked through the spotting scope. It took him a minute to find them, then he saw a flash of red. They were on the trail, fifteen hundred meters. The cop was in front, carrying a rifle of his own, the girl with a red t-shirt was next, and then the woman. She also had a rifle, slung on her back.

The cop was the threat.

Wouldn't be long now.

# **C**hapter **54**

Smokey stopped at the edge of the burn area. In the sun the place seemed surreal – Mt. Jefferson dominated the western landscape with glaciers on the south and east side. He looked at the blackened area, a strip hundreds of yards wide and five miles long in the middle of paradise, a dark and twisted lunar landscape in the middle of green. For the next half mile, the area resembled the dark side of the moon.

Laurel threw her pack down and took a long drink from her water bottle. Sweat streamed down her face.

"Dad, must be a hundred up here," she said, blowing her breath out.

"Two hundred," Jennifer said, working her water out. She raised it to her lips and looked over the bottle at Smokey.

He turned and watched them as Jennifer shrugged her pack off as well. She pulled her bottle down and looked over the valley in front of them. She stayed in that position, frozen, and Smokey followed her stare.

She pointed.

"There!" She said, the excitement in her voice coming to Smokey.

"What?" But he knew as he looked. The rock wall, partially obscured by burned trees was across the valley from them.

Jennifer's heart pounded. She forgot about the heat. She was back again, lost on the mountain, staggering around, scared out of her wits, trembling after running headlong in the twilight. Now she knew that the thing she wrapped in the cloth wasn't her Nanna, but was a thing too horrible to accept. She knew at some level that her mind just wouldn't let her see what it really was, that she needed her doll to survive, so she made the awful fleshy artifact her doll.

There it is, the place she had dreamed about all these days, the place where she found the hand, the place where she had seen something too horrible to remember. Something that had put her at the center of a violent group of criminals. Something that meant a lot of people died, including some of the innocent people on the reservation. The hand.

*It was dark, Jennifer. It was too dark to see.*

Close your eyes and go back to the dark time. Close them and see what you found.

She closed her eyes, unaware that Smokey and Laurel were watching her.

*It's dark now. I'm holding Nanna, looking down at the ground at the base of the rock cliff. It's getting cold in the night, the darkness, what's in the darkness making bumps on my neck? I'm afraid to turn around. Things here I don't want to see. Open your eyes.*

And she opened her eyes, standing on the trail with Smokey and Laurel, seeing only darkness.

Jennifer didn't see Laurel step over to take her hand, and Smokey motioning his daughter away, putting his arm around Laurel as they watched.

Jennifer was standing on the trail in mid-afternoon, feeling the cool of the evening a week ago, looking into the darkness. She saw it, the thing she blocked, coming back to her in the dark. A moonlit night, the scene below the cliff, a place she wandered upon while running from the body of the man, running, screaming, and finding something too horrible to imagine. When you are lost.

*Jennifer, you know what was there. What you left there. The thing they wanted.*

*The hand attached to the briefcase.*

She could see her flight that night, an almost out-of-body viewing, watching as the frightened Jennifer ran headlong into the cliff, falling down to her knees, and in the moonlight seeing something that did not belong in the woods.

A black square object. Shiny. Leather.

A briefcase.

A severed hand attached. She laughed. It reminded her of diamond merchants carrying their wares, only someone had removed the handcuffs the hard way. A handcuffed hand on an attaché case.

Except now there were no handcuffs.

She touched the hand.

Pretty nails. Glitter.

*Don't look at the end, where the wrist used to be, neatly cut, a surgical cut, or maybe a butcher's cut (I'll take the veal), sharp implement, the tendons white nubs in the flesh, the metacarpal bones orderly and neat, like small white mints sticking out of the flesh.*

*Don't look.*
She caressed the hand.
*Nanna.*
*The hand looked cold, like Nanna. I'm just gonna pry it loose, wrap it in a piece of my shirt, like I used to carry my Nanna.*
*Nanna. Where have you been? I'm getting out of here with you, Nanna. We'll go out together. Away from here.*

Jennifer closed her eyes, still seeing the lost Jennifer with a grisly artifact, not a doll, as the lost Jennifer believed.

She felt the heat of the sun, and gradually became aware of where she was, back on the mountain, this time with Smokey and his daughter. She opened her eyes.

"I know what they are looking for," she said as she walked to Smokey and Laurel. She put her arms around the two people who would save the Jennifer who had been lost before she started on the expedition. Lost and she didn't know it.

Breathing.

Alive.

But not like this.

"What are they doing?" Roberto asked, reaching for the scope.

"They're stopped on the trail. Pointing at the mountain."

Roberto grabbed the scope. "They're not pointing at the mountain, *puta*, they're pointing at that. The cliff. Idiot."

"Keep watching, don't let him see any reflection. We'll be at the cliff when they arrive."

He pushed himself back on his stomach until he was below the small rise, out of sight of the trail where the cop stood. "Oh," he said, turning back to look at the shooter, "kill the cop first, on my command."

Stan was out ahead of Amy, moving cautiously, exaggerating each step to be as quiet as possible. He stopped every hundred feet to look at the screen in his GPS tracker. The blinking light for the location of Bigfoot hadn't moved (if that was what he had shot last night). The animal should be close to the base of the cliff across the way, and he was approaching it as one would stalk a grizzly bear. Careful. Out of sight.

Even though Bigfoot was supposed to be nocturnal, he must be sleeping nearby. With the tracking dart, if they could get a film, they had every chance to get a movie. A new movie would make him more famous than the 1967 film. They could now track Bigfoot to his home, and they would get a film.

He watched his screen one more time and looked for a route that would take them through the trees to the top of the cliff. He looked behind him and saw Amy walking around a tree a hundred yards back. Good girl. She's stepping softly, getting into the game.

There. Movement up ahead. He held the monitor steady.

There, on the trail. Something moved up ahead, halfway to the cliff, maybe a hundred fifty yards. His heart raced. He was going to see, for the first time in his life, a giant biped here in the forest.

*But it's not the one on the monitor. Another one, of course. There would be more than one.*

Proof.

He walked forward, crouching. There. A flash of red.

He stepped around a tree, camera ready. A bandanna, tied on a piece of bitterbrush.

*What the hell?"*

"Amigo!"

The sound came from directly behind Stan. He whirled with the camera, more puzzled than afraid.

A man stood on the trail behind him, holding a knife in his right hand. He wore black pants, the army kind, Stan thought, and a camouflage shirt. Some kind of floppy hat. Black hair on his shoulders.

The man was grinning.

Stan dropped the GPS unit and dug in his pack for the dart rifle.

"Who –"

And he knew where the bodies came from, that this man was responsible. He wished he had a gun for the first time in his life. He backed up the trail and went down, pulling the pack on top of him.

"Noooooo!"

The knife hit his throat and the grinning man jumped on top of him. Stan's blood pumped out down his chest, and he found he didn't have time to be afraid.

"Amy!" He yelled her name. It came out as a gurgle, and he knew it was going to be bad. So much blood. He tried to push the knife out, the grinning man still on top, holding him down.

*Amy, ah, Amy.*

He died on the trail, wondering why he couldn't see Bigfoot.

"Get the camera," Roberto said. "We can record what happens to those who meddle with us."

What a beautiful day, Amy thought. She stopped and looked around, not wanting to get too far behind Stan. She saw him on the trail, his head down, looking at his hand-held GPS.

She gave a little wave, wanting him to look up so he would know she wasn't too far behind. A man materialized on the trail, and from where she was it looked as if he was right behind Stan. Where the hell did he come from?

She wanted to yell, but he had insisted that they remain as quiet as possible.

*Stan, behind you! Look up!*

Amy stood in the trail and watched. At least they were talking. Stan had looked up and was talking to the man.

This isn't right. Stan was walking backward, and then he went down. When the man jumped on Stan she couldn't see the knife, but the sudden spurt of blood made her cry out.

He was killing Stan!

She started to run toward them, crying, she started to yell his name, and then she stopped. Another man had joined the killer on the trail. They stood looking down at Stan, and she was sure that he was dead. She could see the blood on the trail from where she was.

*If they look around, they'll see you.*

She was now only fifty yards behind them, exposed. She took a trembling step behind her. She slid behind a tree to her left, tears streaming down her face. She shook, and forced herself to look out again. The men were bending over Stan. They took his camera, and walked up the trail and out of sight.

*Go to him.*

*No, they'll see you. Kill you.*

*Who are they?*

*People who kill, the ones who kill on the mountain.*

When they were out of sight, Amy hesitated, and then she ran to him. She sat in the trail and touched his face and tried not to look at the horrible gash in his neck. He was weird, but he was her weird, and he hadn't ever hurt anyone that she could remember. She suddenly felt exposed and very alone.

She picked up his pack and looked inside.

*They don't know me. They don't know that I was working in a mill when I was sixteen, out on my own by seventeen.*

She felt the beginnings of anger and let it grow, keeping it tight inside, her mouth forming in a grim thin line. Some people would call it "spunk," but it was a look her mother had said was her "fuck somebody up" look. Amy reached in the pack and found the stock and barrel of the dart rifle. The small laptop was laying next to Stan's outstretched hand. She put the dart rifle and laptop in her pack, stood, took a last look at Stan, tucked away her last sob for now, and started cautiously up the trail.

*I'm going to track them. Follow them. Mark them with a dart. Could track them anywhere then.*

*Gonna fuck somebody up.*

# Chapter 55

Smokey stood in the trail and talked to Nathan on his cell. He was surrounded by the ravages of the forest fire, amazed at the rejuvenation in just a few years. Grass and brush had returned. The burned trees were the reminder of the fire that burned for a month. The cliff was close. They were barely a hundred yards to the end of the burn.

"Where are you now?"

"About two miles behind you, coming fast," Nathan said.

"We'll wait at the cliff that we talked about, Big Brother. Don't get lost out here in the big old woods."

"Just take care of yourself and Laurel and Jennifer until I get there. Like you said, you aren't alone out here. Company somewhere."

Smokey snapped the phone closed and looked at Jennifer. "You up for this?"

She nodded. "Let's get it done and get out of here. I've had enough woods for one summer."

"Yeah, Dad, we wanna go shopping. Move it, Dad." Laurel had her arm around Jennifer's waist.

"Deal," Smokey said. He shook off the dread he had been feeling. *Just stay sharp.*

He pulled the rifle off his shoulder and carried it in a combat-ready position. He was as ready as he could be.

Roberto looked at the cop. They were close enough that he didn't need the scope. It had been apparent for some time that the cop and the woman and girl were heading for the base of the cliff.

Roberto and his men were in a thicket of trees at the south end of the sheer rock face. He knew they were well hidden, but they had to be careful. He had heard what the cop could do. He turned to the man with the camera.

"Got the picture?"

He got a thumbs up.

The shooter covered the cop with one of the assault rifles.

When the cop arrived at the cliff, he was as good as dead.

Amy followed the path uphill, using brush and trees for cover at every opportunity. She knew that at this point, it didn't matter which way she walked. She was probably in as much danger going this way as any other. She was not lost, not with all of Stan's mapping devices, and she knew how to get off the mountain and out of the woods. She had food and water. She was going to find the killers. And she wished like she had never wished before that she had a real gun instead of the dart rifle.

It didn't occur to her to run away, to put as much distance as she could from the killers. Her mom and friends always accused her of being stubborn, and with her mouth set in a firm thin line, she followed along the route the men took. She was scared, but determined. She had the beginning of a plan.

The path took her to the top of a sheer rock face, a cliff of over a hundred feet; this is the way the killers had gone.

When she got to the top, she lay on her stomach and looked out over the edge. The burn area stretched out below She saw movement down and to her right. There, in the trees. One of the killers lay behind a tree, looking through a rifle scope.

She saw more color in the burn area. A man approached, a man carrying a rifle. He looked familiar, and then she knew who he was. He was the cop who had talked to them about the lost hiker. And he has a woman and a little girl with him.

*I need to warn them.*

*They're walking right toward the killers.*

Amy picked up her pack and began assembling the dart rifle.

*It's all I got.*

*And they killed my friend Stan.*

Smokey walked out of the burn area. The trees here were green and alive, untouched by the fire that had raged only a few yards away. The fire had burned up the canyon and left trees untouched on either side. Maybe the rock cliff had blocked the airflow.

"Smokey." Jennifer came up behind him and stopped, putting her hand on his arm. He turned to look at her. She was watching the cliff.

"This where you were, where you found the hand?"

She pointed. "There, that split in the rocks, I was here before, I'm sure of it."

He looked at the area where she pointed, and nodded. Laurel held Jennifer's hand and stood on her tiptoes to see better. Smokey shrugged, pulled his rifle down, and walked up the trail through the trees to the cliff.

*At least it's cooler here, Laurel will like that.*

In the burned area, they were in the direct sunlight. Here at the base of the cliff, sheltered by the trees, it was twenty degrees cooler.

A piece of color caught his eye and he stopped. A piece of cloth, caught on a rock at the base of the cliff.

The smell hit him then, the odor of decay, of rotten flesh. He took shallow breaths through his mouth. Smokey heard a noise and looked back to see Laurel holding her hand over her mouth, gagging.

The animals had made good work out of the body during the past week. This was the final resting place of Kal-leed's girlfriend. Smokey revered the dead, no matter how they lived when they were walking the earth. A few scattered bits of cloth, part of a blouse. Metatarsal bones peeked out of the dirt, half buried. A shoe. A skull, cracked and chewed. A long bone, a femur, and part of the rib cage. What they had come for, the prize, the reason for all the killing, was there, at the base of the cliff. The *spilyay* and the *anahuy* had been here several times. Coyote and Mr. Bear.

Battered.

No longer shiny.

A black metal briefcase.

*It held the secrets to a drug empire, the connection to the terrorists and the cartels. I don't have to open it to know that much.*

"I was here," Jennifer said. She pointed at the ground. "The woman was lying on her side, her hand missing, her . . . her head -." Smokey glanced up at her and knew that she was back to that day, the day of discovery, the day she found a hand and renamed the horror her "Nanna."

Smokey circled the dead.

Roberto pressed the spotting scope eyepiece to his cheek.

*The briefcase.*

Roberto kept his hand on the scope and turned his head. "You have a shot?"

"Si, whenever you say.

"Shoot him, then let's get down there quick, don't want the woman to run off with the briefcase."

Nathan looked down at the valley of dead trees. He had a mile to go, at least ten minutes with the trail the way it was, even humping fast. He heard the others come up behind him. Sarah. Burwell. Kincaid. Sergeant Lamebull. Chief Andrews. He knew they had to hurry. Bad things gonna happen.

The sound of a shot rolled across the valley. The direction of the shot was hard to pinpoint here in the rugged terrain, but he knew it was from a large caliber weapon.

*That wasn't Little Brother shooting.*

*We gotta go now.*

*But we're gonna be too late.*

He led them down the trail, as close to a run as he could make it, reckless, jumping where he could, not caring if the others could keep up.

*Hold on.*

Nathan had a sick feeling in his stomach as he ran. He held his rifle up high and mouthed an ancient prayer for his brother.

Smokey bent over and picked up the briefcase. As he turned to talk to Jennifer and Laurel something slammed into his shoulder, the sledgehammer blow spraying blood out against the rock face.

*Shot. I've been shot. Ah, God, my baby girl.*

Smokey flipped over on his back, hearing Laurel's scream, and then everything went black.

"Daddy!" Laurel screamed and ran to him, crying, dropping her pack and throwing herself down on her knees beside him.

*Oh, Dad, there's a lot of blood, don't die, you can't leave me alone, please Daddy, don't die.*

Jennifer dropped on her knees beside Laurel. She was surprisingly calm, now that it was her turn to be the one in charge, the one who would hold them all together. She didn't know she could do such a thing until now. She pulled a shirt from her pack and pressed it directly on the wound in Smokey's shoulder, blood spreading out under him.

She pulled on his arm and got the shirt around and under him, pressing hard down, the blood slowing.

His eyes fluttered. He tried to talk.

"Sorry," he mumbled. Jennifer bent over him as Laurel sobbed, holding her daddy's hand.

"-care of Laurel," he croaked.

"Don't talk," Jennifer said. She was vaguely aware of people coming up on them, footsteps, people speaking rapid Spanish sentences, then commands.

"Stand up!"

She pressed on the t-shirt, remained over Smokey.

The man with the gun stood over her and screamed again.

"He'll die," Jennifer said.

She was pulled to her feet by her hair and whirled around and thrown down by a dark man, throwing her bloody hands out in front of her to break her fall. She caught a glance of another man with a video camera.

*A video*?

Jennifer shook her head and tried to get to her feet as Laurel threw herself on Smokey, and then the girl was tugging at the pistol in his belt holster, screaming.

"I'll kill you, all of you!" Laurel pulled the gun free.

The dark man took a step and kicked Laurel and the gun went flying.

"Don't touch her!" Jennifer jumped up and was on the dark man. She swung at him, a glancing blow at his shoulder, and he slapped her down with an open hand. She fell beside Laurel, and for the first time, she knew that they would die here. The man with the rifle stood over Smokey, and the dark man nodded. Jennifer pushed herself up and threw herself at the man with the gun.

Nathan came out of the burned area at a dead run. He stopped long enough to rest his rifle on a tree, willing his breathing to slow, still four hundred yards away, and put his scope on the scene at the base of the hill.

With his rifle scope at twelve power, the figures swept into focus, and he watched as Jennifer was smacked down, then Laurel. When the man stood over Little Brother, he knew that he had to take a shot.

*Shoot well, Big Brother. Shoot straight.*

He timed the movement of the barrel with his breathing, and took the shot.

Nathan began to run.

He knew he would be too late.


Amy held her hand over her mouth when the cop was shot. She had flinched at the shot and watched in horror as the cop went down. His blood sprayed out on the rocks.

*Must be his daughter, and the woman who was lost. What the hell are they doing here?*

She watched as the men came out of the trees to her left, two of them with guns, one with a camera.

*Stan's camera.*

The guys who killed Stan. She wriggled forward, pushed the tip of the dart gun over the edge of the cliff and waited for her chance. The man with the rifle stood over the cop and Amy knew then that she had to do something or the cop would be shot again. She lined up the air rifle and pulled the trigger.

The man with the gun went down, and the woman went down on top of him. Got him.

*What the hell?*

Amy pulled the air rifle back and looked in wonder at the small gun.

*Did I do that?*

*This air rifle didn't do that. There, across the burn area. Movement. Someone coming. People running. Someone coming way too late, for my money. At least if they are the good guys I won't have to walk out alone. I can get someone to help me with Stan.*

She slid back away from the edge and watched as the two men who killed Stan grabbed the woman and girl and ran them back up toward the trees, away from the cliff. One of them carried a briefcase.

She waited for the others to arrive, Indian cops from the look of them. When they got to the base of the hill they worked on the cop who was shot. Three of them ran up the hill after the woman and girl, their faces grim as they ran past.

Amy slid back and worked her way down the hill to meet them.

# Chapter 56

Mountain View Hospital
Madras

Smokey opened his eyes and tried to focus. Pain came over him in waves. The faces of his crew, Big Brother Nathan, Chief Andrews, and Sarah came to him. Nathan had blood on his shirt, as did Sarah. She looked as if she had been crying, clean streaks on her dirty face. She took his hand. .

A doctor in a white coat loomed into view. New guy. Young.

"You're lucky," the ER doctor said. "A few inches one way or the other, you wouldn't be here with us. The bullet didn't hit a bone, we can patch this up." He leaned over Smokey.

"Took some meat out of the trapezes. You're headed for surgery, pull things together, you'll be down a few weeks."

Smokey shook his head. He couldn't figure out what happened. Where he had been.

*And where is Laurel? Jennifer?*

Then it came back to him. He'd been shot. At the base of the cliff, Laurel and Jennifer had been with him. He had just found the briefcase and then was shot.

"Laurel," he croaked. He looked around at the others. Sarah wouldn't meet his gaze. He settled on Nathan.

"Big Brother. Tell me."

Amy sat in the small waiting room, waiting to ask someone to help her with transportation to Albany. She had to figure out what to do next. From the looks of it, there wasn't much public transportation in Madras. Maybe the Indians would help. She needed to figure out what to do with Stan's remains. His body would be here in a funeral home they said.

She began pulling things out of Stan's pack, thinking that she needed a shower. Shower first, and then food. That's what I'll do, she thought, get a ride to a motel, spend the night, and work on all of this in the morning.

The trip out of the hills had been fast. Four of them carried the cop, Smokey, out to a clearing, then loaded him on Air Life to the hospital. She had walked with two of them to the landing and they drove like wild people to town. She told them on the way about Stan, and about what she saw from the top of the cliff.

She pulled Stan's small laptop out and turned it on. It came up to the mapping program, and she watched as a red light moved slowly across the screen.

It wasn't working right. She resisted the urge to smack the computer (it worked on her radio) and watched the blinking red light on the display of a map of Oregon. The light was showing in southern Oregon, almost to the Nevada border. But that couldn't be. There was another light showing on the reservation, somewhere near the cliff.

*What the hell?*

The second blinking light, according to the map, was now in Nevada, moving at a high rate of speed.

On a plane.

And then she knew.

Amy held the laptop in front of her like a hot serving dish, and ran for the emergency room, her ponytail bobbing up and down as she ran.

She heard yelling as she got there. The cops were holding Smokey down.

He was screaming.

It took her a while to get their attention.

When she had fired the dart, she explained, she hadn't hit the man as she thought. He was in the morgue. Not moving.

She had hit the woman with her dart.

She could track her.

Anywhere in the world.

In the bedlam that followed, Smokey sat long enough to get taped up, the doctor at first refusing, then arguing until Smokey looked at him.

"I'm not signing you out," the young doctor said, and then added, "this will probably kill you, leaving the hospital."

"Got some killing of my own to do, Doc," Smokey said. There was going to be a lot of singing on the hill before this was over.

*Gonna find my baby, and this good woman, Jennifer. And hell will visit those who took them.*

He listened as Chief Martin Andrews gave orders.

"Get Weasel," Chief Andrews said.

# Chapter 57

Gulfstream Five-fifty

Weasel reached forward and touched the controls of the Gulfstream Five-fifty and sat back, the onboard computer doing everything but gas up the finest business jet in the world. The Five-fifty was a fifty million dollar aircraft, with a waiting list for delivery for even the average billionaire.

He looked over at Charley, his co-pilot and friend. Charley was an Ogallala Sioux, and a former Air Force pilot. They were flying the G-550 for a consortium of Indian casinos, flying high rollers from Asia to a selected few casinos. Weasel was the chief pilot for the leased plane.

Weasel loved flying. He had grown up on the Cold River Indian Reservation, and had escaped by going to flight school right out of high school, courtesy of the tribes. He had flown for Freedom Airlines right out of flight school, and for a time, had almost forgotten that he was Indian. One day a couple of years ago, when he was flying out of LAX, the tribal chairman of the reservation had called him and had him pay what was owed – a dangerous rescue flight to Peru – and an even more dangerous flight back to a reservation under siege. Weasel's landing of a G-5 on a reservation highway had made him a hero at home.

Cindy is visiting my mother, how strange is that? My Šiyápu wife and our boys visiting my mother.

He smiled, thinking of his nine and twelve-year-old sons on the reservation. They had been raised in Los Angeles, so it wouldn't be easy for them, but they would cope. Starting a family relationship with my people. And I have become Weasel again, my childhood name.

"Charley." Weasel looked over at the right seat. Charley raised his eyebrows and nodded.

"I'm gonna go check on the passengers, go to the head, get a snack. You want anything?"

"No, I'm good, I can wait for San Diego."

The passengers were a group of Japanese men, industrialist billionaires, flying around to various Indian casinos, spending money that only the super rich can afford. A kind of VIP in platinum letters.

But hey, it allowed Weasel to fly the finest jet in the world, and be home often.

"Your aircraft," he said to Charley, as he unbuckled.

Weasel went back and nodded at the two groups of men, three around a table playing cards, betting loudly. One reading, and one sleeping.

"Hai!" A short round man threw cards on the table and grinned. He looked up.

"Hello, Captain."

"Everything alright?" Weasel stopped at the table.

"It is fine, Captain. We are enjoying the cruise, waiting to see who wins the most at the very fine Barona casino in San Diego. And we have dates there waiting. Will we be on time?"

Weasel looked at his watch.

"We'll land in ninety-three minutes, if the air traffic control people cooperate."

"Excellent, thank you *captain*."

Weasel smiled, and walked to the back of the plane. When he returned to the cockpit, things began to be less than fine.

"Weasel," Charley said, "you got a call when you were away."

"What call?"

"Someone on your reservation, man called Bluefeathers."

*Oh shit. What does that weathered old man wan? But I can't refuse. I owe. And besides, he is part of me.*

Weasel dialed, then listened, thinking that he has known since that last time that it wouldn't be the end. And he knew the ways of the rez. He was *expected* to be the go-to person, the one they counted on, and he knew that whatever the cost, he couldn't refuse. He had to go. He said one word.

"Yes."

Weasel listened for another minute, nodding, his stomach doing a slow roll. Well, it wouldn't be dull. He waited for Bluefeathers to finish, but the old coot had to take the passengers off his hands.

"I'll be there, Madras airport," Weasel said. "Thirty minutes, and get the red carpet people from the casino to take these passengers off my hands."

He closed the phone and slipped it into his shirt pocket. Unlike the airlines, they frequently used their cellular phones, and allowed their passengers to do so as well.

"Where the hell's Madras Airport?" Charley asked, his voice showing his interest for the first time in the flight.

Weasel gave him the GPS coordinates from memory. "Call Seattle Center and change our flight plan. We're gonna pick up some additional passengers. I'll call the rez and have our casino people take our high rollers to Kah-Nee-Ta, treat them well."

*The bosses, they're gonna kill us for this. Might lose my job again. We'll see how much pull the old coot Bluefeathers has after this. We might as well file an amended flight plan. I think that could be the last legal thing we do with this aircraft.*

Weasel, former airline captain, formerly known in Los Angeles as Leonard Mitchell, spoke softly to his co-pilot.

"My airplane," he said, as he started his descent for something that was sure to be interesting, certainly dangerous, and terminally stupid.

Twenty-nine minutes later, he made the landing at the Madras Jefferson County Airport, eight miles from the rez.

"You ever been a hero on your rez?" Weasel asked Charley. He turned the big plane and found the taxiway, pointing the nose toward a small terminal.

"Maybe a little, being an airforce pilot and all," Charley said, grinning over at Weasel.

"Well you will be one on my rez, after this." Weasel said.

*If you live, Charley. If you live. Because I think on this one, there will be a whole lot of people shooting at us.*

*Sort of like the last one.*

*Only this one sounds like it will be worse.*

*Another foreign country. People with guns.*

*Worse.*

*And it was.*

# Chapter 58

"You really should be in a critical care unit for a day so we can watch you." The doctor checked the tape on Smokey's neck.

"Just make these tight enough to where I can move and not rip them open again."

The emergency room doctor, Doctor Evans's replacement, was on loan from a Portland hospital, and he was not happy. "You need to be back here soon, then, no later than tomorrow."

"I'll either be back tomorrow, or dead," Smokey said, and then spoke softly to himself. "They took my daughter, and there will be a lot of them dead before they get me." He looked at the doctor.

"Help me up."

Chief Martin Andrews stuck his head in the room. "Plane will be at the Madras Airport by the time you get there."

Smokey tried to stand, his head spinning, and he put his hand out for Martin.

*Gotta go, need to get going.*

"Doc, we need to have a meeting in here," Smokey said. The others were filing into the ER room. Sarah wore full battle gear, followed by Nathan, and the young woman Amy, with her computer.

The others crowded around.

"As you know by now," Smokey said, "the cartel has Laurel and Jennifer. We think they flew out in a Lear approximately two hours ago." A sudden picture of Laurel came to him, of her laughing at him when he came home from work, and he stopped.

*She can't die*

He shook his head. "We have a Gulfstream coming to pick some of us up, and we're going to get them back. It won't be pretty. We may have to go into Mexico to do it, and this is strictly volunteer, except for Nathan, I need you with me Uncle."

"I'm going," Sarah said.

"Kincaid and Burwell," Smokey said. "Sergeant Lamebull, Sarah, Nathan, and myself. That's it. The rest will guard the reservation." He looked at Martin Andrews.

"Chief, any comments?"

"We've been down this path before," Martin said. "I'll get in touch with Oakley, not to alert them of your plans, but if you have to cross into Mexico, you'll need them to get you back without getting shot down."

Smokey stood and took a step, then stopped and waited for the spinning to subside. Sarah held up a camo shirt and helped him into it. "Where's the computer girl, Amy?"

"Right here." Amy stepped forward, holding her laptop, looking at the screen.

"Where are they now?"

"Over Utah, I think."

Smokey turned to Martin. "We need to get some expertise here, range of the Lear, where they filed a plan to, might stop for fuel, maybe we can intercept them before they cross into Mexico."

Martin opened his cell and stepped away.

"Amy." Smokey motioned her forward. "Amy, can you show us how to run the program?"

She shook her head. No. "It would take too much time," she said. "Besides, they killed my friend. I'm coming with you, you need me to track them."

Smokey didn't argue. She was right, they needed her.

"How many people will the Gulfstream hold?"

"We can probably take six or eight with gear," Sarah said, "with enough room to bring them back." She put her hand on Smokey. "Hold still."

He turned and held his arm out, unable to move without the room spinning.

"Oakley will help on this end, feebs are starting to track the Lear," Martin said, walking over, cell phone up to his ear. He held a finger up, listening. He looked at Smokey.

"Oakley says to remind you that Mexico is a sovereign nation, that the feds can't help you there if you cross the border."

"Tell Oakley that we are also a sovereign nation," Smokey said, "but that didn't stop them from attacking us."

*We're gonna attack them so fast and hard they will think they are in hell before they get sent there, they harm my daughter further. And Jennifer.*

243

Smokey held his hand out for his web gear and shrugged into it with Sarah's mothering help.

"Let's get moving," he said. "We will get my daughter back."

*In Afghanistan they thought I was crazy, that I fought like a madman when we were shot at. These people who make war on my daughter, they better pray that it will be quick for them, 'cause whether or not I get her back, I will kill them all.*

*I will.*

*They're already dead, they just don't know it yet.*

*Harm my Laurel, I'll kill everyone they ever met.*

# Chapter 59

Southern Utah
Aboard Lear

When Jennifer woke up she knew instantly that she was on a plane, even though she was blindfolded and her hands were painfully bound. The hum and vibration of the engines seemed close, as if they were in the back of the plane.

Jennifer's shoulder ached where Laurel was laying on it. Laurel snored fitfully, murmuring. It hurt Jennifer to move. She tried to breathe through her nose but it was caked with blood, sounded like she was wheezing when she tried. Her mouth wasn't much better; she thought two of her teeth were loose.

She remembered being bound and then kicked, Laurel crying out, screaming, and then being loaded on a small jet plane. After that, Jennifer didn't remember much. She didn't know how long they had been on the plane, but it seemed like several hours.

She had a sudden sense of panic, her breathing speeding up, breathing through her mouth now, and she thought that they would be killed soon. And poor Laurel. A child and a sweet kid.

*I don't want to die, but I will protect this child.*

Laurel shifted and cried out. The voices in the front of the plane stopped, then someone laughed, then they started talking again.

"Shhhhh," Jennifer whispered. She nudged Laurel with her shoulder.

"Jen?" Laurel sounded muffled, her face in Jennifer's shoulder.

"Yes, Honey?"

"Jen, I love you."

Jennifer had a sudden burst of tears, soaking the cloth tied around her face, her welling up of emotion unexpected, too quick to stop. She worked her way lower in the seat, drawing Laurel more on top of her.

"I love you too, Honey. So very much."

"Jen." Laurel whispered.

"What?"

"Jen, what will happen to us?"

"I don't know, but these are very bad people."

245

"Jen, they're in terrible danger."

"What do you mean?"

"Because my daddy's gonna come for us, and he's going to be very mad."

Jennifer wished for the very same thing, but she had seen Smokey go down with the gunshot.

*God, I hope so. I hope so, but I don't see how he can survive the gunshot, let alone find us.*

"Jen," Laurel whispered, sounding as if she were sucking her thumb.

"What, Honey?"

"Jen, Daddy's coming for us. He isn't dead, he's coming for us." She sucked on her thumb for another minute, and then said, "You'll see."

Smokey lurched out of the hospital and into the afternoon heat. The officers ran for their cars, Nathan and Sarah held Smokey up, with Chief Martin Andrews following.

"I'm going to sit this one out," Martin said. "Bluefeathers said it was to be your operation."

"Bluefeathers did, did he?"

"He said to tell you to not forget about Laurel's gifts, her special way of looking at the world."

*I'm her father, how can I forge? I lost her mother, now I have lost her.*

For a moment, Smokey stopped and his knees grew weak. Martin put his arm around him and pulled him upright.

"I know you have to go," Martin said, "even if you should be in ICU right now." As they approached the Suburban, Martin bent and whispered something to Sarah. She looked at Smokey and nodded.

Smokey got into the passenger seat of the car, clenching his teeth as the pain made him dizzy.

"Let's get this thing moving," he said, and Nathan accelerated out of the parking lot, escorted in front by Madras PD.

*We've got a long way to go, Smokey. Gotta find baby girl. Gotta find my baby. Bring her back safe.*

# Chapter 60

Aboard Gulfstream 550

Weasel had the plane rolling as Smokey eased down in a leather covered chair, gear and officers piled up behind him. On another day he would have appreciated the plush cabin and all of the comforts the G-550 had to offer. He tried to ignore the pain of his wound, and waved Sarah away as she started to hover.

"Amy, bring your laptop up here," Smokey said, motioning to the girl. Amy sat across from him as the acceleration of the take-off pushed him back in the seat. She placed the laptop on the table and turned the screen so Smokey could see it. Smokey looked at the outline of the Western United States on the display. Amy pointed to Utah and at a flashing red light.

"That signal is for the dart I shot at the men below the cliff, and I now think that I hit the woman, Jennifer. Each dart has its own code, like a transponder."

"What's that signal?" Smokey pointed at Central Oregon.

"That's the dart we shot the night before," Amy said. "Don't know if it hit anything, but we couldn't find it."

Smokey called for Weasel to join them. The pain in his shoulder flared, as if someone had just stabbed him with a butcher knife, again and again. He pointed to the screen. "Can we catch them?"

"Depends on where they are going," Weasel said. "They are about an hour and a half in front of us. If they operate at normal cruise speed with a Bombardier Learjet 45 they will be cruising about fifty miles per hour slower than we are."

Smokey's cell phone rang. He reached for it and couldn't make his arm work. He could feel blood seeping down his chest. Sarah leaned over him and picked it up, her face a mask of worry.

"Smokey's phone," she said, and listened, and then said, "I'll put it on speaker, he's here."

She placed the phone on the table and said, "It's Oakley."

"This is what we have," Oakley said. "We're tracking the Lear, they are in southern Utah now, and I'm told that you are following them in some way as well. We think that the Alvarez Cartel, with

247

Alvarez himself on board, is taking your daughter and Jennifer Kruger to a ranch north of Hermosillo, Mexico, where they have a meth superlab.

Smokey felt cold. "Alvarez? The YouTube guy?"

"Yeah, that's him," Oakley said. "They have filed a flight plan for Phoenix to refuel, then on to Hermosillo. However we believe they can make the distance without refueling."

"Where the hell's Hermosillo?"

"Hermosillo is only a hundred eighty miles south of the border. Less than four hundred miles south of Phoenix. And, they have their own airstrip on the ranch. Twenty miles from Hermosillo."

"They won't land in Phoenix," Smokey said. "It's a ruse, they can't afford to be caught with two kidnapped prisoners."

"We have HRT gearing up now, heading for Luke Air Force Base, and will be waiting to assist."

It's a ruse, Smokey thought. I know the way this fucker thinks, the YouTube guy; he won't let himself get caught that easy.

"Just in case," Smokey said, "can you send us maps of the ranch, GPS coordinates of the private airport, any contact people who can meet us on the ground."

"On its way," Oakley said. "I'll be in touch every few minutes." He broke the connection.

"Weasel," Smokey said. Weasel leaned over the seat.

"Get me a running clock for touchdown at the meth lab."

"In my head, right now I'd say that we will be there in two hours and fifteen minutes. I'll give you an exact as soon as I get back to the cockpit. We might even make up some time on them if they pretend to make a landing in Phoenix, then continue on."

*The feebs finally help us, huh? Hope so, I sure hope so. If there's ever a time for the feds to help us poor old Indians, now's the time. Ain't ever gonna be another time for me if they don't. And if I can't find Laurel alive, I'll stay in Mexico and kill as many druggies as I can.*

*Now's the time.*

Smokey leaned forward and put his head down. He was aware that the sun was setting. The fight to come would be in the dark. He fought the fear that he would never see Laurel again, fought what it would do to him. He couldn't think about that, not yet anyway. The pain from his wound was making him dizzy. He knew he should take something for the pain. It might make him function better, but he didn't want to lose any edge.

*Make the pain work for you.*

With his head down, he felt a light hand on his shoulder, and reached up with his right hand and covered it. With his head down he spoke, quiet, almost a murmur, so Sarah leaned forward to his chest.

"Sarah."

"Yeah, I'm here. We'll get her back, both of them, Smoke."

"Yeah," he said, his voice husky, a whisper. "When Laurel was a baby," Smokey continued, "I would take her in a backpack in the mountains behind the old place. I would tell her the names of the trees, both in Sahaptin and English. Remember when she was a toddler?"

Sarah nodded. "Yeah,"

"I would walk along behind her, just letting her go anywhere on the trail, exploring. Once, she ran out ahead of me on the trail and ran around a corner. I waited until she discovered she had been going on without me, and she ran back, tears in her eyes, yelling my name."

Smokey stopped, the possibility of losing Laurel hitting him, and he struggled. Sarah squeezed his shoulder, and he shook his head. He loved her, and he loved Nathan and his men, and he knew that they would die with him if that's what it took to get Laurel and Jennifer back.

"Attention in the cabin," Weasel's voice came over the speakers, saving Smokey from a certain melt down.

"The feds have sent us a feed to their fighters in the air, a flight of F-16's out of Luke Air Force Base. They've been tracking the Lear for several minutes now. The Lear's onboard radar will let their pilots know that they are being shadowed. Here goes –."

The speakers crackled with static, then cut into a fighter pilot's transmission.

"...to Eagle Flight leader."

"Eagle Leader.."

"We believe that the Lear should have contacted Phoenix ATC by now for landing instructions so we'll have ATC contact them. If they don't acknowledge, divert them with force to Luke."

"Eagle Leader copy. We're maintaining a visual on the Lear, three miles back."

The static dimmed and Weasel's voice cut in.

"We should know something soon, since the feds have decided that they will not stand by and let Laurel and Jennifer be taken to Mexico."

A great leap of faith for them, Weasel thought, since no one actually saw Jennifer and Laurel being put on the Lear.

"Okay, they're not responding to ATC," Weasel said. "I'll put Eagle Flight back on."

"...is the United States Air Force, please acknowledge on this frequency."

Smokey listened as Eagle Flight leader repeated his directive to the Lear 45.

"Eagle Flight Leader to Command, I'm getting no response."

"We copied. Try a visual on the cockpit."

"Eagle Flight Leader's moving up."

As Smokey waited he turned in his seat, knowing that he had to stand up, stretch if he could, getting so stiff he couldn't move.

"Sarah, help me a second." She put her arm out and Smokey pulled on it, pulling himself off the seat, gritting his teeth against the pain.

"Eagle Flight Leader to command," the pilot's voice boomed over the speakers again, "I have a visual on the cockpit, both pilot and co-pilot of the Lear see me."

"Eagle Flight, they're not responding to my signal."

"Command to Eagle Flight, force them down."

*Force them down how, Smokey thought. What is the procedure?*

Smokey stood, the cabin swimming, holding onto Sarah until the dizziness went away, his stomach churning, wanting his daughter to be out of harm's way.

"Eagle Flight to Command, I'm going to fly in to turn them."

Smokey looked around the cabin at his team, the officers motionless, listening to the drama ahead of them.

"Eagle Leader, he's making a sudden turn to his starboard..."

Aboard Lear 45

As threatening as it was to be on the plane, Jennifer dozed, snuggling with Laurel as well as she could. The blindfold was maddening, but she couldn't move it with her hands tied. The plane made a sudden turn, throwing Laurel away from her lap, and the girl cried out.

Their captors yelled in Spanish, just as surprised as Jennifer was.

The plane righted, and Laurel scrambled back.

"Jen, what happened?"

"Sudden turn, I guess. Maybe we're landing," Jennifer whispered. But she thought that the turn was too sudden for a normal turn to a landing pattern.

*Something's going on, and I hope it's not going well for the assholes who have us. I get the chance, I'll send the one they call Alvarez home to whatever god he worships.*

*Right the fuck home.*

She had a sudden vision of a bearded God holding a quaking Alvarez by the throat.

*Yeah, if God doesn't do it, I'll send you home to Jesus all by myself.*

Aboard Gulfstream 550

The voice from the F-16 came back on the speaker.

"Eagle Flight Leader to Command, the Lear's now following us, heading on our coordinates to Luke, going down to flight level 25."

Smokey thought it might just work, praying for his baby and Jennifer to get low, to keep their heads down when the plane was assaulted by HRT. He closed his eyes.

It seemed to take forever for the plane to land, and during that time, no one spoke. The voice finally came over the speakers in the Gulfstream.

"Gear down on the Lear," Eagle Flight leader said. "We'll shadow from above."

"Roger, Eagle Flight Leader."

Smokey sat up and looked around the cabin. It was dark now, the sun having set in the last half hour. They kept their speed up on the Gulfstream, still hundreds of miles behind the Lear. They would ask for a landing at Luke as soon as Oakley said he had Jennifer and Laurel safely in hand.

It might just work.

# Chapter 61

Luke Air Force Base
Outside of Phoenix, Arizona
HRT briefing

The F.B.I. regional Hostage Rescue Team was assembled, the room noisy as the sixteen team members found seats. Oakley stood at the lectern, looking over the room. If anyone could pull this off, they could. The bad guy might just be willing to be called out of the plane. Oakley waited to be introduced. They had twenty minutes until the Lear would land on the air base. They needed all of that time and more to brief and get out there.

Colonel Pulowski of the 61$^{st}$ Fighter Squadron "Top Dogs," moved to the lectern.

"Gentlemen."

The room grew quiet.

"Gentlemen, while you are here on this operation, we will do whatever we can to assist you in your mission." He motioned for Oakley.

"I'm SSAIC Oakley, assigned to the Bend, Oregon field office. I'm going to make this quick, since the Lear will be landing in," and he looked at his watch, "landing in nineteen minutes."

"We believe that Enrico Alvarez, from Hermosillo, Mexico, is on board, with some of his enforcers. Alvarez runs a superlab in Mexico, crosses the border at will under the guise of being a businessman."

A tall agent in the front row raised his hand. Oakley pointed.

"Sir, is he the YouTube asshole?"

"He's the one. Put film of the heads of police officers his people killed on YouTube to warn other police not to cross him. He's a killer. Enrico Alvarez.

"Alvarez is on board the Lear 45, and we believe that he has kidnapped two people from the Cold River Indian Reservation, a Jennifer Kruger," Oakley put her picture on the screen, "and nine-year-old Laurel Kukup. Laurel is the daughter of Cold River Tribal Police Lieutenant 'Smokey' Kukup. He's in the air in a G-550, about an hour behind the Lear. He won't be a factor here. In your packets you have pictures of Alvarez and his crew, as well as Jennifer Kruger and Laurel."

Oakley held up a packet. "There is also a brief of the assault on the Kukup family home on the reservation. You should know that Smokey and a small team of officers killed eleven bad guys who were armed with automatic weapons and RPG's. His daughter Laurel, shot one of them as he came in the door. We need to do this right. Smokey will do virtually anything to get his daughter back. He was an Army Ranger in Afghanistan. He will lay waste to some bad people to get his daughter, or, to avenge her if something happens."

Colonel Pulowski held his hand up from the side of the lectern and listened with an earpiece. He looked at his watch.

"Gentlemen, the plane is ahead of schedule. We now have fifteen minutes until touchdown."

The team leader stepped up and motioned to the door. The team hurried out to the waiting vehicles. The plan was to force the Lear down on an unused runway, far from the buildings, and surround the plane with heavy vehicles, fire trucks for cover, and call to the pilots to order the passengers off the plane. It was as sophisticated as they could come up with given the short time frame.

Oakley watched as the vehicles sped toward the runway, then climbed in the passenger seat of the colonel's car. They would follow at a distance and observe the take-down.

The operation went as planned, until the moment the door opened on the Lear.

The plane touched down, shadowed by the flight of F-16's, and followed a pickup operated by HRT, with the "Follow Me" signs. The Lear came to a stop at a midpoint on the runway, and the engines spooled down. The HRT members quickly surrounded the plane. The bad guys inside the plane could surely see that they had no options.

After a minute, the door opened.

Oakley watched with binoculars from a hundred yards away. A man with a white shirt stood in the doorway.

The Captain, gauging from his shoulder boards.

Oakley knew that an HRT agent was giving instructions with a loudspeaker, and he saw the captain's hands go up and he walked down the stairs and toward a black Suburban. Another person wearing a white shirt came next, the co-pilot.

*Well at least they can't fly the plane now.*

HRT agents were running for the plane, taking positions on either side of the door, as well as under the nose and tail. An agent was yelling to those inside the plane. One by one the passengers came down the ramp, hands up, to be taken into custody by HRT members.

This doesn't look right, Oakley thought.

HRT agents boarded the plane, fast, clearing the small space in a matter of seconds.

The report came fast over the radio.

"Clear!"

"No, I repeat, no hostages on board. Appears initially to be a group of Malaysian investors," the team leader said.

"Drive up there," Oakley urged the colonel.

*We got the wrong fucking plane.*

*But where was Alvarez, and where the hell are the hostages?*

Oakley picked up his cell phone, and called Smokey. *This was going to get bloody.*

# Chapter 62

Aboard Gulfstream 550

Amy followed the blinking red dot as it made its way south. She didn't know exactly where Luke Air Force Base was, close to Phoenix she thought, but the red dot was moving south of Phoenix on her map, almost to Mexico. She had to tell the others. Something was wrong.

"Uh, Smokey. Lieutenant?" Smokey opened his eyes.

"Smokey, look at this." She pointed to the screen of her laptop Smokey.

"What am I looking at?" he asked. He turned to look at the screen, Sarah and Nathan crowding around him.

"That Lear jet is supposed to be heading for Luke Air Force Base, right?"

"Yeah, so…"

"Well, isn't Luke here?" Amy pointed at the screen, to a spot west of Phoenix.

"Okay?" Smokey wasn't getting it yet.

"Well, according to our tracking device, the red dot is way south of Phoenix, almost to Mexico. It's even well south of Phoenix Sky Harbor Airport, the destination they filed in their flight plan!" She thought about what it could mean, and right now she didn't know, but it felt wrong.

"Uh, sir, I'm not sure what it means," she added.

Smokey went cold.

"How accurate is your device?"

"Stan said that it is as accurate as the military's GPS, within feet. It's being tracked by satellites, sending out a signal that anyone can track with the right codes and frequency."

Smokey knew what it meant. It had been too easy. The druggies were too smart to just be taken down in the United States.

*The feds have the wrong plane. The have the wrong plane, and Laurel and Jennifer will soon be in Mexico.*

*Well, so will we.*

*Alvarez was a dead man, he just didn't know it yet.*

Sarah waved her hand, getting Smokey's attention, holding up his cell phone.

"Oakley for you."

Smokey snatched the phone and listened. He turned cold, his breath coming in shallow gasps, as much from losing Laurel as from the news. He thought Amy was right, but he held out a small hope that she was wrong and the feds were right.

The feds did indeed have the wrong plane.

"How could this happen?" Smokey asked Oakley, his voice harsh, unyielding.

"We don't know that yet," Oakley said. "A lot of planes in this airspace, switched transponder, wrong information, misinformation, don't know."

"What I need from you now, to be sent to my plane, is all information you have about Alvarez's operation, aerial photos, strength of his security, where they might take Laurel and Jennifer."

Oakley was silent.

"Look, I want it now, or what good are you!" Smokey yelled into the phone. The others in the cabin froze. Smokey took a breath and tried to calm himself. It wouldn't help Laurel if he lost it.

"Look, Oakley, I'm not asking you to go to Mexico with me, I just need that information, because we will be landing at that ranch in –." He looked up at Weasel, who held up one finger. "We will be landing at the meth lab, or wherever we track them to, in one hour. We need that information, and some contact people on the ground if you can get it for us, maybe military, create a diversion."

"I'll get you everything I can," Oakley said. "Listen, Smokey, Alvarez has an army there, maybe a hundred or more on duty at any time, but he can get more from his private barracks. Most are former army, police, or long time dopers."

"Yeah, I know," Smokey said. "We met some of them at my mother's place, remember?"

Smokey listened to Oakley's reply, and flipped the phone closed.

"Okay, listen up," he told his team, his voice all business, "the feds have the wrong plane. Nathan, come up with an assault plan on their meth lab, we go into their lab uninvited, going in hot, with hostiles there. Get a plan to get us from the airport to follow the tracking device. We'll need a plane guard too. Weasel, can you join us?"

When they presented the operations plan to Smokey he told them it might just work.

*As far as plans go, it's all we have. As far as plans go, it sucks.*
*Hope some of us make it back alive.*
*Doubt it, Smokey old son. Doubt it.*

# Chapter 63

Aboard the Lear

Jennifer felt the plane bank, slow down, then slow some more.
*We're landing.*
Wherever we are, we're landing. Sure hope it's in the United States. If not, we're gonna be dead, and I can't let that happen to Laurel.
"Laurel," she whispered.
"Mmmmmpfff."
Laurel's voice was muffled, sleepy.
"Laurel! I think we're landing. Be ready to run if I can get your blindfold off. I will try to knock the one by the door down when we get to the steps, and then you run."
"Where, Jen? I don't know where you want me to run, I don't want to go away from you, can't we stay together?" Laurel was whispering furiously, the worry in her voice made Jennifer want to cry.
"We'll see, Honey, we'll see. I want you to rub your head on my shoulder, try to pull the blindfold up, and I'll do the same, right when the plane comes to a stop."
"Okay, Jen. But I don't want to go anywhere without you. Please?"
"Okay, Honey, I'll be right behind you. People are sure to come for us. I think if you can run and hide somewhere, it might give us some time. Maybe you can find someone to help you, I promise it will work."
*And maybe you can avoid being raped. Oh God, what are we going to do?*
She wished later that she had never promised. The last promise she made to Laurel, was broken within minutes. Promises were sacred, or should be, for everyone, but for a nine-year-old, they were life.
The plane landed with a soft bump and chirp of tires, and then they slowed. Jennifer tensed.
"Laurel."
"What?" Her reply was soft, and Jen could hear the fear in her voice.

258

"Laurel, we might not need to do anything, but whatever we do, we will do together. Kay?"

"Okay, Jen."

They taxied for what seemed to be a long time, and then slowed, and stopped. She heard the men on the plane standing, joking, gathering bags from their seats.

*Something was wrong.*

The door opened and warm air from the outside came in through the door. But there was something else, something she couldn't explain. Voices came in through the door.

They were speaking in Spanish!

She struggled to get her blindfold off, got a part of it up over her left eye, and a grinning Alvarez came into her vision.

"Well, my little putas," he said. "Welcome to Hermosillo, Mexico."

They were in Mexico, in the hands of a ruthless, sadistic and powerful drug dealer. Had it not been for Laurel counting on her, Jennifer would have lost it by then. After all of her trials in the past week, this was the end.

*But Laurel, I have to stay strong for her.*

*I have to.*

# Chapter 64

Gulfstream 550
Mexican airspace, 100 miles north of Hermosillo

"Dial in the coordinates for the landing strip," Weasel said. "Figure an approach for us, we'll be landing in thirty minutes or less."

"Already have it," Charley said. "We'll be letting down in ten minutes."

Smokey watched and listened as Nathan went over the plan.

"Maps look good," Nathan said, standing over the printout of material Oakley sent. He briefed the others on the plan. "Burwell, you and Kincaid will form a rear guard, keep this plane intact because we might be coming back in a hurry. I don't have to tell you how important this plane is."

Burwell nodded, and tapped fists with Kincaid.

Sarah gave both of them a hug.

"From the landing, we are in hostile territory, consider everyone a combatant. We will follow the tracking device to Laurel and Jennifer. When we snatch them we'll be coming back to the airport in a hurry."

As Nathan talked, Smokey looked at his crew. Sarah came over and fussed with his bandage.

"You're bleeding again," she said.

"Won't be long now," Smokey said. "Won't be long before we get Laurel and Jennifer and get the hell out of here."

Smokey looked at Amy, seeing her for the first time. She was slight, about five foot one, and had long brown hair, a pleasant face, looked to be very young, about twenty-five. She had a tattoo of a Tasmanian Devil on her left arm. Who was this young girl who was risking her life and more to help them? She looked up at him and he motioned her to the seat next to him, Sarah still fussing with his bandage.

When Amy sat, Smokey reached out with his good arm and put his arm around her. She leaned into him and sighed.

"It's gonna get bad, isn't it?" she said.

"It's already bad," Smokey said, "but I want to tell you something about my daughter. How special she is, what a warm heart she has."

"I already know that," Amy said. "I saw her on the mountain, remember?"

"Amy, I don't know what to say to you. You know we are in extreme danger."

"Well, yeah, but I kinda feel like I know Laurel, and I know you would do the same thing for me. But I'm doing this for Stan. They killed him, and he was a good guy, didn't deserve what they did to him."

"Can you show us how to run that thing now?" Smokey pointed to the laptop."

"I will point the way on the ground, I can move fast. You guys," and she looked at Sarah and smiled, "and gals just protect me, keep me safe, and I'll find them for you."

"I promise you that will happen," Smokey said.

*As it turned out, he had made one or two promises too many, and couldn't keep them all.*

*Not by half.*

*The army they were going up against, they weren't all that good, but there were a lot of them, and they all had guns.*

Hermosillo
Aboard Lear 45

Alvarez roughly removed Jennifer's blindfold, his scarred face close to hers She blinked, the cabin lights bright, glaring. Alvarez jerked Laurel's blindfold off and smiled at her. Jennifer was so close to the large pistol Alvarez carried in the waistband of his pants she thought of making a grab for it. As she reached her hand out he shoved her forward down the narrow aisle. The others were already gone.

"Don't touch me!" Laurel yelled, twisting around and glaring at their captor. He laughed and shoved her up against Jennifer.

Jennifer braced herself in the aisle, hooked her right leg under a seat, and pulled Laurel in front of her.

"Don't touch her, you fucking asshole," Jennifer said calmly. Alvarez laughed again, pointed to the front of the plane.

"You may not understand what I'm saying, but you get the message. Don't touch her."

He pulled his gun and pointed it at Jennifer's head.

"Get the fuck out of the plane, now," he said in English, his calm manner more threatening than if he had yelled at her.

"I'll stay right behind you," Jennifer said to Laurel, ignoring the threat. Her knees were shaking and she hoped the man behind her didn't see it. She couldn't show him, and more importantly, show Laurel how scared she was.

She walked down the aisle, slowly, trying to think about what they should do. She knew that they would be separated as soon as they got to wherever they were being taken. And then they would be without any options, and would be killed or worse.

*Now is the time. Might not work, but what else can we do? Poor Laurel. She has such a life in front of her.*

*And so do I. And Smokey. What would it have been like to get to know him. To love him.*

*Never know, Jen. But you have to save the little one. Do whatever.*

"Get your ass off my plane, you little whore," Alvarez said, crowding up behind them.

Laurel stood in the doorway, looking out. Jennifer came up behind her and looked at the airstrip. The men who had been on the plane were getting into an SUV just off the runway, and another was waiting. There was a building on the other side, and a fuel truck, and some lights off in the distance.

Nothing else.

*Maybe time for Laurel to run.*

"Laurel." Jennifer bent down and spoke softly into her ear.

"Laurel, when I say 'go' I want you to run for that fuel truck, hide, and then run to the far end of the runway, find a place to hide, then get to the large town, find a friendly family, something."

Laurel turned, looking up at Jennifer. "I don't want to go, Jen, but I will. Maybe we should stay together."

"It'll be okay."

"I love you, Jen." And Laurel leaned back against Jennifer and rubbed her back against Jennifer's legs.

"I love you too, Kiddo." Jennifer glanced back inside the plane. Alvarez was walking up behind her, his gun pointed at her back.

"Go," Jennifer whispered. Then she said it louder.

"Go!" She threw herself back into Alvarez. Laurel hesitated for a second, then ran down the steps and bolted across the runway, turning once to look back at Jennifer. She pumped her legs, her bound hands up high, swinging from side to side as she ran.

Jennifer knocked Alvarez back, but the man didn't go down, and he pushed Jennifer forward into the doorway, and swung the large automatic pistol at her head. Jennifer ducked at the last moment and the barrel struck her hard on the shoulder. Pain shot down her arm, and Alvarez kicked her down the stairs.

Jennifer stumbled and pitched forward, bouncing hard on the pavement, the drop only three feet, and she looked up as Laurel ran for the fuel truck in the dark.

Alvarez raised the pistol and pulled the trigger.

*He's shooting!*

Alvarez stood in the doorway above Jennifer and shot at the fleeing girl. Jennifer started to rise, to jump up and get Alvarez, when he shot again. And again.

And Laurel went down.

"Nooooooo!" Jennifer screamed.


When Jennifer said "Go!" Laurel jumped down from the plane and ran for the truck as Jennifer told her to. The truck was just up ahead, a large dark shape looking to Laurel like a rusting elephant on the side of the runway. She heard the first shot. The bullet hit the asphalt in front of her, throwing up sparks, and she veered to her right, running as fast as she could, thinking that her dad would be proud of her, running so fast, and he knew that she didn't like to run. Once on a field day at the elementary school, she had walked through the running events. Her dad was gone, in Afghanistan, killing bad people, and later she felt bad, not running fast for her dad.

*Daddy look now I'm running fast.*

*Daddy I know you're okay you'll come for us.*

*Daddy sorry I couldn't help mommy when you were gone.*

*Daddy, I'm sorry I took the fry bread money from Tutu, Jennifer said you would forgive me, I never told you.*

*Daddy I'm . . .*

The sparks from the bullets hit all around Laurel, the shots loud, even as she ran, one bullet touching the fabric on the side of her jeans. She didn't feel it, and ran on.

*Daddy I'm . . .*

And the bullet took her high up on the top of her head and Laurel dropped.

*Daddy I'm sorry . . .*


Jennifer threw herself at Alvarez, screaming, "Kill you," and he hit her, hard with a vicious backhand that sent her sprawling. She got up on her hands and knees, blood drooling from her mouth as she looked at the crumpled form on the runway. Alvarez grabbed her arm, pulled her up to her feet, and shoved her forward toward a waiting vehicle.

"Pick up that trash," he said, pointing toward Laurel's body, "and bring it with us."

Jennifer turned once to look at the crumpled form on the runway, until she couldn't see Laurel at all.

*I just didn't save her. Smokey, I'm so sorry, I . . .*

And Jennifer sobbed.

# Chapter 65

Aboard Gulfstream 550

"Hermosillo Tower, this is Gulfstream W9873N." Weasel looked over at Charley, and waited for the reply.

"Hermosillo Tower, go ahead Gulfstream."

"Uh, we are declaring an in-flight emergency, are fifty miles out, and request an alternate landing site."

"Gulfstream what is the nature of your emergency?"

"Smoke in the cabin," Weasel said, putting some urgency in his voice.

"Hermosillo Tower, I show a private landing field below."

"Gulfstream that airfield is very private, don't know if they will let you land there."

"I don't think we have any choice, tower, we're going to try to get to that field. Please contact them and let them know that we have an extreme emergency. We have a lot of smoke now, we are carrying an international film crew and equipment. When we land we'll be exiting the aircraft fast, will stay away from buildings, but we need to set down there."

"Roger, Gulfstream."

Weasel looked over at Charley and blew air out of his cheeks. "This is all we have, at least they will know we're on the way."

"Think they will buy it?"

"If they're smart, they won't. Depends on their level of command and control. The people at the airport, if it is staffed at all, may not contact those in charge."

"Well, one thing's for sure, we'll know in a few minutes," Charley said, then added, "runway lights activated, in sight."

"Gear down," Weasel said, and slowed the big aircraft to landing speed. They flashed over the outer marker, saw a group of buildings and a large hanger off to the right, a fuel truck, two vehicles parked at the hanger, and then they touched down.

Smokey stood and felt blood seep down his stomach. He tried to get into his ballistic vest as Sarah held it for him. He doubled over in pain, and waved the vest away. The vest was loaded with UMP magazines, incendiary grenades, pistol magazines, and a radio. With his good arm he picked up his automatic rifle. Behind him Nathan checked his radio and weapons.

Burwell and Kincaid were assigned to meet any initial resistance they faced when they opened the door.

"Okay," Nathan said, "as we talked about, Burwell and Kincaid first out with smoke, make it look like we're on fire, throw a lot of smoke, then I will go next, with Weasel. We'll wait a minute, see if they send a vehicle out to check on us. If they do, we'll take it over and follow Amy's lead."

"I'm going to turn the plane," Weasel said over the cabin intercom. "I'll put the door on the side away from the hangers and office."

Smokey looked over the cabin. As the plane slowed they all stood, Burwell and Kincaid by the door holding canisters of smoke, Nathan and Sgt. Lamebull pulling on backpacks filled with explosives, adjusting assault rifle slings. Lights from the buildings flashed by, and then the plane was turning. The plane stopped and Smokey pointed to Burwell. The big man pulled the latch on the door and swung it down, the outside humidity quickly filling the plane, a sharp smell of hot turbines and jet fuel coming with it. Burwell threw two canisters of smoke, and then was out, followed by Kincaid. They crouched under the plane, their rifles out toward the distant hangers, when Smokey followed Nathan and Sarah down the steps. Amy was right behind him.

"Got the signal," she said, and pointed at the laptop screen, then toward a road that ran past the buildings, a red line on the map.

Smokey looked at the laptop screen, then up at the distant hangers. He heard Kincaid pop more smoke.

"Car coming," Nathan said, pointing at the hanger.

"Okay," Smokey said. He turned back to Kincaid.

"You and Burwell, use all of your smoke as the car approaches, the rest of us will stay on this side of the plane as the car approaches. Nathan and I will take the car. Sarah, stay with Amy, Lamebull, cover us."

As the car approached the runway, the runway lights suddenly went out, putting them in darkness, the light from the buildings the only light Smokey could see. From the headlights it looked to be some kind of van. Smoke from the canisters swirled around them and

Smokey thought maybe they had used too much. The van approached on the taxiway adjacent to the runway and slowed a hundred yards out, the occupants being careful of a plane on fire.

The van approached slowly, the headlights flashing on the plane.

"Okay," Smokey said. "Game time, let's make this quick, not let them radio, Burwell and Kincaid out front, Nathan and I will be in your shadow."

"Yeah, but no one will believe those two buttholes can fly a plane," Sarah muttered, but she said it with a smile.

Burwell, smiling as well, raised his middle finger toward her. She blew him a kiss.

"Careful guys," Sarah said.

Burwell stepped away from the plane, flanked by Kincaid. Smokey and Nathan were right behind, their rifles slung. Smokey held his Glock down by his right leg. He resisted the urge to run up to the van, kill the driver and whomever else was there, and drive as fast as he could to where Laurel was being held. He knew that such an action would put all of his people in jeopardy, so he gritted his teeth. His upper body felt as if he were on fire, and he would find a way to use it to keep him sharp.

"Alto!"

The command came from the driver's side of the van, now less than a hundred feet in front of them.

"We gotta get closer, guys," Nathan said from Smokey's right.

"Roger," Kincaid said, holding his right hand up and smiling, nodding, continuing to walk slowly toward the van, and then he added, "I can see at least one gun, Boss."

Smokey looked around Kincaid's shoulder at the figure beside the driver's side door. The driver appeared to be holding an assault rifle.

They were within forty feet now, the driver yelling something to the shadow by the passenger door.

"Hey, guys," Kincaid said, smiling, "we have a little problem with our plane, got some smoke in the cabin," as he continued to walk, Burwell smiling and walking beside him, "and we maybe need a ride."

The driver of the van moved away from the door, holding his rifle up, bringing the muzzle around to point at Burwell. They were now just twenty feet away, and Nathan stepped to the side of Burwell and shot the driver with a burst from his silenced UMP .40 caliber machine gun, the sound not much louder than an air gun, the bolt clicking rapidly back and forth, and the man dropped, his rifle clattering on the runway.

As Nathan moved to the right, Smokey jumped to his left to clear the front fender, moving around Kincaid and past the headlights and fired at the shadow at the passenger door, a spray of bullets that shattered the passenger door window. The man yelled once and fired a shot on the way down.

"Check the van," Smokey yelled as he ran up to the figure on the ground. Kincaid and Burwell were already moving, drawing pistols from under their shirts, running to the side and around to the back.

"Clear!"

"Get them in the back," Smokey said, hoping they were far enough away from the buildings that the shots wouldn't be heard. The engines on the G-550 had produced some noise. He watched as Kincaid pulled the man to the back of the van and the driver and passenger were loaded. Smokey got into the passenger seat, his chest wet from seeping blood. Nathan jumped into the driver's seat, and drove slowly toward the plane, turning off the headlights as he got close. Sarah and Amy stood off to the side of the wing, Amy holding her laptop. The others were by the open door to the plane.

"Brief here," Smokey said, calling to Sarah. He didn't want to move more than he had to, but to find Laurel, he knew he could move like an Olympic athlete. They crowded around the door.

"They've stopped," Amy said. She handed the laptop to Smokey, and he put it on the center console, the screen up so they all could see. On the screen was a surprisingly good map of the immediate area, showing the runway, taxiways, airport buildings, roads, and further off to the east, a group of buildings. A red trail went from the airport to the group of buildings.

"There's a hill between us and the buildings," Amy said, "and the red dot that we think is Jennifer is in the corner of that cluster of buildings there," and she pointed to the screen.

"According to the feds, that's a meth lab drying building there," Nathan said, leaning in.

"Weasel," Smokey said, looking out at the dark figures by the van.

"Here."

"We'll need your shirt for a while longer, gonna use Kincaid and Burwell to drive to the terminal buildings, see if we can fake out anyone there. Oh, and you'll need to be the guards for the plane."

"Done," Weasel said, "and when you come back, you may be hot, so I'll be at the end of the runway, ready to take off. Call me if you can."

No one spoke on the drive to the airport buildings, the lights from the van shining on darkened fuel trucks, an aging Cessna 182, a Lexus in front of the office.

There were lights on in the small office.

Kincaid and Burwell were out in their borrowed pilot's uniforms, Kincaid holding a Glock down by his right leg as they entered the office. Burwell came in behind him, and within ten seconds Burwell backed out and signaled "all clear."

Smokey motioned to the hanger, and watched as the team entered the side door. Smokey couldn't wait, pulled himself and groaned as he stepped on the pavement. Within seconds, Burwell came out and walked toward the van.

"Clear, Boss. Want to hide these bodies in the hanger?"

"Yeah, is their Lear in the hanger?"

"Yes."

"Put the bodies in the Lear, and then disable it."

Burwell grinned, and spoke into his microphone. Nathan and Kincaid assisted in dragging the bodies into the hanger, and within a minute the team was back in the van.

"Smokey," Amy said, her voice higher, "Smokey, the red dot is moving. They're moving them. We better get over there."

*In a couple of minutes, I'm gonna see my baby girl, and there better not be anyone between her and me.*

Jennifer leaned against the wall and looked around the room. Her hands were numb from the ropes. She had been pushed through a large, well-lighted building. The people packaging a white powder didn't even look up when she was rushed past. Alvarez had thrown her into a storeroom. A light shined through a gap under the door, and she saw barrels and boxes piled to the ceiling on pallets.

She had thought she was done crying, but the tears came again as she suddenly thought of Laurel.

269

*I sure didn't do much to protect her, I got her killed. Should have kept my mouth shut, kept her with me, tried to keep her safe. But I know they will kill me.*

*Kill me.*

She worked against the rope on her wrists and was able to slip one hand out. She pushed herself up and stood, swaying, and then leaned against the metal wall. She shivered and hugged herself, wanting to be away, for all of the last day to go away, to be back to yesterday. She thought of Smokey, thinking that maybe his daughter had joined him, and that brought a new round of crying.

*I should be with them, playing with Laurel, getting to know Smokey.* She hadn't let herself think about a future with Smokey, and now there wouldn't be one, so there it was. Didn't matter now.

*Never gonna happen. Laurel dead, Smokey dead if there was any mercy in the world. He loved his daughter beyond life.*

Jennifer looked around for something to use as a weapon. She found a metal pole, about four feet long, like a broom handle. She took a test swing in the dark, and grimaced.

The first person through the door, that person was going to die.

And the next.

And then the next.

She heard something then, far off, a popping noise, like, sounds like, and then it stopped.

*Sounds like shooting. Automatic weapons.*

*Sounded like someone shooting.*

*Maybe they're just practicing.*

*What, at night?*

*Maybe someone is coming for you.*

*Yeah, right.*

She took another swing with the pole, this time putting some heft into it, right about head height.

*Gonna beat someone's brains down on the floor.*

*Oh Yeah.*

# Chapter 66

Alvarez didn't believe that the plane landing on his private airstrip was an accident. He hadn't existed as long as he had to not take it seriously. If it truly was an accident, it would be a good drill for his men.

The call from the airport described the plane landing with some kind of emergency. He moved the airport guards back to the main buildings. They would meet the plane's occupants with force, overwhelming force, and kill them all.

They wouldn't be from the reservation though. The people there, except for the police lieutenant, didn't do things like rescue people. Even their own. And the police lieutenant was dead.

Alvarez speed-dialed a number on his cell phone. He listened. His men at the airport were down. Someone was coming for him, but they didn't have nearly enough men. He sat in his office and changed from casual clothes to dark fatigues. He pulled an assault rifle, a CAR 15, his favorite, from a closet, and a Beretta in a pistol belt.

"Si," the voice on the phone.

"Get the men ready, surround the buildings, the house, and after they leave the airport, seal the road off."

He listened, then shouted into the phone.

"All of them you fool, all of the men, *pronto!*"

He had a hundred men at his disposal.

I'm gonna put their fucking heads on YouTube.

Tonight.

But first find out what the woman knows, who she told.

Then give her to the men.

Smokey sat in the front passenger seat as Kincaid drove up a small grade and around a hill. The road circled to their left. There was a guard shack up ahead, Smokey knew, and he bent over to look at Amy's screen.

"How far," he whispered to Amy.

"Uh, about two hundred yards to the gate."

Scrub brush lined the roadside, broken up by scattered trees and rock formations. It reminded Smokey of the high desert in Oregon.

"One hundred yards," Amy said. They came around a corner in the road and the guardhouse was up ahead. It looked deserted, the overhead lights adding to the feeling of isolation. A wire fence stretched in the distance on either side. Inside the fence, a series of large metal buildings sat in a row, like a group of large aircraft hangers, one as large as a stadium, Smokey thought, only they don't park planes in there. Just white powder.

The guardhouse appeared deserted.

*Bad sign, Smokey old son.*

Nathan voiced his thoughts.

"Doesn't look good," Nathan said, "don't see anyone around."

"Amy?" Smokey asked.

"First building on the right, they're in the far corner."

Nathan slid the side door open and locked it back, and Sarah opened the rear doors. Sgt. Lamebull sat on the end of the van, his assault rifle at the ready. Kincaid picked up speed as they neared the guardhouse and it flashed by on their left. The buildings came up fast, the galvanized metal shining in the headlights.

"Let's hit the door," Smokey said, "Burwell blow it if it's locked, everyone inside, dynamic entry, they'll probably be waiting for us."

Kincaid slid the van to a stop in front of a pedestrian door. Nathan jumped out the side of the van and covered the approach by Burwell and Kincaid.

Smokey stepped out and almost dropped to his knees, the pain in his shoulder making him cry out. Lamebull came up behind him and lifted him up. He went past Smokey, his rifle pointed down the road between the buildings as Burwell tried the door handle. He nodded at Smokey and the others.

It was unlocked.

"Smokey, they're at the other end, left corner," Amy said.

"Go," he shouted, and ran for the door, ignoring the shoulder and blood running down inside his shirt.

The first spattering of gunfire caught Kincaid as he reached for the door handle again, a burst from the corner of the adjacent building made red blotches on his borrowed captains uniform, the ruse to use the white shirts working against him. He didn't have a tactical ballistic vest on to protect him against gunfire. He slumped down and Burwell grabbed the door handle and jerked it open and disappeared inside.

Nathan and Lamebull let loose with long bursts of automatic weapons fire. Lamebull's squad automatic weapon hosed down the corner of the building.

"Get inside!" Nathan yelled. He fired another burst as a group of khaki-clad men ran down the road toward them, falling and firing, bullets pinging off the metal building like an angry hailstorm.

Smokey moved inside with Sarah and Amy close behind. He stopped inside the door. The room was immense, half the size of a football field, brightly lit, with rows of tables with packaged white powder stacked four feet high on each. There were a dozen workers huddled in the far corner, and Smokey pointed to the back of the room.

"There!" he yelled, and ran down the center aisle for a door where his daughter waited. The sounds of the fight outside intensified, and he was aware of Nathan and Lamebull behind him. Nathan shut the door to the street, and the firing stopped.

"In the corner," Amy said, running behind Smokey, holding her laptop open as she ran.

Jennifer jerked back beside the door as the firing started, holding her pole up like a baseball bat, standing with her back against the wall, a foot from the door. They would pay for killing that baby girl.

They would pay. She heard shouting from the main room. Someone yelled Laurel's name.

Smokey shouted as he ran, his voice hoarse, his rifle up and ready, trying to run through the aisle. As he got to the end of the tables he juked left, almost falling, and then he was around the tables and running for the storeroom door.

"Laurel! Jennifer!"

Sarah got to the door first, and jerked on the knob, yelling Laurel's name as she pulled, and that was what saved her from the swing.

As the door opened, Jennifer started her swing, the pole starting in an arc toward the opening doorway, and it registered all at once what was happening. Sarah's face filled the door, a blackened, streaked face, but Sarah's all the same, holding her Glock out in front of her. Jennifer dropped the pole and it fell to the cement floor with a clang, and she

273

threw herself at Sarah. Smokey lurched in the room and looked at Jennifer. She felt herself go then, and the tears came again, shaking, holding onto Sarah.

Smokey moved past Sarah and looked around the small room.
*Laurel?*
He walked to the corner and looked at the boxes, panic coming up in his throat, and he turned to Jennifer. He knew that his stomach was wet with blood, drenching his belt.

"Jen, where's my daughter?" His voice came out hoarse, a whisper at the end.

Jennifer shook her head.

"Laurel!" He shouted and kicked a box, and turned back to Jennifer.

"Where's my baby girl?"

"They shot her." Jennifer said it louder than she thought. Sarah stiffened, and Jennifer said it again through her tears.

"Shot her. Alvarez."

"Noooo!" Smokey dropped to his knees and put his head to the floor.

*My baby can't be dead. I need her. I need to see her grow up. She needs me.*

# Chapter 67

Smokey kneeled with his head on the floor, his mind numb. He didn't hear the shouting around him, and the movement in the room. Nathan came up and shook him.

"Smokey."

*Go away, I want you all to go away.*

"Smokey," Nathan said, his voice cracking, "Smokey, what do you want us to do?"

Smokey pushed himself up and sat back on his knees, his head spinning. He looked around the room as if he were just seeing it for the first time. He held his hand up and Nathan grabbed it, pulling Smokey to his feet. They put their arms around each other and stood like that for a few moments. Smokey's head turned cold, his thoughts frozen on one thing.

"Jen, you sure?"

"I, uh –," Jennifer said, looking up from Sarah, and then she started crying again. "I, uh, I saw Alvarez shooting at her, she was running, and then she went down and didn't move. Out on the runway, but they took her and put her in the trunk, she wasn't moving. I don't know where she, I uh, I'm so sorry Smokey."

Smokey held out his hand and Jennifer came to him. She held him and cried on his shoulder; her tears ran down his cheek. Smokey pulled her arms from his neck.

*Enough of this, we'll do it later. Got things to do.*

Smokey gently moved Jennifer away.

"Not your fault," he whispered.

"Here's what we're gonna do," he said, his voice surprisingly strong. He turned to Nathan.

"Uncle, you with me?"

"To the end, Little Brother."

"Here's what brother and I are going to do. Find my baby girl, dead or alive, and take her home, or die trying." He looked out at the packaging tables. Burwell and Sgt. Lamebull were approaching through the building, backing through the aisle, their guns trained on the door in the front. They stopped by the group coming out of the storeroom.

275

"Okay, here's what we will do," Smokey said, looking at each of them in turn. "Big Brother and I are going to find Laurel. Lamebull and Burwell and Sarah are going to get Jennifer and Amy back to the plane, take off and get out of here. Kincaid dead?"

Burwell nodded. "He took one in the head, he's gone."

"We'll get his body out with us if we're still alive," Smokey said. "We'll cover you to the van."

"No."

Sarah held her assault rifle with her right hand, her left arm around Jennifer.

"What?" Smokey looked at her.

"No," Sarah said. "I'm not leaving without Laurel either. We're all in this together. I love her too, and I'll die with you trying to get her. I'm staying with you and Nathan, and that's final."

"Me too, Boss, I'm in." Burwell said. "Jim Kincaid was my best friend, and I should have a say in how I avenge him."

"You're starting to think like an In-din, talking about avenging," Smokey said, and touched Burwell's shoulder, nodding his thanks. Lamebull just looked. Smokey knew what he thought. He turned to Amy.

"You didn't ask for this," Smokey said. "We have put you in extreme danger, you coming here with us, and we love you for this, helping us find my baby."

Amy slung her laptop under her arm and Smokey waited, catching her eyes.

"I just don't think we should split up for anything," Amy said. "All stay together, we could die, but we should all stay together. Don't you ever watch movies where people split up? Look what happened to Custer."

Smokey didn't think he could ever laugh again, but he started chuckling, and they were all laughing, grinning, hugging Amy, and then he stopped. He looked at them. Burwell and Nathan, bloody from numerous minor wounds. Jennifer's head was bleeding. Of all of them, only Lamebull and Amy weren't bloody.

"You're a sorry looking bunch," Smokey said, "and I love you all." He picked up his assault rifle, pulled the sling tight, and looked over the room.

"Let's go find Laurel."

He led the way down the aisle toward the door. Burwell came up and grabbed the doorknob, looking to Smokey.

"Hell's awaiting for us out there, Boss," Burwell said quietly.

Smokey nodded, Burwell jerked open the door, and Smokey walked through the opening.

*Amazing.*

*I don't hurt.*

# Chapter 68

In Laurel's dream she was alive, sitting at her desk in her bedroom, her Šiyápu doll in her lap. She bent over her diary and wrote furiously with a pencil, her hand skipping over the page. She wrote to her diary and her daddy at the same time. As she wrote she absently fingered the leather necklace to make her strong.

It didn't hurt so bad, Daddy. Really, I know you have been shot before, in Afghanistan and maybe some other place, and then on the mountain, so you know, Daddy, sometimes it's not so bad. But Daddy, I worry 'bout you now, with me and mommy gone away from you, and no one to take care of you.

She stopped writing and looked around her room. The house was intact the way it had been before the fire, the headboard above her bed overflowing with stuffed animals.

Oh, Daddy, I wish I could see you and Jennifer, maybe she can take care of you now, but you have to find her, Daddy. She went away with those bad men, but she is strong, so you have to come quick, Daddy.

The lights in her room dimmed, and then went out. Laurel wrote in the dark, the pencil lead getting fat, needing sharpening; she wrote on in the blackness of her night.

Dad, sometime carry me up on the mountain with you, find a way to take me to the places we used to go when I was a little kid, when Mommy went with us, so I can see it again. In the summer when the wildflowers are out, and it's warm.

*It's so cold here.*

Laurel wrote until she couldn't see the page, bending over her diary until her nose almost touched it, her hand cramping, slowing, and she stopped.

Smokey jumped through the door and froze.

"Alto!" The command came from the end of the building. He looked down the street and saw what appeared to be fifty armed men, their rifles trained on him, and he slowly turned, his rifle up, his finger ready to fire a long burst, when he saw another large group of men with rifles and pistols pointing at him. Nathan came up beside him and trained his assault rifle on the group down the street. Lamebull stood beside Smokey.

"Just say the word, Lieutenant," he said.

Smokey sensed the others behind him. After the first command to stop, it was quiet, the high overhead lights on the street between the buildings casting long shadows, pools of darkness and light, and no one spoke. They stood like that, neither group moving. Someone coughed at the end of the street. A figure moved out of the shadows, coming toward them.

It was so dark and cold.

Laurel's head hurt so bad she wanted to cry.

And she opened her eyes in the darkness.

She was no longer in her house, couldn't be, her house had been burned down by the bad men. She remembered now, she had been on a plane with Jennifer.

Shot.

She was in the corner of a large building. Lights from the outside came in a window, but it was dark in the corner.

My head hurts.

She put her hand up to her head and screamed, the pain so intense she thought she was dying. She pulled her hand away and looked at the blood, black in the darkness.

She tried a smile.

Daddy always said if you hurt, you're still alive.

That's what I am.

*Alive.*

*Daddy, come quick.*

*I'm gonna find Jennifer.*

Laurel stood, shaking, her head blinding her with pain, and then she remembered shouts and a lot of shooting as she was coming awake.

She smiled. That much shooting could mean only one thing.

My daddy's here. And he's coming to get me.

She felt a certain calmness that she knew she should not have, but she did.

*Daddy's coming to get me.*

*And I know how to help him.*

Laurel began making her way from the corner of the large dark building, walking slowly toward the streetlights where the shooting had come from.

*Coming Daddy.*

Smokey held his rifle up, the pain in his shoulder from his wound making itself known again, and he didn't know how long he could hold it up, no matter how much he willed himself to do it. A figure came out of the shadows, walking slowly toward them.

"Alvarez," Jennifer whispered.

Smokey's finger tightened.

The man wore khaki fatigues, boots, held a pistol in his right hand. He pointed it at Smokey.

"You're apparently a hard man to kill," Alvarez said as he stopped in front of Smokey.

"You won't be," Smokey said. His grip tightened until he shook.

*I'm gonna kill him now, but the others will die. Will anyway.*

He heard a commotion at the end of the building, and then someone in that direction screamed. And then another.

"Serpiente!" And then a chorus of screams.

Lamebull got it first, and his face slit into a wide grin.

Laurel pushed the door open, and she stepped into the street. She stood in the shadow behind a group of men, all holding rifles. She slipped behind them, trying to see what they were doing, what they were pointing their rifles at. She stood at the end of their line and peered down the street. Some people there.

*Daddy!*

My daddy's down there! Sarah and Jennifer. She looked closer and saw Uncle Nathan. She wanted to yell at them, to run to them, but that would be the wrong thing to do now. And then she knew why she was there, what she could do to help her daddy.

*I'll try it on the one next to me. Daddy said that he didn't like it, didn't really believe it, and he once argued with grandmother about it. But I can help him.*

*I can.*

Laurel turned to the soldier in front of her, a large man with a black moustache and long black hair, and she looked at his rifle. She turned slightly and thought about the largest meanest baddest snake she could think of, and looked again at his rifle.

The effect was immediate.

The wooden stock on the man's rifle instantly turned into a large, twisting python. He stared, his eyes bulged, and he screamed. He tried to throw his rifle down, but it twisted around his arm, and she turned to the other men in line, and looked at their rifles, each in turn.

The drug soldier standing next to Alvarez (and that was how Smokey thought of them, *drug soldiers*) screamed and jumped back. A three-foot Coral Snake was twisted around his arm, the red, black and yellow bands glistening in the harsh light. The snake drew its head back and struck so swiftly that Smokey thought he had only imagined it, the fangs hooking into the man's cheek. The druggie pulled on the snake and ran blindly to his left, his legs pumping as he crossed the street and ran full speed into the wall of the money building. He fell to the ground, writhing like the snake he was trying to pull from his face.

A tall drug soldier stumbled past, holding the largest snake Smokey had ever seen, a thirteen-foot Black Mamba, its mouth completely over the druggie's left eye socket. Vitreous fluid spurted out of the Mamba's mouth, the man struggling with a pistol in his right hand.

Smokey didn't know if the druggie was trying to shoot the snake when the man pulled the trigger and blew off the right side of his face, popping his right eyeball out to lay on his cheek. Smokey turned to the cacophony of screams behind him, sounds of an asylum from hell. All manner of snakes were biting, striking, sinking fangs into necks, faces, arms.

He saw a seven foot Diamondback Rattler repeatedly strike the prone form of a druggie, the man not moving. Copperheads, Water Moccasins and a twelve foot King Cobra danced a venomous waltz with the druggies, the flared hood of the Cobra sending a chill up Smokey's back.

*What is happening here?*

Alvarez jerked his gun forward, suddenly holding a twisting snake. Smokey was struck with a hatred, a pure white rage for this man who got rich poisoning the children of others. Alvarez screamed. Smokey fired a burst into the drug leader's head, the face and skull disintegrating and Alvarez dropped straight down, holding onto the snake as he died.

Laurel picked her way through the twisting, screaming druggies, the men busy with their own visit to hell. As she walked, she focused on her daddy. He was hurt, but he looked so beautiful. She was going to tell him that. And she tried to call to him but the words just didn't come out.

*Daddy!*

She tried again, and gave a little wave to Jennifer.

"Daddy!"

Smokey slumped down, the pain from his wound causing him to double over, the grief of his loss coming in waves, and then he saw Laurel.

A dream.

And he heard her call his name.

*Daddy.*

"Laurel?"

She ran to him, twisting her way around bodies and snakes, and he dropped to his knees, his rifle clattering to the ground as she reached him. She kissed him again and again.

"Oh Daddy, you're so beautiful."

"That all you got to say," he said, his face wet with tears.

"Take me home?"

Nathan put his hands under Smokey's good arm and lifted. Smokey grinned at his big brother, thinking that they might get home after all. Laurel put her arm around his left side, and as they limped to the van, Smokey heard Sarah talking to the others.

"Let's burn it."

"Wheels up," Weasel said. He turned to Charley. "Your airplane," he said, and unstrapped. "Just get us across the border."

Burwell and Amy sat together, making room for the wounded, Smokey the most critical. Laurel and Jennifer tended to him, both fussing over him like a couple of little mothers, stopping every few seconds to hug and kiss each other and giggle.

"What did I just see, there in the street?" Amy asked.

"In-din stuff," Burwell said, and after a few moments, she nodded.

Sarah made her way through the crowded aisle. She leaned over Burwell and Amy to look out at the burning buildings below. She pulled back from the window and placed her face in front of Burwell's. She leaned forward and kissed an astonished Burwell on the lips.

"First Šiyápu I've ever kissed," she said, winking at Amy, "and Burwell, you better get used to it buddy, you'd better get used to it."

# **E**pilogue

Five Months Later

Smokey sat on the couch and looked around at bare walls of the new log house. It was still rough, but at least they had a roof and walls. The lamp in the kitchen made a dim glow in the living room, but he was too content to turn on more light. Sometimes at night he had flashes of terror at what he had almost lost, and then he would take deep breaths and creep into Laurel's room and watch her as she slept.

He saw the flash of headlights and heard the car as it stopped in the drive. The front door opened and Jennifer and Laurel came in, noisy, chatting as Nathan followed with his arms full of their booty. As Smokey waved at them he heard his cell phone ring.

Albany

Amy sipped tea after dinner and opened up Stan's laptop. She went to the mapping program and watched the movement of the blinking light at the base of Whitewater Glacier on Mt. Jefferson. In mid-December it was too late in the year to be Mr. Bear, or as Smokey called it, *Mr. Anahuy.*

She had already chosen a Latin name for the creature: *Stanislaus Gigantopithecus Bipedus,* named after Stan. He would like that. She picked up her cell phone and made the call she had been putting off for a week. She had waited until she was sure. She didn't want to tell Smokey something she couldn't back up.

"How's my favorite Indian?"

"I'm good."

"You sound good, all healed and everything. That the girls I hear in the background?"

"Yep."

"You healed up enough to give a ride to a city girl?"

"I'll manage, if I have to crawl. When and where?"

"I'll be on the bus from Portland tomorrow, should be coming through the reservation about noon, give or take because of the snow. This city girl doesn't do snow. Besides, I have a new tat to show you."

"What kind of tat?"

"Smokey, it's an Indian thing. I'll show you tomorrow."

"Amy?"

She heard the softness in his voice. "Yeah?"

"Amy, you're always welcome here. All my life you're family now. What's the occasion?"

"I've got something else to show you."

*Something that doesn't exist.*
*Something that has been here since before time.*

## Author Enes Smith

Enes Smith relied upon his experience as a homicide detective to write his first novel, *Fatal Flowers* (Berkley, 1992). Crime author Ann Rule wrote, "*Fatal Flowers* is a chillingly authentic look into the blackest depths of a psychopath's fantasies. Not for the fainthearted . . . Smith is a cop who's been there and a writer on his way straight up. Read this on a night when you don't need to sleep, you won't . . ."

*Fatal Flowers* was followed by *Dear Departed* (Berkley, 1994). "You might want to lock the doors before starting this one," author Ken Goddard wrote, "Enes Smith possesses a gut-level understanding of the word 'evil,' and it shows." Ken Goddard is the author of *The Alchemist, Prey,* and *Outer Perimeter,* and Director of the National Wildlife Forensic Laboratory.

Smith's work as a Tribal Police Chief for the Confederated Tribes of the Warm Springs Indians of Oregon led to his first novel in Indian Country, *Cold River Rising. Cold River Resurrection* is the second novel in the Cold River series. He has been one of the few Šiyápu to hold that position in Indian Country. He worked as police chief in 1994 and 1995, and even though he is a Šiyápu, he was asked back as tribal police chief in 2005.

He has been a college instructor and adjunct professor, teaching a vast array of courses including Criminology, Sociology, Social Deviance, and Race, Class, and Ethnicity. He trains casino employees in the art of nonverbal cues to deception. He is a frequent keynote speaker at regional and national events, and has been a panelist at The Bouchercon, the World Mystery Convention.

Made in the USA
Charleston, SC
28 August 2012